Down to the Sea

A Mystic Beach Fantasy Rockstar Romance interstitial novel

Aislinn Archer

Mystic Beach Press

For Mace, my literary problem-child, who insisted this "novella" needed to be written, and then demanded a novel of his own, before throwing me some plotline curveballs that turned this from a novella into a novel. You are very, very good. And very, very bad. In only the best ways. Behave. Mostly.

A content review for this book, and others in the series, is available on the author's website at AislinnArcher.com. If you have any concerns about whether you might find the content of this work disturbing, please take a few moments to check the content review on the website and do not read if you think you might find any of the content disturbing. The recommended reading age for this work is 18 or older.

Aislinn@AislinnArcher.com so she can fix it as quickly as possible. Thank you!

Note: Portions of the story in this book appeared in the previous book in the series, "Once Upon a Dream," where they are told from the viewpoint of aMUSEd's rhythm guitarist, Hunter Graves. In "Down to the Sea," those events are told from his friend Brighid's point of view, revealing some significant things of which Hunter was not aware or could only speculate upon.

If you prefer to remain in the dark about Brighid's interaction with Aedan "Mace" Mason that took place behind closed doors or outside of Hunter's view, you'll want to skip this book, because that is exactly the story "Down to the Sea" tells.

Some of this hidden story may appear in a future book in the series, but it will be presented as revealed to Hunter. If you want the full details first-hand, this book is for you. (And for Mace, because he demanded it. And then he demanded an entire novel of his own on top of it. But who could resist this guy? Well, maybe just one person, or two...)

CONTENTS

Chapter 1

Girlfriend

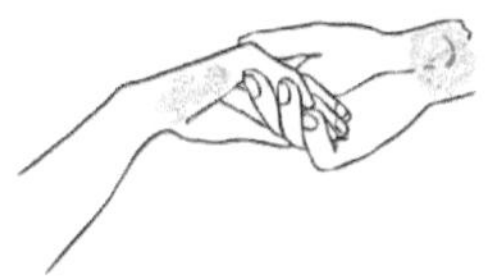

Ellie

The size of the crowd is overwhelming. You see it when you're in the midst of a crowd that big, but looking at it from the stage is a completely different perspective. I can only imagine how it feels to be the one standing on that stage for all those thousands of people, knowing that they're there for you.

That's the not-too-distant future for my very talented lifelong best friend, Hunter, and the rest of his band, aMUSEd. As it stands, without even releasing an EP, aMUSEd has been asked to entertain crowds of as many as 20,000 people, opening for big-name act Telltale Signs. They were a last-minute replacement, but someone had loved their performances at D.C.-area bars enough to bring them on board without so much as a single to promote.

And it seems to have gone over well with Telltale Signs' fans, because they're eating it up while aMUSEd does their shortened set featuring only their as-yet-unrecorded original songs. Declan, their lead singer, is earning his right to his often diva-esque (or dick-ish, depending on the day and who you ask) offstage behavior by tearing up the stage and the songs. He's a tremendously gifted singer, with a range that can't be beat, but his real talent is grabbing an audience from the first note and drawing them in, until they forget everything except watching him entertain them.

Hunter is, as always, in full rockstar mode, taking that green PRS guitar his late mother gave him and making it sing, lighting up in front of the audience as he always does — just on a bigger stage. This is my favorite part of any aMUSEd show: absorbing Hunter's passion, delight and electric energy as he immerses himself in his music and becomes a conduit, taking on the energy of the crowd and then feeding it back to them, enhanced by shining it through his soul, like a lens.

How could any woman see — experience — that and not want to make him her own? I couldn't resist him before he began performing. I definitely can't now. But that's a non-starter, since Hunter had long ago — and repeatedly — rejected me as anything more than a friend, despite a connection between us that seemed to go back more than just this lifetime.

Still, seeing him in his element here, on a stage I know with complete certainty will someday be the norm for him, I'm just plain proud of him. He's worked hard for this, suffered through tremendous loss and painful rejection by his dad, and scraped by (with a little help from a friend) until he's managed to reach this breakthrough moment in a career that shows no limit to the heights it could reach.

When their set is over, I join Hunter and the guys backstage, and Hunter is in the gentlemanly and solicitous mode that I know is behavior his sweet mother had instilled in him. As the concert after-party gets under way at Telltale Signs' hotel, he gets me a soda, sits with me close beside him and largely ignores the overt flirtation from a handful of attractive young women who I suspect would have been sitting in his lap by now if I wasn't here.

He takes my hand and leans into me so I can hear him over the music and chatter, and it's sweet, even though I know it doesn't really mean anything to him. We share a bed as often as not, and sleeping with our arms around each other is about comfort and affection, rather than sex or romance. I'm working on accepting that, as much of a challenge as it has been for the last four years. It's a work-in-progress.

Hunter even walks me to the large hotel suite's bathroom when I ask where it is. Inside, I look at myself in the mirror and sigh. What is it about me that I don't do anything for Hunter, sexually speaking? Is it really just my weight? Are my curves just too ample, my thighs too thick? That aside, what I see when I look in the mirror is a long neck, shapely shoulders, cleavage that isn't exactly overwhelming but is nonetheless what you might expect with a curvy girl, wavy ash-blonde hair that skims over my shoulders and down to the small of my back, and bright violet eyes that are, at minimum, unusual. My bone structure isn't of model-perfect proportions, but there is a strength and uniqueness there that I don't think is unattractive. Overall, I can't see what's missing that Hunter wants, nor what is present that might make me too repulsive to consider, unless it really is just my weight.

Considering the girls in the other room who've been watching him, maybe that's all it takes.

Focused on putting an only-partly heartfelt smile back on my face when I leave the restroom, I don't see the person walking down the hallway until I almost run into him.

"Whoa! You OK there?" the man asks, grabbing my elbow to steady me after the near-collision.

Embarrassed, I smile at him apologetically.

"Sorry about that. I didn't see anyone coming," I blurt, only then realizing who I've all but literally bumped into. *Aedan "Mace" Mason — lead singer for Telltale Signs, universally considered a major heartthrob, according to the entertainment magazines, and the intended target of many a pair of panties hurled onstage at their shows.* Inside my head, my jaw drops, but I somehow manage to keep that to my mind's eye only.

"Do I make so modest an impression as that?" he asks, tilting his head at an angle that pushes his shaggy auburn hair into his eyes. But his smile lets me know he's only joking.

"Well, I nearly made a significant impression on you, in black and blue," I banter back. *Where did that come from?* "So I hope you'll forgive the near-collision. There may be a lot of women looking to run into you, but I usually try to avoid doing that literally."

He smiles at me, his deep blue eyes drifting downward, and I feel extremely self-conscious, wondering how far down he's going to look. But he only reaches as far as the top of my cleavage, where my silver Brighid's cross pendant lays against my skin. He extends his hand and I move to shake it, but instead he holds it, rather than shaking it.

"Aedan Mason — most people call me 'Mace.'"

"Nice to meet you. I'm Ellie."

"Irish?" he asks simply, nodding at my pendant.

"It is. I'm not. At least not by nationality. Just part-Irish. I've actually been working on learning the Irish language, which they're trying to save before English completely eradicates it," I add, feeling like I'm beginning to ramble and prepared for him to make a hasty exit. "There aren't even any monolingual Irish speakers left."

"Oh? That's interesting. I'm actually planning on going to Ireland for a while once the tour wraps up. I want to take some time and really immerse myself in the culture, the music, the mythology, see what it might offer in inspiration for our next album."

"That sounds wonderful!" I reply.

"Which — going to Ireland or the inspiration for the album?"

"Both, actually. I'm actually a devotee of Brighid, which is why I wear Her cross, so that sounds really appealing."

"Oh! You're Catholic?"

"Actually, no," I reply, oddly willing to be candid with this perfect stranger, even if he's a big-time celebrity who I'll likely never see or talk to again after this brief conversation. "Pagan. Brighid was worshiped as a goddess in Ireland long before Christianity was even present there."

"Wow. You always see her portrayed as a Christian saint. People still worship goddesses? How'd that come to be — for you, I mean?"

"I was called to service as Her priestess."

"Now that's fascinating. A religious calling, but to an older god..."

I smile, knowing he's just being polite to the crazy girl.

"What's involved in that?" he asks. And I consider that maybe he really is interested.

"It's a very personalized practice," I explain. "There are some groups that work together. Some of them maintain an eternal flame, handed down from the shrine in Kildare, and they work in shifts — nineteen of them — with Brighid Herself taking the twentieth shift of tending the flame."

"There's an actual shrine in Kildare?"

"Well, that's kind of complicated, because it's actually the shrine to the saint. Some people consider Her one and the same, others look at Her as disparate aspects of the same being —

perhaps evolving as the culture did. And some only worship one or the other."

"And you?"

"I respect the Christian devotion to her. The stories of the saint are actually very inspirational. But, She comes to me as the goddess. She's very prominent in the mythology of Ireland, actually — as a goddess."

"I'm intrigued. Kildare, you said?"

"Yes. I have a candle I use for my worship that's been lit from the flame at the Kildare shrine."

"Now I'm going to have to go there on my trip and learn more."

"Hey, Elle — how're you doing? Everything going OK?" Hunter asks from behind me. It's sweet that he's keeping an eye on me, even if I'm not drinking tonight, like I was at that ill-fated frat party earlier this year where I'd almost — finally — lost my virginity. (What an odd turn of phrase that is... like you could retrace your steps and run across it lying discarded on the sidewalk and just pick it up... like the goal of nearly every adult wasn't to get rid of it...)

I quickly pull my hand from Mace's, hoping Hunter didn't see, only then realizing Mace had been holding it the entire time.

"Yeah, Hunter. I was just talking to Mace about Ireland. He spotted my Brighid's cross and asked me about it."

"I'm planning to spend some time there when the tour's over," Mace explains. "Your girlfriend here's got some great background information on the language and mythology — the exact kind of thing I'm hoping will bring me some inspiration for our next album."

"Oh, we're just friends," Hunter clarifies.

I flinch. I should be used to it by now, but the eagerness with which he corrects people on that common assumption feels a little like he's embarrassed to be thought of as my boyfriend. And that hurts.

"Well, lucky me," Mace says, and I'm not sure if I heard him right. "I won't have to feel too guilty about monopolizing Ellie here while I pick her brain about some of the spots I might want to go to."

OK. Maybe I did hear him right. But I'm the one who needs to clarify now.

"Well, as I said, I haven't been myself, yet," I admit. "But I've done a lot of reading. And it's definitely on my bucket list to go.

Sooner, rather than later," I add, because Mace's interest has me longing to go even more than I had been.

"Don't tempt me," Mace offers, chuckling.

I'm not quite sure how to take that. Is he suggesting that in some other universe we might be going there together? I feel my cheeks start to warm.

"With your permission then, Hunter, I'm going to borrow your *friend* for a little while."

What? You are? Are you sure? Isn't there a model here somewhere who you'd rather be spending time with?

"I'd like to hear more about this duality of Brighid as a goddess and as a saint."

Well, I guess I can do that. I've had a couple semesters of anthropology, as well as all my outside reading.

"Sure," I say quietly, my smile shy. And I take Mace's proffered hand so he can lead me back to what appears to be his bedroom.

What have I gotten myself into here?

CHAPTER 2

SEA OF LOVE

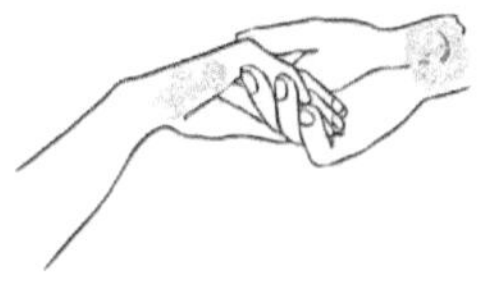

"So, you're *not* Hunter's girlfriend? I kind of thought, the way he was hovering, that you were," Mace says, gesturing for me to take a seat next to him on the bed in what does, indeed, appear to be his bedroom inside this massive hotel suite.

"No. We're just friends. We've been best friends since we were 6."

"And you've never dated or anything?"

I'm surprised by the probing question.

"I'm sorry to push the issue," he adds, looking genuinely apologetic. "It's just you two give off vibes like you're more than just friends. He's not an ex, too, or anything?"

"No. Just friends, really."

"Your expression when *he* said that tells me otherwise."

Busted. *So* busted.

I close my eyes for a moment, steeling myself. When I look up at him, I suspect my expression is more pleading than anything.

"Sore subject, eh?"

"Are you sure you're not empathic or something?" I ask, half serious.

"I've been asked that before," he admits with a gentle smile. My own intuition kicks in, emboldening me beyond the shyness that is my normal behavior with strangers.

"You know more about this stuff than you implied when you were asking me about Brighid earlier."

"And you recognized that way more easily than you should have, priestess," he says with a nod of respect.

Suddenly, it feels a bit like we're two wolves from rival packs who've surprised each other in the same territory, circling each other, aiming to take measure and decide whether the appropriate response to each other's presence is cautious approach, violent conflict or desperate mating.

Because while Aedan Mason is undeniably attractive — especially with my penchant for redheads, Hunter aside — it wasn't until he threw down that gentle verbal gauntlet just now that my hormones kicked in.

I don't just read *Hunter* well, though I read him best of all. Under some circumstances, I read others uncannily well, though less so when it's their feelings about me that are at issue. That feeling is what tells me there's more here than a vocabulary-specific reference to empathy. The man knows things. And he knows I know things, too. And he seems to like that.

I nod at him in my own gesture of respect.

"So, if you didn't ask me back here to talk about Herself and a travel itinerary, what did you ask me back here for, Mace?"

"Oh, I definitely want to talk to you about Brighid," he says, surprising me a little. "She's not one of mine, but I think I need to make Her acquaintance. I've been getting pushed in that direction."

"And when They push, it's never a good idea to fight it."

"No. You are very certain for your age... You're what? Twenty-two?"

"Twenty in a few months."

He issues a low whistle.

"A couple years younger and I'd be in considerable trouble right now," he adds with a smile that's not at all innocent.

"Oh? We've got all our clothes on. You haven't touched any part of my body except my hand. I touch more of Hunter on an average night than that."

His eyebrows go straight up.

"I thought you were just friends."

"We are. If much to my continual lament."

"Yet you're sleeping together? As in *slumber?*"

"We have since we were kids, lots of times. And his mom died when he was 15 and he stayed with me, and it became a habit. And then my mom died right after Christmas, and he's been very determined to be there for me, day and night."

"I'm sorry. You're both young to have had to go through that. I can see where you'd need the comfort."

"You don't think that's weird?"

"Unusual, not weird. And you're wanting more?"

"I've *had* more with him. Just not as who we are now."

I can tell by his expression that he's trying to parse that vague comment. Let's see how intuitive he really is...

"Not as who you are now... which implies it was when you were someone else, before... Past life?"

I nod, though I hedge things verbally.

"I think."

"Tell me."

That inner wolf in me is now wondering if fleeing is the appropriate response at this juncture.

"You don't have to," he allows, observing my hesitation. "And you don't have to tell me all the details, if you'd prefer to be more private with it."

It's disarming, his willingness to listen to something even Hunter could not credit as true. The patient, even, placid expression on his face pulls on the end of the wound skein of experience pooled in my head, and I find myself deciding to let him have — some of — the story.

"I had a dream — a vision — when I was 15. Only it wasn't a 15-year-old's vision. There were things that I'd never seen or done, haven't done... And I was older, married, to someone I recognized as Hunter, but who was also older. And it was a long time ago. Well more than a century, based on my knowledge of clothing styles."

"Let me guess — Ireland."

"Got it in one."

"Well, that explains the easy connection to Ireland and to Brighid, and why you seem much older than your age and know things a 19-year-old wouldn't easily know. You've done this all before, and on some level you remember it."

"It seems so."

"Have you told Hunter about your vision?"

"I like that you just call it a 'vision,' like you accept that's what it was — not a dream or a 'figment of my imagination.'"

"Ugh — now I have that insidious Disney ride song in my head... Quick — tell me how Hunter reacted so I can get it back out again!" he adds with a smile.

I smile back. I kind of like the little purple dragon, but the last time I was there, the ride needed a revamp.

"He... I'm not sure it's that he doesn't believe me. I know he believes *I* believe it, that *I* think it's a real past-life memory. And he doesn't seem to think I've lost my mind. But I don't think *he* believes it. He's not so much disbelieving as skeptical — like somebody who's agnostic, not an atheist."

"That has to hurt."

I tip my head to the side, looking at him from another angle. He *is* extremely intuitive.

"You know it does. The question is whether you know that from personal experience or whether you're reading me well enough to know that's how I feel."

"Either? Both?" Mace suggests, his expression enigmatic.

I lean back, putting little distance between us.

"I think it's time I ask some of the questions here."

His expression shifts, becoming more defensive.

"And that's exactly why," I comment. "I've been warned against letting people know too much about me until I'm certain I can trust them, and I've already told you more than was wise."

"Mom?" he asks, no real concern that the question will hit too close to home, even though he knows my mother is gone.

"High priestess. Though she's more mother figure or mentor than my religious leader."

"So, not a follower of Brighid."

"No. She belongs to another."

"As do I."

"I see... You know who *I* belong to. I haven't hidden it."

"And turnabout is fair play?"

"Not always. But often," I rebut, nodding at him to tell him the ball is in his court.

"You're right. You've shared and I have not. Let's remedy that," he says with a nod of his own. "To even the playing field, I'll give you two names, priestess: Mine — *you* call me Aedan, not 'Mace.' 'Mace' is a rockstar. Aedan is the man inside the frontman."

"OK. Aedan, then," I agree, noting that the request is not casual in tone. "The second?"

"Let's make this a test... Because I'm curious just how much you know at that tender age of yours."

He leans back, crossing his legs with one foot on top of the other knee. A deceptively relaxed pose that belies the tension I can feel in him. This is serious business for him.

"Sea god. Manx."

"Manannán mac Lyr."

He nods in silent confirmation.

"He's not one of mine, but I know Him."

"Oh?"

"Born and raised at the beach... I know most of the sea gods. Certainly the Celtic ones."

"Hunter, too? The beach, I mean?"

I nod.

"And that explains it..."

I raise an eyebrow at him.

"Like recognizes like. As we did."

"I don't think he's Manannán's. Herself has taken a bit of shine to him. Even when he's infuriating me."

Aedan laughs aloud.

"They don't much seem to care when our people refuse to cooperate, do They? It's always up to us to make it work anyway. Probably why She's tasked you with waking him up."

"You think that's what this is?"

"I think you either resolve your issues from past lives in this one or you'll just have to do it again next time out."

"That makes this even more frustrating," I say with a growl.

He chuckles.

"Been there. Doing that."

"So you've got a lady who's refusing to unpack some baggage with you?"

"You're making an assumption that it's a woman. It's more complicated, but you're more or less correct. And we're not together right now. And won't be anytime soon. I've got time to spend on other things... other people..." he purrs, looking at me with keen interest that seems to have little, if anything, to do with our spiritual discussion.

He reaches for my face, tracing my lower lip with his thumb. I'm frozen in place. Waiting with bated breath for what he's going to do next.

"OK, my young priestess of Brighid..." he says, dropping his hand. "How are you handling the situation with Hunter?"

"Wanting him badly, loving him completely, endlessly frustrated that he doesn't see it, wounded that he seems embarrassed by the idea of anyone thinking we're more than friends..."

"I doubt that's the reason, Ellie. That boy has some current-life baggage weighing him down. It's going to take something big — an epiphany — for him to drop that baggage, to look around him and see what's really there. ... You're not *waiting* for him, are you?" he continues.

I break eye contact, not wanting to admit it.

"You *have* been..." he observes.

"Yes. And no. Mostly no lately. But... he kind of busted down a door to keep me from..." I let the statement go unfinished.

"Ha!" Aedan bursts into laughter. "I can picture it now. Hunter's physically imposing, but it's very out-of-character for him, eh?"

I nod.

"Yeah. He's wound up but he can't really see why. He's going to have to get a very loud wakeup call before he will."

I look down at my hands in my lap. He pulls my chin up, forcing me to look in his eyes again.

"He's not going to bust down that door, is he?"

I look over at Aedan's door.

"Highly unlikely. He knows I'm sober this time..."

Aedan looks irate as he realizes I must not have been sober the last time.

"And I can't imagine he'd be willing to risk getting thrown off the tour over me," I add to assure him Hunter really isn't about to burst through the door. "His bandmates would excoriate him."

"Ooohh! Spelling-bee word! I like it!" Aedan comments enthusiastically, with an undertone of something more visceral. "Well, if we can be certain he's not going to get himself in trouble, I'd like to make you a proposition."

"A proposal, you mean? I mean, not marriage, obviously," I splutter, knowing I'm making a fool of myself now. My cheeks flame.

"Settle, little Brigidine. I used the word I meant..."

"I'm not little," I point out automatically, only then realizing the import of his statement of careful word choice — proposition... Does he?

"No, you're not. But already you are one of the most intriguing women I've ever met, and I find this whole package very alluring. There is an otherworldly wisdom about you that tells me that, whatever the experience level of this body," he says, gesturing at me, "you remember much, much more, and you're ready for some experience in this lifetime that Hunter can't give you now. And that I'd like very much to explore with you, while both of us are waiting for our others to wake up."

His gentle expression has slid toward hunger, and my heartbeat begins to pound in my neck, arms, and ... elsewhere. Tempting... But...

I look back at the door, in the direction of the room where I expect Hunter is waiting.

"Still waiting, eh?"

I sigh.

"Alright... So, just hear me out. Here's my proposition: You come back out to the party with me, sit with me, enjoy the party, and if Hunter doesn't read our body language and come to reclaim you, then we come back in here and talk. If it's enough of a shove to wake him up, you win, and I will offer you both all the blessings I can convey.

"If it's not..." he says, again steering my violet eyes into his deep blue ones. "You don't have to keep waiting around for him. Because I'm awake, and I'm not blind, nor am I — despite what the tabloids would have you think — so shallow or limited of vision that I can't see exactly how attractive you are, inside and out. And I think we've already demonstrated that the chemistry is there between us..."

He's right. But I'm loathe to believe this is what it appears to be, no more and no less. So, I ask the question.

"Why? Why me? The last guy made it pretty clear he was very fond of 'cherries,' as it were. Is that all this is?"

He reaches for my face again, holding it between his hands.

"Ellie, it's not often I get a chance to let down my guard. I have to walk around, all day, all night, pretending to be nothing more than 'Mace,' the lead singer of a very successful rock band. Being open about who, and what, I really am, poses risks. To me and everyone associated with me. The pressure on me isn't just to perform or act as the frontman of a band. I have a lot of people relying on me to keep this train running. I'm responsible to a band, dozens of staff members, a label, its employees, hundreds of vendors, venue employees and contractors... Not to mention the music and the fans. And my lady.

"Being 'out of the broom closet' is a risk I can't afford to take," he continues. "Not on their behalf, and not if I want to be free to make the kind of music the gods give me. Because, as has already been proven, when a rock musician is out as Pagan, or Wiccan or Heathen, or whatever word they use, they become a 'posterchild for witchcraft.' And that not only risks losing fans and label support, tour support, it locks you into that role and that public perception, with no room to evolve, personally or musically, because years later, all they'll remember is that you're that rockstar who's a witch.

"And, quite frankly, my beliefs are none of their business. If I'm going to keep anything about my private life personal, it's going to be my religious practices. That and my intimate relationships…" he adds, with the extended meaning of that statement sitting between us now.

"You know *I'm* not going to out you."

"I do. And I know you probably don't want the paparazzi following you around, wanting to know if you're sleeping with me. And gods forbid they get hold of the information that Hunter sleeps in your bed. Because then we've got a love triangle — and within a single tour — and they just love that shit. Trust me. I know. So, this… whatever we say or do here, or anywhere else… it stays between us," he says firmly, but it's a question, not a statement.

"Agreed."

"And you understand what this is, right? Between us?"

"Passing some enjoyable time together, as friends and likeminded folk, since both of us are already spoken for. Even if the people who own our hearts aren't awake enough to realize it."

"Exactly. See — like recognizes like. Are you worried Hunter will have a problem with this? I really don't want to have to toss him or his band off the tour. We've only got four dates left before the next opener comes on for the dates down south, and I'd actually like to work with these guys again. They're extremely talented. Which I think you know. Maybe better than anyone."

"I do. Hunter almost stopped playing when his mom died. It was pure coincidence, or fate, that the day I got him to pick up his guitar again, the Carter brothers happened to walk by and hear him, and decided to join in. I knew he'd be a star, and I knew they would, too. And they've only gotten better since they added Rhys and Alex. Even if it tends to go to Declan's head."

Aedan chuckles heartily.

"The kid has a major case of Lead Singer Syndrome. Only time will tell if he gets treated for it early enough that he'll avoid doing damage to his reputation."

"We practice regular pin-pricking of his ego, just to keep it under control," I admit.

"Well, he's got the vocal chops, and he's got the charisma to be a compelling frontman. Find him someone to ground him, and he could settle in to a solid career and, if he works for it, maybe even become a legend. He's that good, Ellie. As are Hunter and all the rest of them. They're lucky they've had you looking out for them. Because you have been, haven't you? Especially Hunter."

"Honestly, I'm not sure they actually like me, excepting Hunter. And maybe Alex, who seems to have a soft spot for me, but I don't know him very well yet. Rhys... well, Rhys loves everyone," I add with a smile. "But I suspect as soon as they really take off, I'm going to be watching from the sidelines. And that'll have to be enough."

"You're making a life for yourself, too? Not waiting around for Hunter there, too? Tell me you're not."

"No. One of the gifts I've been given is a talent, a calling, for spinning and weaving."

"Let me guess — that past life."

I nod. "I did the senior-level fiber-arts course content last year, as a sophomore. I finished all the content from the lower levels in a single year. Someday, I want to have my own shop. And there's talk of a gallery show."

"Wow. That's great! See — I knew you were special. Promise me, when your work gets into a show — and it will — that you'll invite me."

I'm looking at him shyly now, which feels kind of odd when the man is openly propositioning me for sex and the sex part isn't what has me feeling shy. As instinctive as I've been with him, I still don't quite trust that what I'm seeing is what I'm going to get.

"You want to go to a gallery show of weavings made by a not-yet-20-year old?"

"No. I want to go to a gallery show of works made by a master weaver, which I suspect is what you are. Not to mention that I'd be one of the few people who might realize that there's more woven into those pieces than just some yarn," he adds with a wink. "So, invite me. I'll be there. And I'm going to be offended if you don't, so make sure you remember."

"You're kind of hard to forget..."

"Aedan. Say it. Say my name, Ellie. Because while I'm hoping we're going to be friends for a long time, in the short term, I'm really looking forward to hearing you scream my name while you come on my tongue."

Pardon me. I'm going to just sit here for a minute, and try to re-learn how to breathe. Gods, the man is hot, and it's not all in how he looks.

"You really want to do this, Aedan?" He smiles with satisfaction. "With me?"

"Very definitely. This connection, this chemistry — frankly, it's really hot, and in my experience, it's really rare, believe it or not. I'm not going to let it pass me by if we're both feeling it. And I think we'll be good together, however long it lasts. It feels right. It feels intended. I think you get what I mean."

I nod. "An interlude that ties parts of the symphony together, adding to the beauty of the whole."

"The Muses definitely like you, my lady. Or is that Brighid's 'fire of inspiration'?"

"Maybe a bit of both," I admit.

"Well, I like you quite a lot myself, so you'll forgive me, I hope, if I'm cheering for Hunter to stay asleep tonight, almost as much as I'm cheering for you to wake him up."

"Hunter will do what Hunter's ready to do. I've always known that. There's no dragging him into anything."

"Not even when the biggest prize of all is staring him right in the face, it would seem."

I blush.

"Ah, there we go... I'm already picturing the glorious contrast between your present-life innocence and your past-life knowledge. The seductress who blushes at the slightest compliment and the innocent who knows exactly what she wants, exactly what she needs..."

He trails his knuckles down my cheek.

"Yes, indeed. Now, let's go see how awake your Hunter actually is."

CHAPTER 3

JEALOUS AGAIN

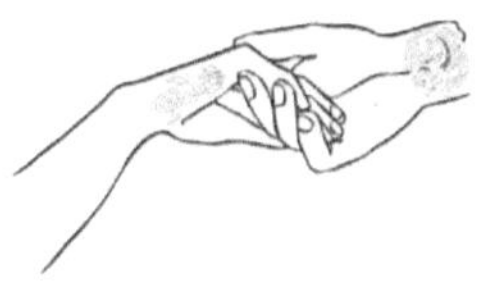

We've been in Aedan's room for nearly an hour. I'm not sure what I'm going to find when we get back into the party. Part of me suspects Hunter will have some skinny girl on his lap, or some other portion of his anatomy.

"He's going to be sitting by himself, sulking. I can promise you," Aedan says quietly in my ear, speaking answers to the worries I haven't voiced. "In fact, I bet you. If he's not sulking, you'll owe me a blowjob."

I think I'm blushing from head to toe now.

"Oooh... That's a new thing in this life, too, eh?" he says, his hand on my hip and following me close behind as we near the living area. "I'll just have to reawaken that old knowledge, then... Stick with me, kid. I'm gonna show you the world!" he promises with a laugh as we reach the open central room. I can't help but look back at him over my shoulder, laughing out loud as I picture us flying high over the world in a hot-air balloon, him navigating and me on my knees in the basket below, my lips wrapped around him.

An hour ago, that would have been so impossible a prospect that even the idea of it would have merited a laugh at the joke. Now, it's a promise of pleasure to come, even if it would be a consolation prize in a game I'm expecting to lose.

"Don't look over at him," Aedan purrs in my ear. "You owe me a blowjob, because he's sulking. Actually, he looks like he'd like to slice me into small pieces, saving the mincing for my dick, for its daring to have noticed you."

He steers me over to a chair on the other side of the room from the sofa where Hunter is sitting. Alex talks to Hunter briefly before going for another beer. I let my eyes skate over Hunter, taking in the sulky posture that Aedan so accurately predicted.

My would-be lover sits down in the chair and positions me on the armrest, his right hand on my lower back, and his left accepting his own bottle of beer from one of the approximately three hundred and eighty-seven people in this small room. It's a good thing he's seated me on the arm of the chair, because there is nowhere else to sit.

Whether it's because of that or just the way things go, I notice quite a few of the girls who'd been watching Hunter earlier now pressed up against one wall or another by a guy. None of those guys are Hunter, of course, because he's still sitting across from us, watching us with an expression somewhere between sadness and longing. I'm instantly feeling sorry for him and ready to run across the room to comfort him.

But Aedan seems to sense that I'm ready to cave and go to Hunter, and he runs his hand up my spine, making me shudder and turn to look at him.

"Don't," he warns quietly. "Wait. Lean down and whisper something in my ear."

"What should I be whispering?" I whisper, as commanded.

"Well, if you want to work on a lesson in talking dirty, you could start there, gorgeous," he whispers back, his voice lower in tone and more gravelly than I remember it being since we started talking. Again, I shudder, this time from his voice alone.

"You are a bad, bad man," I say, putting a purr of my own into my voice.

"In only the best of ways," he replies, his eyes traveling down and his gaze dipping into my cleavage, showing no signs of trying to hide his interest.

It's entirely possible I could sit here on the arm of the chair, with him just lightly touching my spine, and orgasm simply from listening to him speak. The man may serve a sea god, but he is fire. I begin to wonder if I could actually ignite, erupt into flame, just from the proximity. The gush between my legs is not nearly enough to put out this blaze. I take a deep breath and try to get hold of myself again.

"Are you wet?" he asks, his lips touching the shell of my ear.

"You sure you're not a telepath?" I ask, again only half kidding.

"You're putting out enough pheromones to draw half the men in this room straight to your pussy," he informs me. "The only thing keeping them in place is my hand on your back. They won't cross the big dog in the room."

"Is that a size reference?"

"I hope you'll get to find out," he replies, chuckling with a deeply sensual tone.

He raises a hand and catches the attention of the guy who brought him the beer. He whispers in his ear, and the guy looks over at me and at Aedan's hand on my back and nods. Aedan distracts me with another sweep up my spine.

"Sensitive there? Is that an erogenous zone for you, beautiful?"

I'm rendered mute and only reply with a nod.

"I'll make note of that," he says, with a tone that suggests that could be a threat, or a promise.

A minute later, the beer guy returns with a soda for me. Aedan opens it and hands it to me.

"I don't want you even a little tipsy tonight," he explains. "I want no questions about this being entirely consensual and mutual, and I want your mind sharp and focused on what we're doing, what we're feeling... because it's going to be glorious." *That's* a promise.

I sit sipping my soda while people converge on Aedan. His magnetism isn't just sexual. It's the frontman's gift. A thing far beyond charisma that engages people and makes them want to be around him. And the only thing about it that I question is why I'm the one sitting here, practically in his lap, with his hand drifting down toward my butt.

A few of the other women in the room are looking over at us, their expressions resentful. But they don't approach. It seems Aedan's overt claim on me tonight is enough to deter even the most avaricious groupie, as well as Hunter. I glance over at my best friend, finding him still watching us, seeming increasingly anxious. It's verging on torture to watch.

I lean down to Aedan, saying quietly, "I'm not sure I can keep this up. He looks like he's ready to burst, like a water balloon that someone's sitting on. Someone like my weight and not one of these petite little groupies you all seem to collect."

"Patience, priestess," Aedan urges. "The more anxious he gets, the more likely he'll wake. Give it a little longer. It won't hurt him."

I know he's right, but that doesn't make it any easier.

The number of people around Aedan — and me, since I'm sitting on the same chair — fluctuates. Sometimes they leave us alone in silence, and then sexual tension stirs, feeling like it should be a visible force between us. And sometimes they walk up to engage him in conversation. In those moments, he's relaxed and warm, and while I don't have much to add to the verbal intercourse, his hand never stops moving on my back. I can feel a portion of his attention is centered right on me, no matter who's talking to him, and it adds to that sexual tension — not with more sexual tension, but with a feeling of being desired, appreciated... and I suspect he knows just how badly I needed that.

After we've been back in the party about an hour, it occurs to me just how much time has passed since aMUSEd left the stage. I'm used to being up late for their gigs, especially when I help with load-out, but my sleep schedule has been all over the place lately, and I yawn, trying to hide it behind my hand so Aedan doesn't think I'm going to pull a Sleeping Beauty on him and just slump into slumber.

"You ready to call it a night, Elle?"

I'm not sure how Hunter appeared so quickly in front of me. I'd barely finished the yawn and he was already there. But I don't want to yield to his prompt, not any more than I wanted Aedan to think I was going to renege on our agreement, let alone the bet he'd made and I'd lost. Even though I hadn't bet anything and even though I suspected both of us would be winners in this game.

"Not quite yet, Hunter. I'm having a good time. It's been a long time since I've had this good of a time," I tell him with a smile. It's the truth, at least minus what is increasingly feeling like a "How long can we torture Hunter?" component to the evening.

"I haven't had this good of a time with someone in quite a while either, Ellie," Aedan says, putting his hand on the back of my neck, under my hair. I push into the sensation, which I find I quite like. "Thanks for bringing her tonight, Hunter. She's one of the most interesting people in the room, for sure."

"Why, thank you!" I smile, having no problem now believing that he means that.

"Can I borrow you for a minute, Elle?" Hunter asks. His expression and tone are intense, and I'm a little leery of what he has to say. Have I pissed him off and he's going to bail on me?

Is he wanting to take one of the other girls off for some sexual tension of his own? Or was Aedan wrong and this little torture test of his has gotten Hunter thinking about him and me?

Chapter 4

You'd Be Mine

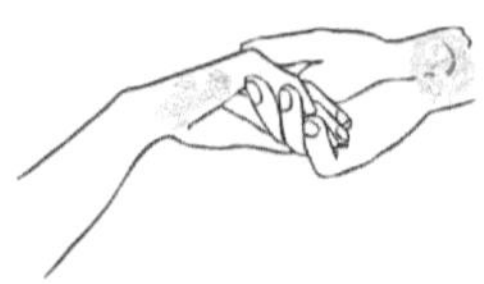

I nod and take the hand Hunter offers me, sliding off the arm of the chair. I kind of miss the feel of Aedan's hand on my back and neck, and I find myself a little astonished that I've let things with him move so far so fast, that I'm that comfortable with him and with him touching me so intimately.

Hunter leads me out onto the balcony, which is vacant and all but silent compared to the noise of the party. He turns me so his back is to the room, which feels protective.

"Hi," I say, feeling a little shy after having been on display with Aedan for the last hour and having been locked in his bedroom with him for an hour before that.

"Hi," he says back. I'm waiting for him to speak, but the silence continues.

"Uh... Hunter? Did you want to talk to me about something?"

"Yeah... Um... How are you doing?"

"I'm fine. Why wouldn't I be?" I'm a little perplexed here, truly. Is he worried that I'm too tired to stay? Is he worried I've been drinking again?

"I don't know... You were in Mace's dressing room for a long time... alone... with him... together."

I raise an eyebrow at him. He's telling me things that are self-evident. What is he getting at?

"I was," I acknowledge.

"And you're OK?"

"Of course I am. Why wouldn't I be?" I mean, I'm standing right here with him, intact and looking untroubled, except for not understanding what the heck he's trying to say.

"I didn't bust the door down this time."

Now he's being at least a little clear about what he's driving at with this stilted conversation. But part of me I can't believe he's actually asking me about this at all. What the heck am I supposed to say to such an overtly intrusive inquiry?

"You're... You... I... We... You're asking me..." I'm starting to get angry, and I can feel my face start to flush. I can't ever stay mad at Hunter, but I sure as heck can get there in the first place. "I really don't know what to say to that."

"Are you saying you didn't?" he asks.

"Didn't what, Hunter?"

"You know..."

How old are you, really? Use your grown-up words if you're to ask me intrusive questions about my sex life.

"I think you had better spell it out for me."

"You know — with him. Together. *Together* together."

I notice that he's using the same wording I used when telling him about him and me in that outlandishly erotic first vision I had of us together before. *Together* together.

"More words, Hunter. Preferably with a verb."

"Sex, Elle. Did you have sex with him? With Mace?"

"I don't think that's any of your business, Hunter."

Because it's not. Not at this point.

"But... I... But..."

"But what?"

He sighs in frustration.

I'm not sure where this goes if I don't throw him a lifeline to try to finish what has become a very uncomfortable conversation.

"Hunter — I wasn't drunk. I haven't had anything to drink tonight except soda. I didn't do anything I didn't want to. No one forced me to do anything. No one seduced me into doing anything I didn't want. I'm 19, almost 20, well past the age of consent, and I've had my full faculties about me all night."

"That's not an answer, Elle."

No   kidding,   you   contrary,   oblivious,   blind, still-fully-fucking-asleep rockstar, you.

"No. It's not. And as I said, it's none of your business. You're not my boyfriend. You made that very clear again tonight, to Aedan and to me," and I am both wounded and irate about that. "And if I want to spend some time with an attractive—"

He flinches.

"— intelligent, creative man who happens to find me interesting and wants to spend time with me, behind closed doors or not... then that is none of your business."

Darn tootin'.

He frowns. Did he actually think that, after all these years of me watching him go through girls like he has, I was just going to do a kiss-and-tell with him (of all people!) less than an hour after what he clearly (and correctly) surmises would have been my first time having sex?

"I never asked you about you losing your virginity, Hunter. Even though you're my best friend and even though you and I at this point have probably shared a bed more nights of our lives than ones we haven't. And even though I freely admitted the content of that vision I had when we were 15."

He looks a little uncomfortable now, even though he clearly still has no idea how much it cost me to admit that back then. I wanted him to figure it out with me, and instead my best friend just shut me down and then started to pull away, even though he'd said it wouldn't affect our friendship. This isn't even close to parity.

"I never asked, and you never opted to tell me, even though I assumed — safely, I think —" Though it's more like I *know*... "— that you had slept with someone in the last four years. And probably a lot of someones at this point." The content of that hotel suite tonight being Exhibit A.

"I can't keep doing this, Hunter." He clearly has no idea how hard this is for me. "*You* can't keep doing this. You can't keep trying to leap to my defense every time a guy looks at me with something other than platonic interest. I'm not your sister. I've got a platonic guy friend — you. What I don't have is anyone who looks at me like *that*. For whatever reason. Whether that's because you're running interference or because they think I'm too fat to be worth fucking."

"Elle!" he objects. But if we're honest with each other, we both know it's true.

"Don't think I'm naive, Hunter. I may not have had the degree of experience you have. I probably never will. But that's fine with me. I know a lot of guys don't find me attractive because of my size." And how it hurts to admit that, even to myself, let alone speaking the words out loud in front of him, the one who's rejected me more than all the others combined.

"But if someone looks at me and actually finds me attractive, and I'm so inclined, I'm going to have sex with him." And I mean that. I'm not waiting anymore. I wasn't really waiting by the time we got to that frat party, even if my judgment about that particular set of circumstances was lacking. "You don't factor into that decision," I tell him. Because I can't let him factor in anymore. I've waited, intentionally or otherwise, more than long enough. Long enough to make a fool out of myself countless times and alter the trajectory of my life in some pretty significant ways. "And you've got to find a way to be OK with that, because I've broken my heart a million times on the rocks of your rejections, and I can't do that for the rest of my life.

"Someday, someone will want to be with me." And, apparently that day is today, and that someone is one of the Sexiest Guys on the Planet. Literally. He was on the list last year, which I've been trying to pretend I didn't know, because then I'd chicken out on this, and I really don't want to do that. "And whether that's for an hour or a lifetime, it's my decision to make."

"This isn't easy for me, Ellie. I don't really know what I'm supposed to do here."

He's seriously not doing this right now, right? I'm trying to make my life *less* about him, and now he's going to play the "troubled Hunter" card. Does he think I'm going to just knuckle under and take care of him when he's the one who started all of this by asking me about things that are none of his business? Any filter I had is lost to the flood of emotion rushing through me.

"It isn't easy for *you*? You have *no idea* how hard this can be, how hard it is on the other side of the equation. None at all. You think I don't see all those girls in there, hanging on the other guys? The short skirts, the barely-there tops, the fuck-me heels and the blow-you lips? You think I don't understand that that happens every night on a tour? You think I don't have it stuck in my head how many of these girls, or whatever selection is available that night, you've fucked, screwed, eaten..." What's the verb to use for being in receipt of a blowjob? Oh, screw it. "...whatever? And you have the unmitigated gall, the *balls*, to tell me this isn't easy for *you*?"

Well, I've done it. I've rendered him speechless.

In retrospect, I can see how this tirade could come as a shock to him. How often have I stood up for myself with him? How often have I pushed back? How often have I even called him on his shit with the groupies, the party girls... the cheerleaders? Does he really think I'm so naive that I didn't know what he was doing?

Is this really the life he wants to lead for the rest of his life? Anonymous quickies, shallow one-night stands, hot-and-cold-running blowjobs, as I've heard Declan mention repeatedly? Is the appeal of that really so strong for Hunter that he can't see he has a woman standing in front of him who loves him with everything she has in her and wants to help him build an empire that we can both enjoy? Doesn't he see that he's falling into the same patterns his father did, with a woman who loved him dearly and who was always left feeling she was never enough? I refuse to go down the same path his parents did. I deserve better than that. He deserves better than that, whether he realizes it or not.

"I'm sorry, Elle. You're right. I'm not your boyfriend."

And there it is. It's not like he should need to be reminded of that fact, because he's the one who keeps saying it. I don't ever want to hear those words again. And maybe, after this, I won't have to. Because he's really leaving me with next to no hope that he will ever really wake up and see me, see us, for what we are. Maybe Aedan was wrong there, even if he was right about tonight not being enough to wake Hunter up.

"It's not my business who you sleep with. Even if it's Aedan Mason," he says, and I can't tell if he means that as a dig or a compliment. I want to chalk it up to jealousy either way, but that doesn't change the fact that he's drawing that line between us again. "So, I'm sorry," he says. "I won't interfere anymore."

Great. Can we throw a party? Oh, wait! There's one ten feet away already, where the guy who'd actually like to screw my brains out is sitting while you're out here beating your chest when I could have that guy's tongue in my pussy.

"But I want you to understand one thing: You are my best friend — one of the most important people I've ever had in my life. And I want the best for my best friend."

Suddenly, I'm a lot less angry. I'm actually in danger of starting to cry. Ugly cry. See — this is how he does it to me every time. Can't fucking stay mad at you, you glorious asshole you.

"So I hope whoever you decide to sleep with, now or ten years from now, will be as good for you as you deserve, which is the best. You deserve someone who will treat you well and love you with at least as much love as you offer him, which is pretty much limitless, as I know very well."

Yeah, well... Aedan and I have an understanding, and he knows already that he's not getting my heart, just like I'm not getting his. So, limitless or not, he'll be getting exactly what he gives.

You, meanwhile... Oh, gods fucking dammit, Hunter! Just wake the fuck up! Look at me — see me! I don't look the same as I did a hundred and however many years ago. But it's still me. Still us. You're destroying the chance we have to be that to each other again. What are the chances we'll find each other again in a future lifetime, let alone that one of us figures this out in such a clear fashion? I managed to figure it out, and you refuse to listen. Why? Why can't you just believe me, trust me? Give me enough credit to just give it a try? Why can't you see this? Is this body really so much of a disappointment that you can't find your soulmate inside?

And now the crying begins... Because he's taken away the one thing I had left: hope.

He notices the tear I couldn't keep from escaping my eyes, which is now running slowly down my cheek. And he does something I couldn't ever have predicted. He wipes it away with his thumb and then sticks his thumb in his mouth. My salty tears becoming part of him.

It doesn't matter how many times we've slept in the same bed, how much we've shared. It's a level of intimacy that he and I share with no one else. And it's a tiny speck of hope after all he's dashed tonight. But it's there. And it's a reminder that as stupid and senseless and counterproductive as this whole refusal to see is... We still love each other, if only as friends, and we will always have that.

He drops his forehead to mine, looking deep in my eyes, as if that has never been uncomfortable for us for even a moment. Then he wraps his arms around me, so tight that I feel like we could meld together. That thought instantly relaxes me, relieves this tension and makes it feel once again like we are still each other's safe spaces, each other's home. And I thank the gods for that, because I don't know what I'd do without my Hunter, my home.

We stay like that for a minute before we release each other. He grabs my hand and turns to lead me back into the party, where I know Aedan is waiting.

Except he's not.

There are actually two people standing in the doorway to the balcony — Aedan and Alex, both of whom appeared to have overheard some portion of that scene between Hunter and me. Alex's soft spot for me appears to be on full display, his eyes full of sympathy to the point where I suspect he's also feeling sorry for Hunter.

Aedan... I'm trying to read Aedan now, and it's more challenging, as if things have gotten more complicated now that he's seen Hunter and me alone together, heard us air our dirty laundry with each other, and maybe gotten some insight into where I am in the context of the agreement he and I had made.

I told Hunter I wasn't letting him factor in to my decisions on that front anymore, and I meant it. And I had every intention of following through on my decision to enjoy myself with Aedan, who — list-rating sex-symbol or not — genuinely seems to want me, who he's now seen in all my emotional glory. If he still wants me amidst the debris that's littering this balcony now, I'll know it's because he understands, perhaps better than anyone, what this bizarre set of circumstances is like, from the inside.

And, yes, like recognizes like. Like calls to like. And no matter how different his rockstar and celebrity life is from the life of the very-average college student that I am, he and I understand each other on a deeper level, where priest and priestess stand on equal footing. And if his goal in making his proposition was to help me merge my inexperienced current life with the woman in those erotic visions, I strongly suspect I was right about this being a win-win for us both.

Aedan's attention is on Hunter, to whom he gives a sharp nod that suggests respect, and I'm glad to see it. After that scene, some men would have judged Hunter and perhaps have lost respect for him. And what I see here, in Aedan, makes me think

Hunter's actually grown in his estimation. I still love Hunter. I always will. And having Aedan in his corner, even if Aedan's relishing the idea of having me be his for a while, is a good thing for my burgeoning rockstar. That tells me even more surely that Aedan understands. And while I'm sad that Hunter is so determined to deny what we are to each other, I'm surprised by how comforting Aedan's understanding is. Priest, indeed. Like to like.

"My Lady, I would like very much to continue our earlier conversation, if you're so inclined," he says with distinctive formality.

I am very much so inclined, as I think he well knows. Even if there's likely to be less conversing than the words would make it seem. And it is something to genuinely look forward to.

"I'd like that very much."

I take his hand to follow him back inside, headed to his room.

But one more thing needs to be said between me and Hunter tonight.

"Hunter, I'll let you know when I'm ready to leave," I say gently, trying to convey to him that our friendship will survive whatever happens here tonight or in the future. "I can still play designated driver if you'd like to sleep somewhere other than a tour bus, and then I'll drive you to Virginia Beach tomorrow afternoon, as planned."

He smiles back at me, and my heart soars, just a little, when I hear him say, "As you wish..."

CHAPTER 5

SENSE THE ADVENTURE

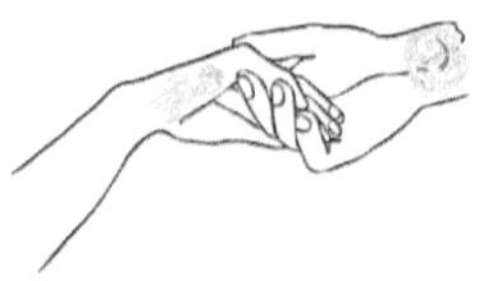

"How are you?" Aedan asks as he shuts and locks the door behind us.

"I appreciate the concern. But I think you have a pretty good idea how I'm feeling after that. How much did you hear?"

"Nearly all of it. And I apologize for the eavesdropping, but I wanted to make sure I understood where Hunter was coming from, how far he is from realizing what a tremendous treasure he's so tantalizingly close to having, or losing."

"And?"

"He's got some work to do. And, yes, some of the baggage is from this life. He's under a heavy burden that's not his own but that he's taken upon himself because he feels he deserves to be burdened."

"Guilt. He still blames himself for his mother's death, because he didn't stay with her that night. And because he was with me when she did it."

Aedan looks at me with a very grave expression.

"That does not go further than between you and me. Ever," I tell him pointedly. "Very few people know, and certainly no one involved in the industry. He has never fully dealt with her death, let alone his grief and guilt — guilt he clings to, despite the fact that it was his father who spurred it, with his horrible treatment of her. And I'm telling you this priestess to priest. So, let's pretend we're Catholic after all and say this is under the seal of the confessional. Even if it's his secret and not mine."

"Understood. And agreed. That burden alone would be enough to make him avoid committing to anyone, which — if

I am to be entirely honest — seems to very much be his modus operandi, at least for now."

"As I told him, I assumed that was the case."

"And it still hurts." It's a statement, not a question.

"It does. As much as I'd like to pretend it doesn't. I'm trying to think of it as exposure therapy," I add with a note of dark humor.

Aedan folds me into his arms, and I'm struck by how similar the sense of safety and comfort is to when it's Hunter who's holding me. There's a level of trust that has seemed to exist between us since the moment we both realized what the other was.

"Been there," he says quietly, and I know that he has.

"It sucks, doesn't it?" I say bleakly.

"It does. But I think both of us, after considerable waiting and more torment than would seem fair, are going to find that the wait is worthwhile. That doesn't mean it'll be easy or that we won't lose hope. But I think we'll eventually find ourselves at the end of this very dark tunnel. And, in the meantime, I'd propose — no, not marriage," he adds with a chuckle. "I'd propose that we help each other get through the darkness by sharing some light. If that idea still appeals after all that. I'll understand if you've changed your mind or need time to process."

I give it some thought, because it's a serious enough decision to merit that. And I can't think of anything that will change the decision I'd already made when I'd left this room earlier tonight. Hunter and I have restored some degree of equilibrium to our relationship and redrawn some lines, and I feel now like our paths march alongside each other more than being a single path that we share. Only time will tell if that continues to be the case. And I've been patient with him for this long. I can be patient a while longer. Especially with Aedan apparently still prepared to explore this attraction between us.

"I'd decided before we left the room the last time. I haven't changed my mind, nor do I find there's any reason why I might even want to change it. I'm not going to look a gift horse in the mouth, especially when I've got a long road ahead and my feet are tired," I add with a smile.

"So, I'm a horse now?" he jokes. "I'm sure we could work a little cowgirl-time into the itinerary for our little world tour," he adds with a smirk.

The heat he surely wanted to generate with those words strikes home, putting images in my head of things I'm not sure I'd have dared dream were possible for me, let alone with this man. I flush more than I'd like to, and Aedan doesn't fail to take note.

"There she is... that innocent girl with the seductress' soul," he says, with a note of delight. "Yes, we'll definitely put that on the list."

He circles me now, taking me in from toes to the top of my head, and not for a moment do I feel like I'm being judged, let alone found wanting. His expression is one of hunger, but hunger restrained, as if measuring small bites of delightful food to ensure the experience lasts as long as possible and can be enjoyed as thoroughly as it deserves.

There's an expectant feeling growing inside me. Something is about to happen here, and it will be very, very good. And probably not a little bit bad.

"Let's be plain with each other, Lady," Aedan says. "What have you experienced — in this life — and what yet remains to be enjoyed? Be honest, because I plan to be very thorough in our exploration, and I need to know where to proceed slowly and where more... vigor... would be appropriate."

I chuckle.

"Bear with me, because, as we've established, this is not a current area of expertise for me."

"Leave the expertise to me, Ellie. You just relax and tell me what you need, what you want. Let's start with the most basic question... Are you still a virgin?"

"I think we've established that already but, yes, my experience is nearly non-existent. The guy who told me he liked 'cherries' — he was pretty much it."

"And you were drunk at the time?"

"I'd have said tipsy. Hunter said drunk. I think he was closer to the truth."

"It can be useful to help you relax when you're uncomfortable, but I'd much rather find other ways to help you relax that also let you fully enjoy the experience and recall it fondly later."

He leads me back to the bed again, urging me to sit before sitting down next to me.

"Ellie — Do you prefer Ellie or Elle, or is it Eleanor?"

I laugh.

"My father is very adamant that my name is Ellen. But no one other than him has called me that since I was a child. Nearly everyone calls me Ellie. But it seems a little childish now. Hunter usually calls me Elle."

"Are you comfortable with me doing that as well? We are adults, doing adult things, and you deserve to be called by an adult name that you feel fits. Is that Elle?"

It's odd, because I'd never even considered whether Ellie or Elle fit me, any more than I'd questioned whether Ellen ever did.

"Actually... would you mind calling me Brighid?"

He looks a little surprised.

"Taking on the name of a goddess... Bold, but in your case, entirely suitable, I think. She'd tell you if She didn't like the idea."

"It's not that, actually... In my visions — yes, more than one — Hunter called me Brighid. I think that was actually my name."

"Then it's one connected to those experiences we're trying to tap into, and that would seem extremely fitting. So, Brighid it is, my Lady."

"I can hear the capital L when you say that."

"Of course! You've earned the title."

"You are being very respectful of a 19-year-old girl who fancies herself called upon by a goddess."

"I think you and I both know you're not just a 19-year-old girl. And there's no fancying involved. You're called. Like recognizes like. I keep saying that. Perhaps you needed to hear it."

"I know I recognize it in you. Instinctively. I haven't met many — well, any, really — Pagan men, let alone one who knows what it is to serve as priest."

"Your Pagan friends are all women? You mentioned your high priestess."

"It's her circle, her group. Eclectic — Wiccans, more generalized Pagans, a Druid or two. And I'm not formally a part of it. When they do ritual, they usually do it without me. I come for discussions and social events, but I'm not usually there for anything formal."

"You're a solitary."

"I am. You?"

"Yes. As I said, being out of the 'broom closet' poses issues. That's one reason you've been such a delight to get to talk to today. And I, too, seem to instinctively trust you. It's a good basis for us to work from. Now, my Lady, Brighid," he adds with a nod, "let's see where you are and where we want to go."

I take a breath and dive in.

"I had one slightly drunk fratboy kiss me and slide his hands into my panties. Right before Hunter broke down the door," I add with a wry chuckle. "So, I am only barely on this road at all."

"Nonsense. Getting on this road we're taking doesn't start with the body — it starts with the mind. And you've already told me you experienced that vision of you and Hunter back then. What did that Brighid do? How did she feel? What did she want?"

"She was very much in love, and in lust, with that Hunter."

"Much as you are now."

I nod in agreement.

"And what did they do together, that Brighid and that Hunter? Tell me... I need — but far, far more, *you* need — to learn what excites you, discover what you enjoy, learn what your body wants. And you need to learn to talk about that, ask for it."

I take a deep breath. Aedan seems to understand that this is a challenge for me. But he's waiting, patiently.

"He embraced her from behind..."

"You, Brighid. He embraced you. Own it."

I close my eyes, bringing the images back again, fresh.

"He embraced me from behind..."

"Does that appeal to you? Does it make you aroused, being approached from behind? Having a man's chest pressed to your back?"

"Yes. It does. I think we've established that my back is an erogenous zone for me. Especially my spine."

"Lips or fingers? We've already tried fingers, and you seemed to enjoy that."

"Fingers was very... good," I reply with a smile. "Lips — those are better. Tongue..." I shudder.

"Good. We're getting to know you. What did he do when he embraced you from behind? Did he kiss your neck? Play with your breasts?"

"Yes," I confirm with a laugh. "Both. He pinched my nipples between his fingers."

"And they got tight and hard and sharp, right?"

It feels almost like that's happening now. My breathing is speeding up, my pulse starting to pound.

"That's good, Brighid. Keep going."

"He kissed and sucked on my neck, leaving marks there, bruises... he wanted to mark me for later, mark me as his."

"Does that arouse you? Do you like being claimed like that?"

"I do. That way and..." I'm hesitating now... this is beyond just admitting that I liked Hunter putting his mark on my neck.

"You like knowing you have his cum in you... on you..."

"Yes."

"Say it. Tell me why."

"I like knowing he was inside me. I like being reminded of it afterward. I like knowing that I made him aroused enough that he came inside me. I like the feeling that he's left something of himself behind, part of him in me. I like having that evidence of him on my thighs, between my lips, running down between my butt cheeks..."

"Does that excite you? Being touched there?"

"Yes. He had me bent over, pressed down into the mattress, my butt up in the air, where he could do whatever he wanted to me, and he was fucking me..."

"Hard or gentle?"

"Slow and firm, then fast and hard." I am so unbelievably aroused right now, and that's just from reliving that one vision and describing it to Aedan.

"You're wet already, aren't you? Right now. Here. In the present."

"I am. I can feel it."

"How does that feel, knowing you're wet from just telling me about what turns you on?"

"Like we're going to have a very, very good time once there's more than words involved."

"Yes, Brighid... we are," he says, and I realize his voice is coming from behind me now, so close to my ear. He'd moved behind me without me even realizing. And I shudder.

He sweeps his hands over my shoulders, sliding the thin straps of my sundress down my arms. He places his hand on my back, running it from my waist to my shoulder blades before taking hold of the dress' zipper and sliding it slowly down. It feels like it could go on forever, moving inch by inch, loosening the dress around me, peeling it away from my body. When the zipper is open down to my hips, he pushes the straps down my arms, leaving me bare from the waist up.

"I'm going to touch you now, Brighid. I'm going to reach my arms around you and I'm going to touch your breasts, your nipples, just like you like."

"OK..." I can't imagine telling him no.

And just as promised, he slides his arms around me, his hands reaching up for my breasts. He weighs them in his hands, squeezing them lightly, and then takes each nipple between thumb and forefinger and pinches them sharply. I moan aloud. And then he twists. Just lightly. And they're so sensitive, so tight, so hard...

"How's that feel?"

"Amazing..."

"And how about this?" he asks before nuzzling my neck. Then he licks from my collarbone to my earlobe. I moan.

"You are so amazingly responsive, Brighid. You are so utterly sensual, sexual, by your very nature. I find it hard to believe no one else has seen this before, that no one else found you as irresistible as you are to me right now. I find it incredible that no one has bent you over a bed and fucked you, and eaten you like you were their last meal..."

He says all of this purring his words into my ear, while continuing to fondle my breasts, soft and sharp, massaging and pinching, and then pressing kisses along my nape, from spine to hairline, lifting my hair off to the side and then sucking the skin into his mouth, between his teeth, and biting down lightly.

"You're mine now, Brighid. I've marked you. And I'm going to mark you lots more. Over and over again."

I moan louder and longer this time. I want him to do that.

"I'm laying claim to this extraordinary woman. But not to her heart," he says, turning my face to look into my eyes. "Your heart is already given away, as is mine. You understand that, right? Before we take this any further."

"My heart belongs to Hunter. Always has, always will. And yours to your lady. But my body is my own to give as I choose, and, for at least a while, I'm giving it to you. If you want it."

"Oh, I want. So, want. What an amazing gift, even if it's just for a while..." He kisses along my jaw, turning me toward him before running his thumbs over my eyelids. "Look at me, Brighid. See me."

I open my eyes once again, and my breath is taken away in a rush, as I meet the intense blue of Aedan's eyes, so different from Hunter's green, and I find I don't so much mind the change. It's like Hunter and I — I've hit the pause button to let him work on what's his to deal with. And with that on pause, I can focus on what's in front of me now, which is one of the world's most desirable men, whose appeal to me is less in his admittedly stunning looks and more in this meeting of the souls and minds. Yes, this is going to be very, very good.

"Are you seeing me, Brighid? Are you seeing Aedan? Not Hunter, then or now? Aedan."

"Yes, Aedan, I see you. Hunter and I are for later. You are here and now, and I'm planning on enjoying every moment of it."

"Good. Because I am, too. And I plan on ensuring you experience every ounce of pleasure you can possibly have. I know you're wet, you're wet for me now, aren't you?"

"I am. Drenched."

"Practical matters... Are you on birth control, Brighid?"

"Yes. Just in case."

"Good." He goes to the dresser and digs under some clothes, withdrawing a piece of paper, which he holds out to me. "I get tested once a month and I never have sex without a condom, so I know I'm clean. Do you believe me? Do you trust me? Enough to know you're safe if we have nothing between us?"

I unfold the paper and scan across the contents. It's a panel of tests, all negative, dated three days ago. I look him carefully in his blue eyes again, seeing only honesty, earnestness. I ask for guidance, for surety. And I feel a hand on my back that isn't Aedan's, propelling me ever so slightly forward. Benediction.

"What does She say?" he asks, tuned in to my mind as he's done from the first moment we met.

"She approves."

"And do you?" he asks with a laugh. "Your consent is what I'm after."

"I do. I trust you." I hand him back the paper, which he sets back on the dresser before sitting down next to me once again.

"Then, I want to spend the next few hours exploring with you. This won't be the last time. And I'd much rather we had more time to do this. But if we wait for that, we'll be waiting weeks or months, and I don't want to wait. Do you?"

"No."

"Then I'm going to mark you a few more times on your throat. And I'm going to eat your pussy until you're dripping for me.

And I'm going to suck your nipples and run my tongue up your back..."

I shudder yet again. He's tapped straight into my deepest desires, without even trying hard.

"I'm going to stick my tongue down your throat. And at some point, I'm probably going to spank you a couple times, too. Does that sound good? Does that excite you?"

"Yes."

"When you are flying high on sex and sensation and this meeting of the minds, I'm going to fuck you... slow and gentle, and then hard and fast. And then we — both of us — are going to come, together, and I'm going to fill you up with my cum and leave you dripping with it as you lay panting under me, sated. Is that what you want?"

"Oh, yes... Yes."

"Today is just the start. But there will be more. I'll be back. Heck — come to Ireland with me when I go in a couple months."

My eyes go wide... Does he really mean that? I think he really does.

"We'll fuck each other in every county and every town, and we'll invent new ways to pleasure each other, until any notion of Brighid as a naive virgin is completely gone. You'll be a radiant goddess of sex. You're already halfway there. All you need is someone to hand you the keys to your own freedom. Do you want that?"

"Yes. I very much want that. All of it."

"Then let's get started."

CHAPTER 6

I HAD ME A GIRL

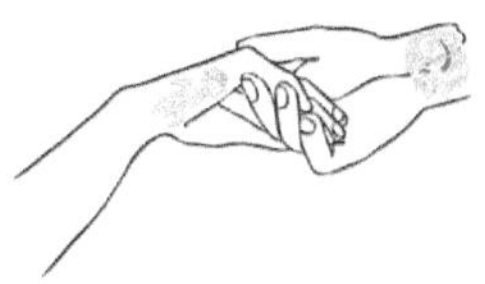

"You remember when I talked about other ways to ensure you're relaxed without having to be drunk?"

"Yes."

"We're going to work on that now. You're already aroused... wet... That's a start. But I still sense some tension. Let's fix that."

His hands return to my shoulders, his thumbs digging into the muscles, calluses brushing against my skin.

"I can tell you play guitar."

"I do," he says. "We're only a four-piece, unlike aMUSEd, so I play on at least some of our songs. And I write most of them. That's one reason I want to go to Ireland, spend some time there. I'm feeling like the well is a little dry, and it's time to refill it. Now, you noticed the roughness of my fingers on your soft skin. How about this?"

There's a gentle sweep of flesh across my left shoulder.

"Your lips..."

Now, warm, moist, firm...

"Your tongue..."

"Yes... And now?"

Now the sensation is running up from between my shoulder blades to the nape of my neck. My mouth falls open, wordless.

"Yes... definitely an erogenous zone," he comments with a low chuckle.

"Stand up."

I hesitate, because with my dress unzipped so far, I know it will just slide right off when I stand up. He's asking me to strip down to my panties for him.

"Yes. You will be nearly naked. Do it."

He's commanding but not demanding. I know I have the ability to refuse, which makes it all the more difficult to do what he's asking, because if I do, I've chosen to do it, and to follow his commands.

"Brighid..." He moves back in front of me, once again steering my eyes to his own, with no escape. I'm lost in the deep sea shining from his face, pools of blue so intense that it feels like being swallowed by the ocean. I'm a beach girl. But this is nothing like getting pulled under and thinking you'll drown. There's no tide, no wave, just peaceful blue, with an eddy of desire running through it.

"Brighid... You're safe here. You're safe with me. That seductress inside your head, in your memory — let her loose, let her come out to play. Borrow her confidence, her sense of self as a grown woman, her knowledge, her certainty that she induces lust in men, brings out their passion, their desire, because it's what's inside of her that does that. Put away the fears and the self-consciousness — just be. Be yourself, here with me. Now. And trust me that you are beautiful and desirable and capable of commanding a man with your mind and with your body. Because men will fall at your feet once you do.

"Stand up, Brighid," he says, half commanding, half cajoling.

I find myself rising to my feet and my dress does slide down to my toes, revealing me to his gaze, except for the small scrap of fabric that is barely containing my wetness now. Aedan' eyes have left my own, dropping lower as if pulled by my now-shed dress. He licks his lips, and his hunger is naked on his face now. His hands move to my hips, and he pulls me hard against him, pressing his hardness into me through the thin fabric. My eyes fall closed.

"That's for you, my Lady," he tells me, rolling his hips to press into me again, and catching my gaze once again.

He slides his thumbs under the sides of my panties and begins to pull them slowly downward, over my hips, down my thighs, moving ever lower with them, until they are on the floor and he is, as promised, on his knees in front of me. His eyes are now focused directly on my pussy, where it lays directly in front of his face. I begin to blush under his undisguised attention.

"Stop," he says, without taking his eyes off the scene in front of him. "This is a treasure. Don't ever forget that. Don't ever let anyone imply otherwise. If they do, they're lying. You serve a goddess. Own the sacredness of your body. It's a temple any sane man would die to worship in."

He presses his lips to the top of my mound. A gentle kiss atop it, again like a benediction. His arms wrap around me again, only this time, it's my hips, my thighs, my ass that he seeks to pull against him. And it's no comparatively chaste kiss he's giving. He's delivering open-mouthed kisses to my lower lips, my pussy pressed to his face by eager and determined hands. The sensation is overwhelming. And then he licks me from my opening to the top of my slit. My legs start to go weak, and he pulls his mouth away to look up at me.

"How has no one eaten this pussy before? How has no one devoured you and your sweet juices?"

I reach down and run my hand over his cheek. He catches it and presses a kiss to my palm.

"Teach me what you like, Brighid. Guide me to where you want my mouth."

He presses my palm to the back of his own head now, grabbing the other and placing it on the other side.

"Show me," he urges, bringing his mouth back to my core, breathing me in. He licks my clit. Once, twice, and I start to lose myself in the sensation. My hands instinctively guide his head as he licks, sucks, tongues and even nibbles his way around my center, until once again my knees, my thighs start to fail me. He growls against my pussy, grabbing my leg under the knee and pulling it up over his shoulder, leaving me standing on one leg, with the rest of my weight balanced on one of his broad shoulders.

He presses his mouth harder against me, his arms tight around my hips, his hands kneading my ass. He moans into my mons, and the vibrations shoot right through me. I can feel my inner muscles starting to tighten, the tension almost unbearable. And then Aedan pulls away, dropping my foot back to the floor.

I'm left panting and groan in frustration.

"Aedan... Tell me you're not going to leave me hanging here..."

He chuckles, just a hint of sadism in his voice.

He licks up the middle of my slit again, across my clit. My hips jerk forward.

"Did I tell you you were a bad, bad man?"

"You did. And I told you 'only in the best of ways.'"

He puts his palm against my pussy, his thumb rubbing against my clit. And he pushes me backwards with the pressure against my clit, my lips. It's like he's found a handle upon which my entire body balances, and he's using it to move me where he wants me to go. Which is back to the bed, I realize, as the backs of my knees hit the mattress and I find myself seated on the edge, my legs spread to accommodate Aedan' shoulders.

"I don't want your legs to go weak on you — which, trust me, they are going to do, very shortly here — and both of us end up on the floor. I'd rather save that for the third or fourth time we do this," he adds with a laugh that again suggests something somewhere between threat and promise. "Right now, I just want to eat you. Consume that glorious pussy. Sip from the sacred well..."

I raise an eyebrow.

"Too much?" The laugh is straightforward now. "But it's true. Source of all creation, sweet fount of liquid lust, center of the universe..."

"I think Neil deGrasse Tyson would disagree."

"Perhaps, but he would be lacking imagination, and firsthand experience of the wonder that is Brighid. Which is how it will remain, because you're mine now, remember?"

He nibbles at the inside of my thigh, pushing them even farther apart.

"Flexible. Nice," he observes with a chuckle. "We'll have to see just how much when we've got more time... But now, I've worked up an appetite, and I'm going to gorge myself on this pretty pussy."

From there, I lose track of the sensations, as his lips, tongue, teeth and fingers touch every part of me, laid out on display like a buffet, and he's acting like a starving man. I'm dripping under his attention, and he takes notice, sitting back on his haunches and running his fingers up and down my slit. He slides one inside me, and I gasp.

"There we go, my girl," he says. "Hungry pussy needs to be filled. And we'll get you there very, very soon now." He pulls his finger out, again sliding around my drenched opening, playing in the juices of my arousal. And then he slides the tips of two fingers inside me. I whimper.

"So hungry... Just as hungry for my fingers, my cock, as I am hungry for this gorgeous glistening pussy..."

He begins to work his fingers slowly in and out of my opening, and I can't even think anymore, the sensation overriding any brain function not directly related to arousal. And, of course, he picks that moment to ask me questions.

"So wet... Have you had anything else inside you besides my fingers? Your fingers? A toy?"

"My fingers. Just my fingers," I manage to reply, panting.

"So, you know what you like in that way, huh?"

"Kind of," I admit.

"We're going to explore that some more soon, too," he says. "But I'm asking because you may experience a little bit of pain the first time. 'May,' because not every woman keeps her hymen intact until she loses her virginity, contrary to popular belief. Modern women do too many vigorous activities for that to be the rule anymore. I want to make sure that if it's going to hurt at all, we go slow and gentle, regardless of what either of us might want right now. So, I'm going to do a little exploring with my fingers first."

"OK."

He inserts two fingers inside me again, this time probing around inside. The feeling is different from what I'm used to. The inability to predict where or how he'll touch me adds an edge beyond what I might have given myself. And just as I'm getting used to the sensation, he pushes both fingers straight inside me, going deep this time, and again I gasp. This is new... and it's wonderful...

My hips press forward, seeking more. He gives me more, curling his fingers inside me to caress and then tap a spot on the front wall, sending my whole body into a spasm against his hand.

"There we go... That's your G-spot, my luscious Brighid. Wonderful little bundle of nerves that does wondrous things if you can manage to hit it... with fingers or a cock. And since you haven't so much as winced, I'm going to conclude that your hymen is already broken. Which is going to make this a lot easier and more fun for both of us. But I'm still going to ensure you're ready for me. I'm not small," he warns. "Not bragging. Just reality," he says. "More lubrication is better. On several fronts."

He returns his mouth to my pussy, licking and sucking, pulling on my clit with his lips and probing it with his tongue. And all the while, he's working those two fingers in and out, in and out, at an ever-increasing pace, all sense of slowness and gentleness sliding away as my hips begin to thrust against his fingers. That tension is there again, feeling like I could split in two at any moment.

"That's it, my Lady... Let go... Lose yourself in it... Give me your pleasure."

My inner muscles are fluttering against his fingers, getting tighter and tighter, and my hips buck wildly against his mouth. I feel like I'm going to explode. And then suddenly, he sets his fingertips to target my G-spot and sucks my clit inside his mouth and I do explode, crashing in pieces held together only by the feeling of his fingers inside me and his mouth on me and the feel of my inner muscles grasping so hard at his fingers.

"There's my girl," Aedan says. "Ride it out..."

He continues to milk the contractions from me, sucking on my clit and fucking me with his fingers, tapping that little bundle of nerves inside until I can't do anything other than pant, my mouth open and unable to form words. Slowly... oh, so slowly, the contractions start to subside, and I'm left feeling gloriously high and with my whole pussy throbbing deliciously as he slides his fingers from inside me.

He sits up, leaning over me as I lay sprawled on the bed, and claims my mouth with his own, feeding me the taste of my own pussy, combined with the unique taste that is all Aedan Mason. He tangles his tongue with my own before I feel him smile against my mouth.

"I'd ask you if you enjoyed that, but the evidence is dripping down between your ass cheeks," he teases.

"Thank you," I tell him. "That was... amazing. I had no idea how much ... more... it would be with someone taking care of things for me."

"I'm going to be doing a lot of taking care of things for you, Brighid. But don't thank me. You probably can't fully appreciate it yet, but that was just as pleasurable for me as it was for you. Your expressions, your reactions... Sexiest thing I've ever seen. Truly."

He presses another kiss to my lips and lets his fingers trail down between the lips below. My hips lunge for him of their own accord.

"Wow."

"Your body knows what it needs. And it wants more. And I'm going to give it to you. Especially now that I know I can do it without needing to worry about hurting you."

"You realize you still have all your clothes on, and I'm lying here on the bed in your room, entirely naked."

"I do realize that. But I'm about to remedy that. Or, rather, you're about to remedy that..."

My eyebrows go up.

"Next lesson: Getting comfortable undressing your lover."

Aedan grabs my hand and pulls it to his waist, tucking my fingers around his belt buckle.

"Undo it, Brighid. My cock is very eager to make your acquaintance. Help him out."

My fingers refuse to work, and it's not because I'm drunk this time.

"Look at me, Brighid," he commands. "Unbuckle my belt."

I swallow and begin to pull the belt through the buckle, now using my other hand to pull the latch free, and I pull the belt through the loops of his jeans, laying it on the floor.

"Keep going," Aedan urges, a catch now in his voice.

Feeling a little bolder, I grasp the bottom of his T-shirt and pull it upwards. The movement lifts my breasts, and I see his eyes flicker down. He grabs my wrist and stops me from finishing removing his shirt. Instead he moves his mouth to my breast and pulls the nipple inside, thrashing at it with his tongue and then sucking it to a point before pulling it free of his mouth with a pop. My head drops forward, and I find his forehead pressing against mine.

"Just perfect. Just utterly perfect," he murmurs.

"I'm going to be very honest with you, Brighid. I've had a lot of women in my life. All sizes, shapes, colors... But this, with you... I'm not sure I've ever been this aroused before I've even gotten my shirt off," he admits with a chuckle. "This is not me flattering you because you need more confidence. This is me being open about exactly how desirable you are. I'm still marveling that you're mine. Even if it isn't forever."

"You've been so wonderful, Aedan. I'm not sure I could have asked for a nicer first time for all of these things. Things I've wanted for so long..."

"You'd have enjoyed it more with Hunter. You and I both know that," he says, and I concede the point with a nod. "But you can't keep your life on hold while you wait for that stubborn guitar player to wake the fuck up. So, I'm taking the keys from his sleeping hands and handing them to you. From here on, you have agency. You decide what your life is going to be like. Not him. Not me. Not any man. Just you, priestess, goddess in the making... Now, finish stripping me out of my clothes so I can climb inside you and make us both feel even better."

My whole body shudders, from the top of my head to my toes.

I grab for his shirt once again, now suddenly in a hurry to get Aedan naked. He chuckles at my newfound urgency.

In one motion, I'm pulling the shirt over his head, marveling at the sight of him before it even touches the floor. Solid muscle, defined but not from hours spent in the weight room. This is a man who looks like he has spent half his life toting amps and moving heavy metal flight cases, even though I know he has roadies to do that all for him now. My gaze drifts downward, the direction suggested by the chiseled V running from his waist and into his jeans, and targeted with a scant trail of hair leading directly to the top button of his jeans.

"My eyes are up here," Aedan jokes, tweaking one of my nipples.

"Sorry. I may be a beach girl, but this is a totally different context from seeing guys on the beach."

I reach toward his chest, grazing a thumbnail across the flat button of his nipple and then doing the same to the other one with my other hand. My hands slide south, taking in the underlying muscles and the feel of his skin under my fingers. I look up into his eyes, which are gentle and knowing, with an underlying heat that I want to take inside me. My hands reach into his hair, pulling him to me and pressing my lips to his. My mouth opens and I lick at his lips, coaxing him to open up to me, and he does, his tongue tangling with mine as we taste each other and relish every moment of it. Something as simple as a kiss, and how big that moment felt...

"That's the first time you've ever kissed a man, isn't it?" he asks. I start to correct him, but he continues. "Not the first time you've been kissed, but the first time you've been the one initiating it..."

"I suppose so," I acknowledge. "I hadn't really thought of it that way... I tried..." I take a deep breath and sigh. "I tried to kiss Hunter right after the first time I told him about my vision of us.

I'd wanted to do it for years, and I'd even tried to kiss him when we were little. He ran away," I admitted, a wry expression on my face.

Aedan' expression slides toward sadness, and perilously close to pity.

"He came back and told me I was his bestest friend, but that kisses were yucky and I shouldn't try that again," I add with a smile. "He had... He *has* no idea how difficult it was for me to even try it again, all those years later, with so much more on the line."

"It hurt you, when he stopped you."

"It did. I'd been so nervous about it — I just couldn't get myself to close that small distance and touch my lips to his, and it was eating me alive at that point, weeks after the first vision. I finally broke through that invisible wall. And he erected another between us in the space of seconds."

Aedan smooths my hair away from my face.

"He's asleep, Brighid. He doesn't really understand what he's doing. He doesn't see the import of these things, which seem to mean so little in the context of a single life but grow bigger when they follow us from life to life. But he will wake up. Someday. I promise you."

"I'm going to hold you to that," I joke.

"Sweet girl... you need this so badly I don't think even you understand that. But I'm going to make sure you have it. We'll try to undo some of the hurt, as much as I can. Some of it is Hunter's to undo, and nothing I could do or say will change that. But the rest of it... I'm going to do my best."

"Why do I believe you when you say that?"

"Because it's the truth," he says, sighing. "Look at me... You and I — this isn't the intensity of the eye-fuck, though we've had that, too, and will plenty more. But it's more comfortable, more serenely spiritual than eye contact is between you and Hunter. There's less deep emotion involved, rushing at you like an untamed bolt of lightning. You and I — it's a safely insulated high-voltage electric cable. I'm actually kind of surprised I didn't feel you from a mile away tonight — good mental shields you've got there... Until we touch or we look in each other's eyes. This is important, you and me. I think I need this almost as much as you do."

He leans into me and captures my mouth again, leaving me gasping, and before I can get my equilibrium back, he's taken hold of my hand and once again placed it at his waist, this time on the top button of his jeans.

"Undress me, Brighid. Undo the buttons and let my cock out so we can play together."

This time, there's no real hesitancy in me. What little reticence I retained after he fucked me with his fingers and ate me into oblivion is gone in the face of that thrumming connection, which transmits the energy between us but doesn't pose a terrifying risk.

My fingers find confidence as they work the buttons of his fly, one by one. And I don't have to go far before I realize there's nothing between him and me but the fabric of his jeans. My jaw goes slack, my mouth liquid.

Once again, he grabs my hand. But this time he pushes it down, turning my palm to cup him through his jeans. So hard... So big... So close...

"Take it out, Brighid. It's all for you. Let it loose so I can get inside you. I'm so hard, so painfully hard, poking through my jeans to get to you. Take me out."

I can't resist the plea. I undo the remaining buttons on his fly, and with just a moment of hesitation, I slide my hand inside, grasping his cock firmly and stroking it from root to tip.

"That's nice... So nice... You've got wonderful hands," he says. He pulls my hand free, and for a moment I wonder what I did wrong. But then he stands up, his open fly now even with my mouth, and my mouth waters at the proximity.

"Take them off me, Brighid. Take my jeans off. Make me as naked as you are now, sitting in front of me, with that sexpot mouth and those soulful eyes eating up what you can already see. See the rest of me now. So hard for you. So eager for you."

I put my hands on his hips, unable to resist the temptation to run my thumbs along the indentations of that V. His hips jump forward at my touch.

"Don't play with me, Brighid, or I won't be able to wait. And I don't want to just pull out my cock and fuck you." My inner muscles tense and I can feel it right in my spine. "I'd much rather take my time with you this first time. But *you* have to take off my pants. *You* have to strip me naked. I won't do it for you."

After that, I don't wait. I pull his jeans down around his hips and his cock juts out from his body, hard and erect, the tip already glistening in his eagerness for me. I pull the jeans down the rest of the way, and he steps free of them, standing proudly in front of me.

"Touch me. Gently. We'll play more later. But right now you need to be comfortable with my cock."

He pulls my hand to him, again cupping my hand over his dick. But this time there's nothing between me and that rock-hard staff covered in warm, velvety skin. He slides my hand up and down, his hips pushing forward against my palm.

"All for you, Brighid. All for you... Are you still wet for me?"

I nod, feeling the renewed rush between my legs, my body preparing me for what it wants very badly now.

"Show me. Use your fingers."

I'm past the shyness now, immediately doing as he asks and feeling my pulse racing faster as I do.

"Oh, yes..." Aedan drawls. "We're definitely going to do that... You like me watching you, don't you? It makes you even wetter. Touch yourself for me. Touch yourself how you'd want me to touch you."

I slide my fingers down to my opening and gather some of the moisture there. I circle my clit with my fingers and find I'm rocking against my hand, seeking more stimulation. My fingers travel south again, this time entering me.

"Beautiful... so beautiful... so sensuous... sex goddess..." Aedan muses, his jaw slack and his eyes gone huge and dark. He's stroking himself lightly as he watches me with my fingers inside me, now moving slowly in and out as his had before. "Show me your fingers. Show me how wet you are."

I slide my fingers free, and they're glistening with my arousal. Aedan grabs my wrist, pulling my hand upward. His lips drop down and the next thing I know, he's sucking my juices from my fingers, slowly and sensually, seeming to relish every taste.

"I said you were sweet. I meant it," he says, his voice low and full of heat as he continues to slowly stroke himself. "My tongue and my fingers have had their tastes of you, and now it's time for my cock to have some of his own."

His expression is beyond hungry now as he steps closer to me where I'm still seated on the bed, my legs splayed from letting him watch me play with myself. I instinctively move back, and

Aedan is on me in a second, pulling my hips back forward toward him. He runs his cock along my slit, coating it with my moisture. He slots it between my lips, the head poking above my clit, and he rolls his hips back and forth, running his length across that spot, and watching it raptly, and it instantly sends my desire into the stratosphere.

"Too good... too hot... almost too much," he murmurs before sliding back. "Lie back, Brighid," he urges, pulling me upwards when I don't move fast enough for him. "Open for me," he encourages, pushing my thighs apart, and I let my legs fall to the side, giving him full access.

He growls now, and unintelligible expression that combines hunger and aggression restrained. He strokes himself again before climbing onto the bed on his knees, between my legs. Again he slides his cock up and down through my center. He leans down and takes one of my nipples in his mouth, sucking until it become a tight point, then moving over to do the same to the other. My back is bent, feeding my breasts to him, wanting him to devour me whole. Again he releases my nipple with a pop, a last little bit of suction and sensation to drive me wild.

And now it's my mouth he wants. He leans up across me and just instantly owns me, pressing his lips to mine before demanding entry with his tongue, and I give it to him gladly as we taste each other and moan into each other's mouths. I feel him move his hand down below, grasping himself and aiming directly at my opening. He hesitates there, catching my eyes with his, a question clear in his expression. Once again, we have an instinctive understanding of each other, and I nod, pressing my hips up toward his.

He returns to my mouth, taking control of the kiss and of me, ravaging my mouth and turning my arousal up from boil to boiling with the lid on. And just when I think I can't take anymore, I feel him start to press inside me, and the sensation is exquisite, not the same as any I've felt before, not my fingers, nor his, nor his tongue. It's a desperately welcome invasion as his cock caresses my interior walls as it slides slowly, ever farther inside me, until he's buried deep within me, up to the hilt, and I can just feel the tip of him brush my cervix.

He runs a finger over my cheek, again offering intense eye contact that asks a question, this time asking if I'm OK, if I'm ready for more. And I can honestly say I've never felt better. No hint of pain, no real discomfort, only the sensation of being filled by something warm and hard and wonderful. I attack his mouth with my own, giving him his answer, and he begins to pull back. I relish the sensation but nonetheless feel the loss. That sense of fullness, of knowing I had this glorious man inside me, like this was meant to be... It slides out of my grasp again, and I want it back. I push my hips up at Aedan once more.

"Patience, my greedy one. I'm not going anywhere until this has reached its natural conclusion, and even then, I'm thinking it's going to be very hard not being inside you every moment of every day. Delicious..."

His mouth dips down to suck on my neck, and I can feel the little bruises he's leaving behind, making me wonder if he's sketching a constellation of his own making on my skin, for the world to see and marvel at, as surely as the Great Bear or Orion's belt. And as I picture that, Aedan has pulled out of me except the very tip of himself. He braces his arms to either side of me, and I know what's coming.

He pushes into me in one hard thrust, and he swallows my ecstatic moan with his mouth before pulling slowly out again. When my hips begin wiggling under him, seeking to have him back inside me again, he chuckles once more.

"Greedy, impatient, hungry, hungry, *so* hungry, this pussy... You'll get what you want. Enjoy it in the moment, every sensation, every touch. We won't get the chance to do this again, not like this, not the first time. Never again the first time for you, not for this. Relish it. Let me pleasure you, let me make this perfect for both of us."

He's looking into my eyes once again, and this time I nod my assent. Once more he slams home, and my legs wrap around him, pulling him deeper. My head is thrown back — too much sensory input. He brushes his lips across my throat, grazing me with his teeth and I silently scream, unable to make my vocal cords work and express in words how good that feels.

He's captured my eyes with his now, gazes locked together as he begins to move rhythmically in and out of me, the snap of his hips at the end of each stroke making his cock tap against the nerves inside me.

Our eyes penetrate each other as surely as his cock penetrates my core, conveying something with wordless meaning that we both innately understand. And we're in a shared space —

not this room, nor the space inside my body that we now both inhabit, but sacred space that's created here yet exists beyond this physical world, amidst cloud and fog, sunlight and moonlight, our minds and spirits in an endless, timeless dance, cavorting together in a realm beyond form or function, where there is only existence in the moment and a liquid flow of one into the other, one through the other, separate and yet one.

Wordlessly locked together in body and spirit, we dance in the earthly realm as well, coming together not gently, but with passion and heat and desperation and glory and an instinctive push-pull that rises like the crest of a wave as he plunges within me over and over again, ever faster, control sliding away from us both as the wave reaches a peak, our eyes finally unleashed from one another, and we both scream into mouths now once again locked together.

Aedan collapses onto me, panting just as I am.

I close my eyes and look away, trying to recover myself after feeling like that mutual explosion hurled parts of me across the entire universe.

Looking back again, I see that Aedan, too, seems a little scattered, the placid priest's mind replaced with something more closely resembling a rumpled bed after a night of passionate sex. Suitably. Aptly. Appropriately. And there's the moment when my brain comes back online.

"Wow."

"Yeah. Wow," he agrees.

"It's not like that all the time?"

"No. It's not... Wow."

"Where'd we go there at the end? Or was it just me?"

"No, not just you. That was a dance well beyond the physical one we continued here."

"You know it's not..."

He chuckles. "No need to worry about me giving you my heart, priestess. It still belongs to another."

"As does mine."

"But that was something... unique... special... And I don't think it was just because it was your first time. I think that was us. Whether it will continue is another question. One I can't answer. But I can't wait to find out!" he adds with a radiant smile.

"Tha..."

"Ahh-ahh-ahhh — none of that, my Lady. This was, as promised, for both of us. That it worked out tremendously better than either of us could have predicted doesn't change that. So, I don't want to hear that word. Not regarding this or any future meeting of the minds, and more."

"Agreed."

"Wow."

"Yeah. Wow."

"I guess I don't have to ask if you enjoyed that..."

"Since you were all but inside my head for a portion of that, I don't think that will be necessary."

"I enjoyed the inside-your-body part, too, Brighid. Speaking of which — I've marked you again, claimed you as mine again."

He pulls out of my body, languidly, liquidly, and it's both arousing all over again and a keenly felt loss.

"Felt that, did you?"

I chuckle. "Of course. I'd almost gotten used to having you inside me."

"Now you see what I meant about expecting I'd not want to be anywhere else anytime soon."

"I'm glad it's mutual, at least."

"Most definitely. And, back to my original question — do you feel that?"

My expression must convey my confusion. Aedan grabs my hand and pulls it down between us, tracing along the skin of my inner thighs and his as well.

We're, both of us, dripping with our combined release. He has indeed marked me again, claimed me in yet another way that no one else has. At least not in this lifetime.

"You've marked me as well, priestess. You've got me until you tell me you don't want me, or until my lady wakes up."

"You don't have to..."

"It's not a matter of having to," he says. "It's a matter of is. Can you tell me, after that, after what we just experienced, that you'd want anyone else inside you?"

"Other than Hunter, no. I can't say that I would."

"Someday, you and I will move on, release each other. But I'm in no rush to get there. I said we could share the light until we reach the end of the dark tunnel we both find ourselves in, and I have no plans to do otherwise."

"Wow."

"Wow, indeed."

"We keep saying that."

"I think it's merited under the circumstances."

"Agreed."

"At some point, over practical concerns, I'm going to have to wash you off of me, and you will have to wash me off of you. Now — don't look so sad. That was always inevitable. I'm not really looking forward to slipping back into my jeans. But I'm also not ready to wash you off me yet. So that sensation will remind me, for a while, what we shared here and what we will continue to share until our time together has passed."

"It's a little easier with a dress on, I suppose."

"I would think so. Speaking of which... We have so much more to explore, but time has flown past in this little bubble of ours, and I think you'll find it's time for you to go. But I have a suggestion."

"What?"

"Assuming he's as willing as I think he will be, take Hunter home with you tonight, as you had planned. And do not wash me off of you."

"Why?"

"You already smell of sex and of me. My seed between your thighs — he'll notice it on some level, and it may remind him what he's already given up and again give him a push to wake up before he's in danger of losing it all."

"I don't think he's going to have much trouble realizing that we weren't exactly having a philosophical discussion in here the last couple hours," I remind him, gesturing to what is already looking like a Grade A collection of love marks on my neck and chest.

"He'll see them and know you had fun with another man. But he'll never know whether I just marked you up or whether I had you completely. Don't tell him. Let him wonder. And when he finally wakes up, he'll be the beneficiary of our explorations, whether he realizes it or not."

"You really want me not to tell him? Ever?"

He sighs.

"When you and I no longer belong to each other in this moderately limited way, and if he has woken up, tell him if you wish. But be sure he won't feel compelled to come retroactively knock down my door. I'd like to return him to you minus a police record. If he can be trusted not to do that and not to let the tale go any further than between us, I suspect he and I will need to sit down and have a beer or three and compare notes. Because you, my Lady, are already extremely memorable," he adds with a smile that makes my insides warm. "Now... let's get this clothing situation taken care of, and you can go reclaim your sleeping soulmate. Have him at the venue by 6:30 for their soundcheck. And then you and I will see what other kinds of terrain we wish to explore together," he adds with a lascivious grin.

"Tomorrow? Again?"

"We won't be anywhere close by for at least another month after that. So I say one more night to tide us over. Agreed?"

"Yes, please," I say sweetly.

"And Brighid — I was serious about Ireland. I'd like to experience that with you. I have a feeling that trip will be extremely inspiring. So, please, plan to come with me. In two months' time. Get your passport in order, arrange for a Hunter-sitter or whatever you need," he adds with a wink, "pack a bag and bring your traveling shoes. Oh — and a nice dress. Something sexy like this one," he says, handing me back my sundress. "One of these days, I'm going to have you go without panties, and I'm going to fuck you outdoors. Preferably on a beach, so both of Them can see what they've wrought."

I chuckle, but the image has kickstarted my arousal once more. Which is probably exactly what he intended.

"You're getting aroused just thinking about it, aren't you?" he says knowingly.

"Of course. You have that effect on me."

"Because you're a naturally sexual creature and like recognizes like."

I slip on my dress and pull the straps back up. Aedan moves to zip it before I can even lay hands on the zipper. He runs his hands up my sides again, and I shudder once more.

"So responsive..." he murmurs, and I smile.

"Now I just need my panties."

"They have been confiscated."

"Confiscated? Why?"

"Because it'll keep you aroused, and because I want a reminder of what I do to you, because I'm going to have to deal with what you do to me every day we're not together."

"So you're planning to jack off in my panties."

"I hadn't been until you mentioned it. But now that you have, I think I'm going to have to do just that. You, my Lady, have a very dirty mind for a girl who just lost her virginity an hour ago."

"I do. And I did, didn't I?" I reply, unexpectedly proud of that turn of events. And that's before we even get to the fact that the man who claimed my virginity is this rockstar with the soul of a priest.

"Oh, you really, really did. And that seems to please you."

"It does."

"Good. It was inexplicably overdue. Stupid boys and their lack of insight..." He shakes his head and smiles warmly at me. "But, once again, lucky me."

"I'd tell you that is very nice to hear, but I expect you already know that."

"Not flattery, Lady. Gods' honest truth. I was a very lucky man tonight. I hope to remain that way for a while to come," he adds, sliding his hand up under my skirt. "So wet. And so tempting. I could bend you over and have you again right now. I could make it quick... but I'd much rather savor you tomorrow. Or maybe I'll take you up against a wall... And you still owe me that blowjob. So many things left to try," he adds with a leer.

"I'm looking forward to it."

I smile as he slides his hand back out from under my dress.

And with that, he pulls me hard up against him.

"That's for you. Yours," he assures me as he places my hand on his renewed erection. "Don't forget." He grabs my neck and pulls me in for a torrid kiss that threatens to melt me into a puddle in my shoes, before pulling back and looking me deep in the eyes once more. "Wow." He shakes his head, that lovely auburn hair falling into his eyes again. And he offers me his arm and escorts me back to the other room.

CHAPTER 7

GO INSANE

When I find him on a sofa in the living room, Hunter is... well, he's drunk. Drunker than I can remember ever seeing him. But then I didn't see enough of him after all those parties during high school — the ones that I wasn't invited to — to know whether this is normal for him.

"Hunter — it's time to go. We need to go get some sleep so you can do the show tomorrow night in Virginia Beach."

"We're going to the beach? Can't stay with dad... Bastard..."

"No, you can't. But we're not going back to Mystic Beach. You've got a gig in Virginia Beach."

"Oh! Well, that's OK then. Where's the bus?"

"You're coming back with me to get some sleep while everyone else is going to take the bus to the venue. Telltale Signs has some PR to do early this afternoon. So they need to get going here soon. I'm going to drive down with you after we've gotten some sleep...

"And after you've had a chance to sleep some of this off..." I mutter.

"You need any help? I can send one of the security guys with you," Aedan asks.

"No. I'm going to have a hard enough time getting his drunk ass into the dorm without waking anyone up, even if most everyone is already gone for the summer. A big hulking guy dragging him around after me won't be an improvement. But thanks."

"Let me know if you need help after all. You've got my number."

"I do. Thank you. I'll have him there by six. Good luck with the PR stuff today."

"Thanks. It's old hat at this point."

"I bet it is. Nothing much left to surprise the jaded rockstar, eh?"

"Well, I still get surprised every once in a while. Takes something rare, though," he adds with a smile that's intended solely for me.

He helps me lever Hunter up off the sofa and get him moving down the hallway, giving me a small wave before pulling aside one of the security guys and telling him to go with me.

"I really do have it covered," I tell him. "I've been taking care of Hunter for a long time."

"Longer than most people would believe... I know. But Barry here is just going to see you to your car, just in case."

"OK. Thanks. I'll see you later."

He winks at me.

Stop that! Bad, bad man... Deliciously bad...

I get Hunter to my car and buckled in without any problems, giving Barry a wave of thanks. When we arrive at the dorm, I leave Hunter sitting outside the locked side door and come back to open it from inside and bring him in with me. I dump him on the bed and take off his shoes, in the process realizing he reeks of alcohol. Must have spilled some on himself. I roll my eyes and strip off his shirt, trying not to admire the view.

"You throw up on me and I'm going to be pissed, Hunter. I've still got to get you to Virginia Beach in like twelve hours. And I need some sleep."

"Not gonna throw up. Come. Sleep," he commands, holding his arms out to me from where he's already lying down in my bed.

The man is so baffling sometimes. He's cuddly and annoying and stupid and amazing all at the same time.

But I can't just lie down with him right now. If for no other reason than I don't have on any panties... Yeah. Going to have to remedy that. Boy, would that be a surprise for him. Of course, I'm not sure how much of this he'll even remember. But I head into the bathroom with a tank top, yoga pants and, yes... panties! Darn Aedan and his little panty fetish... But he's right. Even thinking of the fact that he's got my panties is making me horny all over again. Thinking about what he might be doing with them is too distracting to let happen.

I go to clean up a little, turning on the faucet for just an instant before remember Aedan's suggestion. Alright... let's see how this goes.

I put on my clothes and crawl into bed with Hunter. He pulls my back up against his chest and snuggles up spoon-style. He pauses for a moment and gives me a sniff.

"You use a different soap?" he murmurs.

"No. Actually didn't wash up at all. Too tired. I'll shower in the morning."

"You smell differen'. Don' like it."

I have no idea what to say to that. Part of me wonders if he doesn't like it because I smell of Aedan, who predicted this would happen. I decide not to say anything, and we both fall asleep.

Later that morning

"U p, Hunt! Get up!"

I'm already showered and dressed. I had to carefully pick my outfit, because so many of my favorite clothes have spaghetti straps or bare shoulders, and with the mottled appearance of my lower neck and shoulders this morning, wearing any of them would send a not even vaguely subtle message about what I'd been up to last night.

I smile at that thought. Aedan marked me, because he knew I liked it and because he wanted to. It's very strange to me to feel wanted, to feel claimed, and even more so when there's no goal of a happily-ever-after with him. He and I both know this is not that. But we also both recognize that it's something very good and very needed by both of us.

It's hard to believe that the Sexiest Guy guy not only doesn't want a bevy of groupies in his bed every night but somehow, for some reason, wants me to be the one who's in his bed when there's anyone there at all. He isn't lacking for "just sex" partners. But then we're not truly just about the sex. There's something more there, whether it's friendship, understanding or just a deeper chemistry than the physical.

And he marked me. Because he wants that with me. For however long we both do want it. Which is seeming like it might be for a while.

I'm not counting on it, but I'd be lying if I said I wasn't looking forward to it.

So, I've pulled a keyhole top out of my closet. It covers up most of the marks Aedan left. Just the edges of a couple of the little bruises show along the inner neckline, with the rest hidden under the shoulders and mock neck. If I don't move around too much, it's unlikely anyone will even notice. Not that I'd mind in general, but I don't want to have to lie to Hunter about this any more than necessary.

I haul Hunter up to a seated position on the bed. Man, he's gotten heavy with all the muscle he's put on in the last few years! And I give him some ibuprofen, with orders to take them — which he follows for once — and then toss a cold washcloth at him to help wake him up.

"Wake yourself up. We've got to go."

"Where are we going?"

"Virginia Beach."

"Weird time to go to the beach, Elle."

Really? He's still on this?

"You have a gig — remember, rockstar? You're opening for Telltale Signs in about eight hours."

"Oh. Right. My head hurts."

"Which is why you just took some ibuprofen."

"Ah. Yup. It's all coming back to me now!"

Wait. What is all coming back to him now? Is he remembering seeing me with the first hint of all of those little bruises last night?

"Don't worry. I'll be fine."

I'm hit with a twinge of guilt over the subterfuge and over having left him alone last night, getting drunk, when I was having my little cherry-pie sexfest with Aedan.

"The ibuprofen will kick in soon, and as soon as this headache wears off, I'll be good to go. Maybe after another couple hours of sleep…"

He lies back down, and I lose patience with this.

"Hunter! Wake up!"

I drop the wet washcloth on his face again, hoping it's still cold enough to get him moving.

"I'm up! I'm up!"

I grab a T-shirt from the closet. Pausing and frowning a little when I see which shirt it is. Hunter Graves is where my concert tees go to disappear. It's one reason being a big girl with a male best friend can suck. They just steal all your cool shirts.

"Here — put this on," I tell him.

"Is this your favorite Fleetwood Mac concert T-shirt? From the show my mom took us to in Hershey in...?"

"It was 2004."

The year before she died, which I'm not going to remind him of.

"Good times... a day at the amusement park and a concert by one of the best bands of all time."

One of Hunter's mom's favorites, and both of ours in turn.

"With no Christine McVie," I note, recalling how sad she'd been that they'd said there was never going to be another full Fleetwood Mac reunion. "But Lindsey kicked ass."

"Yes, he did. Made me want to buckle down and get better."

"And you did. And look at where you are now..." Which makes me look at my watch. "Which is three hours from where you need to be in about four hours. Mace said your soundcheck is at 6. Put that on and let's get moving! Your limo awaits, rockstar."

"Fits like it was made for me." He pats the shoulders as he settles the shirt over his chest.

"Oh, I don't think so, mister!"

"What?"

"Just because your best friend isn't so petite you can't wear her concert tees doesn't mean you get to appropriate them! I want that back. Washed. Or there will be retribution."

I have no idea what retribution. But I'd find something. Probably. Maybe.

"Sounds like fun!"

I throw the washcloth in his face again.

"Get your shoes on. We need to go."

"I need more sleep, Elle."
"Yeah. You probably do."
I hand him a travel pillow from the back seat of the car.
"Go ahead. Take a nap. I'm driving."
I spend the next two hours and change with an endless whirlwind of thoughts running through my brain.
Hunter.
Aedan.
Love.
Sex.
Placid priest brain-space rumpled in a sex-filled bed.
Sweetly sleeping with his arms around me.
Sweetly sleeping next to me.
Fingers inside me.
Aedan's cock inside me.
Keep your eyes on the road, girl. Let's not kill the rockstar before he gets his first Grammy, as tempting as that has sometimes seemed...
Hey — I'm giving myself credit here. What 19-year-old freshly-deflowered virgin wouldn't be a little fixated on the experience less than twelve hours later? And that's with any old 19-year-old guy. Not the list-making rockstar. Who turned out to be as sweet and caring as any teenage boy would have been, with a ton more expertise and a wisdom beyond even his 30 years of life.
Yeah. I'm a little besotted with him. But probably a little more so because I'm not in love with him and have no plans to be. It takes the pressure off. I get to just enjoy the time we have together, explore and learn, talk about spiritual matters and even use him as a sounding board where Hunter is concerned. Win-win, as far as I'm concerned.
I turn up the stereo a little, spurred by the earlier Fleetwood Mac conversation to play some of their music while I drive. I'm listening to Lindsey Buckingham's virtuoso live acoustic

performance of "Go Insane" for the fourth time when Hunter wakes up.

"I love this song." He stretches as much as his long arms can manage inside a car.

"I know. It's probably one of my favorite songs of all time. If it was just the guitar playing, it would be incredible. But the vocal performance. Just riveting, devastating... One of the best things they ever recorded, and it's purely him."

"People always assume you love Stevie, with that long blonde hair and the witchy style..."

"She's fine. I like her. The vibe between them is odd, though. You can tell there's something there that comes before..."

"Before?"

I've avoided mentioning this to him before, because the "before" I'm referring to is the same kind of "before" he and I have, which he can't deal with. So I let the silence do my talking.

"Oh."

"Anyway — we're nearly there, and it's perfect timing, because you're going to go wow them on that stage yourself in a couple hours."

"That I am. I hope."

"Head OK?"

"Better. The sleep helped. Thanks."

"It's not that long of a drive. About the same as back home, but with a concert at the end instead of a cranky parent."

"You're staying, aren't you? I got your backstage pass and everything."

"Mace gave me a tour lanyard last night."

He had. He said he wanted me to be able to go to any of Telltale Signs' shows for the rest of the tour, without needing to worry about tickets or backstage passes arranged in advance. It puts me oddly in the "not quite the girlfriend" zone with him. Which is, even more oddly, exactly where I've often ended up with Hunter.

"Oh?"

"Yeah. He wanted to make sure you hadn't forgotten me."

Which was what Aedan had said. And meant, he made clear, in both the short term and the longer-longest term. The desire for me to have an awake Hunter was one we shared, and I felt the same about him and his lady. He deserved to be truly happy, just as he said *I* did.

"I'll *never* forget you, Elle," Hunter says, squeezing my hand.

I smile back at him, but the thought in my head is that he already has, has forgotten our own "before," or we wouldn't be at this place in our relationship. Moreover, just as I'd said to Aedan last night, I was being a realist that aMUSEd was going places on a scale that would eventually match Telltale Signs, and I knew when that started to really happen for them, I was going to be left behind. Maybe not entirely, but Hunter and I wouldn't be anything like we'd been for the bulk of our lives, not with him on the road so much and me running my own business, I hoped.

So, promises that he'll never forget me ring a little hollow in that context. I adore that he wanted to make the promise, but I'm not going to hold out hope that he'll be able to keep it.

"We OK?"

He seems concerned. And I appreciate that he knows me well enough and cares enough to ask.

"Yeah, Hunt. We're OK. I've just got some things I need to adapt to."

My head is still so all over the place that I know I've got a lot of mental and emotional adjustments to make. Aedan has turned a significant portion of my world upside-down. And taking in the full import of my conversations with him, and with Hunter, last night is going to take a while.

"You and Mace had a good talk, then?"

Among other things. That I can't tell you about...

"Yeah. We did. He's a very spiritual guy, it turns out. We kind of clicked over that."

Which is true. There was a strong spiritual component to everything between us last night. And that's all I can even acknowledge, since I promised him I'd keep his secrets.

"Well, that's cool. I'm glad to see someone appreciating you in the way you deserve."

It's a bittersweet sentiment, but I smile anyway, because I know he meant it as a statement of caring and appreciation of his own.

Pulling in to the venue, I grab my lanyard and show it to the security guard outside the gated parking area where the tour buses are visible. He sends us on our way, and I park alongside the buses.

"You, sir, need to go get showered and ready for soundcheck. Mace said yours is right after theirs, which is in less than an hour."

"First in, last out," Aedan had explained last night, meaning that the opening act's gear was put on stage after and soundchecked after the headliner's was put in place and was checked, because most or all of the opening act's gear had to come back off the stage before the headliner performed. It was an amazing feat of logistics to put on a show like this.

"You coming?"

Speaking of which...

"I thought I'd look around the venue a little, grab something to eat. I'll meet you backstage after soundcheck."

I kind of want to see the empty venue from the audience's perspective. I've seen so many places — most of them smaller, granted — from backstage, and many others when the audience was packed in. I kind of want to get a feel for the empty room.

"Sure. Have fun!"

He moves to give me a hug, and I notice that he's looking down at my chest, at the small section of skin that's not covered by my top, and I realize that my shirt has shifted just enough to reveal the edges of some of those delightful little hickeys that Aedan left me with. Yeah... Don't like that word. Love marks? Bruises of passion? Well-earned welts? I smooth my shirt back into place, hoping he didn't actually see them or at least that it's not so obvious what they are that it will be clear to him what — or at least some of what — Aedan and I got up to last night.

His expression suggests he's suspicious and maybe even a little upset, angry...

"Elle?"

"Hmm?"

"Uh. You and Mace..."

Nope. Not going there. We established that this was not your business, and even if you think you've figured it out, we're not having this discussion.

"We had a nice philosophical conversation last night. Yes."

This is a thing that is true. And it is a thing you will believe because I say it with utter conviction. Because it is true.

And when all else fails, change the subject.

"Hunt — you need to go get ready. I'm going ahead in. I kind of want to get a look at the stage from the audience."

"Oh. OK. Well, come find me if you get bored."

Considering Aedan's in the building and specifically requested to see me tonight, I don't think boredom is going to be a problem.

"I don't think I *could* get bored here."

He pats me on the arm and heads off to get ready for soundcheck. I think I may have succeeding in diverting his attention and averted a likely scene. That takes a load off my mind.

With my lanyard around my neck, I head into the venue, which again is sized to hold many thousands of people. The scale of it versus Hunter's bar gigs is astonishing. I head down into the audience area, glad to see there is actual seating here, and I take a load off in a seat near the back while I take in the scene around me.

Lighting techs. Sound techs. Riggers. Instrument techs. Security. People are scrambling all over the place, on stage, behind me, down in front of the stage, in and out from backstage. Everyone has a task. They all know their jobs like I know my loom, maybe better.

Even the local crews that are doing the load-in jobs that don't require technical expertise are working their butts off, but as parts of a tremendous organized effort to bring joy to so many people tonight in this one place. Music is such a gift, whether it's me sitting in my bedroom listening to 13-year-old Hunter learning Beatles songs, a bar crowd on a Friday night listening to a local band or one of the masses who will be here tonight to enjoy Aedan, and Hunter, and their bands on a much larger scale.

I think this is part of what my father has never gotten about Hunter, or about my devotion to Hunter. This isn't a matter of fame and fortune, it's a matter of the creative drive to make something that makes people's days better. That lifts them up when they are low and offers sympathy when they struggle or a way to celebrate when they are happy.

It may be a bunch of guys with electric guitars, but it's art, just the same as Chopin at the piano or Michelangelo with paints and canvas or a chisel and stone. And it offers the same gifts to humanity. It is a precious thing and should be treated as a treasure, supported. And, for Hunter, I know it is not just his career he's working on, but his passion. And watching someone like that — immersed in their passion — is a gift over and above whatever they create. And I never want to lose the joy I take in seeing that.

A commotion on stage shakes me out of my philosophical moment, and I see Telltale Signs coming out for soundcheck. Their techs hand Aedan and Robbie their guitars, and Chris his bass, while Izzy hops behind his drum kit.

I didn't watch much of Telltale Signs' set last night, but I've seen them before, with Hunter, from the audience, and I know how hard they work to put on a great show. Aedan is the ultimate frontman, exceeding even Declan's ability to master a crowd and bring them with him into the music. And the energy level from his bandmates is just as contagious.

Now, though, it's a little different, because they've essentially got an audience of one, plus all the tour personnel, most of whom have seen this hundreds of times over several tours. The energy is lower, more contained, more casual, but no less compelling for all that. Their mastery of their instruments gets the spotlight now, with the "show" put on hold for a few hours. And I am again struck by the creative fire that they each contain, kindling it from a tiny spark into a roaring bonfire that could keep entire cities warm. It is a gift. It's also a well-honed craft. But the gift is what gives it life.

Soundcheck is, by its nature, disjointed. One instrument at a time, levels are set, balance and tone tweaked, frequencies adjusted to bring out the exact desired result, with each subsequent instrument adding to a rich whole, topped by Aedan's powerful voice. It's no less impressive now that I know him, if just a little, and is perhaps even more so. The man, the priest, the lover — they all combine with this performer on stage, the musician at the peak of his skill, and it's an amazing thing to behold, watching all of who Aedan is come together before my eyes and ears. And not just them.

Halfway through their third song, when things are seeming nearly complete, I watch Aedan prowl across the stage, his guitar slung behind him and an old-style microphone pressed close to his lips. In an instant, his attention shifts from the mic and the stage, and lands squarely on me.

I had purposely sat near the back of the floor seating, both to see the room at a distance and to stay out of the way. No one has acknowledged or even seemed to notice my presence. And I usually like things that way.

But when Aedan's gaze snaps onto me, from all that distance away... There's a different kind of spark and a different kind of heat. Even from here, his eyes light up, his mood shifts from focused and worklike to pleased and intense. He's now performing for an audience of one: me. It doesn't matter how many people are in the room, this is a message aimed directly at me, and as he's reminding me with every move, every word, every growl, what we did together last night. And he's making it clear, without saying so much as a word, that he wants me again. Now.

My skin feels hot, my pulse fluttering in my chest, but also lower, like he's got a laser-focused ability to reach across the space and touch me, without moving so much as a finger. His eyes deliver caresses the same way his hands did hours ago, and I've never wanted the ability to instantly transport myself from Point A to Point B quite so badly.

As the last notes of the song fade away, he snaps the tension between us, looking away from me and at his bandmates on stage.

"All good?" he asks, to nods and words of agreement.

"All good on the house sound?"

The sound engineer gives him a thumbs-up from his spot mid-floor.

"Then it's time for a break and some food before we put on a show here in a couple hours. That means everybody! Local crew included! Enjoy, all!"

"You, gorgeous — come here," he orders into the mic, crooking a finger at me before he pulls out his in-ears.

I smile and make my way toward the stage, invoking my inner Marilyn Monroe with a sway in my hips as I take my time getting there, letting him wait and watch. I have no idea where this sultry persona came from. It seems to be new since last night. Maybe Aedan really did unlock some doors to my inner seductress. Regardless, she's on full display now, and I watch as his bandmates exchange a look, remarking on the interplay between us.

When I reach the stage, Aedan bends down on one knee, leaning toward me, saying with a quiet rasp, "Nicely done, my Lady. You are truly a natural at this."

I smile and nod, trying not to blush at his praise. Something about this man and how he responds to me just sets me free. But...

"I think perhaps we're not being quite as circumspect as we might like. Your bandmates seem to sense there's something going on..."

He looks back at them, where they're handing off their instruments to their techs, and gives them a nod, which they return.

"Not a problem. They know you're a friend of mine and of Hunter. They won't think anything of it, and if they do, they won't say anything."

"Why does that sounds like a 'bro code' thing that comes up when you're fucking someone you shouldn't be, or when you don't want the person you're fucking to know what *else* you get up to?"

"Because it is. Or, rather, it can be," he corrects when he sees steel creep into my eyes. "But, since you and I have an agreement, with higher things binding us than any 'bro code,' the latter does not apply here, and the former is for your protection and Hunter's, not mine. It's one thing to tease him with the idea of us. Forcing him to confront gossip of us is quite another matter."

"I agree. Well said."

"Thank you. Now, how has your day been?"

"A challenge getting Hunter up and moving, but he seems to have recovered. I sent him for a shower before their soundcheck."

"And then came in to watch me on stage..."

"Actually, I came in to see what the venue was like with no audience, just the view of the stage. I was just lucky enough that you came out while I was here."

"I'm not going to call it luck. I'm going to call it providence, because I have been looking forward to having you all day..."

"Having me *here*?"

"Here, backstage, on the bus, in the hallway... wherever you like..." he says with a voice just dripping sex.

And I'm rendered momentarily speechless.

He winks at me, gesturing to the side access to the backstage area. I head that way while he sets his guitar down in its stand.

I just get behind the curtain in the doorway when I'm grabbed around the waist and pulled off to the side, where there's a small nook just off the corner of the stage, concealed by a double layer of curtains that separates the stage from offstage and the access-way from the offstage area. I'm pressed chest-first up against the far wall, where the curtains seem to conceal everything. I recognize Aedan's scent, which I lamented washing off of me this morning, and he presses himself against me from behind, letting me know that I'm not the only one who's anticipating our coming together again.

"Aedan! Someone's going to see us!"

"No, they're not. I just told everyone to take a break. Union rules are half an hour to eat, minimum, and they all left when I said it. You didn't even see my guitar tech out there a moment ago, did you?"

"No... but aMUSEd has their soundcheck..."

"In half an hour. When the crew will be back. There's no one here right now but you and me..."

He licks a trail up the side of my neck and presses himself harder into my ass.

"You really *are* happy to see me, aren't you?"

"Happy to do more than *see* you, Brighid," he says, rolling his hips against me. And I melt. "You up for some more travels on that road of ours?"

"Here? Now?"

"We've already established that both this place and this time are our own. I've got half an hour to lead you down the path to bliss, and I intend to do that. At least once," he adds, gently biting my earlobe.

My body instinctively leans back into his solid presence and the sensual stimulus he's offering.

"Still hungry for me, I see..."

"Yes..."

"Well, I can feed that hunger. But first — not sore? No second thoughts? No qualms or questions?"

"Not sore. No second thoughts. You've addressed any qualms I've considered, and as to questions — I think a lot of those will have to be answered between the two of us as time goes on. As long as we are exclusive until we're done, I'm still very much on board for this ride."

"You realize that, being exclusive, I'm going to have to have you a lot more often, right? Are you ready for that?"

"I think we've established that my sex drive is high, and I can handle extended and repeated stimulation."

"Oh, yes, indeed you can... Deliciously."

"So let's take a step forward."

He literally takes a step forward, pushing me firmly against the curtain-covered wall in front of me. He raises my hands along either side of my head, pressing them, too, to the wall. Finally, he presses my hips into the wall, not with his hands, but with *his* hips, reminding me of exactly what he seems to be planning here.

"Aedan... I..."

"You want this? You want me to take you up against a wall? Where someone could see or hear us, even if that's unlikely?"

I shudder. He rolls his hips against me again, pushing his erection into my ass.

"Answer, Brighid. Do you want this?"

"I do."

"Good. Because I'm going to give it to you..."

He slides one hand up under my top, reaching straight for my breast, which he cups firmly before giving my nipple a pinch. He's got me so worked up already that I'm panting.

"There's my girl... let that seductress come out and play..."

I reach for his hand, but he pulls it out of my top and uses it to place my hand back up against the wall by my head.

"Leave them there. This is an exercise in surrender. We pushed you to act last night, to touch me, undress me, show me how you like to be touched. This time, it's about letting go. Letting someone else have control. Trusting them to make you feel good. And, oh, am I ever going to make you feel good..." he purrs in a seductive promise I can't resist. My hands will stay where they are.

"Are you wearing panties? Or were you hoping to get back the other pair once you got here?"

"You said you were keeping them, were going to use them..."

"Oh, you can be sure I did. Having you once last night wasn't nearly enough, and I only have so much self-control when you've got me worked up like this..."

Again, he presses himself into me, and I moan, trying to keep as quiet as I can.

"So, panties?"

"Yes, I have some on."

"Good. Then I'll just take them off."

My jaw goes slack as his fingers creep up my outer thigh, under the full knee-length skirt. When he reaches the side of my panties, he slides his fingers underneath, only to slip them toward my center and down and then cup my mound possessively.

"Mine, yes?"

"Yes," I gasp.

"Did you wash me off of you?"

"Not until this morning."

"Good. Did he notice? Did he realize you were coated inside and out with my cum?"

I shudder again. He's very good at this...

"He noticed I smelled different. He said he didn't like it."

"Good. Exactly as it should be. Are you wet for me now?"

"I am..."

"Let me see how much you're wanting this..."

He slides his fingers between my lower lips, and I can feel the slickness as they move.

"Soaked. Already. Oh, what a glorious gift you are, Brighid..."

I swallow as his fingers slide back up through my slit and graze over that central spot.

"I'm not going to be able to go slow and soft this time, my dear. It's all I can do not to come on your back right now, just from touching you like this. Are you ready for hard and fast? It's probably the best way for this anyway..."

"Yes... please..."

"Oh, how nicely you ask... I like it."

His other hand slides under the other side of my shirt, again cupping my breast. He takes the nipple between his fingers and gives it a solid twist, I gasp, but it's a feeling of pleasure overriding the pain. I'm panting again. And then his tongue again sweeps up my neck, leaving a trail of wetness behind, just as I'm leaving one on his fingers.

He pulls my head to the side and claims my lips, taking without asking what is nonetheless willingly given. Our tongues tangle together, and when he pulls away, we're both panting.

"Sweet, sweet girl... such delights to savor... but so little time, unless you want to be discovered..."

"No... I..."

"You kind of do, do you? Part of you? Admit it. We'll learn from it."

"I... I do... but not..."

"Not right now. Not this time. Good. Because I intend to have you before anyone is here to hear you scream my name as I fill you up while you stand right here against this wall..."

I moan.

He grabs both sides of my panties and pulls them down in one swift movement. He lifts my left thigh, and they drop off over my left foot, freeing my legs, which he then pushes apart with his own feet. I'm now standing, legs apart, no panties, dripping, with my breasts pressed into the wall in front of me and my hands and face immobilized by the sheer force of his personality.

"Relax, Brighid. This is going to be rough and fast, but it's going to feel very, very good."

I take a deep breath, bracing myself. I can fell his hand move between us, taking his cock out. He lifts the back of my skirt out of the way and rubs himself between my thighs, presses his cock into the crack between my cheeks. Just pressing against me. His fingers travel around my belly, under my skirt, where they caress my clit in time with the rhythmic movements of his hips.

I can feel him fit his cock against my opening. He circles my clit one more time before putting his hands over mine where they rest against the wall. And with one thrust of his hips, he's impaled me, all the way to my core.

I can't help but cry out, a gasping moan of pleasure too deep to express with words.

"There you go... That feel good, Brighid? That give your hungry pussy what it needs?"

"Oh, yes, Aedan. More, please."

"See — begging me so nicely. Make sure you're ready for it, because once I start moving, I'm not stopping until both of us have come. Hard and fast. You ready?"

"Yes..." I exhale.

He pulls back and then sinks right back to my core again, his hips hammering into mine, The rhythm is fast — a frenetic, driving beat, in and out, over and over, punctuated by little grunts from both of us as the impact of each thrust hits home.

This is fast and rough and not nearly as quiet as I'd hope, with the rising volume between us surely loud enough to give away exactly what we're doing here. Anyone walking past would never mistake it for anything else. But it's delightfully, wickedly primal, and I want it badly. I feel like we're chasing after elusive quarry, running faster and faster together in pursuit of a singular goal. His hips smash into me, faster and faster, his cock going deeper, pressing harder, building the friction between us to the point of igniting. I feel the tension rising inside me, pulling ever more taut and hovering just outside the breaking point.

Aedan is panting hard in my ear now, his lips fastening themselves to my neck, as if he fears flying free of a spinning earth if he doesn't clamp them onto me, the only thing keeping him anchored. I cry out as the pleasure-pain hits me, pushing me over a cliff where we both break free and fly.

"Aedan," I cry out, and he swallows down his own name with his lips on mine.

"Oh, gods, Brighid. I'm coming... can't wait... so hot, so perfect..."

He gives a deep, guttural grunt next to my ear, his hips spasming, out of control, nailing me into the wall, over and over again.

Suddenly, I'm awash in a sea of white. Light all around me, with Aedan carried along with me. I instantly picture a spotlight turned on us, but that sensation fades as I hear the pounding of the surf on a rocky shore, all foam and mist, reflecting light, blotting out the world around us. He slams into me one last time, slowly... exhaling with more than the air in his lungs. His eyes come open behind me, and he seems both startled and in awe, suddenly grasping my hands and wrapping both of our arms around us.

"What have we done?" he asks. "Where have we gone?"

"On a trip," I tell him, suddenly realizing that's exactly what we've done. I laugh with delight. "Exactly as we set out to do... Now, hold on — it's time to go home..."

I pull his hand to my mouth and press a kiss to his palm, then lick a drop of salty sweat before sinking my teeth lightly into his thumb.

And, like a bubble popping in the summer sun, we drop back into ourselves, clasped together against the wall in a curtained corner of a very large music venue, where I hear the first stirrings of people returning to work.

"Time to go, Aedan."

He snaps out of his abstraction, pulling out from inside me and tucking himself back in his pants. Before I can reach down for my panties, he's got them back over both feet and is sliding them up into place. His arms once more wrap around me, and he presses a kiss to my shoulder.

"You are far more than you seem on the surface, my Lady," he says, with a smile and a shake of his head.

"This isn't just me," I tell him, certain of it in that moment. "It's us. And Them. A little something for priest and priestess while we bide our time."

He turns me to him, looking deep in my eyes.

"God-touched," he says running his hand down my cheek with an expression of wonder.

I chuckle.

"What else did you expect when you suggested this pact between us?"

"I honestly do not know, my Lady. But I suspect I was led by the hand into it just as surely as you were. Gods be praised. Because that was astounding. Again."

He kisses me quickly on the lips, and pulls me along behind him, checking before darting out from behind the curtain and walking us quickly to his dressing room.

With the door shut behind us, he presses me up against it, again seeming to marvel.

I just shrug, because I know as little of what's happening as he does. Only little twinges of knowing, suspecting, wondering.

"Yeah. We're going to have to keep doing this..."

"I thought we'd already agreed on that," I tell him.

"We had. We do. But I'm going to have a very hard time trying to finish this tour without another chance to see you, see where this might take us."

"Flatterer."

"I think you know I'm not."

"I do. It's magic, Aedan. It's not just me. Don't let yourself be fooled into thinking it is. I know it's not. Just like it's not just you. It's a chemical reaction on a spiritual plane. Aptly. Because I really think we're just supposed to enjoy the ride, whether it's a train through a dark tunnel or a long flight into the night sky."

"Wisdom beyond your years."

"You said that from the start."

"And I was right. Thank the gods for that." He starts chuckling now. "You realize you're coming with me to Ireland when this next leg of the tour is done, right?"

"I am?"

"Yes, you are. I wouldn't miss this for the world. And neither should you. So, plan ahead now. August in Ireland. We'll see what there is for us there. It's calling, and we must answer."

And in that instant, I know he's right. I have to go. We have to go. And I'm going to make it happen. That and so many other things that need to happen for me.

Aedan demands I take off my top so he can see his handiwork from last night.

"Lovely. Like a reverse starfield."

"I was thinking constellations while you were doing it."

"Then I wasn't doing it well enough. Because if I was, you couldn't have managed to think at all," he says with a laugh.

"You did just fine. I mean, we've had sex twice and had out-of-body experiences both times. I don't think anyone is going to fault either of us. At least I hope not," I add, suddenly self-conscious.

"No, no, no — none of that, priestess. You have acquitted yourself admirably, for an expert, let alone a near-virgin. Never let anyone — including yourself — say otherwise. If you do, it'll eat away at that goddess inside, and then we'll have to go excavating to find her again."

"Can't have that."

"No, we can't. So don't forget. Even after this thing between us has run its course."

"I will try, priest."

"Good girl," he tells me, wrapping me in a warm hug with more camaraderie in it than sex. And that's just fine with me. I'm still coming down from the last round.

"Hunter's going to be wondering where you are. They're probably doing their soundcheck as we speak."

"Come back out with me to watch. He's so good. I like to see other people who understand what that means see it in him, too."

"Just for a minute. Then I need to get back in here and get my game face on. Otherwise, I'll let you ensorcell me all over again and we'll have no concert tonight."

He kisses me sweetly, almost chastely, and I suspect it's a carefully measured gesture to keep things from going any further while we both have other priorities.

"You're coming to Ireland? Promise me!"

I sigh.

"Yes. I'll come. I'll have to make a bunch of arrangements, including a passport. And tell a passel of lies to cover my ass."

"And a fine ass it is, naked or covered!" he jokes, smacking my bottom.

"Watch it there, buddy, or we're going to get ourselves back into something that's supposed to be over for the night."

"Did I say the night? Well, I guess it technically *is* done for the night. It'll be after midnight when we're done with the show." He gives me a serious look. "Come back to the hotel with me. We're staying overnight this time. One more for the road. What do you say?"

"I say you said that about *this* one. But it sounds nice. Let me see how things go with Hunter, and if I can, I'll stay over. Just one more night. That'll have to hold you until Ireland. And I can't believe I just agreed to go to Ireland with you. For a month!"

"You did, indeed. I've got it marked down in my book and you are committed. No going back on your word. And now, let's go see how your Sleeping Beauty is doing with soundcheck. Briefly. Then you're on your own for a while."

We go back out to the side stage, where Hunter is in his usual spot in front of Alex. They're well into one of their newer originals, "That Night," and Hunter doesn't notice us standing there. I smile, once again feeling so proud of him.

"He's blind, not seeing the way you look at him and realizing he's the luckiest man on the earth," Aedan says from behind me. He presses a kiss to the top of my head before it occurs to me that we're not in private. I look back up at him, a little frantic, but he just shrugs.

My eyes go directly to Hunter, who's still playing toward Declan's position at center stage. Thank the gods.

I glance around at the rest of the guys and find a smirking Rhys and a pensive Alex. Somehow I doubt the bro code applies in this case. I'm just going to have to hope that one chaste, if affectionate, kiss isn't going to send either of them running to tell Hunter. I give them both a pleading look. Rhys shrugs and goes right back to his drums. Alex gives me a gentle nod and looks at Hunter again with deep sympathy. He's got a story, that one, and it's about more than a clingy girlfriend.

Chapter 8

Dream About Flying

"**C**ome here. Sit."

It's not a suggestion. It's an order. And I comply without thinking about it, sitting on the bed in Mace's hotel room in Hampton, just outside Virginia Beach.

I bade Hunter goodnight after the show and told him I was headed out. I didn't tell him I was headed out with Aedan in my car, nor that we were headed for his hotel. Together. Me and Aedan Mason. Who's my lover. This "Sexiest Guy on the Planet" contender is, somehow, my lover. Little old me... Well, neither little nor old, but still... me. The gods have been kind to me this week. I don't know what I did to earn such largess, but I'm going to enjoy it while I can.

"Take your panties off."

Again, not a suggestion.

I slide my hands up under my skirt and loop my fingers under the fabric.

"Stop."

Wait. Did I do something wrong? Have I already messed this up?

I freeze and look up timidly at Aedan, who is still standing in front of me at the end of the bed. He looks... unhappy.

"That pout, that sad expression. I want it gone."

"OK... but... Did I do something wrong?"

"Because I stopped you taking your panties back off?"

I nod gravely.

"That's why I had you stop. That right there."

Aedan kneels in front of me, so we're eye to eye, sea-blue eyes full of storm clouds to my gentle violet-blue.

"Why did you sit on the bed?"

"Because you asked me to." I shrug, confused.

"I didn't ask you to. I told you to. And you just did it, without thinking."

OK. I see his point there, but why does this seem to be a problem for him? He's Mace Mason. He could order a stadium full of women to take off their panties, and most of them would do it, just because it was him telling them to.

"Why?" he asks.

"Why what?"

"Why did you do it without thinking? Why did you follow an order without considering what *you* want to do?"

"I didn't object to sitting. And you asked— *told* me to," I correct myself at the renewed frown on his face.

"And what I want is more important to you than even considering for a moment what you yourself want?"

"Well, no..."

"Then why?"

"I don't know. It's just what I do."

"And that's why I stopped you." He sits down on the bed next to me, taking my hand in his. "Brighid — it's fine to be submissive, if that's your nature. Just as it's fine to be dominant — so long as consent is given. *Reasoned* consent. But you've developed a very bad habit of following both orders and requests without thought, of putting other people's needs and wants above your own — especially when that person is Hunter Graves, or even just a man. Goddesses bend, Brighid — they don't fold. And they bend when they want to, not because some man told them to."

He raises an eyebrow at me, clearly waiting for me to confirm I get his point. I nod.

"Now, take off your panties."

My fingers move automatically, but this time I catch myself before they start to slide my panties down. I flex my hands to relieve the tension of wanting to do it and not wanting to do it just to comply. Aedan pulls my hand to his mouth, kissing the back of it, then unfolding my fingers to take two of them into his mouth. My breath halts. This man... it takes so little to get lost in him.

And then I realize that's exactly the point he's making. He doesn't want me lost in him. He wants me on my own two feet, consciously choosing to be there with him. And I want to be. Boy, do I want to be.

My fingers slide under my skirt again, pulling my panties down as I lift my butt up to let them slide to my knees and then off my bare feet.

The look in Aedan's eyes is naked hunger. For me. I'd say, "Pinch me," but I suspect he would choose my nipples as his target and I'm not sure I could handle that right now.

"There you go…" he purrs into my ear. "This time — because *you* want to."

I nod.

"There she is…" He turns my head to face him, pressing a gentle, sensual kiss to my lips. "Brighid, you let Hunter hold the keys to your sexual self for far too long. I want you to take agency of yourself — in bed and out. Be with me because you want to, not because I overwhelmed you. I do that," he admits. "People find me appealing, and it becomes like a spell — they're enthralled. I don't like it, not offstage."

He looks genuinely uncomfortable.

"The opposite of Declan, then. At least offstage. He wants the whole world arrayed at his feet in a posture of worship." I chuckle.

"He may say that. He may even think he wants that. Trust me — he doesn't really want it. And if he thinks he does, he's going to find out — probably sooner, rather than later — that it isn't what he thought it would be." Again, a look of substantial discomfort. He sighs. "I just want someone to treat me like a partner, or at least a friend — not a sex toy or a god. That's hard to come by these days. It's why I don't often sleep with fans anymore. They look at me as a sex toy *and* a god, all in one."

I'm tempted to joke about how hard that must be for him, but I can see in his expression that this is a subject of deep distress for him.

"So I should act like a goddess but not let people worship me like one."

"You should do what you want, what makes you happy, Brighid. But don't let that happiness default to giving happiness to others. If I impart just one thing to you, let it be that. I've seen people destroyed by their own giving nature, by their submissiveness to the needs and wants of others. I've seen people sacrifice everything for the people they love, sometimes with no love given in return. You shouldn't cross oceans for people who wouldn't jump over a puddle for you. A mermaid should get that."

Surprisingly enough, I do get that, now that he's pointed it out.

"You stood up for yourself with Hunter last night."

I shrug. "I was angry."

"As you should have been. He acts like your sexuality is his to control, to police. And that's fine if it's what you want, if he's giving as good as he gets. But he's taken on this bizarre martyr's cloak of his and made you both pay the price for it. He'll realize that someday. But in the meantime — take agency for yourself. It's the only way you're going to be able to have a healthy relationship with him when he does finally wake up and really see you. Or with anyone else between now and then."

"Including you?"

"Especially including me." His hand cups my cheek. "You may be younger, less experienced, but you're on equal footing with me. I like it that way. I like that sassy seductress who puts me in my place when I try to get away with shit. And I do — believe me. I steamroller over people without even realizing I'm doing it. That's half the reason I made you the offer I did. I can be myself with you, but I know that priestess part of you will kick my ass if I lose myself in the mythic Mace persona."

"Part of you loves it." I don't know how I know that. But I do.

He looks just a little stricken.

"Has anyone ever suggested you might be claircognizant?"

"My friend, the high priestess."

"She's probably right. I don't have that skill. I read people very well. I play parts very well, in the context of my life. But I'm left in the dark more often than I'd like."

"Sometimes I just know things."

"Literally what claircognizant means. The trick is knowing when you Know and when it's just your subconscious thinking out loud."

"You're deflecting."

He chuckles. "I am."

"You love being Mace. At least part of the time."

"I do. I have a healthy ego. Probably too healthy at times. And I'm used to getting my way. Not getting my way irritates me. But I also know that that way lies madness — which Declan Carter will figure out one of these days, if I'm half as good a judge of character as you are."

"But you don't want me to do as you ask."

"Sometimes, when it's fun for both of us, sure. But not because you're swept up in the force of my personality. Equal footing, my Lady. You do what you want, even if that's doing what I want. And I will endeavor to remind you that what I want — what anyone else wants — can't come before what you yourself need."

"And if I were to say I needed... say..." I freeze up. Can't get the words out past my lips.

"Say it, Brighid. Own it."

I swallow and take a deep breath.

"I need you to fuck me. I need you to show me that you want me."

He pulls my hand to his crotch, and he's hard. We've had a long, introspective conversation after I took my panties off — of my own free will — and he's still hard. His cock twitches under my fingers.

"Does that tell you anything?" he growls. "I find you alluring, Brighid. You're a challenge, a puzzle with a delightful finished result just waiting to be fully appreciated. I want to help you set those corner pieces in place so you can do the rest yourself. Sometimes, all you need is a little help getting started."

He rocks his hips into my hand before grabbing my face and pulling me in sharply for a hard, almost bruising, kiss. As his tongue strokes against mine, I stroke him with my hand, enjoying the fact that I have permission to touch this beautiful man like this. Beautiful not just because he's handsome (because the gods know he is), but because he's so giving himself, despite his warning me against being too much so. He moans into my mouth, then breaks the kiss, both of us panting.

He scoots back on the bed, lying flat on his back.

"Come, sit up here."

He pats his hip.

I shake my head.

"Don't say it..." he warns. But I can't help myself. If I'm going to be stuck on this, I'm going to at least be honest about it.

"I'm too heavy."

"You're not."

"I am."

"You're really not. Trust me. You trust me, don't you?"

"Yes... but..."

"No buts. Except for the butt that should be sitting on my cock right now. I'd make it an order, but you'd still have to decide to follow it."

I sigh. I want to trust him. Moreover, I want to *know* that I can do this and not have it be the nightmare scene in my head, of poor Aedan crushed between my thighs...

I crawl farther up the bed, next to him. He strokes the outside of my thigh, gently encouraging me to lift it across him so that I'm straddling him. I can't quite get myself to do it. His hand wanders toward my center, gently stroking between my lips, just teasing. My hips seek his hand as I get more and more aroused by his touch. He pulls at the inside of my thigh, prompting me to straddle him, and my knee raises off the bed, swinging over him. I'm tall enough that with my knees on either side of him, my legs still support most of my weight. I'm not sitting on him so much as straddling him. Or something in between, as he goes back to playing under my skirt, between my lips, and my hips drop toward the sensations.

"There you go... See? I'm fine. Better than fine," he says, pushing his hips up at me, rubbing his hard cock through his jeans against my very naked pussy. He delves between my lips, caressing my clit until my hips rock against him, swiftly approaching a point of no return. I'm going to come draped across Aedan's hips if he doesn't... As if on cue, he stops, his fingers tracing their way from my crotch to the sides of my bare hips. I whimper.

"Patience. You'll get your orgasm. We both will. But right now, I want you up here," he says.

Incredibly, he's gesturing to his mouth. He can't be serious.

"I want you to come on my face."

Wow. I guess he is serious.

"Now. No more hesitating. You can do this. We both know you can."

"The *you* part of 'we' is a lot more certain of that than the *me* part..."

He scoots down between my legs, my knees now on either side of his chest.

"Just a little farther. You have to do this for yourself. I promise I'll be fine."

"You realize that if I smother you, I'm going to have to watch my back for the rest of my life, because all your fans will want me dead."

He chuckles.

"Then we had better make sure it's safe. By trying it out..." His smile is wicked, his eyes twinkling mischievously.

Again, I heave a sigh.

"Here goes nothing... or everything, depending on whether you survive."

I shift my knees until they're positioned above his shoulders. He's looking straight into my crotch, which he quickly unveils by tucking my skirt up over its waistband.

He licks his lips.

He actually licks his lips.

Like I'm dessert or something, and not the instrument of his imminent death...

"Brighid — I'm not doing this *for you*. You have to make the decision. Prove it to yourself." His tone is amused but firm. Hel is the Norse goddess of the underworld, and the name of Her realm. And... Oh, what the Hel...

I settle in over his face, still plenty of room between my pussy and his mouth. He grabs me around my thighs and pulls me down against his lips. His tongue slides straight inside me. And I moan like I've never moaned before. And I've done a lot of moaning in the last couple of days...

Aedan's fucking me with his tongue, his hands keeping me in place as I start to writhe against his mouth, his chin. He licks me from opening to the top of my lips, circling my clit with his tongue. I'm panting for him already, chanting his name like it's the mantra that will save me... from what I'm not even sure. He sucks on my clit, his hands tracing their way down my bare ass this time, brushing against that opening, and my hips jerk in response. I've dreamed, had visions of being touched there, but the reality of it, now, in this body, is overwhelming.

I can feel Aedan chuckle under my pussy. He releases my clit from his mouth just long enough to say, "Soon," in a tone that sounds almost like a threat. My pulse races faster.

He resumes eating me, seeming to savor it, and it sets me to writhing against his face, seeking out the most intense and exquisite of sensations among all he is offering me. The tension in me builds quickly. His obvious enjoyment of having me on him like this, having me gyrating against his mouth like he truly is a sex toy, only makes it hotter, more arousing. The pull of my approaching orgasm only gets stronger, like it'll pull me apart if I resist, but I'm past all resistance to this idea. Way past that...

Aedan pulls me harder against his mouth, feeding on me while my arousal feeds on his, his quiet moaning and the subtle, sensual, liquid sounds of his lips and tongue working me to a peak. And that's what sends me over — that sound, of this glorious man absolutely rapt in his worshiping of my pussy, that it's as arousing to him as it is to me...

I see stars all around. It's like I'm sitting in a planetarium as Aedan lies under me, licking me through the strong waves that take me over. And that notion makes me unaccountably even more aroused as he draws out my orgasm with his tongue and lips. The spasms go on and on, leaving me weak and ready to collapse.

In an instant, Aedan pushes me over, my legs too weak to resist. I land with my back flat on the bed, still dazed and seeing the afterimages of a night sky. Aedan's out of his clothes in an instant, almost supernaturally fast, as if granted a dispensation from the rules of physics for just this one moment. Or maybe I'm just so out of my head with lingering pleasure that I don't perceive time passing.

In seemingly the blink of an eye, he's gone from ministering to my pussy from underneath to poised at my entrance with his cock hard and in his hand. I moan in anticipation, and he plunges inside, straight up to the hilt in one movement. I cry out in surprise and delight, reveling in the roughness of his pounding into me, a degree of madness about him now, like he's been driven wild with lust. And then I realize he has been. He is. He's fucking me hard and fast, and it's as amazing for his obvious loss of control as it is for the physical sensations. Can the man really want me this badly?

"You're thinking. Stop it," he instructs between panting breaths, keeping up a punishing pace that I want to go on forever. He leans down to kiss me deeply, his tongue spearing into my mouth, his lips sucking on mine, his teeth grazing across my bottom lip as he groans. His mouth feels cool, and yet somehow also warm, against mine, still slightly slick, and I realize what I'm tasting now is a mix of Aedan and me. And that's more arousing than I could have anticipated.

The slow spiral back up to that peak rockets suddenly upward, and I'm on the verge of another orgasm. I'm astonished that he's kept up this pace for this long.

"Almost. There," he grunts as he plows into me hard enough to split me in two. "Come for me again, Brighid..."

His wish is my command — if a mutually and consciously desired one — and I tumble over once more, the sound of Aedan's panting quickly lost in the crashing of waves against a cliff face, his eye widening to encompass an entire ocean, his auburn hair transforming into the wings of a raptor, strong muscles pulling them upward before pressing them down against the air and pushing me, us, aloft again. Together, we're soaring over that churning sea, born aloft on the air, watching the green land and brown stone slip away behind us.

It's nothing like the hill that rolls gently down to a beach below a little cottage built by Hunter and surrounded by our sheep. Where there was peace and warmth and a deep feeling of comfort, here there is excitement, adventure and the edge of fear from the pounding waves and the land growing so quickly distant, no safety net, no stopping if you get tired or afraid — you fly free and trust your wings, or you fall from the sky and drown. And flying I am, if not entirely free, because I can feel Aedan with me once more, the two of us on this adventure together. It's companionable, if not comfortable; the more dangerous heat of the flame instead of the comforting sun; the delight of exploring a new place rather than the comfort of home. And in that moment, I'm certain. I'm going to Ireland with Aedan Mason.

CHAPTER 9

LEARNING TO FLY

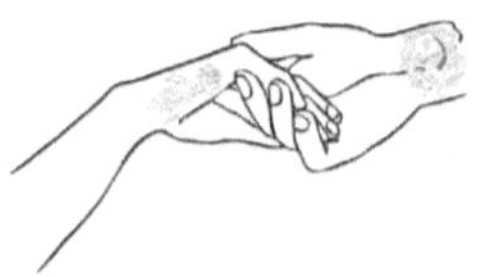

I wake just before dawn, an arm lying across my hip. My first thought is that it's Hunter, but I'm naked and that's not Hunter's arm, traced as it is with images of the sea, a horse twined with Celtic knotwork, a three-armed spiral triskele... then a sword, a shield, an armored breastplate, and on his shoulder there's a boat with no sail or oars, a blue heron — a bird so familiar to me from its constant presence back home in Delaware...

My brain refuses to process that I'm lying here — naked! — in the sleeping arms of one of the biggest rockstars on the planet (who is also naked!). Instead it fixates on the colorful artwork engraved into Aedan's arm from mid-arm, up his shoulder and beyond.... In this quiet time, with no one else around, no awakened Aedan putting me through my increasingly expansive sexual paces, I have the leisure to examine his tattoos in detail.

How on earth could anyone take in the symbology on this one arm alone and not know this man belongs to the Manx sea god? Come to think of it, I can't remember seeing many, if any, photos of Mace with his shirt off, despite his "Sexiest Guy" reputation and photo shoots, despite the sweaty job of performing like he does. His shirts fit tight across his chest, yes, his strong arms clearly defined beneath his sleeves, even while they remain mostly covered. I'm sure some of his friends, employees have seen him with his shirt off, and certainly some of the many women he's slept with, but it seems he does keep his faith largely to himself, even though he's got his devotion marked permanently into his skin. Not that I would mention it to anyone. I mean — who would I mention it to, except perhaps

Hunter, and I can't exactly tell Hunter how it is I came to be spending time with a shirtless Mace Mason and cataloging his tattoos at five-something in the morning. Naked. In his bed.

I smirk, feeling a little self-satisfied, and otherwise satisfied, for that matter.

"I can feel that brain working," he murmurs sleepily against my ear. "What *are* you thinking about at such an ungodly hour as this?"

"Just looking at your tattoos..."

"Ah... those..."

He lifts his arm from around my waist and sits up, stretching, the sheet sliding low around his hips, causing me to shiver.

He chuckles.

"See something you like?"

I blush.

"Eyes up here, Miss Brighid, unless you're prepared to have your mouth follow them..."

I grimace in embarrassment but look him in the eyes, instantly riveted. A stormy sea, indeed... Like the one on his arm.

"You keep them hidden, don't you? Most of the time?"

He sighs.

"Nearly all the time."

"I'd ask why get them if you have to hide them, but I think I understand better than anyone what it's like to have your faith be so important to you that it must be expressed in some way, even if it causes some problems."

"Have you had such problems?"

"Lost a roommate. Two, actually. Well — that could have been because Hunter sleeping in my bed half the time freaked them out, and him climbing in through the window..."

"He climbs in the window?"

"Dorm rules."

"Ah."

"But this last one... I suspect it was my Brighid statue and my books..."

"I'm sorry."

"I'm kind of used to stuff like that."

"I'm sorry about that, too."

I laugh, despite the serious subject of religious and other discrimination. Aedan raises an eyebrow.

"If those people could see me right now..." I laugh again, shaking my head.

Aedan's expression is serious.

"No — I'm not going to tell anyone about us," I assure him. "I have no more interest in the fallout from that than you do."

"I didn't think so," he says, kissing my bare shoulder and then rolling onto his side, his arm around me once more. "As for my tattoos... You're one of a handful of people who've seen them at length since I started getting them."

"Really?"

"Really." He nods sharply.

"Despite all the photo shoots, the concerts in summer heat, the backstage free-for-all, the many, many women you've had in your bed?" I'm skeptical.

"Not in my bed."

"Wait — what? What do you mean 'not in your bed'? You brought me back to your room quickly enough. I mean, I'm here..." I gesture at myself — yes, naked — in Aedan's bed.

"I don't have women in my hotel rooms. I go to theirs, or the dressing room, the tour bus — we trade off the bedroom on the bus, so that's not my bed exclusively. I don't consider it my bed, and their stay is limited there, because they have to get off the bus before we go to our next stop."

"So this... with me..." I gesture at myself again, for an entirely different reason this time.

"You and I are together. It's temporary. But we have an arrangement. And my tattoos — among other things — are secrets I need not keep from you. I like that." He nuzzles into my neck, and I'm suddenly very warm.

"But you keep your shirt on during all of these... encounters?"

"Pretty much."

He looks a little uncomfortable, almost embarrassed. Mace? Embarrassed about sex? How has this shoe gotten on the other foot?

"Listen — you know I have someone..."

"And you can't have her right now."

"Yes." He face is grim but he shrugs it off. "I have no interest in relationships. I'm already in one, as one-sided and dysfunctional as it is right now."

"And you're a one-woman man."

He nods.

"Always have been."

"Just like me."

"Only I didn't sit around the last several years waiting for her to get that lovely blonde..." He pauses, clearly realizing he said more than he meant to.

"I won't tell anyone. I swear."

He knows I mean that literally.

"—for her to get that lovely blonde head of hers out of her ass. She's just as stubborn as Hunter, just slightly less stupid about it."

I chuckle. It's nice to have someone else think Hunter's been stupid about us.

"I waited for her long enough," he says. "I can tell you from experience that it's not healthy to keep holding on like that."

"Hence your determination to break me out of my one-woman convent..."

He nods.

"Partly anyway. I meant everything I said about this connection between us, about trusting that I can be myself around you. I really needed that. More than I'd even realized."

I look back over my shoulder at him, and there's a vulnerability that I suspect even fewer have seen in him than those who've seen his tattoos. He groans.

"A healer... That's what you are... Her gift made tangible in you."

I blush.

"I'm really not. Not yet. I'm going to get some training, though — Reiki, herbs..."

"I don't mean physically — at least not just that. You have a healing nature. It works on emotional wounds, too, I'd say, based on what I've experienced."

Huh... that's new. Except...

"Hunter needs that. It's one of the reasons you two are so close, beyond the past-life ties. You make him feel better. And he wants to *be* better when he's around you. He's just got a fucked-up idea of what better means in that context."

It's food for thought. I have no way to digest it right now.

"So when you're with these women..."

"It's mutually pleasurable, but it's quick, efficient, detached. Bodies, not minds or hearts, let alone souls... A very different thing from this, from us..."

"Minds and souls, not hearts."

"Mostly. We're friends. I feel like we're friends, anyway."

"We are." I trail my fingers over the ink on his upper arm.

"We're... intimate. In a way I've never allowed myself with anyone else. Not since..."

I'm touched. My eyes start to well. After all these years of beating myself up on the rocks around Hunter's heart, the last thing I ever expected to have was an *intimate* relationship with someone like Aedan. I never thought I'd be interesting enough for even a frat guy to want me for more than a place to stick his dick. Hunter, I know, loves me. We're beyond intimate, despite the platonic nature of our physical relationship. But if *he* doesn't want me, how could I possibly be attractive to someone else? Anyone else. Part of me has come to accept that. And maybe that's why I waited. At least part of the reason...

"We're a sorry pair, aren't we?" he observes with wry laugh.

"Not anymore."

He's quiet for a moment.

"You're right. This has been a tremendous gift. For both of us, I think... Speaking of which... Did we fly off a cliff last night?"

I laugh.

"Yup. Straight off and no safety net."

"Don't need one. You've got to learn to trust your own wings."

"I'm learning that."

A edan and I get in one more round of mutual pleasure before it's getting perilously close to the time he'll have to get on the bus and head south.

In fact, we're just out of the shower and getting dressed when someone pounds on the door. My breath catches as I picture Hunter on the warpath, busting down *this* door.

Aedan gestures at me to stay quiet, but suddenly he pulls off my towel and wraps his arms around me before tweaking my nipples. He's making it very hard to stay quiet. On purpose. And then he slides his hand down between my legs. I bite my lip, trying to keep from whimpering aloud.

"Mace! You up, man? It's almost time for bus call! If you want breakfast, it's now or never!"

"Yeah, Iz. Just finishing packing up my stuff. Don't want to leave anything important behind!" He smirks at me over my shoulder.

"Idiot check!"

"No idiots in here, man. I'll be down shortly."

Aedan is still playing with my clit, teasing and caressing, when the hallway goes silent once more.

"You're terrible!" I squeal at him, shaking my head in amused irritation. "What if I hadn't been able to keep quiet?"

"Iz wouldn't tell a soul anyway. Though he'd have been surprised that I'd brought someone back to my room. He knows how unusual that would be. Really, I just wanted to see how desperate I could make you without you screaming out loud."

"And now what are you going to do? Leave me like this?"

"Tempting..." he drawls.

"Aedan!"

He chuckles.

"The rest of the band and crew are downstairs eating breakfast right now. I think I should do that, too." His grin his somewhere between amused and predatory. He pulls me back to the bed and lays me out, my legs spread wide, settling his shoulders between my thighs. "It *is* the most important meal of the day..."

Aedan and I keep in touch, talking almost daily, if only a text when he gets up. He insists that I come to at least a few of Telltale Signs' shows later in the month, now that aMUSEd has finished their regional opening slot. In fact, he buys me plane tickets to get to the shows in Raleigh, Atlanta and Orlando. Once he's done that, I can't bring myself to say no. Especially when he tells me he's got two free days in Orlando, and he wants to take me to Disney World.

You haven't seen sexy until you've seen Mace Mason in mouse ears.

All of that weight lifted off his shoulders for just a day or two, and he grinned like a kid — we both did — as we did rides (and, yes, we did do the ride with the little purple dragon and the overly catchy song, three times) and saw shows and watched the fireworks from a VIP area. With his hair tied back and tucked under a safari hat, sunglasses on, no one recognized him, and we were free to just have fun together. When I left him to head back home, there was a visible lightness in him. And I was glad I could help him find that.

I had to tell my dad and Lindsey that I was visiting Kara and Maire in Virginia for a couple days so I could get out of town without further explanation. But I'd already told them I was going to be spending all of August in Virginia, so they didn't blink. Things have been tense enough with Dad that I don't want any suspicions about my plans to add to it.

The rest of my time is devoted to work and ironing out my plans for my own shop, my healer training later in the fall — all so I can focus on my time in Ireland once August arrives. The weeks fly by. I have my passport in hand, flight arranged, a reservation at a little boutique hotel off St. Stephen's Green in Dublin for the first few days after I arrive and again for the last few days of the month, coinciding with Telltale Signs kicking off their European tour in Dublin. Mace had the timing all planned out so he could spend all of August in Ireland before they get back on the road.

And so it comes to pass that I'm sitting in the shade on the green, green grass of the park, reading my visitor's guide, when Mace plops down on the grass next to me.

"Hello, beautiful!" he says, beaming at me, almost as light of countenance as he was when I left Orlando. He presses a soft kiss to my lips, and there's a mix of excitement and comfort in it. The only man I've ever kissed treating me so tenderly after having been apart for a month.

"Back at you! How did you find me?"

He gives me a mischievous smile.

"You enthralled the hotel staff, didn't you..."

He looks like a kid caught with his hand in the cookie jar.

"I may have signed a few autographs and offered a few tickets to the show here in Dublin..."

"At least you did more to earn the information than just flash that famous panty-melting smile of yours..."

"This one?" he asks, giving me a smoldering look worthy of the camera at one of his photo shoots. "Is it working?"

"I haven't seen you in more than a month, Aedan. I got used to those marathon sessions of ours. My panties were pre-melted today."

"Then maybe we should do something about that..."

He slides his hands up along my waist, cupping my breasts just overtly enough that I look around to make sure no one is looking.

"I assume your autographs paid for discretion about *your* whereabouts and your choice of traveling companion."

"And a pretense of deafness should there be any screaming of my name in the middle of the night..."

He brushes his thumb across my nipples, through the thin cotton of my top.

"You thought ahead. That's nice..."

"I think I even charmed them enough that they'd overlook someone screaming my name in the middle of the afternoon."

"I see..."

"I think we should test that theory."

"For the purposes of collecting data on exactly how charming you are in the context of Irish hospitality..."

"Naturally."

My nipples are sharp points under his fingers, barely disguised by my top and the lacy bra underneath. I splurged on nice matching lingerie when preparing for this trip, and now I'm going to see whether Aedan appreciated the effort.

"**Y**ou should give yourself permission to buy lingerie more often," Aedan muses as I lie in his arms in the soft bed of the hotel room. "Better yet, you should let me buy it for you. Preferably after a fashion show that culminates with me pressing you up against a dressing room mirror and fucking you from behind while we both watch."

I shudder at the image he paints.

"You don't think some shop clerk would call the tabloids and sell them video of a closed dressing room door and loud moaning and thumping coming from inside, interspersed with my screaming your name? Probably with some surreptitious still images of the two of us taken with her cell phone?"

"Hey — a man can dream. And if you insist on bursting my bubble, I may just have to see whether I can charm a lingerie store clerk into locking the door, flipping the closed sign and taking a long lunch."

"Promises, promises."

He smiles and kisses my temple.

"So — what's on your non-dream list of things to do, now that we're both here?" I ask.

"I figured a few days here in Dublin — a little shopping, sex, some good food, sex, a pub or two, some more sex, a museum, sex..."

"I see a pattern forming."

"Hey — I warned you my sex drive was very high, and that I'd need to have you often if we did this..."

"And I never even flinched. Because my sex drive is as high as yours. So you're not hearing me complain."

"Good. Because then I'd have to work even harder to make sure you're enjoying every moment of having my cock, my fingers, my tongue... inside you."

His hands trail up between my legs.

"We're never going to make it out of the hotel room at this rate."

He sighs and frowns slightly.

"We *have* both been looking forward to exploring the country for a long time. I suppose I can drop down the fucking-you-senseless component of the itinerary to just three or four times a day..."

"Such restraint!"

"You have *no* idea... What time is it?"

"Around six, I think."

"Is that a.m. or p.m.?"

I shake my head at him. "It's too light outside for it to be morning."

"I kind of lose track of time when I've got your mouth on me."

"Good to know…"

"Dinner?"

"Gods, yes — I'm starving."

"We worked up an appetite."

"That we did."

The next three days are a whirlwind of touristy activities, most of which Aedan never did during his prior tour stops in Dublin. We stop at Trinity College to see the Book of Kells. We go shopping on Grafton Street. Aedan jumps in to sing with a young girl busking with a guitar, who appears to recognize him, even with a ball cap and sunglasses, because she goes straight into one of Telltale Signs' biggest hits. He winks at me and lets her take the lead on the verses, joining her to harmonize on the chorus. We start to draw a crowd — OK, it's definitely *his* crowd, not ours — and he drops a large tip in the girl's guitar case, accepting applause with a humble nod as we head quickly away.

We have lunch in the Stephen's Green shopping center near the hotel, though I'm so enamored with the architecture that Aedan has to keep prodding me to eat.

"I think I could live here," I tell him. "With the park nearby, I'm not sure I'd ever need to go anywhere else."

"What about the beach?"

"OK — here and the beach."

He chuckles at me. "Mermaid."

"Guilty."

A mischievous Mace then insists on going to one particular pub, knowing it's famous as a hangout for the members of U2, being just down the street from the Windmill Lane studios. Sitting next to me near the bar, he loudly criticizes the band's latest album as I cringe, watching the barman polish glasses with ever-increasing vigor.

"He's winding you up, man," one of the apparent regulars finally tells him, just as I begin to fear for the drinkware. "That's Mace Mason, lead singer of Telltale Signs. He's a friend of the band."

Mace grins widely and shakes the man's hand, buying a round for the entire house to make it up to them and leaving the irritated barman a tip so large that he might be Mace's new best friend.

I just sit quietly out of the way and shake my head. Finally, he comes back to sit beside me, pressing a brief kiss to my lips.

"You're not worried about them telling the press you were in here kissing an unknown chubby blonde woman?"

"You're not chubby."

I raise an eyebrow at him. "I am and you know it. And that's the polite term for it."

"You're curvy. You have an hourglass figure. You're soft and feminine — voluptuous, which I happen to like, especially on you. And I happen to think you're hot as Hel, and no one — not even you — is going to make me feel bad for thinking that."

"You didn't answer the question — aren't you worried about someone seeing you kiss me?"

"I'll tell them I tripped and fell onto your lips."

I giggle despite myself.

"It's a great way to break a fall. I should trip more often," he says.

He kisses me again. Longer this time.

"Aedan…"

"I'm having a good time. I refuse to alter my behavior just to avoid a hint of rumor about my friendship with a beautiful young woman. It'll be fine, Brighid. Plus, these guys are regulars at a pub where legends stop daily to get a pint. We can trust them to be discreet."

I'm skeptical. But keeping our arrangement secret was his idea, even if I agreed that it protects me, too. If he thinks this is an acceptable risk, I'll have to take his word for it.

CHAPTER 10

ONLY THE LONELY

A few days later, we begin a rambling journey around the country, Aedan driving since he already had an international permit and experience driving on the left side of the road. I'm happy to navigate. We pick a hotel or B&B whenever we decide we've had enough for the day, planning ahead no further than that. The only concrete goal we have is to get to Kildare to visit the Brigidine sisters' shrine. I'm a little leery of visiting a shrine to the Christian saint, but I've heard the sisters welcome all comers with open arms, regardless of which of Brighid's forms they connect with.

Aedan can't resist the wealth of live music, and honestly, neither can I. So we usually end up in a pub in the evening, Aedan more often than not joining in to sing or play a borrowed guitar. He's an instinctive musician, following along even on songs he doesn't know, and his vocal range means he can fit in nearly any song. Having seen him on a stage in a stadium, entertaining tens of thousands of people, it's in the pubs of Ireland that I truly appreciate his musicianship. The charismatic frontman is left behind, in favor of the love of story and melody. It's impressive. Almost as impressive as...

I pull myself away from the thought, unwilling to think longingly of my best friend, to whom I lied about where I am, while on the vacation of a lifetime to... And there it is again — thoughts of... And here I'm traveling around the place I believe he and I once called home. With another man.

But as I watch Aedan smiling widely as the impromptu pub band challenges him with an ever-increasing pace, I refuse to feel guilty about it, even if part of me feels disloyal to Hun... Hmm...

We've reached the Munster Gaeltacht, where many speak Irish as their first language. The Dingle Peninsula is gorgeous, the coastline very different from that of Delaware — rocky at the edge of tall hills, sloping sandy beaches at the toes of the rocks that aren't already in the water. Aedan and I are both enraptured, distracting me from my plan to use as much of my Irish as I can. It isn't a lot. But I worry about my pronunciation and my grammar. The bolder Brighid who has been unleashed since I first met Aedan retreats, managing just a few words here and there, despite Aedan's encouragement.

I'm more vocal in the bedroom. I think Aedan's autographed and free-ticketed his way through nearly every place we've stayed. And still I've seen a few amused looks from B&B proprietors and hotel staff when we've headed out in the mornings.

On this night, Aedan is unusually interested in the solid wood construction of the four-poster bed. Before I can ask him why, he pulls from his suitcase some silky ropes, smirking wordlessly at me.

A shiver goes down my spine. We haven't discussed taking things in this direction, but it's certainly something I've been curious about.

"Who's tying up whom?" I ask.

"Whichever you prefer," he replies languidly. "I'm an equal-opportunity bondage enthusiast, even though it's not a regular thing for me."

"I don't honestly know. I want to try... but I have no idea what to do."

"It might be easier to let me tie you up first, so you can get an idea of what you like or don't like, whether it appeals to you at all. Once you've seen me do it, you may find it easier to do it yourself."

I nod.

"You're going to have to use your words here, Brighid — clear consent needs to be given, and you need to be able to tell me if you want me to stop."

"A safe word."

"Yes. And we don't have to do this if you're at all uncomfortable. No pressure. It's just a place we haven't gone yet in our explorations."

"No — I want to try it. I'm curious..."

"Then pick a word you wouldn't say during sex or any related context."

"Spacefruit."

Both of his eyebrows go up.

"Spacefruit?"

"There's a visualization exercise I do, trying to construct, in my mind, a fruit that does not exist, visualizing it in such detail that it feels real and tangible to my senses, even if it's not."

"That's a good exercise. Manifestation of something you don't yet have."

He gives me an odd look, speculative.

"What?"

He shakes his head.

"Nothing... Just had a thought. Nothing concrete. Yet..."

"So... spacefruit?"

"Got it. Strip down to your bra and panties. Quick. That's an order. Unless you want to stop now."

"No!"

He chuckles at me.

"So, you really *do* want me to tie you up..."

I nod emphatically, trying to keep my nervous energy from taking over, making me shake.

"Strip, Brighid. Now."

I pull my clothes off as quickly as I can, leaving me standing in front of Aedan in the violet bra and panty set that was my favorite among the new purchases.

"On the bed. On your back. Legs spread wide. Quick."

I scramble up and lie down, my breath already coming fast. He's watching me carefully. I can't decide whether his expression is hungry or scrutinizing. Maybe it's both. I just know I don't want to disappoint him.

He pulls my legs farther apart.

"Keep them there. I'm not tying your legs yet. You'll have to keep yourself in position."

Tension starts to build in my limbs, and he hasn't even touched me.

Aedan grabs my hand and pulls it to his mouth, kissing my palm before licking up the side. It's incredibly erotic, and I close my eyes to try to control my reaction.

Aedan's hold on my wrist has changed. Because he's no longer holding it. He's tied the soft rope around it. He pulls the rope taut, tying it securely around the bed post. There's enough play in it that it's not pulling on my arm, but I can't do anything with it. He repeats the process with my other wrist. I instinctively pull against the bonds, a thrill rushing through my veins when I realize I really am tied in place. Aedan has total control, and I've willingly given it to him.

I can feel a rush of arousal between my legs. The tension in my arms creeps downward, and I find myself wiggling my legs about nervously.

"Hold still," Aedan orders. "If you can't do it on your own, I'll have to tie your legs, too."

The image is more than I can take, and my hips lift up, my knees pulling up, my toes pushing me off the mattress.

"If that's the way you want it... naughty girl..."

Aedan slides his hands slowly down the inside of my thigh. I'm ready to trap his hand between my legs, but he pulls my legs apart again. Then my ankle is tied and he's reaching to attach the other end of the rope to the nearest bed post.

I only have one leg free. My muscles twitch with nervous tension. I can't move, therefore I need to move. Have to move. Instinctively, I pull lightly against the three ropes that secure me in place.

"Do you want me to stop? Untie you?" Aedan asks.

I shake my head almost frantically.

"Words, Brighid. Do you want me to untie you?"

"No! Please!' I'm whining with the need I can't express. But Aedan knows what I want, what I need.

He grabs hold of my free leg, forcing it to still. His other hand traces from the very top of my inner thigh down to the ankle. Gentle caressing. A sharp contrast to his firm hold on my ankle.

I'm biting my lower lip. I can't do much of anything else, tied down. My muscles spasm, and I can feel my arousal starting to drip from me.

Aedan takes his time tying the rope around my ankle. He seems to almost enjoy it. He releases my leg, but I can't move, because he's drawing the rope taut around the final bed post. He ties off the end and stands back to admire his work. And in that moment, I lose the battle for self-control, pulling against the ropes securing all my limbs in place.

He smirks at me, but it's a mirthless expression, without mercy, without any hint of softness.

And the adrenaline hits my veins, sending me into a frenzy as I fight against the ropes.

Aedan's hand reaches for my inner thigh again, and it's like he flipped a switch. My struggles cease, my limbs relax. All I feel now is anticipation. And my body is anticipating the need for copious lubrication.

I'm drenched. I know it. I can feel it. And Aedan knows it, because his fingers are diving under the edge of my panties, swirling around in the puddle forming between my legs. My pussy chases his fingers, wanting them, his cock, his tongue, whatever I can get inside me.

"Aedan..."

"What do you need, Brighid? What do you want?"

"You — any part of you. Inside me. Fucking me. Make me come."

"No."

His tone is firm. I frown back at him. My hips writhe as much as they can when I can't move my arms or legs.

"Aedan... please!"

I'm begging him. Literally. I'm so aroused at this point that I can't think to do anything else.

"You trusted me to tie you up. You trusted me to take control of your body, your pleasure. And now you have no choice but to trust me... Unless you want me to turn you loose. Stop all of this."

"No!"

I'm struggling against the ropes again.

"You want me to make you feel good, Brighid? You trust me to make you feel very, very good?"

I nod frantically.

"Words."

"Make me feel good, Aedan. Make me come. I need to come, so badly."

His fingers have continued their light tracing through the liquid pooling between my legs, and my pussy seeks more, chasing after him.

"If you want me to touch you, you're going to have to stay still. As soon as you move, as soon as you struggle, I stop touching you. Do you understand?"

I nod, but answer verbally when he frowns at me again.

He places his hands on one of my hips, playing with the side of my panties. And he rips them apart. I gasp. Whether it's in shock or arousal, I couldn't say. He moves his hands to the other side, repeating the destruction.

"Those were my favorites."

"I'll buy you new ones. I'll buy you a hundred. Right now, you're mine, so they're mine. And they were in the way. In the way of me touching you, making you come. You still want me to make you come, right?"

"Please!"

He nods curtly at me. This is a new side to Aedan. Not the confident, encouraging instructor. Not the charismatic rockstar. Not the affable friend, nor the wise priest, nor the mischief-maker, and definitely not the sweet lover who's opened up to me on a deep level. He's domineering, detached, almost cruel. And I still find it incredibly arousing.

He reaches behind my back and unhooks my bra, leaving it loose around my chest. He pushes it up, my breasts bared with my arms tied away from my body. He crawls up beside me, lying casually on his side. His demeanor says he has all the time in the world, because my urgent need for an orgasm isn't even on his radar. He starts idly playing with my breasts, tracing circles around each one but avoiding my nipples, which are aching for his touch.

I want to push my breasts into his hands, but his warning to stay still rings in my mind. I force myself to relax, to simply watch as Aedan Mason does as he pleases with my body, I don't know how much time passes, but the sensation of his touch on my breast changes. Not the callused fingertips, but a gentle press of lips, an insistent probing of his tongue along my nipple. First one, then the other. My nipples are hard peaks, teased by his touch. And then it stops.

Again I fight instinct that tells me to pull against the ropes. I let him continue his languid exploration.

His fingers trace down my chest, circling around my bellybutton and then dipping down once again between my legs. He slides one finger into me, then two, and three... So full... I feel so full of him. My hips wiggle against his hand, begging for more. And he gives it to me, pumping his fingers in and out in a relentless rhythm. I'm already so aroused that it doesn't take more than a few moments to send me back up to the peak. And then he withdraws his fingers.

I'm left empty, aching, wanting, desperate. And I start pulling against the ropes again.

"Stop it, or I'll untie you."

"That should *not* be a threat. It sounds ridiculous."

He chuckles at me, and I see that warm Aedan peeking through the cold, distant mask. "You really are delightful — you know that?"

And in that moment I see what the mask was really hiding.

Aedan Mason likes me.

He talked of Hunter feeling better when he was with me, of him wanting to be better when he was with me. And now I see he said that from some part deep within himself that recognized what Hunter needs from me is also what Aedan himself needs.

I know this. I Know it.

He's looking at me with those sea-blue eyes of his, and it's like the clouds have parted, the stormfront has blown away and the sun sparkles on a fresh, clean world.

"Untie me."

I'm not sure he hears me at first.

"Untie me, Aedan."

His eyebrows quirk up at me.

"Spacefruit, Aedan. Let me loose."

There's surprise in his expression.

"Are you sure? You haven't had your orgasm."

"I'm sure. I need to be free to move right now, to use my hands."

He nods, seeming uncharacteristically uncertain. He starts untying the ropes from my wrists and ankles. One by one, I get use of my limbs back. But I sit still until he's untied all four of them. Given the choice between taking off the bra that no longer has matching panties and sitting here with just a bra on, I toss it away.

"Sit."

This time it's me giving the order.

He's curious, but he complies.

I scoot up close to him. I feel odd, sitting here naked while he's still fully clothed. But it feels symbolic in some ways. Because Aedan has broken his promise to me. The promise to be honest with me. And with himself.

My hand goes to his cheek. I steer his eyes to mine. That incredibly strong force of personality... He's never had a problem meeting my eyes. Not like Hunter and me. But he's subtly dodging me now. Like he knows I've seen something in his eyes that he'd rather I hadn't.

"It's OK," I promise him. "It's going to be OK." He seems to need the reassurance.

"Do you know that, or do you Know that?"

"I Know it. Capital K."

"What else do you Know?"

I take a deep breath.

"You like me."

He nods. "I've been very clear about that. You wouldn't be here if I didn't. We have a lot in common, despite all the things that are different."

"That's not what I mean, and I think you know that..."

He can't meet my eyes now. He's not even trying.

He sighs.

"I'm sorry. We had an agreement, and I broke it."

"It bothers me a lot more that you hid this from me than it does that you... broke the other part of our agreement."

"I am sorry about both."

"Aedan — look at me. Really look at me."

He pulls back to look at me. His eyes drop down, fixing on my breasts.

"My eyes are up here," I tell him, grinning wryly. "Unless you're prepared to have your mouth follow..."

"I could really get into that."

"I know you could. So could I. But I pulled us out of that headspace for a reason."

Those strong shoulders of his, muscles honed from hauling equipment and kept that way with long hours performing, used to carrying the weight of an entire tour... his smooth skin bearing his statements of his faith... those shoulders sag. There's a feeling of surrender in his posture. He's given up the pretense.

"Is it just me?" He meets my eyes now, without trouble. The masks are off.

I give him a small smile. "No. It's not just you," I admit.

"The one thing you and I both knew was absolutely certain. That we wouldn't fall for each other. Because we're already in love with other people."

"Sometimes the universe feels it necessary to surprise us."

"Surprise! Your comfortable fuck-buddy relationship just got very complicated."

I chuckle. "Unfortunately, this is par for the course with me. If things can go bizarrely wrong, they will. I should have been called to serve Murphy, because his law owns my ass."

"Hmm... owning your ass..."

Aedan leers at me. Still naked here... So not fair!

"OK — seriously — either let me get dressed or take off your own clothes. This is utterly unfair."

He looks me up and down, no pretense of not enjoying the view while he remains fully clothed. At no point in my life did I envision I would be objecting to being ogled by a rock god.

He appears to ponder the decision for a moment. Then he reaches behind his neck and pulls his shirt off, tossing it behind him.

I look at him expectantly. He just sits there.

"There's still a decided lack of balance here."

He smirks at me and stands up to remove his jeans. He catches my raised eyebrow and, laughing, strips off his last remaining piece of clothing.

"You realize that, except for having my tats on display, I have no issues with being naked. You know that, right?"

"I do. Comes as part of the package of being drop-dead gorgeous, I would imagine."

"Well. *You* tell *me*... You should be naked all the time. All soft curves and long legs and those shoulders..."

He bends down to kiss my shoulder, sliding his tongue sensuously along my skin as he pulls away.

"Aedan... I am n—"

"Don't. Please don't."

I go silent in the face of his deep-felt earnestness.

"Yes, you're bigger than average. But I think you're beautiful. I meant it, what I said back in Dublin — I'm not letting anyone shame me over finding you attractive. You're overdue to have someone tell you that. So I'll keep saying it until you believe it."

"You sure that isn't... a complication? A symptom of the complication?"

"Pretty sure, yeah. This snuck up on me. And I'm really sorry if this messes things up."

"This doesn't have to change anything. Nothing else has changed. It really will be OK."

"How can you say that?"

"Because I Know it. I can't tell you how or when or why, but I Know it."

"So, where do we go from here?"

"Kildare."

"I meant you and me."

"I know. That's still the answer."

Chapter 11

Lonely in Your Nightmare

Things are tentative between Aedan and me. I've never seen the man anything less than confident — until now, with me. He's his usual self with everyone else. Well — the relaxed vacation-Aedan who sits in with folk bands, buskers and local cover bands, and never gets within a hundred miles of diva territory, even when people ask for his autograph.

But with me, he's now quieter, softer, less self-assured. How on earth have I — of all people — managed to undermine Mace Mason's self-confidence?

There's nothing overtly wrong with how he's behaving. It's just not the Aedan I know, let alone Mace the rockstar.

And I feel horrible about it.

I called him out on the pretense of not feeling something more for me because once I'd seen through it, I hated that pretense. I felt we owed each other true honesty, even as friends. It was not because I wanted to strip him as naked emotionally as he had done to me, physically and otherwise.

I look out the window of our hotel room, appreciating the Galway skyline after so many days in the country. It's late, and we've just gotten back from the near-nightly pub excursion. We should be exhausted, but we're both restless. Aedan walks up behind me and wraps me in his arms, taking in the view. But I can tell he's on edge.

"Beautiful," he says, his head resting alongside my neck, his mouth near my ear.

"It's a lovely place. I think I still prefer Dublin, but I'm glad we stopped in the city for a couple days."

"I wasn't talking about the skyline."

I sigh and lean back into him, my hands on his as they rest around my waist. From almost the moment I met him, Aedan has seemed nearly as safe and comfortable as Hunter. We understand each other on a deep level, despite all the differences. And I think we both needed someone exactly like that — someone outside our own daily experience who nonetheless provided something we were missing. On a basic level, I think Aedan was just as lonely as I was, if not more so. At least I had Hunter. From everything he's said, Aedan doesn't share his true self with anyone, except maybe his lady, and she's not around these days, though he has yet to tell me much of anything about why that is or about her. And I think that's the root of this complicated circumstance we find ourselves in now.

Aedan is lonely. And he's been lonely for a while.

It *is* "lonely at the top," and Aedan *is* at the top, a dominant force in rock music, a pop-culture icon and head of a musical juggernaut with countless people watching his every move and so many others relying on him to ensure their continued success. I'd have crumbled under that kind of pressure. But *I* also saw the priest, the man, behind the facade. No need for the two-dimensional mask to hide the three-dimensional man. He wanted that — wanted to shed that mask he wore 24/7 with everyone else. And the relief of being able to do that safely and still connect with another human being — it holds a deep emotional appeal for him, even beyond that connection we share.

So it should be no wonder that things have shifted in this direction. It still *is* a wonder to me. But it shouldn't be. If Hunter hadn't still been in my life on a nearly daily basis, would I have just straight up fallen in love with Aedan? But if I'm honest with myself, aren't I a little in love with him anyway?

"Aedan... I..."

"You don't know how to take a compliment, do you?"

"I don't have a lot of experience with them."

"I'd like to change that."

I turn in his arms, looking into his eyes, full of raw, naked emotion.

Oh, I could *so* fall for this man. I mean, who wouldn't? But Hunter still fills my heart. I'm not sure there's room for anyone else.

"You *are* changing that," I tell him. "I've never felt so beautiful, so appreciated as I have since we arrived here. You've treated me like I mean something to you, like I'm special."

"You do. You are."

"Thank you."

"There — that's better. That's how you take a compliment."

His lips dip toward mine, delivering a soft, sweet kiss that carries far more affection than sex. I can't tell if I was just blind to it before or if he's thrown away that mask with me now that I've seen behind it, if he's simply given in to how he's feeling.

"Aedan... I'm not sure this is a good idea."

"What?"

"Us. Like this. I'm... I could get very attached to you if I let myself, and we both know that won't end well."

"It doesn't have to end badly. It doesn't have to end at all."

"But it will. We both know it will. Because we're both still in love with other people. She'll come around, and you'll be so blissfully happy that you'll forget I ever existed."

"I won't. You're my friend. One of my closest friends."

"Aedan — I know nearly nothing about you, your childhood, your family, what you're like at home in New York..."

"What's my favorite color?"

"Blue. Ocean blue."

"And my favorite band? Telltale Signs aside," he adds with a wink.

"Zeppelin."

"My favorite guitar player?"

"Stevie Ray. Or Charlie Sexton. Always Austin blues-rock."

"My favorite food?"

"Scallops, with risotto."

"What's my ritual before I go on stage?"

"Shower, meditation, prayer, get dressed, vocal warmup, then music that raises your energy level, then you make sure everyone and everything is in place."

"Because..."

"You're a control freak, and you don't trust anyone else to do it the way you want it done." I chuckle at his expression of mock offense. "Well, it's true!"

"It is." He nods and gives me a smile.

"How do I sleep?"

"Naked. Soundly, unless something is bothering you. On your side."

"With my arms wrapped around you."

I swallow. Hard.

"See — you *do* know me. Probably better than anyone has in a long, long time. And I know you as well as anyone except Hunter."

"What three things do I save in a fire?"

"Your spinning wheel, your Brighid statue. And... something that reminds you of Hunter — probably a photo from when you were little."

"From when we were 16, actually. One of the last times we went to the beach with my mom."

"Who you miss like crazy because she never judged you for being who you are, or for loving Hunter."

My eyes well up, and I nod.

"We're good friends, if nothing else, Brighid. Close, *intimate* friends who enjoy giving each other pleasure."

There's that Mace smirk, spreading across his face as he runs his thumb over my bottom lip. His eyes displaying all the confidence of the rockstar who can have any woman he wants — except the one he really wants. And that's a wound in him that won't heal. But he also wants me. A bandage to stop the bleeding, a salve to make it hurt a little less. That's all this is, right?

"We have to be honest with each other, Aedan. And ourselves. This isn't just fuck-buddies or friends with benefits. Surely, you can admit that."

His eyes drop from mine. He's thinking, considering. Finally, he takes a deep breath, that vulnerability back and pouring off of him.

"I'm a little bit in love with you, Brighid. I still love *her* so much it hurts. But I love you a little bit, too."

"And I'm still head over heels for Hunter. Always have been, always will be. But you're very special to me, Aedan. I don't expect this to change anything over the long term. But I'm a little bit in love with you, too. And I'm OK with that, now that I know it's mutual."

"Me, too."

I lean into him, tracing the planes of his face with my fingers. The storm clouds are back in his eyes, but there's also a hint of sunshine.

"Make love to me. Aedan. No secrets, no lies, no masks. Just you and me, as we are. Come what may."

"If fucking sends us out of body, what's making love going to do?"

I laugh.

"Let's find out."

It's a study in soft sensuality, connection, affection. If Aedan was attentive before, he's utterly devoted to my pleasure now. Fingers tracing along skin, from head to toe. Hands wrapped in my hair, stroking my face. Lips pressed to mine, nudging them open, making way for his tongue to slide inside my mouth and brush roughly against my own. Sweet kisses down my neck, into my cleavage, tongue working in slow, sensual circles around my breasts, laving across my nipples. His hand travels south and caresses my inner thigh, pushing it aside so his fingers can delve between those lower lips, teasing touches building slowly, inexorably toward that peak, at a lingering pace, as if every second, every millimeter of the journey was being savored, marked into memory.

My fingers likewise trace across his back, memorizing every ridge and ripple of muscle, the sensual feel of strength under smooth satin, my lips fastening themselves to his collarbone, as if I could absorb the essence of the man through the ink on his skin. He's already found his way inside me. Not physically — yet, now. But into my heart and soul. He may still one day forget me, but I won't ever forget him.

He slides down, his lips joining his fingers to tease and taunt, an ache building inside my core, tension, a vacuum, calling for the one thing that will satisfy that need. I want him in my hand, my mouth, but he's too far away.

"Aedan... gods... I want my mouth on you, my hands on you, but I don't want this feeling to stop..."

He looks up at me from across my mons, his eyes glazed with pleasure, but I can see an idea form in his head. He smiles so sensuously that I nearly come just watching the expression spread across his face.

"You don't have to choose, Brighid. We can do both..."

He repositions himself with his feet above my head, his tongue still delving between those lower lips as he pulls me onto my side. The silk-clad steel of his erection lies within easy reach now, and I take him into my mouth, mimicking each lick, each thrust of his tongue into crevices filled with nerves that are now on fire from his efforts, from my efforts now, too. He moans, and again I'm ready to ride that sound right over the top, especially as the vibration hits my pelvic bones.

But I focus on what's literally at hand, caressing his balls while I suck hard on his tip. His hips jerk forward, pressing him deep into my mouth.

"Gods, Brighid... that mouth of yours is just heaven..."

I moan my appreciation, this time accepting the compliment gracefully, if wordlessly. He cries out.

"You're going to have to stop that, or I'm going to turn making love into fucking your face, and while I want to do that at some point, that's not what I want for you, for us, right now."

I release him slowly, sensually, pulling him from my mouth while still applying suction. He shudders, panting as if trying to control his breath, and his hips buck toward my face again. I smile, pleased that I've learned enough from him to elicit that kind of response.

He growls.

"You're a fast learner, my Lady."

"So I have been told." Now it's me doing the smirking.

He laps between my lower lips before prodding my clit with his tongue. My hips return the compliment, not that his skill was ever in doubt.

He shifts back up on the bed, another sweet kiss delivered, tasting of Aedan and of me, of us. I revel in it, wishing again that I could absorb the essence of this wonderful man, to savor later, after... I shake my head free of thoughts of the future. Aedan looks at me, curious, clearly perceiving the intrusion of reality into our little bubble of romance and sensual delight.

"It will all be OK," he assures me. "I've been told that by someone who Knows." He smiles warmly, looking gently down on me, a bit of wonder in his eyes. I know that feeling. I'm feeling it, too. I brush my thumb over his cheekbone, my fingers trailing along his jaw. My eyes hold his for a long moment before settling on his mouth. He dips down again, and our mouths meet, consuming each other like there's no other sustenance in the entire world.

He presses against my core, seeking entrance to the place he seems right now to belong. Not on stage, not signing autographs or having his photo taken, not even on a stool in a pub with a guitar on his lap. But here, with me, inside me. He slides slowly home, his eyes glued to mine, every tiny bit of the movement, the sensations of it, savored by us both. And when he's seated deep within me, there's so much in his expression — comfort, excitement, wonder, delight, adoration and, yes, just a little bit of love. I hope he's seeing that reflected back at him, because I'm feeling it, too.

He begins a lingering dance, withdrawing and then pushing slowly back in again. My thighs wrap around his hips, reluctant to allow the retreat. I could lie here forever with him inside me. I let that thought drift away as his pace increases, his breath coming faster and mine matching it. We're in the here and now, lost in the physical sensations of it and the shared emotion — warm, intimate, sensual, affectionate, a layer of adoration and...

Our mouths collide, mimicking our coming together below, and everything speeds up, a frantic edge of need growing sharply in both of us. I can feel it coming, that peak, that cliff we keep throwing ourselves off of, reveling the moment of leaping from the earth as much as the sensation of gliding out over that ocean, literal or symbolic. And then it hits, Aedan plowing inside me in a frenzy and me clinging to him with legs and arms and lips as the first of the spasms hit, intense and gloriously real.

I dive below the crashing wave, rising again behind the crest, gasping with the exertion, full of adrenaline after escaping the tumult of water. I look back toward the shore. It's familiar. Sandy, not rocky. Sloping, no cliff in sight. A wooden boardwalk just visible to the north. Home...

I duck under the next wave in the set. It's not as big, but breaking too close to be surmounted before it crashes over me. Something brushes against my leg. Instinctively, I pull away, but it grabs hold of me, sliding up from my calf, up my thigh, around my waist, up my back. As panic fades, the touch is familiar, comfortable. Hunter does this all the time — sneak up on me and pretend he's a shark or an octopus, getting my pulse racing so I'll race him back to shore. But it's not his golden blonde head that emerges from the water, not his piercing green eyes looking up at me. Dark, dark red, almost brown, eyes the same color as the water around us.

Aedan.

His arms wrap around me, kisses dragging along my neck, eyes full of delight. He's a welcome sight, and yet...

I look back at the shore. I can see a figure on the beach now. Shirtless, tall, wearing board shorts, not naked like Aedan is now, pressing his hardness into me as our legs kick in time, holding our heads up above the water. The man on the beach has long hair, dark blonde, a short beard, both just a little longer than Aedan's... The man looks familiar, but I can't place him. But he's home, on this familiar shore, and it feels like he's important. Like I need to go talk to him.

Aedan is kissing the back of my neck, sucking on it, leaving a mark. I shudder, reveling in the sensation. But I'm drawn back to the man on the beach. Who is he? So oddly, inexplicably familiar.

Aedan's arms pull free of me, and I turn from the shore in time to see a massive wave coming at us, looming over Aedan, who's closer to it but watching me so intently that he doesn't notice it coming. I cry out to warn him, but just as he seems to hear me, a pair of arms reaches out from the wave and pulls him back into it.

I scream his name and dive under, avoiding the crashing water but opening my eyes in time to see an unconscious Aedan being dragged away, his auburn hair lost in the midst of golden tentacles. No — long golden blonde hair, long enough to reach my feet if it was on my head and not... A flash of face from behind Aedan. Sharp, almost pixie-like, but with a solid kind of strength to it that belies the otherwise delicate features. Haughty, domineering almost. Decidedly unfriendly. Until she looks at Aedan, and then her mien softens, fills with affection and... concern. Guilt?

I don't get the time to analyze it, because she turns, and with a strong kick of her legs... no, her tail! ...she jets away, taking Aedan with her.

I strike for the surface, gasping for air and looking for any sign of her, of him... and there's nothing. The sea has gone flat in an instant, the only waves the ones now rolling into the shore. I've got to find Aedan! I call for help, hoping the man on the beach will hear me. Only, he's walking away, back up over the dune, unable to hear me, no matter how loudly I scream. No! Don't go! Don't leave me!

I wake in Aedan's arms, tucked into his side, my head on his chest. He sleeps peacefully, no sign in him of the terror of that dream, or was it a vision?

I shudder, remembering how helpless I felt, trying to rescue him from that... mermaid? I mean, I've always considered myself a spiritual mermaid, but this was the real thing. Or at least she was in that vision. And she was *not* happy to see me. Almost... possessive.

Could it be?

I shudder again, recalling the moment when I realized the blonde man was walking away from me, couldn't hear me, wouldn't come help. I'd turned back to look at Aedan, and the man had just walked away, not giving me a chance to come closer and see who he really was. And it was important. Who could he be? The only blonde man I know is... Hunter. But Hunter's thinner, his hair shorter than that, and he's clean-shaven. Though he wasn't always; not in my visions of us from that time before. Could it have been Hunter, but from another time? In board shorts, of all things anachronistic?

Aedan stirs in his sleep, snuggling into me.

"Love you," he mumbles.

Oh, gods... what have we done? What have *I* done?

"**I** need to get to Kildare. Today."

"I thought you wanted to go to Donegal first, see if you recognize anything from your visions."

Aedan is clearly confused by my sudden need to change what little plan we had.

"I know. But I need to get to Kildare. Now. I'm being pulled there."

Aedan absorbs this. He nods. "When we're called..."

"We follow."

"Alright, I'll let them know we're checking out early."

I grab my suitcase from the closet and start packing my things. I emerge from the bathroom with my toiletries to find Aedan on the phone.

"Right. I see. Thank you for letting us know. Can you have someone bring that up, please, when they come up for the keys? ... Thank you. Yes, go ahead and charge the card. We'll get some food along the road."

He hangs up and sits back down on the bed, looking troubled.

"What's wrong? They want to charge us for another night?"

"No." He shakes his head. "No — they were understanding that our plans had changed. That's fine. But they were just getting ready to call up to let me know there was a different problem."

"And..."

"One of the tabloids... They've got a photo."

"Of?"

"Me and a 'mysterious blonde companion.'"

"Oh, crap."

"Yeah. They're bringing us a copy, but they wanted to let us know that there are some members of the media camped outside."

I sigh.

"They're going to let us go out through the service entrance. It's gated."

"Hunter... If he sees that photo... He's going to know I lied to him."

"What are the chances he'll hear about a tabloid photo of me with a woman?"

"I have no idea. Declan likes to check the tabloid sites to see if they've made it big enough yet to end up on them."

"Idiot."

"Diva, more like. But he's got a point."

"Let's see how bad it is before we panic."

Another horrifying thought occurs to me.

"Oh, gods... what if my dad sees it? Me and the 'Sexiest Guy' guy, a rockstar who's more than a decade older? He'll lose it."

"Are you embarrassed to be seen with me? Am I that ancient?"

I laugh. It's a silly question, but his expression is uncertain. I sit down next to him on the bed, grabbing his hand in mine.

"You, my dear, are on that *list* for a reason. Short of Hunter, sexiest man I've ever seen. Or probably ever will."

I kiss the end of his nose. He smiles. All of my panic — both from that vision and from this tabloid thing — melts away under the need to reassure Aedan. I've felt that before, with Hunter. How on earth did I end up in love — even just a little — with two men, two rockstars, at once?

I need to get to Kildare.

There's a knock at the door, and Aedan goes to answer it, handing over the keys to the rental car.

"We'll be ready to go shortly."

Aedan sits down with the tabloid in his lap, turning pages. He doesn't get far. Page five.

"Mace spotted with mysterious blonde on Irish vacation!" the headline screams.

OK — it wasn't screaming in giant type, and there was no exclamation point. But it's the dominant headline on the page. At least it's inside and not on the cover, where Hunter or my dad might see it in the grocery store.

The photo... It's of me and Mace walking down Grafton Street on the day we ended up in the pub near Windmill Lane. His arm is around my waist, and he's kissing the top of my head. There's no question it's me. My favorite boho top, the short circle skirt over leggings, the wavy flaxen hair down my back. Anyone who knows me would find it at least familiar.

The saving grace? It's shot from behind. Someone was trying to be discreet about taking it. Probably a fan. Oh, it's recognizably Mace. That auburn hair is a dead giveaway, even in Ireland, and he'd taken his cap off while we walked, revealing his profile to the camera as he turned his face toward me to press that kiss to my head. The same gesture of affection Alex and Rhys had seen him make backstage two months ago. That had worried me then. Only now I was caught while on vacation in Ireland with Mace. My plausible deniability is wearing thin.

This isn't great news. But it could be worse. Except now there's a horde of media waiting to catch Mace and his traveling companion together, with the chance to put a name to my face. That can't happen.

"It'll be fine," he promises.

"We keep telling each other that. I'm starting to wonder."

He grabs me around the shoulders, kissing my temple.

"It will be fine. You can wear my cap when we go out, and we'll go straight to Kildare. It's quiet there, you said. And usually the Irish press doesn't pay much attention to celebrities. That's one of the reasons I wanted to come here on this break. This is a British publication. The press outside is probably foreign, too, or at least hired from outside the country. We'll lay low for a couple days, and they'll forget all about us. You'll see. It'll blow over."

I frown and sigh.

"Maybe I should call Hunt and confess before Declan throws this in his face."

"Don't. Chances are he won't ever see it. Don't borrow trouble. Besides — what's he really going to say if he puts things together and realizes you and I are involved? I hate to be blunt, but he rejected you, Brighid — again. You opened that door for him another time, and the best he could do — even after demonstrating just how jealous he was — was to tell you to go find someone else."

"That wasn't quite all there was to it."

Aedan sighs.

"I know. But I'm trying not to remind myself that he wanted you to find someone who'd be devoted to you and support you to the exclusion of all else. Because... I'm finding myself both admittedly unable to do that and really wanting to do it anyway."

"Oh, Aedan..." I scrub my hand over my face. "What a mess we've made..."

He pulls me into his chest, rubbing my back.

"It will be OK. You told me you Knew it would be OK."

"I did."

"And are you ever wrong about this stuff?"

"Just about Hunter and me..."

"You weren't wrong about that, even if things have changed a bit. Let's get to Kildare and regroup, get you some time at the shrine. It'll give you some perspective."

I already needed that, just to try to sort out this mess with Aedan and me... and... was that mermaid, in the vision, was she his lady?

"Aedan?"

"Hmm?"

"You said your lady... that she was blonde, right?"

"Yeah — not at all like your hair, though. Golden blonde, lighter than Hunter's hair, and down to her hips."

I shudder.

"You OK?"

"Yeah. Just trying to find some answers to this situation."

"Let's get packed up and get on the road. It will be fine. You'll see."

"I hope we're both right about that..."

Chapter 12

Paparazzi

It's less than three hours from Galway to Kildare. In that time, I've twisted this strand of hair — the one that never stays in my ponytail — about a million times. It's not a nervous habit of mine. Well, maybe it is now.

We didn't exactly make a clean getaway. The service entrance was gated, as promised, but the gate was openwork steel, and about half of the paparazzi who'd turned up out in front of the hotel were now holding their cameras through the spaces between the bars, hoping to get lucky with an angle and timing as they click-click-clicked their rapid-fire shots. Aedan went out first, aiming to distract them with the overt display of his presence while I hid myself behind him (harder than you might think, since he's not much wider than I am at the shoulders and probably thinner at the hips). I kept my head down, the bill of his ball cap tipped in front of my face, praying that I could pull off subtle for the first time in... well, ever... as I slid into the passenger seat.

I have no idea if it worked, and I'm about ready to pull the rest of my hair out worrying about what the photographers caught as they shouted their questions at Aedan, and at me.

"Is this your girlfriend, Mace?"

"Who is she, Mace?"

"Hey, darlin' — how'd you land the Sexiest Guy on the Planet?" (If anyone has the answer to that question, feel free to let me know.)

"Mace — over here! Let's see the lovebirds together! Give the girl a kiss!"

Aedan frowned at them for an instant as the questions flew at him, then turned on that famous smile of his and waved.

"Great to see you all! I'm just getting to know the country a little ahead of the big kickoff of Telltale Signs' European tour in Dublin in a couple weeks. Great, great place. Wonderful people. Really amazing music. It's nice to get in some downtime before the tour gets going again!"

He never acknowledged their questions about me, let alone answered any of them. And as he pulled out toward the road, with the hotel security manning the gate, I kept my head down, my arms over my face. One of the paparazzi tried to follow us on a motorbike, but Aedan lost him in traffic and then doubled back to take a different route out of the city.

"You OK?" He glances nervously at me, his hands tight on the steering wheel.

"Yeah. Yeah. I'll be fine." I'm apparently less convincing than I'd hoped, because he finally releases the wheel with one hand and clasps it over my right hand where it sits on the center console. My fingernails are making dents in my palm, and he uncurls them with his fingers before pulling my hand to his mouth and kissing it. I resist the urge to pull away.

This isn't his fault, and I've already let this go too far. I won't hurt him by pulling away, physically or otherwise, but I don't want to encourage him either. I need to get myself sorted out before this gets to a point where there's no going back. We ride in silence for a good half-hour before he breaks down and puts on some music. Not rock. Quiet, meditative vocals over a spare accompaniment of flute and violin, in Irish. I have no idea where he got this. But it's exactly what I need.

"I bought it in Dublin, before I found you on the green that first day. I was going to give it to you when we got to Kildare. So we're only a little ahead of schedule."

I didn't ask. He answered anyway.

I look over at him, and he glances nervously at me again. But there's more there now. The priest has risen to the surface, sharing Aedan's eyes with that concerned... friend? boyfriend? What are we at this point? Do either of us even know?

I take a deep breath.

"Thank you. Truly."

He squeezes my hand again. He never let go, from the first moment he took it.

"Is She talking to you?"

"Not at this point. I'm too freaked out. I need... I needed this." I gesture at the car stereo.

"Close your eyes and rest, even if you don't sleep. I'll get us there." He runs his thumb back and forth across my hand, and between the music and that soothing sensation, I finally relax. I even fall asleep for a little while.

"**B**righid. Sweetheart. We're here."

"Hmm?"

"We're here."

I sit up and stretch, blinking the sleep from my eyes and the fog from my brain. Too much adrenaline too early in the day. I flash back to the drive through the gate, the crowd of photographers, and I shudder.

"Oh! We're *here* here!"

Aedan smiles at me.

"We are." He nods.

I look around me, not quite believing it. We're sitting in a small parking lot on a narrow Irish lane, with a path and bunch of trees. I've seen photos of this place. We're at the well. My anxiety melts away, in favor of a peaceful kind of excitement.

Aedan is beaming at me, his expression kind of like a proud parent.

Wait. Did he just call me "sweetheart"?

We got here none too soon.

"What are you waiting for? Go!" He shoos me out of the car.

I open the door and take a look around, my excitement returning.

And then I bend back down, looking over at him, still that proud expression on his face.

"You coming?"

"I can..." He seems uncertain.

"Aedan — you were called here the same as I was..."

He looks at me, incredulous.

"You said you'd been told to make Her acquaintance, remember?"

He nods. It's been less than three months since that night that changed everything. It seems simultaneously an eon ago and like yesterday. My heart melts all over again. Things between us *have* gotten complicated. Perhaps this reminder of a time when they were simpler, clearer-cut was needed.

"You sure? I can come back and pick you up later. Or I can wait here."

"Aedan — come."

"Yes, my Lady." There's that smirk again. I can't tell if he's enjoying whatever double-entendre he's got floating through his head or if he's just enjoying me giving him orders. So, yeah, a few things have changed since that night.

He gets out of the car, and I grab his hand, pulling him along behind me down the path. He chuckles. I stop and turn to look at him.

"What?"

"Sometimes I forget how young you are... You're an old priestess in a young woman's body."

"I'm not sure how to take that."

"It's a compliment. There are days when I feel ancient. It's good to see that excitement in someone's face, and to know it's on a spiritual level I understand."

"You've been alone too long."

His smile fades.

"I have. I wasn't sure you'd realized."

"I did. I do. It'll still be OK. All of it."

"You Know?"

"I Know. Now, come on — let's go see!"

W e've seen everything here. If I was here as a tourist, I'd have taken my photos and been ready to go. But I'm not here as a tourist. I'm here as a priestess, because I was called here. And I have a thing I need to sort out in my head, and my heart, and it seems I'm supposed to do that here.

It's a warm summer day, for Ireland, anyway. It's topped 70, and I'm enjoying the sun as I sit on the grass near the well and the statue. Aedan's sitting behind me, leaning back on his hands, his eyes closed, with that distinctly feline attitude of relaxation in a pool of sunshine. I think if I stroked his head right now, he'd purr.

"What are you thinking over there? I can feel it from here. Are you ogling me?"

"Do you want me to be ogling you?"

"Of course." He chuckles, and I roll my eyes at him, my affection for him apparent in my smile.

I scoot back next to him, and he reaches around me to pull me back to lean against his chest.

"You can't ogle me when you're not looking at me."

"Nope. And probably better this way for just that reason. We are in a shrine, and not an overtly Pagan one, even if the sisters are very open-minded and welcoming."

"You Brigidines seem to be that way, Pagan or Christian."

"Are you feeling welcome here?"

"I am. Surprisingly much. It's a different feeling than I'm used to. Warmer, feminine, firm but not harsh. I think it was important that I came. Are you feeling like you accomplished what you wanted to here?"

"Not yet. I have some things to sort out."

"One of them being us."

"A bit."

He tone becomes serious.

"Don't shut me out, Brighid. I meant it when I said whenever either of us wanted to call an end to this, we could. No strings. If you aren't comfortable with where we've been headed, tell me. I don't want to lose my friend."

"Nor do I. But we'll get it figured out. I'm sure of it."

He kisses the top of my head, and I instinctively look around us. There are a few other visitors here, but they're all engaged in their own explorations and meditations. No photographers, not even a cell phone pointed in our direction. They're all focused on the statue, the well, the trees with their clooties tied on them. I didn't know we were coming straight here, and I don't have anything to leave. I'll have to think of something before we go.

"Did you want to leave something?" I ask. "It's tradition."

"I noticed the bits of cloth tied to the trees."

"And a few baby booties, some coins, bits of jewelry — something tied to the people who left them. Some of them belong to people in need of healing, others — it's kind of a thank-you for what the shrine offers to people, from the water from the well to the peace and healing they take away with them."

"I'll decide on something to leave before we leave Kildare. As a matter of fact, if you want to stay a while longer, I can go get us checked in at our hotel, get the bags to the room, and come back for you in a couple hours, if you like."

"That sounds perfect." I turn to look at him, and I'm struck by his expression. Soft, warm, peaceful. He captures my mouth with his own. It's not simple affection anymore. Not just friendship overlaid with sex. And I don't know if that's OK or not. I know it will be OK. I'm just not sure how we get there from here.

"Aedan... Thank you. For encouraging me to come, for being my traveling companion, for bringing me here to the well when I needed it most, without me even asking. And that's before I get to all the rest of what you've given me these last two months."

"You deserve it, and a lot more. It was past time someone gave you what you deserved. And now I'm going to go take care of some practicalities while you, my dear, get some quality time with Herself. I'll be back in two hours."

He kisses the top of my head and gets up with the same feline grace he exuded in that pool of sunshine. I have to admit, I watch him as he walks away.

"Brighid?"

He's stopped after a few yards and turned back to face me.

"Hmm?"

"Are you staring at my butt?"

"I decline to answer on the grounds that I may embarrass myself."

He chuckles.

"Good. Because I'm planning to return the favor later. Two hours, my Lady!"

CHAPTER 13

WATER TO THE WELL

I spend the next hour or so in quiet contemplation, enjoying the sunshine and the feel of water pooled in the nearby well, the soft sounds of people moving around the shrine. I close my eyes and just listen, focusing on the whisper of the breeze, the liquid sound of water dipped from the well, murmurs of prayer and conversation. It's a peace like nothing I've ever experienced before, except perhaps sitting on the beach at night or lying in Hunter's arms... I sigh.

I need answers. I need a solution to this dilemma that's now invading my dreams. Hunter and Mace. Mace and the mermaid. Mace and his lady? Mace and me? Me and Hunter? What's the right thing to do? What am I being told to do? This all seemed so clear when Aedan and I first met. As soon as Hunter made it clear I'd be a fool to keep waiting for him, it seemed obvious what I was supposed to do. Now, it's no longer obvious. In fact, it's utterly murky.

"That's a real dilemma you've got there."

My eyes pop open to find a woman looking down on me from above. I shield my eyes against the glare of the sun from behind her.

"Sorry — the sun." She moves off to the side, and I can finally see her.

She's tall, probably about my height, solidly built, but not curvy like me. Strawberry-blonde hair falls straight and past her shoulders, her eyes kind — a green-brown hazel that reminds me of changing leaves.

"Hi." I'm not sure what else to say. Did she ask me something? I was so deeply focused that I'm not even sure.

"You were thinking very hard." Her accent tells me she's Irish, maybe a Dubliner? "Sorry if I interrupted. I should have left you to your thoughts. Your expression was... troubled?"

I nod.

"Trying to puzzle out some things."

"This is a good place for it. Only one better that I can think of."

I cock my head, curious. "Where would that be, if you don't mind me asking?"

"There's another well. Just down the way. Actually, there are dozens of Her wells all around the country. But I meant the other one in Kildare."

"Why is that one better?"

"This one's newer, belongs to the sisters here, as lovely as they are to all their visitors. The other one... it's... older."

"It's..."

She nods.

"Thought it might suit you better."

"But you're here."

"I visit both of the wells, nearly every day."

"Equal opportunity worship?"

She chuckles.

"She doesn't seem to mind. The sisters don't. Why should I?"

I nod in understanding.

"Makes sense."

"They call it the Wayside Well. I can give you directions, if you like."

I pull a scrap of paper and a pen from my purse and offer them to her. She writes something down and hands them back to me.

"Thank you."

"My pleasure. I hope you find your answers. Blessings."

"Thank you. And to you."

She walks back off toward the parking area.

"So, you want me to go to the other well..."

I say it aloud, even though I know it doesn't need to be.

"The other well?"

Aedan drops down on the grass beside me.

"You're back early."

He wraps his arms around me and kisses the side of my head.

"I got us all checked in. And I wanted to make sure you were OK."

I find that simultaneously comforting and troubling.

"I'm fine. Really. Being here has been... peaceful."

"You get things sorted out?"

"Not yet."

His mouth drops down by my ear.

"You don't have to decide anything right now. You have all the time you need. No pressure. I mean it. If you want me to get a second room, or a suite, I'll do that."

I sigh and nuzzle my face up against his.

"That's not necessary."

"Are you sure?"

I nod.

"I don't have my answers yet, but there's no reason we can't share a bed. You've been so good to me, Aedan. I don't want things to be uncomfortable between us just because things didn't stay inside their predefined boxes."

"Sometimes, it's easier if the lids stay on the boxes. It's less messy that way. But you don't learn as much, about yourself or others."

"That's pretty profound."

"People tell me I should be a priest or something..."

"It would suit you. You should give it a try."

We both chuckle.

"You hungry?"

"Starved."

"Then we should go take care of that... Can't leave you wanting..."

His voice is a purr in my ear, and my heart races in response. He's been downright feline today, but it's no house-cat sprawled next to me now, instead a panther coiled and ready to pounce. And yet the thrill in my blood holds no fear. He's safe. Aedan himself is safe. The risk is in letting what we're just starting to feel for each other run free and overwhelm us. It's a risk that could pay off, or destroy us. And I need to know which it's likely to be before I decide how to go forward.

But, in the meantime, there's no reason not to enjoy the comfort Aedan's friendship offers.

With the close call we already had with the paparazzi, we don't take the risk of dining together in public. But the hotel staff bring some really good food up to us from the hotel restaurant. After dessert, Aedan excuses himself and I close my eyes to ponder the things that are still weighing on my mind.

I refuse to give up Aedan's friendship. I may be a prime example of the old saw that men and women can't be friends, but what's happening between me and Aedan is lightyears away from what exists between me and Hunter. Centuries away, more accurately. And maybe that's the core of the issue. I already have two lifetimes' worth of love for Hunter. And as much as we understand each other on a soul-deep level, Aedan and I are still getting to know each other. And that's before we even get to the feelings we both have for other people. Maybe this is just an outgrowth of the frustration over having our feelings spurned by the people we love. Maybe on some level we're transferring some of that love onto each other. It would make sense, even if I'd like to think we're both self-aware enough to recognize that if it was the case to any significant degree.

Aedan calls my name from the bathroom. I cross the threshold to find him standing next to a spacious bathtub full of hot water and bubbles, lit candles dispersed around the darkened room.

This may be the sweetest thing anyone has ever done for me. No — second to Hunter's refusal to leave my side after my mother died, and his determination to be at her funeral. But this might be the most romantic...

And my heart twists just a little.

Aedan's arms come around my waist from behind.

"Would that there was room for two. But I thought you might like some relaxing time alone anyway."

He kisses the side of my neck, and I'm hit with that same feeling of deep affection for him that has started to become something stronger.

"Thank you."

I turn in his embrace and throw my arms around his neck, brushing a kiss over his lips. He returns it with fervor, and I allow myself to get lost in it, just for a little while.

"You really are an amazing kisser," Aedan murmurs as he breaks the kiss.

"Natural talent." I chuckle, looking down demurely. "Either that, or it's all this practice I've been getting with this amazing teacher of all things carnal."

"Hmm... Could be." He winks at me. "But you were already an excellent kisser the first time we kissed."

A shudder runs down my spine.

He delivers another sweet kiss to my lips.

"You should go have your bath before the water gets cold. And before I strip you naked myself and we end up in bed instead of you getting your bath."

I sigh, an unlikely mixture of contentedness and wistful wanting. It feels so nice being treated this way, like I'm treasured and not just tolerated. I'm reminded of how often I've felt tolerated, especially where aMUSEd is involved. And I consciously choose to shake off that feeling, reveling instead in the candlelight and the scented bubbles and the water waiting for me, drawn by an amazing man. This is what Aedan knew I needed that night we met, to feel appreciated and cherished as a woman, and I'm not going to shortchange either of us on that count.

"I'll be out here," he says, backing out of the room and pulling the door to behind him with a little bow.

I smile. He's so cute. As devastatingly handsome as he is, as undeniably charismatic, as powerfully as he commands a room or a stage in front of thousands, there's also a sweetly endearing quality to him. How is any woman able to resist his charms? It's a familiar refrain, my brain again asking me why Hunter doesn't see me like that. And I know that, right now, it doesn't matter why. What matters is sorting out this complex web of emotions that's fogged my mind the last day or so.

I get undressed and slip into the hot water, the bubbles up to my neck in this deep tub, despite the rest of its dimensions being modest. Maybe someday I'll have a bathtub big enough for two, even when one of those two is me.

I let my mind go blank, aiming for that relaxation Aedan suggested I needed right now. And he is, as usual, entirely correct. I've never been one to be able to keep a quiet mind. But dragging my thoughts away from busy places has become a well-honed muscle for me, and the next-best thing. In the little bit of thought that creeps in around the edges, my mind goes back to the time I spent today at the Garden Well and my encounter with the woman... priestess? who mentioned the Wayside Well. I already feel drawn to the place, and I haven't even seen it. Tomorrow, I'll go there and see if I can find some answers.

When the bubbles have started to thin and the water to cool, I pull a bath sheet from the pile of towels Aedan left near the tub and wrap it around me. I expect he'll want to go to a pub tonight, even if I'm more inclined to stay in. But I should get dressed regardless, and my clothes are all out in my bag.

"Aedan, thank you again for that. It was..."

My mouth stops moving of its own volition, my brain skidding to a halt and the words piling up on my tongue like a throw rug under sliding feet.

Aedan is lounging on top of the bed. Naked. Like something out of a women's pin-up magazine (not that I've ever seen one). Half of my brain sends signals to my cheeks to flush in embarrassment, and the other half is a millisecond short of just throwing me on top of him.

"Cat got your tongue?"

Aedan's grin is decidedly cat-like, so perhaps a cat did get my tongue... or will, soon enough.

This is exactly what I needed. A bath to relax me, and some lighthearted fun to engage my senses and keep my mind from getting preoccupied with things I clearly can't puzzle out on my own.

In a measure of how much my body-confidence has improved under his influence, I turn away from him and drop the towel, returning his grin over my shoulder.

"Is this sufficient for your ogling needs? Or should I walk over to the window?"

"I'm not sure there is such a thing as sufficient ogling opportunity where you're concerned," he says, "but I don't want to wait any longer to get more than my eyes on you."

He pats the bed in front of him, and I re-enact that slow Marilyn-esque saunter I made to him after his soundcheck in Virginia Beach. The distance is shorter, but the apparent impact just as strong. As soon as I get within reach, Aedan sits up and grabs me, pulling me onto the bed with him. I start to object, but he's already ahead of me, issuing a repressive look that keeps me silent about my being too heavy for that.

He pulls my leg across his hips, leaving me straddling him. His hands reach up and cup my breasts. His expression is somewhere between fond and spellbound. His thumbs brush across my nipples, and I lean into his hands. He pushes his hips up against me, and I can feel him, hard, beneath me.

And I pause, considering...

"What?"

A grin breaks out across my face.

"What?" he asks again.

"I just had an idea..."

"I'm listening."

I take his hands in mine and push them back against the mattress, holding them down by the wrist and shifting enough of my weight onto my arms that he's pinned there, unless he chooses to make an actual effort to get loose. Even then, that solid build and those big bones of mine are a bit of an equalizer in a little playful wrestling between lovers, or... this.

His expression shifts from curious, to surprised, to hungry. He wants this.

"Where did you put those ropes?"

Five minutes later, with some careful instruction and a pair of medical-grade safety scissors on standby, I've got Aedan's arms secured to the bed. He's relaxed, not fighting it at all, but his breathing is rapid, his expression eager, his cock hard under my hands as I stroke him lightly with just my fingertips. There's a twitch as my fingers finish their run up the ridge on the back side, and I marvel at it. I usually have my hand wrapped around him or my mouth on him in a moment like this, and I've never seen this before.

I look up at him.

"You look like you've just discovered fire," he tells me, panting a little.

"I discovered fire two months ago. His name is Aedan." The look he gives me is full of that heat.

"You know, Aedan means—"

"'Little fire,'" I interrupt. "The diminutive for the old god Aodh — a god of the underworld, eldest son of Lyr, who is also father to Manannán."

"You have no idea how hot it is that you know that," he says, still panting.

"I looked it up after we met. You use the Manx spelling. Aptly."

"Yeah, I do..."

I lick up the same path my fingers just traveled. His hips push up, and I take him into my mouth, savoring the feel, the taste of him. My movements are languid, teasing, much as his were the night he bound me with these same ropes. He's not pulling against them like I did, but his muscles are tense, on edge, like he's longing to break free. But he doesn't ask me to release him.

"Gods, I love that mouth of yours..."

"It's mutual," I reply, licking around his tip.

"But if you keep doing that, I'm going to come."

"I thought that was the goal."

"The goal's whatever you want it to be."

"What do *you* want it to be?"

"Not up to me. You're in charge right now. How's that feel? Being the one making the decisions? Being the one in control? Being the one who decides what happens?"

"I kind of like it."

"As much as you liked being tied up?"

"Actually, yeah..."

"More than neither of us being tied up?"

I shake my head. "I like it all."

"Gods, you are just perfect..."

He's grown even harder in my hand as I stroke him, and his hips are pumping short strokes inside my grip.

"Ride me, Brighid. I want to watch you work yourself on my cock, make yourself come."

I only hesitate a moment, rising to straddle his hips, sliding my slit over the hard line of him.

He pulls on the ropes now.

"I want those glorious breasts in my hands. I want to touch you, make you come on my mouth, my hand... But I need to see you fuck me. Fuck me how you want to fuck me, no thoughts of my pleasure. Because all I want to see is what makes you feel good. Show me."

I fit his tip to my opening, savoring every bit of the sensation as I slide slowly down to the root of him.

"Gods above and below..." he breathes, his eyelids drifting closed over those pools of deep blue that are his irises.

I start to move, hesitantly at first, keeping most of my weight off of him, just rocking a little, forward and back. My mind is focused within, on the feeling of him filling me, caressing me. I chase sensation, shifting forward and back, twisting my hips a little, making short dips down from above and then sliding down again. I whimper a little as I hit bottom, my opening fully sealed against him.

"Keep doing that. Fuck yourself hard on me. I can tell you like it," he says, lifting his chin in encouragement. "I can feel you fluttering against me. Make yourself come. Let me watch you come on my cock."

I settle into a steady rhythm, pressing him hard into my center and sliding slowly up, just to do it all over again.

"Cut me loose, Brighid. I need to touch you."

His expression is earnest and desperate. I don't even ask for the safeword. I snatch the scissors from the bedside table and cut the ropes at his wrists. His fingers move just above where we're joined, and he starts circling my clit. I drop back into that driving rhythm, quickly rising back to that near-peak. He turns his hand, his palm and fingers grasping my hip while his thumb continues to rub me in the most delightful ways.

"Come for me."

I do. Not because he told me to. Because I wanted to.

I half-collapse on top of him, but he flips me over on my back and comes right back inside, smashing his lips into mine, licking at my tongue. My arms wrap around his back, my legs around his hips. That deep pressure, him plunging inside me, I revel in it, rising back up, meeting Aedan at the peak as he groans and smacks his hips into mine one last time, and I fall over the peak... falling forward, stunned by the distance between me and the water. I stretch my wings to catch the wind and fight the pull of gravity, but there are no feathers, just skin — normal human skin on normal human arms, and suddenly I'm plunging from the top of a cliff to a churning sea far below. It's a literal nightmare, falling and knowing I won't survive the landing, even if water is a little more forgiving than land. Only a little.

I have just enough presence of mind amid the panic to pull my arms together to help break through the surface of the water, and in an instant, I'm underneath, body shocked by the impact and the decided lack of air down here. I swim to the surface, my joints aching from the force of hitting the water but feeling relieved there were no jagged rocks to be dashed upon.

I break through to the air, gasping for breath and prepared to swim literally for my life lest I be smashed up against the bottom of the cliff. But there's no sheer cliff face in front of me — just a wide stretch of sandy shore that looks and feels familiar. I know this place. Home. And I've been here before — and not just in my waking reality. This is the beach where I saw the blonde man, the one who reminded me of Hunter, but older, and yet not a shepherd living in a cottage on a hill overlooking the sea.

I scan the beach for any sign of life. Gulls flying overhead, piping plovers scattering as a wave breaks and rushing back to the water line in search of food when it retreats... Someone sitting at the crest of the beach, well above the tide line. Yes — the blonde man, bearded, broad of shoulder and slender at the hips, his long hair trailing down onto his chest as he leans forward, looking troubled. That I can see the discomfort in his expression from this far tells me just how troubled he must be. I need to help him, whoever he is.

I start swimming for the shore, thoughts of falling and drowning now far from my mind. I have to get to him, talk to him, figure out who he is and why he's so important, why he's in such deep distress.

"Brighid!"

I reach the back side of the breakers. I have to time my approach to the land so I don't get caught up in the crashing waves and pulled back under.

"Brighid!"

The voice is coming from behind me, and I turn around to see Aedan struggling amidst the deep swells. I can't let anything happen to him. In a decision that's as much instinct as it is thought, I strike out for Aedan's position. If I can just get to him in time, I can get both of us out of the water and onto the beach, and I'll be able to sort all of this out and keep everyone safe, help everyone.

I cut through the distance with efficient strokes, nearly to him now... Almost there...

I pull up short as something rises to the surface directly in front of me, all teeth and claws and... tentacles? No. Long ropes of golden-blonde hair. The mermaid!

This time she's not pulling Aedan away into the depths far from shore. She's placed herself between him and me, almost protectively. The impression of teeth and claws is just that. She's grimacing at me, hands raised up to keep me away.

"Brighid!" Aedan calls again from behind her.

It's like he can't see her, that she's keeping me from coming for him. I try to go around her, and she strikes out at me, narrowly missing my face with her nails. I tread water with just a foot or so between us. Her expression becomes less feral, more somber, and I consider my options. She can cover any distance in the water faster than I can. And she's clearly prepared to get violent to keep me from him. And while he struggles in the waves, she appears to be protective of him. She won't let him drown, right?

Just then, he sinks below a swell, coming back up sputtering. I launch myself around her, the threat she poses be damned, but she hurtles herself backward in that same moment, diving below the surface, and suddenly Aedan is wrapped in her arms, towed along from behind at a pace I can't even begin to keep up with. Quickly, they're out of range, and I'm left shocked and horrified, treading water with no idea what to do next.

I turn back to the beach and find the blonde man still sitting on the crest of the beach, his head now weighing heavily in his hands. I look back at where Aedan once was, and once again, there is no sign he was ever there, and if he was, what could I even do about it? I swim for the shore, determined to get to the blonde man this time, if nothing else. But I'm caught up in the rushing water as I reach the breakers and am pulled under, that familiar and yet terrifying feeling of being caught up in the washing-machine cycle that rolls me under and pushes me down into the sand, abraded and searching desperately for the surface.

I wash up on the beach, feeling scoured and gasping, relieved to be on solid ground again. I lumber up onto my feet, trying to get oriented and looking for the man. Only there is no man. There's no sign anyone was even on the beach.

I collapse onto the sand, exhausted, physically, mentally, emotionally. My eyes slide closed, and...

I wake cradled against Aedan's chest, his arm around my shoulder. Again, he sleeps peacefully while my heart races, my blood full of adrenaline from a fall from a cliff, a near drowning, a rush to the shore, an attempted rescue, a confrontation with a mermaid, another near drowning and dragging my dream-world ass onto the shore.

Making a spur-of-the-moment decision, I ease Aedan's arm from around me and sit up gently, praying that he will not wake this time. Luck, or the will of the gods, is with me, and I manage to get out of the bed, silently gathering up a change of clothes and retreating into the bathroom, where I get dressed and ready to go out. I scrawl a cursory note on the notepad by the telephone, telling Aedan that I've gone off to Her well and not to worry. I grab my day bag and room key, and let myself out into the hall, breathing a sigh of relief when there's no sign of Aedan waking.

My need to get to the well is so strong that when the desk clerk tells me it'll be a while before a taxi can get to me, I start walking. It's not that far. And the walk won't hurt me. Well, no — it may well hurt. It's not a short walk. But I could stand to walk off last night's dessert, even though I got some exercise in afterward...

A little more than twenty minutes later, I've reached the Japanese Gardens, where, curiously, the ancient well is situated. I follow the priestess' directions to find the well, which is situated in an alcove literally off the beaten path. The surrounding stones are traced with moss and plants, the water itself topped with shed flower petals and pollen. It's early enough that no one else is here, and I settle myself on a stone wall nearby, pulling my focus within, yet still acutely aware of the liquid energy of the nearby well.

When I open my eyes, it's not pavers and stone walls and a ground-level well that I see. There is a well, but it's raised, with a bucket and dipper alongside. I take a drink from the dipper, and it's sweet and cool and pure, the best thing I've ever tasted or likely will ever taste. I squint up into the sun, which is now high overhead, and then down the grassy hill. The tide is out, and the rocky parts of the shoreline are revealed. I pick up my basket and head down to collect seaweed from the rocks. Hunter ate the last of the dillisk butter with his oatcakes last night, so I'll be making some more today while he's out with the sheep.

I clamber carefully over the granite rocks, which are slick with sea lettuce and other seaweeds. The dillisk here grows most fervently in pockets along the rock pools, so I have to navigate carefully across the more exposed rock faces. I set my basket down on a high spot and pull my little harvesting knife from the pocket of my apron. I carefully cut the dillisk from its roots so it can regrow on the rock face and then deposit it in the basket. When I've harvested a few clumps from this pool, I move onto the next.

"Brighid!"

I turn back toward the sandy beach, expecting to see Hunter come back unexpectedly early, but there's no one there. My imagination is running away today. I continue to the next pool.

"Brighid!"

This time, it's coming from behind me, which is impossible, because not even Hunter would be swimming in the ocean on a cool day like this. My feet are already half-frozen. But I look nonetheless.

It's not Hunter, whose golden mane can be spotted from shore, even soaked dark with seawater. But there is a man out in the water, and he seems to be in trouble, his reddish-brown hair cascading over his forehead and into his eyes. I drop the basket and hurry to the edge of the rocks. And that's a mistake. My heels slip out from beneath me, and I crash onto my back, my head hitting the rock hard enough to rattle my senses. My left hand, still clutching the knife, is the next point of impact, as the sharp inward-curving blade bites into the webbing between my thumb and forefinger. My vision goes hazy and then...

"Brighid!"

I frown. I try to sit up. Ow. That may have to wait.

"Bridge!"

I blink and look up, now blinded by the sun, but seeing the silhouette of a man. That red-haired man must have pulled himself from the sea after my fall. We're both lucky the tide was at near full-ebb, or he might have been swept out to sea and I might have drowned, unconscious on the rocks. As it stands, I'm chilled to the bone. I reach up for his extended hand and find mine grasped gently, rather than being used to lever me up. He tears a strip of cloth from his shirt and uses it to wrap my hand, which I now remember has met the business side of my knife.

"Thank you."

"You're welcome, sweetheart..."

Sweetheart?

"I'm sorry, sir — you're being over-familiar. I thank you for your aid, but I am married."

He chuckles.

"I know that, Bridge. I married you, after all."

I blink again and cock my head to look up at him again. No red hair. Golden blonde.

"Hunter?"

"Who else have you married, my love?" He chuckles. "How hard did you hit your head?"

Hunter grabs my right hand and pulls me up from the rock. My head is pounding, but I feel even more confused than seems warranted after that. I could have sworn...

"There was a man... red hair..."

"Apparently very hard," he observes. "There's no one here but me, and you were lucky Crógan ate my lunch and forced me to come back for sustenance, or you could have drowned there. Take greater care when you're gathering, Brighid. I can't lose you."

He kisses my forehead and then my lips. My legs falter under me. He sweeps me into his arms and carries me across the rocks and onto the sand, where he sets me down at the edge of the grassy hill. He goes back for my knife and basket, and then kneels down next to me.

"How are you feeling, Brighid? Should I go get the healer?"

"No — no, I'm fine. Just a little bump to the back of my head." I touch it experimentally, wincing but finding no blood.

"And your hand," he reminds me.

"And you tore your shirt."

"A worthwhile sacrifice." He kisses my hand just above the cut, where my thumb and forefinger meet. I stare at the spot. Something about it...

"Let's get you out of these wet clothes..." His eyes are full of mischief. "...and warmed up by the fire. Or something..."

I chuckle and shake my head. Only my husband would go from rescuing me to thoughts of ravishing me in the space of a moment.

My husband...

I thread my fingers through his hair. His blonde hair. Blonde. Not red. My fingers trace over his beard. A bearded blonde man on the beach... but Hunter's hair isn't that long, and his beard is a bit longer than the one on that other man's face, which is barely more than a scruff...

I look up into those sparkling eyes. Green, like the grass of the hill behind me... Green, like the moss on the rocks around Her well...

My eyes snap open, and I find myself sitting directly next to the Wayside Well, staring deep into the water. The sun is high overhead. How long was I lost in that vision? Of Hunter and our home on the shore. And the red-haired... Aedan...

I don't have all the answers I needed. Yet. But I have more than I did this morning. I send silent thanks to Herself for the insight, and I dig into my bag, pulling from it the tiny blown-glass vessel that has contained a few drops of seawater from home since I left for college. I uncork it and dip it into the channel that feeds the well, a prayer on my lips. I return it to my bag. On impulse, I tear a strip of cloth from the hem of my shirt, the simple white cotton almost perfectly matching Hunter's shirt from my dream... vision. This was a vision, given to me in my waking life. I shake my head and rise, moving to a nearby tree and tying the fabric to a small branch with another word of thanks and another silent prayer, this time for guidance to answer the remaining questions in my mind.

The act reminds me of a promise left unfulfilled, at a time and place not too far distant from here. I give a nod of respect to the well, and I start walking again. Not nearly so far this time.

CHAPTER 14

MEMORY SONG

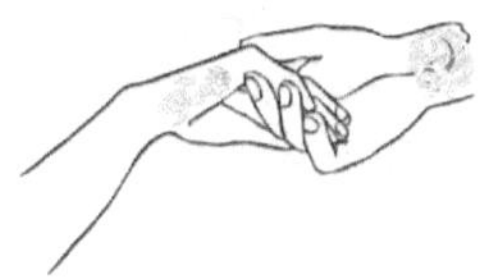

As I walk up the path from the parking area, I head this time directly toward the clootie trees. I pause to tear another strip from my shirt and walk up to tie it to a branch. But there's a familiar head of auburn hair and set of strong shoulders ahead of me, already tying his own strip of cloth to a branch. Lavender, curiously...

"Aedan?"

His head, bowed, raises and turns to me.

"There you are!"

He gathers me into a hug, clutching me tightly.

"I was worried! You said you'd be at the well. I've been waiting for more than an hour. Hoping you'd come back. Are you OK?"

I blink, confused. Then I realize that I didn't tell him in my note that I was going to the *other* well.

"Yes. I'm fine. I'm sorry I worried you. I went to the other well. I've been there all morning."

"Thank the gods." He kisses my head. I pull free. Thoughts... memories? of Hunter doing that are too fresh in my head. And I know what I need to do now.

I walk up to the branch and tie my own strip of cloth to it, another prayer of thanks and one for answers.

When I turn back toward him, Aedan's looking at me curiously.

"You get your answers?"

I nod. "Some of them."

"Care to share?"

"Let's go back to the hotel. It's been a long morning, and I'd like to get out of the sun for a bit."

He nods and pulls me into his side, his hand at my waist. We walk back to the car and drive to the hotel in silence. Once back in our room, I sit down on the freshly-made bed. Aedan stands in front of me, looking at me with trepidation.

"Come sit, Aedan."

"I feel a 'We need to talk' coming on."

I nod solemnly. "Not every 'We need to talk' is a break-up talk." That idea bothers me. Sometimes you just need to have a serious talk. It doesn't have to be an ending.

"And we're not exactly dating," he points out.

"No, we're not. But I think we both know it has been headed there."

He nods, and he sits next to me. We look at each other, the eye contact painful but necessary. There's more pain in his eyes than I've seen in the past. He's hidden exactly how much his loneliness has worn on him — from the world, and from me, and probably from himself to some degree. I can only pray that what is to come for him will make up for it, as much as I hope my life will eventually make up for my own pain. I pull his hand to my lips and press a kiss there.

"You are my friend, Aedan, and I think you always will be. I want that. I do. But this has started to get more complicated than either of us foresaw or wanted. You know that."

He nods.

"I need to go to Donegal now. The rest of my answers are there. And you can't come with me."

His frown deepens, his eyes stormy skies again.

"I don't like leaving you on your own."

"I'm not. I've been called. I have to answer. And the one thing She's told me is that I can't bring you with me. I have to do this on my own. You're too much of a distraction." I smile warmly at him, reaching out to cup his cheek in my palm. He turns to kiss it, grabbing my hand and holding it as he brings it to his lap.

"I'd like to think I'm more than a distraction..."

I chuckle and smile at him, pouring all of the affection I feel for him into the expression.

"You are *far* more than a distraction, Aedan. You're one of the closest friends I've ever had or likely ever will. You're the man who saved me from my self-imposed sexual confines and made me believe that maybe — just maybe — a man can actually find me attractive."

"No maybe about it."

"Thank you." I squeeze his hand. "I love you dearly, Aedan." His eyebrows go up. "As a friend." His face relaxes, and I can't tell if it's in relief or from expectations met. "I don't think I've ever said those words to another human beyond my family, and Hunter. And I mean them. I just don't know whether they can, or should, mean more than that."

"I understand."

"You do? Really?"

He nods. "I'm feeling the same way. And I have more experience and distance to put that feeling into perspective. I understand why you need some time to sort things out. I really do."

I lean forward and kiss him gently on the lips.

"Thank you."

"I'll call and make some reservations for you in Donegal, arrange for a car to get you there."

"No. Thank you, but I want to do this on my own. You've done enough for me on this trip. It's time I do things under my own power."

"You got to Dublin on your own."

"I did. But that was the easy part. I need this to require effort. I need to feel like I really did it on my own."

"OK. But I want you to promise me one thing... Well, two..."

"Alright..."

"First, if you need anything, you contact me. Period. Do not hesitate. Got it?"

"I won't need to. But I can make that promise. And?"

"Second — I want you to come to the show in Dublin, as planned. You've got nearly two weeks before then, and you're already set to go back home the next day. I've already got a VIP tour lanyard for you. I brought it with me in case you wanted to come to some more shows on the European leg of the tour. And you're welcome to do that."

He squeezes my hand.

"Until the day I stop touring, or the day I die — which will probably be the same day," he adds with a chuckle, "— you have a standing VIP pass to all my shows. Just give your name at the box office or security entrance, and they'll let you right in. That's no matter what happens with us. You understand?"

"Yes. Thank you. And don't act like this is an ending, Aedan. It's really not. Not to our friendship, at least. The rest... the rest I'll have to figure out."

"I understand."

He holds his arms out, inviting me into a hug that lasts so long I lose track of the time. Just sitting there with him holding me, in silence. Peaceful, and feeling loved. In all the ways that matter for us right now. After a while, I start to pull away, and he grabs hold of my chin, pressing a sweet kiss to my lips.

"Take care of yourself, and remember what you promised me."

"I will. Thank you, Aedan. For everything."

"And thank you."

I sigh and stand up, packing up my bag for the trip to Donegal. I haven't even figured out how I'm getting there. But I have enough money to get me there, stay and then go back to Dublin for my flight home. That much I know.

Aedan is pensive, but with that placid, almost distant, expression that tells me he's withdrawn into his priestly self.

I perform my own small version of the "idiot check" the guys do when packing up after a show, ensuring nothing has been left behind.

Aedan stands and meets me at the door, drawing me once more into a hug.

"Blessings, my friend," he says solemnly, kissing my forehead. "I'll see you in Dublin."

I nod and head out the door, refusing to look back, even though I can feel him watching me walk down the hall. It's time for me to go. To Donegal. *Back* to Donegal. Where I've long suspected Hunter and I lived in that time before. And where my answers, if there are any to be had, are to be found.

I step onto the beach near my hotel in Narin, northeast of Donegal, on the Atlantic coast. It took me two days to get here. Only six hours of that was getting from Kildare to Donegal, which I managed via a combination of train and bus. I spent the night in Donegal, and the next morning I threw a non-literal dart and just asked the desk clerk at the hotel if she had any idea where I might find a place along the coast with green hills that could graze sheep and a sandy shore with some rocks where seaweed might be harvested, or at least some place that might have been like that in, say, the early 1800s.

She said she'd once visited Inishkeel Island, just off the coast, where there's a historic site with the remains of an abandoned monastery. She said the area around there was a lot like what I'd described, said she'd walked Portnoo Beach up to the north, and it sounded a lot like that.

That afternoon, I headed out to Narin, the nearest town. I'd checked in to a hotel there, with a tentative reservation of a full week. It was too late when I arrived to go searching an unfamiliar area where I didn't know the tides, so I again talked to the hotel staff. A little bit in Irish, even, because this is part of the Donegal Gaeltacht. They agreed that the area to the north sounded like what I described. They also told me that a number of yarnmakers had historically been in the area, encouraging me to get in touch with some of the locals who still raised sheep for wool here.

The next day, I walked a ways up the beach. It had a familiar feel, though nothing quite matched what I'd seen in my visions. I got sidetracked by a large farm on a hill overlooking the beach, making friends (yes, me!) with the grandmother who'd been raised there and who had herself made handspun yarn before her arthritis made it too much of a challenge. Thankfully, Gráinne speaks English well, so we're not reliant on my smattering of Irish, though she encourages me to use it. She was thrilled to see a young woman — an American, even — so passionate about the old craft and handed me her remaining supply of wool roving, some dyed and some undyed.

"These girls are after becoming video game designers and rockstars," she tells me, gesturing dismissively at her tween granddaughters.

"Both potentially lucrative professions," I tell her. "I know a few professional musicians. It's not easy to get there, and the work is still hard even once you make it, but it's a wonderful contribution to the world and an amazing life if music is your passion."

"Tell Orlaith about that hard work part," she begs me, pointing at the younger of the two. "I keep telling her she'd have a solid living making handspun and selling it to the shops in Donegal."

"That's what I've been doing for my job. Part of it, anyway," I tell the girl, who's been eavesdropping since I said "professional musicians." "I've done well enough that I could afford this trip."

"But it's boring! And gran's hands hurt her something fierce. I don't want to have my hands hurting like that."

"Then you don't want to become a guitarist, either," I tell her. "My friend's guitar teacher has been playing for more than twenty years professionally, and he's always talking about having to retire because his hands just can't do what they used to."

She looks down at her hands, her enthusiasm clearly chilled by my revelation.

"Yeah — but I'd wager he'd do it all over again if he had the choice."

"I'm sure he would. I know my friend wouldn't be who he is today without his music."

"Is he really a professional musician?"

"He is. They just got their first record deal. And they just finished touring with a very well-known band."

"What are they called?"

"His band is called aMUSEd. He's their rhythm guitar player. And he writes some of their music."

She looks at me skeptically.

"Who'd they tour with?"

"They opened up for Telltale Signs in May and June."

"Telltale Signs? They're amazing!" she enthuses. "Did he get to meet Mace?"

I try to suppress my smile a bit.

"He did. And he introduced me to him, too."

"You've met Mace! You're so lucky!"

"What's he like?" the elder one, Niamh, says, joining in on a topic that clearly interests her at least as much as her video games. "Is he as tall as he seems? Is his hair really that amazing ginger color in person?"

I chuckle. Her grandmother scoffs and rolls her eyes.

"We've lots of ginger-haired boys around here, raising sheep and looking for wives who know how to spin..." she says, pointedly. But her granddaughter ignores her, still waiting for me to answer.

"Mace is very nice. He's smart and funny, and he's a deep thinker. Yes, he's quite tall, though my friend is a little taller. And, yes, Mace has amazing auburn hair."

Saying the words conjures images of my fingers combing through those auburn strands as he's licking me. But I shake myself free of it. See — he *is* a distraction. And he's not even here!

Under pressure from the seanmháthair and keeping in mind traditions regarding hospitality, I stay for supper with the family. Full of stew that tastes much like the one from my visions, I bid them farewell an hour or so later, walking back to the hotel as the light begins to fade from the sky.

I may not have found a spot that exactly matches my vision, but the feel of the place, the people, the tone of their speech — it's so close as to be indistinguishable. It's as much of a confirmation of my vision as I could hope to get, short of finding the little cottage on the hill or being transported back in time after touching a standing stone and finding myself right there. I fall asleep easily, exhausted from the walk and feeling both content and excited.

The next morning, I repeat my walk, getting farther this time. I reach a spot that has all of the hallmarks of the coast I saw in my visions, just in a different formation. If it's real and it's not nearby, I'd be surprised. I head back before it gets much later.

"Miss Brighid! Miss Brighid!" I hear called down the hill above me. It's the girls, the younger one blonde and elder brunette, but otherwise near carbon copies of each other. They race down the slope so fast that I'm worried they'll tumble. But they seem to be half goat (or at least half sheep) as they handle the terrain like they were born to it. Which, of course, they were.

"Miss Brighid!" the elder one says breathlessly as she grabs onto my arm to pull herself to a stop. "We saw you walk by earlier, and Gran said we were to invite you to supper again if we were to see you. Will you come? Will you come?"

I laugh aloud in amazement over this enthusiastic welcome. They seem happier to see me than anyone other than my mother, Hunter and Mace ever have been.

"If your seanmháthair told you to invite me, then I am obligated to comply," I tell them.

They half-drag me up the steep hill — which, thankfully, I did not try to scale the day before, having met the grandmother on a lower slope to the south.

"Tell me more about Mace!" the elder girl demands as we come through the door.

"Girls, where are your manners? At least let the poor girl get her coat off and sit a spell before you pester her with questions."

"Yes, Gran," they groan in harmony.

"Let's get her a nice cuppa. Honey, dear?" she asks me.

"Please." She nods to the girls, who seem to have the process mastered.

"You're not a coffee drinker like so many Americans, are you?"

"No, ma'am. The lady I work for at college, her daughter is a papermaker and dabbles in herbal teas as well. I've tested many a blend of hers. I always hedge my bets with honey, though," I add, laughing.

"Wise girl. I hope the girls don't make too much of a pest of themselves. They're fascinated with this Mace fellow..." She glances over at the girls at the stove, dropping her voice low. "I take it you two are more than friends?"

My shock must be visible.

"How... What? I, uh..."

"I'm 70 years old, dear. I know the look in a woman's eyes when she's talking to strangers about her lover."

"Oh. My. Gods. I'm that transparent?"

"And a follower of the old ways, too, I take it." She chuckles.

"I'm sorry — I know people aren't always fond of... less conventional faiths... here. I'll leave if you'd prefer."

"Oh, no, dear!" She pats me on the arm. "Don't tell the girls — or the neighbors — but my own gran was half-pagan herself. Da insisted I go to Mass at least once a week, just to ensure I didn't take after her. But she's the one who taught me to spin and weave. And I see that Brighid's cross around your neck. There's a reason devotion to her in all her forms has persisted in this country. You're safe here."

I relax visibly.

"How did you know? About Mace, I mean."

"Your eyes go soft and your mouth takes on an affectionate smile when you talk about him."

"We're not... I mean... We're friends. Things are complicated right now. My best friend... I... He doesn't... and I... Mace... We...

I came here to get some clarity. I'm supposed to meet Mace in Dublin next week before their concert, and..."

"You're meeting Mace!"

"In Dublin!"

"And you're going to their concert?"

I cringe. Half from the volume of the girls' shrieking and half from having been so careless. I look over at their grandmother. She shrugs.

"Can you get us an autograph?"

"Can we go, too?"

The simultaneous vocal eruptions of the two siblings takes a moment to process.

"Girls, Miss Brighid is just here for a few days. I'm sure she has plans that don't involve taking two overly demanding children to a concert, or even taking the trouble to get them an autograph to send across the country."

"Please, Miss Brighid! Please!"

Never say I'm not a soft touch.

"Girls, your parents would have to approve you going hours away, to a concert, with a stranger. I can't see how they'd approve."

"Ma'll let us! She likes you. Gran likes you!"

I look over at her for help. She smirks and shrugs again.

"Oh, you're a big help..."

"I'm an old woman. I've got to get my entertainment somewhere."

"I don't suppose you want to play chaperone to these two should I agree to this... Someone would have to bring them back. I'm flying out the next day."

"I'm spry for 70. Too many days spent chasing sheep... I can handle two bus rides and a little while on my feet. Girls, we'll discuss this after your parents come in for supper. Go finish Miss Brighid's tea. I can hear the kettle ready to boil."

The girls run off, chattering excitedly between them.

"Besides, I'd like to meet this young man they're so fascinated with, and who puts a twinkle in your eye."

That thought all but snuffs out that twinkle, though, as I recall the decision I need to make. And why that's such a challenge.

"The other one — your friend. You've got feelings for him, too?"

"Mace and I... it was supposed to be short-term, friends... Hunter... he's my best friend. And he doesn't think of me like that."

"I find that hard to believe."

"I kind of do, too, but he's been very adamant about it."

"Which is why the ginger is a dilemma for you."

I nod.

"Tell me about this Hunter, then."

Tea delivered, she sends the girls outside to finish their afternoon chores. And I spend the next half-hour telling her all about Hunter. Everything except my visions, which I no longer trust anyone but Mace to believe.

"You have a photo of this one? The girls showed me what the ginger looks like last night after you left. He'd be hard to compete with."

I give her a look of surprise.

"You think I became a grandmother by not appreciating a handsome face?" She chuckles.

"There's no denying he's handsome. Half the women on the planet would drop their entire lives just for a night with him."

"And deservedly so, I take it."

I purse my lips and look discretely at the ceiling.

"I'll take that as a yes."

"He's very nice. Truly. A sweetheart. A good friend."

"Of course. You wouldn't go for a bad-boy. You're too nice yourself."

I shrug.

"So, let me see this boy."

I pull a photo of Hunter and me from my bag. It's the one Mom took of us on the beach a couple years ago.

"He's a couple years older now. We both are."

"And fated to be together."

If my look was surprised before, it's shocked now.

"Why do you say that?"

"You two look right together. You just fit."

"And Aedan — Mace?"

"He belongs with someone else."

"And you know that how?"

"My gran... People said she had the Sight. Knew things before they happened. Knew about things that happened far away. Da frowned upon anyone mentioning it, but she used to tell me stories. And every once in a while, I know a few things I shouldn't either."

I look at her, analyzing her expression. It's earnest, confident, placid, wise, and tiny bit amused.

"And now I know why Hunter always looks at me like this—" I gesture at my face. "—when I say things like that."

She smiles back at me and laughs heartily. "I should have known."

"So, I'm not wrong? About him and me? It's not just wishful thinking?"

"I think you're right that there's a connection. But people sometimes fight what is fated for them. Whether your Hunter will do that until it's too late is a question I cannot answer."

"And that's half the reason I'm here."

"Hard to hold out hope for something you've been told repeatedly isn't going to happen. Much easier to take something that's both attractive and offered freely."

"A bird in the hand is worth two in the bush."

"Just so. But you'd rather have the one in the bush, no?"

I look at my feet. I know the answer to this question. I shouldn't be hesitant to say it. Not even to — especially not to — a stranger. So why is it so hard to get the words past my lips?

"Do you trust him?"

"With my life."

"Do you love him?"

"More than anything."

"Does he love you?"

"He says he does. Sometimes. But that he's not *in love* with me."

"Do you believe him?"

"That he loves me, yes. That he's not *in love* with me? I don't know. It feels wrong. But I believe he means it."

"There's more you're not telling me."

I nod, slowly.

"That's why you're here, isn't it? Why you came *here* to sort this out..."

I nod again.

She looks at me, scrutinizing.

"You've given me enough of your secrets. You can keep that one. But I'll remind you what I said — you're fated to be together. It takes a lot to thwart fate. Mayhap this blonde guitarist of yours is pigheaded enough to pull it off. Mayhap your ginger is charming enough to make it easier for you to give up and move on. In the end, it's up to you to decide. I know plenty of women who'd take the ginger and run, if just for a while."

I can hear the girls approaching the house again, the bright chatter carrying through the heavy door.

"Can you tell me... Is there a place around here where a hill slopes down to a cottage and then down to a sandy beach with rock pools off to one side? Somewhere that might have been a small sheep farm two hundred years ago? Maybe with a family that produced yarn?"

"That could describe any number of places, including what today are portions of *this* farm."

"There's a cottage?"

"Was. It was abandoned a century ago. Burned down when I was a child, even younger than these two." She nods at the girls, who have rushed straight into the kitchen for a snack. "All that's left now is the old stone well."

"There was a well?"

"Well, there was a well on every farm back then."

"Of course."

"I can take you there tomorrow, if you like."

There's a sense of relief, like a weight has lifted off my shoulders.

"I'd like that very much."

CHAPTER 15

DREAMS

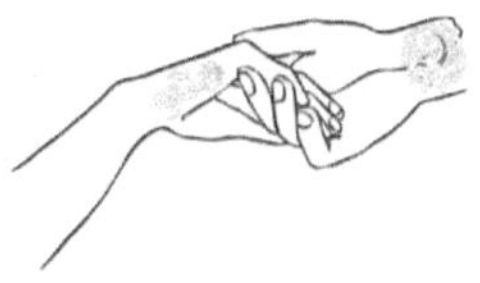

Just after breakfast, I'm walking back up the beach, eager to meet Gráinne and see if, by some miracle, the place in my vision is the one she knew. She's waiting for me at the foot of the hill. I find myself hoping she didn't come straight down that slope on her own. Maybe the whole family is half sheep...

"The girls wanted to join us, but I told them we had grown-up things to discuss and if they really want you to take them to that concert, they should respect that."

"I can't believe their parents agreed to it."

"They're off school for another week or so, and they're right — their mother likes you. We all do. Plus, I think Ciara might like your ginger a bit herself, though she'd never admit it."

"We'll have to get her an autograph. He *is* pretty irresistible."

"And yet here you are..."

"Yeah. That I am."

"Let's go see that old well."

We hike up the coast, going just a bit past where I stopped the day before. There's a rock pool that resembles the one from my vision. The coastline could be the same one.

"The well's up here. It's been capped for a long while, for safety. But it's still here."

I follow her up the low slope. Half of me wants to close my eyes so I can see it fresh from the last view I had of it in my vision. The other half is hungry to take in the entire scene at once, to see if it matches my first visions.

I compromise and keep my eyes on Gráinne as she leads the way. She comes to a stop at a flat spot halfway between the beach and the crest of the hill. A round metal plate covers the top of the well, which is the same shape and size as the one in my vision.

"The cottage was up there." She points to an uneven spot closer to the hilltop. "The barn was over here, with the sheep pen next to it." She points to a spot to the side of the well.

I walk around the stone structure, standing on the back side of it, and look down toward the beach, the rocks. And then I sit on the side of the well, because if I don't sit, it's entirely possible I'll end up on the ground.

The shoreline is subtly different, worn away by what would have been nearly 200 years of erosion. But the rocks are where I saw — where I *remember* them being. As I turn to the north, subtle variances in the flat grassy area point to where the barn and sheep pen once stood. And behind me, to the east, is the same vista I looked upon so many times — the scattered trees atop the hill, the subtle dip to the south where Hunter would take the flock most days. The only thing that's missing is the cottage.

I take a deep breath and stand up, walking to the spot where I know the cottage should be. Again, the subtle unevenness in the terrain. A cluster of stones where a hearth once stood. Where *my* hearth — *our* hearth once stood. This time I do drop to the ground, if less precipitously than I'd feared.

"Are you unwell, dear?"

For a few moments, I had forgotten Gráinne was even here.

"I'm... I'm fine. I just... It's exactly the same. All of it. I mean, the wood structures are gone. But the well, the hearth..."

I shake my head in disbelief.

"You walked straight to it. Like you knew it was there." She sounds spooked. She's not alone in that.

"I did. At least, I thought I did."

"You didn't know that from an old photo."

"No, I didn't. I haven't seen a photo of this place before. If I had, I'd have come straight here."

"And I'd have missed seeing this. Something that I'm having a hard time believing. You're not winding me up, are you? Having a joke at the old lady's expense?"

"You're not that old. And I wouldn't do that. To anyone."

"I know. Which is why I think *I* need to sit down now."

She retreats back to the well, sitting in the same spot I had before.

I look around me again. I can picture it all. The floor by the hearth where Crógan would lie, the table where we ate our meals, the chairs by the hearth where Hunter would sit and play his penny whistle at night while I sat at my spinning wheel, the heavy wooden bed in its little alcove... The visions all come rushing back to me, like I had them yesterday, like I had been here, with Hunter, just yesterday. Everything is where it should be, except what was made of wood. So, nearly everything. But the stone bits... the subtle remnants of posts that were embedded in the soil for so long... They're right where they belong. Where *we* belong.

A shiver runs down my spine.

I know two things now.

My dreams — my visions — are true. I — we — lived here, in this very spot.

I also know Hunter will never believe me.

Maybe someday, if I can bring him back here — maybe then he'll remember on his own. But short of that... I can't keep talking about my visions. I barely mention them anymore anyway. But now I know I can't keep pushing him. If I tell him I came here and saw this, he'll chalk it up to my imagination and wishful thinking. Or, worse, he'll decide I'm making it all up in some bizarre effort to persuade him to be with me. And he'll fight it even harder. I'll drive him away. And that's the one thing I could not handle. I'm already terrified of what his burgeoning career will do to us. My pushing him away is the only thing that would be worse.

I have to let this go, let him go. If he comes to this on his own, that's one thing. But I can't lead him here, let alone push him here.

I have my answer where Hunter's concern. And that answer is no. It has to stop here. It has to stay here. And I will just have to wait, be patient... and live my life as if none of this happened. Until something changes. If it ever does.

And now I have my answer where Mace is concerned, too.

Leave the bird in the bush. Take the one in my hand, knowing it will someday fly away, and hope — desperately hope — that after it does, the one in the bush will come to me of its own free will.

Gráinne and I make our way back down the beach an hour or so later, long after my butt has grown sore from sitting on what's left of the hearth. I spent that time trying to fully absorb what has happened, knowing that my memories are rooted in reality and yet also knowing that any visions I have of this place in the future will be influenced by having seen it with my own eyes, in this lifetime.

Before we leave, I take a few photos — OK, a *lot* of photos — planning to put them away for sometime in the future, when Hunter or I need to see this place again. I can't indulge myself in looking at them anytime soon. That I know.

"Do you want to come in for some tea, dear?"

"Thank you. But no. I think I need to be alone for a while. See if I can absorb this enough to move on."

"I understand. You're welcome anytime, Brighid — we're not from the same family that owned that little farm back then, but you still feel like you belong here. Come back and see us when you can."

"I'm not leaving yet, Gráinne. I'm not ready to see Mace again yet. And I promised the girls..."

"No one would blame you for heading back to Dublin now. The girls would understand."

"No. Things are as they're supposed to be right now. I was led here, to see what I've seen, and I'll be ready to go to Dublin and see Mace when it's time. You and the girls should still come. They'll love meeting him, and he'll enjoy the story of our little adventure."

"He knows?"

"He's the only one I've ever told, other than Hunter. And he's the only one who believes me."

"Not the only one now."

"No? Do you have any idea what I'm even talking about? I know how crazy this sounds."

"You recognize a place you've never been before. I know what that means. And you and Hunter... It would explain things if you'd been here together."

I give a slight nod.

"Come for supper tomorrow. We'll discuss the plans for next week, and I'll give you some of the things I learned in more than half a century of spinning and weaving. Come every day until we leave for Dublin, if you like. I'd like to pass this knowledge onto a younger generation, and you're the best candidate I have."

I give her a smile.

"Thank you. I'd like that. Very much."

"Get some rest tonight, dear. Take whatever time you need. You'll find a way through this."

"I know. Thank you for everything you've done for me. I can truly never thank you enough. But I want you to know I really do appreciate it, deeply."

"You're welcome. We'll see you tomorrow."

I bring a heavy lunch back up to my hotel room, planning not to leave the room again tonight.

As the sun sets, my phone pings.

Aedan: *How are you? I'm trying not to worry.*

Aedan has respected my need for space and hasn't texted or called since I walked out of the hotel room in Kildare. And I know he has to have been concerned about me being off on my own. And probably about the decisions I've been trying to make.

We've been in near-constant contact since the day we met. And he truly has become one of my closest friends. It feels strange to be out of touch with him. And I don't like even the idea that my asking for space makes him feel rejected or unwanted. Because neither is the case.

Brighid: *I'm fine. It's been enlightening. Still working my way through what I've learned.*

Aedan: *Still coming to the gig in Dublin?*

Brighid: *That's the plan. I may have a few people with me. Is that OK?*

Aedan: *Leave it to you to make friends in a place where you know no one.*

Brighid: *That's sarcasm, right? You're supposed to do a winky face to let me know it's sarcasm.*

Aedan: *I'm not THAT old, Brighid. I know about the winky thing. It wasn't sarcasm. You're very likable.*

Brighid: *And extremely awkward. I break potential friendships even more easily than I make them.*

Aedan: *You underestimate yourself. But we both knew that already.*

Aedan: *I miss you. I miss my friend. I miss having you in my bed. But I miss my friend more. It's not nearly as fun going places without you.*

Brighid: *I miss you, too. But I was right about you being distracting. You're not even here and you're still being a distraction.*

Aedan: *Is it OK if I'm happy to hear that?*

Brighid: *You wouldn't be you if you weren't. And I like you as you are. So, yes, it's fine. But I've got some more thinking to do, so I'm going to call it a night. I'll see you at the gig.*

Aedan: *Be safe and well, sweetheart. I'll be eagerly awaiting your arrival.*

I shut my phone off to avoid the temptation to reply again.

I've made my decision. I just need to absorb it before I talk to him about it. And this is the best place to do that. And I'll gladly accept every bit of knowledge Gráinne wants to give me. I never dreamed that would be part of what I'd take away from this trip, but the more I think about it, the more it seems like fate, or Herself, had a hand in my landing here, in meeting Gráinne and her family. And I'm so thankful for it.

CHAPTER 16

AN CAT DUBH

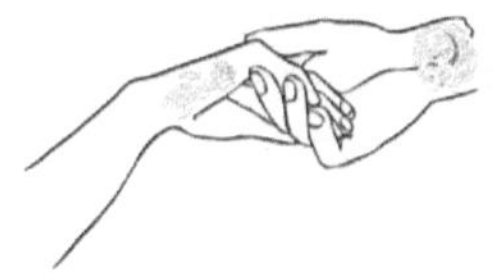

It's been an incredible week. What Gráinne has taught me in this short time changes everything about my approach to spinning, and most especially to weaving. I have a concept for a series of works that will pull inspiration from my time here in Ireland, and I have really high hopes for their success.

Gráinne has given me enough of her leftover roving to create a dozen pieces, and she's given me the contacts to get a steady supply of roving from her friends and neighbors.

Her son Cían, the girls' father, drives us all to the bus station. The girls and Gráinne each have an overnight bag, while I'm toting along all that I have had with me this entire time I've been in Ireland. I've stuffed a carryon-sized bag with my most important things, displacing some of what was in my suitcase to make room for some of the roving and some sample pieces I made with Gráinne's oversight. I also packed up the rest of the roving and shipped it back to Kara's shop so I can start working with it when I arrive home in two days.

The month has flown by so fast, with so much learned, so much realized, understood, so many things that have changed.

I miss Hunter. I need to go home and spend some time with him, get us back on solid footing, even if it's not in the exact place I'd like. As much as Ireland — especially that little section of coastline — has felt like a second home, what I know now is that anywhere Hunter is is where I feel at home.

That I feel some of the same things when I'm with Aedan is also telling. And that's what I need to tell him tonight when I see him. I'm already picturing that wonderful smile of his, the affection in it, the wanting, and the little bit more that I'd seen in his expression when he looked at me in the last week or so before we parted. I'm not taking that for granted, nor am I going to let things with Hunter stand in the way of us seeing what this wants to become.

The ride to Dublin also flies by, with the girls and I listening to Telltale Signs in our headphones, while Gráinne takes in sights she hasn't seen in years. We check in to the same hotel Aedan and I stayed at when we first arrived, drop our bags and freshen up a little. OK — I do a little more than freshen up. I'm dressed up in my most flattering dress, my hair loose around my shoulders, the tiniest bit of makeup.

"Miss Brighid — you look so pretty! Do you have a boyfriend who'll be there tonight?" Niamh seems to have reached that stage where boy-crazy is just over the horizon, if it hasn't officially arrived yet.

"Niamh..." Gráinne admonishes her, likely in deference to what she knows of my situation.

"It's fine," I tell her. "Some of my friends will be there tonight, Niamh, and since it's my last night in Ireland, I thought I'd celebrate a little bit by dressing up. That's all. But thank you for the compliment."

We head off to the gig, and the girls are practically jumping out of their skins, so I decide to hire us a car for the trip to Croke Park, in deference to Gráinne's age and their flightiness. They float around us like butterflies, flitting away and then returning to hover.

Once we reach the stadium, I ask the driver to take us to the backstage entrance, where I flash the tour lanyard Aedan gave me when we parted ways in Kildare. The security team lets us in, and we're escorted to the hospitality suite. The band's nowhere to be seen, though some of the members of their opening act — a band I hadn't heard of before — are socializing with the VIPs who are already backstage.

"Ellie! Good to see you!"

The girls give me an odd look as Izzy approaches, pulling me into a hug that I'm not quite expecting.

"You couldn't have gotten here at a better time," he says quietly in my ear. "Mace is about ready to chew his arm off worrying over you... and... well, I'll let him fill you in."

Izzy seems perturbed, and it sets my teeth on edge. Is something wrong with Mace?

"Izzy, these are my new friends Niamh, Orlaith and their grandmother Gráinne. The girls are huge Telltale Signs fans, and Orlaith wants to become professional musician."

"Wow! That's great!" he enthuses. "I bet you all would like a peek at the stage. Why don't you come with me, and Ellie can wait here for Mace? You can get some photos and autographs with everyone when we get back."

"Why is Mr. Izzy calling you Ellie, Miss Brighid?" Orlaith asks.

Izzy gives me a curious look.

"Mr. Izzy met me with my friend Hunter, who calls me by the name I used when I was younger. Mr. Mace calls me Brighid, since he met me by asking about my Brighid's cross. So I go by that name sometimes, too."

"Oh. That makes sense."

Gotta love kids.

"If you ladies will follow me, I'll take you back behind my drum kit and you can look out over the whole stage from the back. And Mace should be out soon, Ellie."

I nod and smile in thanks. And as they leave the room, I shake my hands, trying to disperse the nerves that have suddenly hit me as I wait for Aedan.

Finally, I can't stand it any longer, and I decide to go find him. Presumably, he's still in his dressing room. I head back in what seems a likely direction, and it seems my instincts were right, because I can hear Aedan's voice coming from a half-open door.

"I didn't have anything to do with it, Cat! I didn't have a clue about the change until an hour ago."

Aedan is shouting. I've literally never heard him so much as raise his voice. It doesn't fit at all with his usual priestly placidness.

"Don't lie to me, Mace — there's no way management strong-armed us into this opening stint without your knowledge and approval. Nothing involving Telltale Signs happens without your say-so." It's a woman's voice, and I'm at a loss as to what to do. Was this what Izzy was talking about?

"Not this time, Cat! I swear! You asked for space, and I've given that to you. In spades. I haven't even spoken to you or been in the same room in three years! What more could I do to prove it to you that I've stayed out of your life like you asked?"

I peek around the door just enough to see cascades of golden-blonde hair above a slender set of hips and long legs encased in tall high-heeled boots.

"You could have not dragged me into a European tour right after getting photographed with some fangirl clinging to you. It's beneath you, Mace."

"So you've been paying attention to gossip about me?"

"*That's* what you took away from that? That I'm paying attention to some British rag that publishes paparazzi photos of you on vacation?"

"So, you did see the story..."

There's a scream of frustration.

"Stop it, Mace! I may have to do this tour, but I don't have to be in the same room with you, and I definitely don't have to talk to you. Go back to your fangirl, whoever she is. And maybe try a brunette next time, so it doesn't look like you're still stuck on me."

"Brighid may be blonde, but you two are night and day. And you know how I feel about you. It's not the same thing at all."

My heart thuds.

"That's her name? Brighid? Some Irish girl you met? Why isn't she here, then?"

Well, she is. Not that either of you seem to have noticed that...

"This isn't about her, Cat. It's about you and me. You can't tell me you've forgotten already..."

He pulls her against him, and she struggles for just a moment before melting into his arms.

And the heart that had stopped beating in my chest falls out into the hard concrete floor.

I turn around, ready to flee to I don't know where. And there stand Izzy, Gráinne and the girls. I'm not sure what the girls are making of this overheard argument, but the looks on Izzy's and Gráinne's faces remind me far too much of how Alex and Aedan had looked at me that night almost three months ago, after Hunter had rejected me yet again.

Why do I keep handing my heart to men who don't want it? Did I not at least learn my lesson after that night with Hunter? At least this time I figured out where I stood before I got around to telling Aedan that I'd decided to give us a chance. A chance we never really had, it seems, despite his claims to the contrary.

"I'm sorry, girls. I'm not feeling very well. I think I'm going to go back to the hotel and rest up before my flight home tomorrow. Maybe Mr. Izzy could introduce you to Mr. Mace and make sure you get your autographs and one for your mom?"

"Sure, Ellie. No problem," he says. "Why don't we go back in here and get you three a drink and let your grandma sit somewhere comfortable while we wait?"

As he passes by, he speaks quietly to me.

"I'm sorry, hon. I didn't think that was going that way, or I'd have said something before. He's not himself right now. You can see that." He shakes his head.

"Don't tell him I was here, Izzy. Let him think I didn't come tonight, that I just sent Gráinne and the girls. I'm going to get an earlier flight out if I can get one. I need to get home."

"I understand. I'm really sorry. Have a safe trip. Tell Hunter I said hi, and tell Rhys I've added two toms to my kit. I'm going to catch up with him!" His smile is wan, but I appreciate the effort at levity.

I glance behind me, seeing Mace still holding onto the woman I am now all but certain is his uncooperative lady. It seems his relationship with her is even more fraught than mine with Hunter.

And it's past time I get home to my best friend. I need to make up for the lies, especially when it turns out they were all for nothing.

"**B**righid — wait..."
Gráinne has come after me as I head for the exit.

"I really can't stay. I'm sorry."

"No — I understand. I just wanted to tell you I'm sorry how this worked out. Trust what fate has in store for you. Oftentimes, it's the most challenging things that take us where we need to go."

I nod, unable to put what I'm feeling into words.

"Thank you again for all you've done for me. Please enjoy the concert with the girls. I'm going to try to get an earlier flight out, so I likely won't see you again before I go. The room is paid for, so enjoy it, please."

"We will, dear. But I'll be thinking about you. Remember — you're always welcome in our home. Don't be a stranger. You haven't been that since you walked up the beach that first day."

I pull her into a hug. She can't know how much that means to me. Even if I never make it back to Ireland, I know I have friends here who I can trust.

"Have a safe trip home."

"You, too."

My eyes are full of tears by the time I get outside. I ask the security guard to call me a taxi for the ride back to the hotel, and I wait in the shadow of a cargo truck parked near the gate. When my cab arrives a few minutes later, I dart inside and close my eyes for the trip back to the hotel.

A half-hour later, I've changed into travel clothes, packed my bags and caught a ride to the airport. I've got a good five hours before the first flight for D.C. will leave, but I've gotten my flight changed and I'm sitting in the waiting area, the novel I haven't touched since I arrived here laid across my knee. I can't concentrate enough to read it, but it's there.

A day ago, I was excited to get back to Dublin and see Aedan, to tell him I wanted to give things between us a try. I was prepared to let things with Hunter take their own course over the years to come. My reasoning for that hasn't changed. But my understanding of my relationship with Aedan has changed. Dramatically.

Cat. It's an unlikely name for a mermaid. But I have no doubt it was her I saw in those visions. The ones I never shared with Aedan. The ones that clearly, in retrospect, weren't so much pushing me to choose between Hunter and Aedan, or even warning me against getting more deeply involved with Aedan, as they were warning me that Cat stood between us and was going to be making her presence felt.

I don't know their story. He never told me much about them at all. Clearly, she's in whatever band is opening for Telltale Signs on this leg of the tour. And clearly, they have a history that's trying to work itself out between them here and now. And that's OK. It's not like I didn't go into this with my eyes open, aware that he was already in love with someone else. This was just the wakeup call that no matter how things seemed to be shifting between us — toward something more than just friends with benefits — in his case, at least, there was no real chance of anything more. And, really, was there ever much chance of that with me, either? No matter how much I'd come to appreciate him. It would have been nice to remain friends, but maybe it's just better this way. For both of us.

Around 3 a.m., my phone rings. It's Aedan. I send the call to voicemail. Two minutes later, it rings again. I turn it off. I move to the most hidden spot I can find near the gate, just in case. As far as Aedan knew, my flight doesn't leave until noon. He's going to expect me to be in a hotel room somewhere, resting up for my flight. I might get to the airport around 8 or 9 for that flight. I'll be in the air over the middle of the Atlantic by then. And he'll be flying out on a big chartered jet soon, bound for London and the second concert of their tour. With his lady by his side. I wish them well. Truly. He was a good friend, and I only ever wanted the best for him. Just as Hunter said of me.

And now it's time I got home to Hunter and my real life. I've learned a lot here. It has been an experience I'll never forget. I might have done a few things different if I'd seen where things were headed, but it's been a necessary lesson for me. All for the best. Time to move on. On a lot of fronts.

I leave my phone off until I'm back at the dorm, unpacked and settled in. When I turn it back on, I have a dozen calls from Aedan, eight voicemails and thirty texts. I mark them all as read or listened to, without actually doing either of those things. Aedan has a tour he needs to focus on, and, hopefully, working things out with Cat, finally. He'll forget about me soon enough.

I pass the next hours spinning some of Gráinne's roving into yarn. It works up so beautifully. It's a finite resource, too, since she no longer dyes her own. But such glorious colors. And the things I'm going to make with them...

I collapse into bed, exhausted from traveling and the focused work at the spinning wheel, as well as another less-than-promising start with a new roommate. Hunter's arrival startles me enough that I nearly smash his hand in the window. But he just crawls into bed with me, like we're 15 again, just enjoying being around each other, being close. And that's something I'm never going to stop wanting. Someday, he will, I'm sure. But I'm going to enjoy every moment with him in the meantime. And I push thoughts of anything other than school and my best friend from my head.

CHAPTER 17

COME TO MY WINDOW

Two months later

A edan hasn't stopped calling and texting, though the frequency of his attempts to reach me has decreased. He tries about once a week now, sometimes twice, and I let everything go unanswered, un-listened-to and unread. I can't bring myself to block him. I miss him too much to think I'll never want to hear from him again.

But he needs to move on. I've tried. I've refocused on school and especially on my works for the winter art showcase. I've allowed myself one indulgence where Aedan goes. No, no checking the gossip sites for pictures of him and Cat, no tour reviews, even. But I've started work on a new weaving, which I'm calling "Soul of the Deep Sea," a companion piece to the work that is the core of my new style, "Soul of Ireland."

"Soul of the Deep Sea" is inspired by Aedan. It carries the russet tones of his hair, the deep and sometimes stormy blue of his eyes, the sea tones of his god's domain and those of the blue heron etched into his skin... there's a thread of passion and of his joy in music, a swath of humor and a warm wave of his caring heart. It captures him, I like to think, in much the same way "Soul of the Hunter" does my best friend, my soulmate — an essence of the man, made tangible.

When winter break is rapidly approaching and I find out that my works have made it into the college's very selective juried showcase, I invite Hunter to come to opening night with me.

And that reminds me of the promise I made to Aedan the first night we met — that I'd send him an invitation when my work debuted in public. I think of all the work that went into the piece he inspired, how much of him it captures, and I know I'm honor-bound to at least invite him, even though I know his tour schedule will prevent him from attending. And maybe it's better that way.

He hasn't texted or called in two weeks now. It may be that he's given up. But I send him a text anyway.

Brighid: *I promised I'd invite you when I made my debut in a gallery exhibit. The college art showcase is coming up just before Christmas, and I have a few pieces that got selected for the exhibit.*

Brighid: *Just thought you might want to know. Hope you are well and happy.*

I send the text before I can reconsider.

There's no reply.

I can't say that doesn't make me a little sad. But I don't blame him. We both needed to move on.

"**E**llen, this is entirely unacceptable! You haven't been home since July. And it's one thing to further your business experience by working with your employer and another thing entirely to be hanging around there with Hunter and that 'band' of his."

I pray for added patience. It isn't instantly granted.

"Dad — for the thirty-third time: I am not staying here to hang out with Hunter. I am staying here because my work was selected for the college art showcase, and the exhibit opening is a holiday gala scheduled during the break."

"Just more nonsense, Ellen! That Hunter has been a terrible influence on you — dreams of cushy artsy jobs, fame and fortune. Nothing is ever that easy. Success requires hard work, long hours, sweat, working your way up over time. Nothing that lasts happens overnight."

"Neither of us is expecting success overnight, Dad. Hunter's been working toward this career since he was a kid. I've been putting in hour upon hour, honing my skills, for several years. Any success we get, we have earned."

"Having some yarn monstrosity hanging up on a wall in a student exhibit isn't success, Ellen! Your finger-paintings got hung on the wall in elementary school. That was meaningless then, and this is meaningless now."

I opt not to remind Dad that even my finger-paintings won awards.

"I understand the appeal of that lifestyle to a young man — 'sex, drugs and rock-and-roll,' and all that. But it's not a suitable environment for my daughter. And I can't imagine that Hunter and his friends are going to tolerate you being a hanger-on when they've got a bunch of centerfold types lining up to be seen with them."

Centerfolds? Do they even have those anymore?

"I shudder to even think about you backstage at one of these concerts of theirs, half-clad girls showing off their... assets... while your much more... ample... figure..." He voice trails off, as if he can't think of even a vaguely polite way to say I'd suffer in that comparison.

Wow. Thanks, Dad.

"Any man who's paying attention to you in that environment is after only one thing. Otherwise, he'd be paying attention to the other girls. If he tells you anything otherwise, he's lying, just to get you into... a compromising position."

OK, then.

"Dad, again — I'm staying because I have work in the very selective *juried* art showcase. It has nothing to do with Hunter, or drugs or sex, regardless of how ample my 'assets' are. No one's lying to me about anything, because I'm not involved with anyone — musician or otherwise."

"If that were true, you'd be coming home over the break. Instead, you follow Hunter around like a lost puppy. Have some self-respect, Ellen! Your mother would be ashamed. Boys like that will use you and throw you away as soon as something better comes along."

I can't help it. Despite the fact that he is, again, wrong about my mother, his words invoke images that unsettle me — images of Aedan holding a slender woman with long golden hair and high-heeled boots. It doesn't matter that I was the one who left that night, putting an end to whatever it was that Aedan wanted from me. All it took was me putting a little space between us, and he was right back with Cat, despite all of his talk about her not wanting him. Aedan really has no idea how it feels to be rejected by the person you love. Even the one woman he said rejected him came back and threw herself right into his arms.

And as much as I think he's wrong about Hunter, maybe Dad has a point. I can't compete with these women who throw themselves at the musicians.

"Ellen? Are you still there? Tell me you've reconsidered this ridiculous plan to stay there over the break surrounded by pipe dreams and debauchery."

If I'd been inclined to change my mind, any such impulse flies out the window with that comment.

"No, Dad. I'm the same ridiculous person I've always been, and that means I keep doing ridiculous things. Best you not waste your time and breath trying to talk me into being anything other than ridiculous. Because that would be ridiculous! And you are definitely not ridiculous! Have a ridiculously festive holiday!"

I hang up. I can see the steam rising from between his ears from 150 miles away.

I'm not sure what it would take to prove to him that I can be successful, that Hunter can be, but I'm pretty sure that it would stifle both of our spirits. And that will never be something I'd consider successful.

I cannot even believe it. I won top place in the entire showcase! And a cash prize. The two pieces I put up for sale sold for record-setting prices. In one fell swoop, I'm approaching the point where I can afford to open my own shop.

The whole thing is so overwhelming that I nearly faint under the press of people. Twice. The second time, someone has to guide me out of the room for some air, and I'm so overwhelmed that I don't even see who it was, and then they're gone. I'd hoped it was Hunter, who'd promised to be there, even though he had a gig tonight. The thought did count here, and I know he will have tried.

But I've had more people tonight than I can take, and I head back to the dorm to get some rest and digest what has happened. I'm too tired to even change into my usual tank top and yoga pants before I go to bed. I just strip off my clothes (thank the gods for an absent roommate) and climb right into bed.

I wake to a noise over my desk, by the window.

Hunter! He must have wanted to hear how things went. What a shock he's going to get when he hears!

I suddenly realize I don't have any clothes on, but the window is already up, hands reaching through, so I just wrap the sheet around me and sit up to wait for his arrival. This is what he gets for not warning me he was coming. Did he not learn anything from the hand-smashing incident?

Only it's not a golden-blonde head that comes through the window. The lights from outside pick up the red cast to the dark hair. It can't be...

"Good morning, sweetheart!"

"Aedan? How? Why?"

"You're good with those interrogatives." He chuckles as he slides over my desk. "And I see you were expecting me after all. I love the look," he says, gesturing at my bare shoulders and the cleavage barely covered by the sheet.

"What are you doing here?"

"So you weren't expecting me? You weren't expecting some other man to pop in on you, were you? I know it's been a while, but I've been hoping you hadn't found yourself a third devastatingly handsome rockstar to join you in your bed."

"Aedan! What are you doing here?"

"You invited me to your show!"

"I did. True. But I didn't really think you'd come, and I didn't see you there."

"I was keeping a low profile."

"I'm not sure that's even possible."

"It has to be, because you didn't see me, did you? Not even when—"

"You! It was you who took me outside when I was feeling faint!"

"Ow. I really am too old to be crawling through dorm room windows..." he groans, before finally sliding off my desk and sitting next to me on the bed. "Yes, that was me. I didn't want you to get hurt."

I look away from him.

"Brighid — I really didn't mean for you to get hurt. Not tonight and not back in Dublin. What you saw — it wasn't what it looked like, what it probably sounded like. And I had no idea you'd actually come to the show until your friend Gráinne read me the riot act well after one in the morning — with little girls half asleep on either side of Izzy — having waited around just so she could call me out."

I laugh at the image of Izzy and the girls.

"He's going to make an excellent dad someday."

"Not anytime soon, I suspect. But that's beside the point. I tried to explain all of this to you, but she refused to tell me where you were staying that night, and you didn't answer my calls or texts..."

"I never read or listened to them."

"Then you don't know..."

"Know what?"

"Cat — she... Izzy said you saw her with me, overheard that argument. She was furious with me over something I had nothing to do with. So furious that I spent an hour after the show trying to find a replacement opening act so she could get out of the contract her manager had signed on her behalf. They had to do three shows. But by the time we got to Paris, she was back in New York. Still pissed at me. Just a little less so."

"That's her, isn't it? Your lady?"

He nods.

"I saw her."

"I know. And I'm sorry about how that happened."

"No — I mean... I saw her in a vision." I take a deep breath. "The last two times we were together... what did you see?"

"Nothing. I fell asleep with you in my arms, passed out from a lovely orgasm, I assumed. You're telling me you had a vision. Both times?"

I nod.

"Well, tell me. Because clearly I missed something significant."

"The gist of it — we ended up in the ocean, and there was a blonde man on the beach who looked kind of like Hunter, but not Hunter now and not Hunter from my visions of our past. I still don't know what that meant. But when I tried to get closer to him, you were suddenly there and drowning..."

"I swim like a fish. I'm not sure I *could* drown at this point." His expression is reflective.

"I don't think it was literal. It seemed at first to be about me making a choice between the two of you. If I chose him, you were drowning, and if I chose you, he left me behind."

"It wasn't a dream, Aedan. I saw her. I saw *her.*"

"Cat?"

"Yes. Or at least I assume it had to be her. That long golden-blonde hair... Only she was a mermaid. A very, very angry, protective mermaid. She didn't want me anywhere near you. Kept taking you away when I tried to rescue you."

He looks stunned. He pauses before replying.

"It may have looked like Cat, but it doesn't sound like her. At least not in this lifetime."

"You never told me about her, not really."

"No, I didn't. Not because I wanted to keep it from you. It's just... there are some secrets that are not mine to tell, not even to you, as much as I'd like to be able to share..."

"It's OK, Aedan. It all just made me realize that we'd gotten off track as soon as things stopped being friends with benefits and became something more."

His expression deflates. "Oh."

"You don't agree?"

"What did you plan to tell me when you saw me that night?"

I take a deep breath.

"That I wanted to give things between us a chance, to see where they might go."

"And I ruined that when you saw me with Cat."

"*You* didn't. But *it* did, I think. I... I really can't see us like that now that I've seen you with her, in person. It made it all very real."

He sighs.

"I was afraid you'd say that. Because I had decided the same thing — that I wanted to give us a chance. And that's not possible anymore, is it?"

"I don't think so, Aedan. I'm sorry."

"What about what we'd agreed to before... before things started to shift?"

"Friends with benefits, until one of us calls it off?"

"Cat and I aren't together, Brighid. I don't know that we'll ever be at this rate. And I meant what I said — I miss having you in my bed. And I miss my friend even more. Far more even than I'd realized when I said it, because we'd only been apart a week then, and now it's been..."

"Months."

"Yeah."

He leans into me, brushing his lips against mine. Almost tentatively. I've never seen him do anything tentatively. And then he's not tentative at all, pulling me hard against him, the sheet sliding down over my breasts as I wrap my arms around him and return the kiss with fervor of my own.

"Gods, I missed you," he says.

"And I missed you."

"So, no new boyfriend?"

"No. Not a rockstar one or otherwise."

"But you do have a rockstar in your bed, if you still want him."

"Just friends with benefits? Nothing serious?"

"If that's what you want."

"It is. All the rest... it's just too complicated. I hope you can understand."

"I can. I can't say I don't wish circumstances were otherwise. But as long as I don't lose your friendship, I'm happy. So... about those benefits..." He gives me a wicked grin, and I chuckle in response.

"This bed is a little small for what we do to each other. And the neighbors can't be bought off as easily as your hotel staff can. The resident advisor is on the other side of this wall."

"Well, we can't be getting you in trouble with the dorm police. You and Hunter push your luck too often just to get your cuddle thing on. So put on some clothes and come back to my hotel room with me. Or you can come naked if you prefer. I won't object."

He winks at me.

"We still need to discuss a few things." His finger traces across my nipple, sending a surge straight to my core. "But we can get to that later. Move — I need to get dressed."

Two minutes later, we're racing to Aedan's rented car.

"Wait — how did you know which room was mine?"

He smirks at me.

"I may have waylaid a lovely young lady in the lobby named Lisa and promised her VIP tickets to our next show in D.C."

"Lisa? Medium build? Dark hair? Wearing a floral robe at this point in the night, I would guess?"

"That would be her."

"She's the RA."

"I guess she's a big fan of Telltale Signs."

"And aMUSEd. She hit me up for tickets when Hunter got caught in the dorm after I got back. She's got a thing for Rhys."

"Or for redheads..."

"I can't exactly claim to be innocent of that myself."

"So, you and Rhys?"

I laugh. "Not happening."

"We still need to discuss you and Hunter..."

"And you and Cat."

"Orgasms first?"

"At least one."

"I'm aiming for two or three. But we can do yours one after the other if you want to save some time."

"Aedan..."

"Is that a yes?"

"It's not a no."

"Then get in the car, woman!"

Did I mention I missed this man? Oh, boy, did I miss him...

I'm barely inside Aedan's hotel room door when he pushes me back against the door, putting the safety latch on with one hand and using the other to push my skirt up my thigh. He sucks my lower lip into his mouth, biting down lightly.

"Gods, I missed this, missed you..." he says, looking at me with something akin to wonder. "Missed watching you come. Missed making you come. Missed seeing you with my marks on you, my cum in you..."

My eyes roll up in my head, and my knees threaten to buckle under me.

"You missed that, too, didn't you?"

"Gods, yes... But..."

"But?"

"I know you said you weren't with Cat, but it's been three months, and you've been on tour... So I don't expect you to..."

"To? I know what you're asking, but I want you to say it, Brighid."

"Do we need condoms?"

"Ask again. Ask what you really want to know." He rubs his thumb along my cheek, staring deep into my eyes.

"Did you sleep with anyone after I left?"

"You know the answer to that. Deep down, you know. You Know."

He's right. I do. He wouldn't be here if he had. He wouldn't be talking about coming inside me if he had.

"Come have a shower with me..."

He pulls me along behind him into the bathroom, with its deep spa tub and a glass-walled shower. He toes off his shoes, unbuttons his shirt sleeves and turns the water on. Then he turns and watches me undress, rapt. I push him back against the glass wall, unbuttoning his shirt with shaking fingers as he unbuckles his belt, undoes his pants and lets them fall to the floor. My eyes drop with them, reveling in the sight of him so eager to have me again. I push the shirt off his shoulders, and he drops his arms, letting it join the growing pile of shed clothing.

He pinches my nipple between his thumb and forefinger, then lets his hand drop, cupping my sex, trailing a finger up between my lips. Then he pushes me under the shower head, which douses me before I even pass under it, and up against the shower wall.

"One to start," he says, dropping to his knees in front of me. He buries his mouth in my pussy, licking and suckling, and sliding his fingers inside me. It's been too long without him, without anyone touching me like this, and having him here now is too arousing. I roll over the peak within moments. He stands and kisses me, the taste of Aedan and of me melding on our tongues. I wrap my arms around him, pulling him hard up against me. And hard he is...

His hand lifts my thigh up around his hip, and he pushes inside me, the cool tile of the wall on my back, the warm water flowing over us and the heat of Aedan in front, inside me. Perfect. It's a slow dance of water and fire, enshrouded in steam and building to a frenzy as his hips pound into mine, the sounds of flesh and liquid the layers of the song we dance to, the accent notes his moaning and the tiny mewling sounds coming from me as I swing up to another crescendo and then sail slowly down, notes on the wind.

"Two," he says as I spasm around him. He smacks his hips against mine one more time, pulsing inside me as he presses me into the tile with his arms around me and his lips pressed the side of my neck, sucking softly on my flesh, then harder, leaving that promised bruise. I sigh, my muscles loose, languid, my mind relaxed, content.

"Come to bed, Brighid..." he says, wrapping me in a towel and pressing a kiss to the end of my nose. And, you know, I could use a nap.

Chapter 18

Magnet & Steel

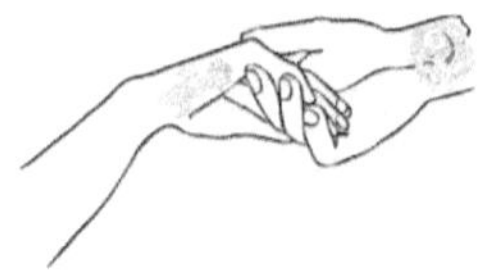

"A edan?"

"Hmm?"

The sound is both content and sleepy, and it makes me smile as he murmurs against my ear.

"Didn't you have a gig today? Yesterday? I thought you all were in Tokyo or something."

"We were."

"You flew back here from Tokyo, to go to my college art showcase..."

"I did."

"You shouldn't have done that. It's such a long way, and your tour schedule is always so tight."

"We had a few days off for the holiday. I just flew out straight after the last show in Tokyo, rather than spending the time there with the guys. With the time difference, I arrived here about the same time I left there."

"That's wild."

"It is. The down side is I lose a full day flying back. And our next show is in three days."

"So you have to leave..." I try to do the math in my head. Keeping track of the patterns in my weaving is easier.

"I have to be on a plane in about a day and a half."

"We could have a lot of fun in a day and a half..."

"Did I tell you I missed you?"

"You may have to remind me."

"I can definitely do that."

Aedan doesn't sound so sleepy anymore. And contentment shifts back into wanting as he rolls me over on top of him, staring deep into my eyes.

"I missed this, too."

It's still there, that something more... And not just for him. It grabs hold of my heart and twists. I break the eye contact.

"Brighid..."

He caresses my cheek, and I instinctively lean into his hand, my eyes closed, reveling in the sensation. He claims my lips in a kiss whose passion is far beyond the physical. And I return it.

We are in so much trouble...

"We need to talk."

"I wasn't fond of it the last time you said that," Aedan reminds me.

"I know. And it wasn't as bad as it sounded that time, and it's not like that this time, either."

"Isn't it?"

"No. Really, it's not." I run my thumb over his cheek. "I think we've both been honest about how we're feeling. And we both know we still have stronger feelings for each other than is probably ideal."

"I'm not prepared to concede that. Not yet."

I sigh.

"Brighid — we had both of us decided that we wanted to give this, us, a chance. We each decided that on our own, with time to consider it. It wasn't an impulsive choice for me. Was it for you?"

"No. It wasn't. I had my reasons, and they still made sense to me when I left Dublin. The thing that changed was my understanding of our relationship, and my perception of your relationship with Cat."

"Neither of which you got directly from me. And I can promise you what you saw, what you heard, didn't accurately convey how I feel."

"So, how do you feel?"

"I find you delightful. I enjoy the time we spend together more than nearly anything else in my life..." He pauses. "If I'm being honest — with myself and with you — I love you. I say that knowing how loaded that phrase is for you." He tucks my hair behind my ear. "I'm not going to pull a Han Solo on you. Or a Hunter. I *am* in love with you. Maybe it's just a little bit. Maybe it's early. But I feel that way and I openly admit it."

"And Cat?"

"Cat and me — it's complicated. More so even than you and Hunter. And everything I've done to try to fix things between us, get them back on track, protect her — it's all backfired. She's felt pressured, and she resents me. So I gave her the space she asked for. Years of space. I hadn't seen her in more than three years before that night in Dublin. Some ambitious young staffer in the label's A&R department decided putting her band on our tour would be perfect, without running it past me or anyone else there — all of whom would have said it was a non-starter. It was a last-minute replacement after the Irish act we'd booked as the opener broke up just a day before. No one involved knew what had happened until we were staring at each other across the dressing room."

"And still you ended up with her in your arms."

"I wish I could explain better, Brighid, but I'm sworn to say nothing about the circumstances. I have to ask you to respect that. You know I wouldn't keep it from you if I had a choice. But the bottom line is while I do love her, as deeply as you love Hunter, she's conflicted about me, and there's no middle ground with her. She's either resentful and fighting me or she's forced to admit she needs me. And that hasn't been a healthy dynamic for either of us. It's one of the reasons I was willing to give her that space. I can't even consider being around her unless she's there of her own volition and happy about it. And, believe me — she was not."

"I got that impression, at least at first."

"Her breaking down and accepting a hug from me is the exception to the rule. And I both know that all too well and am still wounded by it."

"Like me with Hunter."

"I told you I know how it feels. I really do."

"I found it. I found the place where Hunter and I lived together. The place from my visions."

"You did? You found the actual physical place?"

He's both shocked and excited.

"It's part of the farm that Gráinne's family owns now, along the coast northwest of Donegal. She said the farm had been abandoned for a long while before the cottage burned down, which happened when she was a child. But the well, the hearth, the coastline — even the remnants of where the structure of the house and the barn were — they were all exactly as I had seen them."

"Have you told Hunter?"

"No. And I'm not going to."

"Why not? Wouldn't that persuade him that you've been right all along?"

"You tell me — has that worked out well with Cat?"

His shoulders slump.

"No. It hasn't."

"Hunter doesn't believe in my visions *now*. And even mentioning them puts him into flight mode, or at least denial. If I come to him claiming I have proof my visions are real, why should he even believe me? There's nothing to prove what I saw matches up with the real location. He hasn't seen it himself, which would be the only way I *could* prove it to him. And now that I've been there, what is there to prove that I didn't just pick a likely spot and then embellish my supposed vision to fit? At best, he'll think I'm lost in the 'woo.' At worst, he'll think I'm making it up to manipulate him. And that will not go well for either of us."

"No, I guess it wouldn't." He sighs. "I'm sorry, Brighid. I know you were hopeful that this was the key to waking him up."

"And instead, it's the latch on the deep-freeze that he's consigned that part of our relationship to."

Aedan pulls me into his arms.

"I'm so sorry."

Tears spill from my eyes. Aedan kisses my forehead and then tucks my head under his chin.

"Nothing's really changed. It's just been made clearer to me. If anything, it takes the pressure off me to make him understand."

"And it frees you to pursue other things until something really changes where he's concerned."

"It does."

"Which is why you felt you could give us a chance."

I nod. "The universe takes with one hand and gives with the other."

"It closes a door — at least for now — but opens a window."

"You *are* pretty decent at climbing through windows. For an old guy."

He pushes me away from him and holds me at arm's length.

"Decent? I don't think anyone has ever called me 'decent' at anything."

"We can't all be rockstars at everything we try."

"Maybe not. But this 'old guy' has learned a trick or two in the decade I have on you..."

"Oh, really? If you're going to brag about it, you're going to have to offer some proof. Do you have references I can check?"

"I can offer a free demo, if you like. No commitment."

"Like a money-back guarantee on the quality of your labor?"

"If you prefer..."

"Then demonstrate away..."

"Oh, you..." He snatches a kiss from my lips. "You're going to get a demonstration alright..."

He presses me back into the mattress and earns his five-star review.

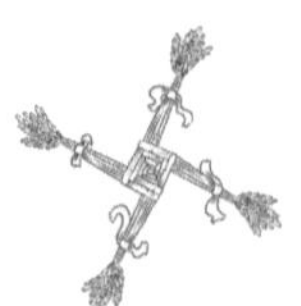

We haven't left Aedan's hotel room since we got there Friday night. We made it out of bed only to get in the shower — which then led to additional showering — and for Aedan to bring in the room-service cart full of our favorite foods. Gotta love a guy who knows you well enough to order for you without even having to ask what you want.

Gotta love him...

At least a little.

I want to say we're back where we were when I set out for Dublin that day in August. But while I believe what he's said about him and Cat, and how he feels about me, the reality is it's changed things. Cat is a real person in my head now, with a real relationship with him, however fraught that relationship is. She's not just an ex who's no longer in his life, even if she might be back in it someday. And she may not want Aedan any more than Hunter wants me, but I also trust what my visions have shown me enough to know that Gráinne was right — he belongs with Cat. Someday. Not now. But someday.

And I know that means there will come a day when I'm alone. Hunter will be off living his rockstar life, and Aedan will be with Cat. I have to start building that life I want for myself, because someday in the not-too-distant future, it will be all I have.

"You're pensive again. What's wrong?"

"I... Aedan — I can't..."

"Take your time. I'm listening. You don't have to get the words perfectly. Just tell me what you're feeling, what you want."

"I can't trust the universe not to take you away from me. It doesn't feel like you're mine. So, as much as I do want to give us a chance to see where things will go..." I falter again.

"You don't want to commit to that, because you're not sure it will work out. And you don't want to get hurt. Again."

"Or hurt you. Or let it mess up our friendship. I missed you too much before, when I felt like I had to let you go."

"So, we'll keep it casual," he suggests. "We'll keep the baseline at friends with benefits and just let the rest go where it wants, when it wants. No pressure. No expectations. Just promise me one thing."

"What?"

"Don't shut me out again. We're friends, and we'll stay friends. If we stop feeling what we're feeling, that's fine. If we find other people we want to be with — whoever they are — that's fine. But we're friends first. Bottom line. And we talk things out and forgive each other when we make mistakes. You do that with Hunter, right? Give me the same chance."

"I try to. Doesn't always go perfectly."

"No one's perfect. We're going to screw up. It's inevitable. But nothing is ever broken so long as you're willing to try to fix it."

"There you go, being profound again..."

"I really should look into that priest gig. Could be my ticket to real success. So, what do you say? Friends? With or without benefits?"

I nod. "Now, about those benefits..."

"I offer a generous package."

"You did not just say that."

"I did."

I fall over on the bed, laughing.

"Does everyone know you're this big of a goof?"

"Just my closest friends."

"I feel honored."

"Not nearly as honored as I am to be your friend."

"Now you're just kissing up to me."

"Well, you're half-right about that..."

No, we're not leaving this room anytime soon.

"**B**righid..."

"Hmm?"

"It's Sunday morning. I have to head to the airport soon. You want me to order breakfast?"

"That sounds wonderful."

He kisses me sweetly on the lips and then puts in the order.

"I'd ask if you really have to go. But I know you do."

"I do. As much as I'd love to stay in this bed with you for a few more days."

"You're off to... Australia?"

"Macau, Singapore and Abu Dhabi. Then Latin America. A month or two off, to film videos for the upcoming singles, and then Australia and New Zealand."

"I can't fly around the world to go to your shows, not like I did when it was just the Southeast."

"I know. It's OK."

"You don't have to..." I can't bring myself to say it. I try again. "Aedan, you don't have to..."

"Stay exclusive with you?" I nod. "Do you really think I'd sleep with anyone else after all we've been through the last few months? I really did think I'd lost you there for a while. Izzy keeps joking about my 'Vitamin E' deficiency.' I kept telling him it was 'Vitamin Sea' that I was lacking. He's going to know something's up as soon as I get back, grinning like an idiot for no apparent reason. So, fuck yes, I'm staying exclusive with you."

"You're sure? It's a long time to go without... when you've got so many... other options."

"Non-options. It's not the same. And I'm an adult. I can keep my dick in my pants when there are other women around."

"But the guys..."

"Are barely in their 20s, and brand new to touring and rockstar treatment. I've been doing this for a decade. Any wild phase I had is well over. That's not the case for every musician my age, but it's the case for me. And that's all that matters where we're concerned. Assuming you still trust me."

"Of course I do."

"Then that's settled."

B reakfast. Making love. Shower. Fucking in the shower. More shower. Getting dressed. A quickie in the bed. Getting dressed all over again... It was a busy morning.

By the time he's ready to leave, Aedan is already cutting it closer for his flight than either of us like, though he's less worried about that than I am. I don't know — maybe they hold flights for first-class passengers, or maybe they just hold them for Mace Mason...

He drops me back at the dorm, staying in the car when I insist he doesn't have time to walk me to my room, or for the things we'd be tempted to do if he did. We end up spending the same amount of time *that* would have taken in saying goodbye in the car. Otherwise known as making out. When I finally tell him he has to go, my lips are swollen from his kisses, my cleavage abraded by his short beard, my panties wet from his teasing.

"You *have* to go now, Aedan. You've got no time left to spare."

"I've only got one carry-on. I can sail right through the VIP entrance and straight to the gate. It's fine. I promise. One last kiss for the road. It's going to be a while before I can see you again. I need to stock up."

"You and that megawatt smile of yours... I really fear for the world if you had bigger ambitions than rock-and-roll dominance. If you had political ambitions, we'd end up with an emperor in very short order."

"...I'm sorry. I got distracted when you said 'dominance.'"

"Aedan!" I smack him on the shoulder.

"And here comes the sadism..."

"Aedan!"

He grabs me up in a tight hug and kisses me hard. Then softer. Then slow and sweet.

"I really should go."

"You should."

"Take care, sweetheart. I'll be back before you know it."

"Take care of yourself, rockstar. Tell Izzy I said hi."

"Nope. Can't do that. He'll gloat over the source of my good mood."

I roll my eyes at him.

"Be safe. Have fun."

"But not too much fun. Which is fine. I had just as much fun here in a hotel room with you as I do on the road."

"I think you're kissing up again."

"Did you say kissing?"

He dots kisses all over my face, setting me to giggling.

"OK — go. Before we start up again. Let me know when you've landed safely in... Macau?"

"I will."

I reach for my phone as I step out of the car, only to realize I didn't have it with me the whole time we were gone. I must have left it in my room and never even noticed.

I close the car door and step back, watching him drive away.

"My, my... you are a busy girl."

I turn to find Lisa looking at me with an amused smirk on her face.

"It's not what it..."

"...looks like. Yeah. No — not buying that. That was definitely you making out with Mace Mason. Who, by the way, owes me VIP tickets for their next local show."

"He said something about that."

"Love me a redhead. Though that one appears to be taken, judging by what I just witnessed. But that's OK. I have a date with Rhys on New Year's Eve."

"You do?"

"Hunter came by Friday night, looking for you. We made a trade. But how are you juggling two rockstars at once? I'd be exhausted."

"It's not what..."

"...it looks like. Yeah. I heard you the first time. Still not buying it. Anyway, Hunter was freak-out-level worried, so I let him in to make sure you'd made it home safe. The phone and the clothes on the floor confirmed that much."

Uh-oh.

Hunter's going to have questions. And he's probably still worried.

"I'd better go catch up with him."

"If you ever need some help with that juggling act, let me know. I've got a few tricks up my sleeve."

Why am I not surprised to hear that?

Chapter 19

Supermassive Black Hole

Hunter is not happy with my little disappearing act. And I don't blame him. But the most he's getting out of me was that I left my phone behind and got caught up in "things." Again — a truth, if not a whole truth.

I let Hunter off the hook about the exhibit opening, more pleased that he made such a Herculean effort to get there, even if he was late and didn't get to stay long.

I'm less pleased when he tells me about his ride with Rhys to the opening, during which Rhys was apparently fixated on the topic of Mace. Mace and me, to be specific. Leave it to Rhys to accidentally blow this thing up when all he's seen is a pretty platonic kiss to the head. I have to be more careful. And I start that by defusing Hunter's questions about a mysterious man he saw hanging around me at the opening. Maybe it was Mace. Maybe it wasn't. I can't confirm what I don't know. But even then I'm careless, referring to him as Aedan, and Hunter picks up on it. I explain it away, but I've been calling him Aedan for six months now, and it's not likely to be the last time I do so in front of Hunter.

I've been so focused on the showcase and then on Aedan that I've forgotten entirely about the holidays. I'd already decided not to go home, because I had the opening. But Dad was so rude, so quick to blame Hunter for something that had nothing to do with him, so dismissive of me. I can't go back to that. But that doesn't mean I remembered Hunter's invitation to be his plus-one for their New Year's Eve show. When he reminds me of it, though, I know instantly that that's exactly what I need to keep my mind off of... things.

But I'm feeling really positive about... things right now, and I want to do it right this year. I want to get dressed up, celebrate, and knock Hunter's — everyone's — socks off. Maybe I need a few tricks up my sleeve, too.

This is both totally me and totally not me, all at the same time. I look in the full-length mirror, and it's like someone Photoshopped me into a glamorous pin-up version of myself. More makeup than I usually wear, with cat-eyed liner, full red lips, my natural brows elegantly arched, long lashes. My hair is in a classic pin-up 'do, the beachy waves tamed and shaped to cascade down my back, and a white rose tucked above my ear.

The dress is straight-up '40s glam, with a portrait collar to frame my shoulders and cleavage, a fitted waist and a full, crinolined skirt to highlight my figure and disguise those over-ample thighs.

I stop myself at that thought, remembering Aedan tracing his fingers seductively up my inner thigh, the views of his gorgeous face, eyes smoldering with lust, as he looks up at me from between them. Maybe not so in need of disguising after all...

And the blue dress also hides a wonderful little surprise — the main reason I bought it in the first place. I can't wait to see Hunter's face...

I'm already running late after the trip to the salon for this little pin-up makeover. I hope it was worth the extra effort.

"Hi!"

Hunter's jaw drops as he takes me in. A shiver runs up my spine.

"Wow."

And now I blush. I don't think I've ever rendered a man monosyllabic before. Not even Aedan. But then we're on to our usual friendly banter.

"I like the shirt. Geeky, yet rockstar."

Hunt has on a Stormtroopers-meets-Abbey Road T-shirt. It's so thoroughly Hunter that I can't help smiling.

"Thanks again for inviting me."

"No one I'd rather have kick off the new year with me."

My heart flutters a little.

He leads me into a room where the band is hanging out, based on the loud chatter. And then we walk into the room. Rhys lets out a loud wolf-whistle, and the room goes dead silent. All eyes turn to me.

"Whoa... Nice bombshell bit there, Ellie," Alex says.

His girlfriend, Megan, glares at him and says nothing, hitting me with an even angrier glare when she realizes Alex didn't see her glaring at him.

"You look *amazing*," Lisa says. "The salon did a picture-perfect job. I'm so glad!"

"Cool outfit, Ellie," David comments, while Declan's just standing there, speechless.

"Hi, everyone! Glad to be here. And thanks. I think it turned out pretty well." I'm not sure what else to say. I don't think I've ever been the center of attention like this.

Lisa comes over to survey the results of my makeover, clearly impressed with the job her salon did with me.

"Hey, Ellie — where's Mace?"

Hunter was right. Rhys *is* a little fixated on Mace. I do my best to play it cool.

"I'm not sure, Rhys. Why do you ask?"

"Just thought you might have brought him as your date tonight..."

"Hunter mentioned you were a little obsessed with Mace, Rhys... I could see if I still have his number if you'd like to ask him out..." I'm trying really hard to keep a straight face, only partially successfully.

The room erupts into laughter.

"Good one, Ellie!" Rhys replies, coming over to give me a fist bump and a hug.

Wait — is he looking at my breasts?

Hunter smacks him on the back of the head.

"What?" he asks, failing to pull off the innocent act.

Hunter tells everyone about the showcase — my awards, the grants and the record-breaking auctions.

"You sold them all?" David asks.

"No. I kept one for myself. Too much sentimental value."

I haven't even told Hunter that he's the inspiration for the one piece I refused to sell. He hasn't asked. But I can't imagine he hasn't figured it out.

Soon it's time for the band to go on.

"Are you going to watch from backstage?" Hunter asks.

He knows I don't like crowds, which is one of the reasons I try to come early to their gigs, so I can claim a prime spot near Hunter. But the area in front of the stage is already packed.

"For a while, at least, I think. I may go out to the bar and watch from there for a bit later."

"OK — have fun! I'll see you in a bit."

He kisses my forehead and stops to look at me for a moment before he heads out to the stage.

Oh! "Hunter! I forgot the best part!"

I grab the little box in the pocket of the skirt and press a button. The whole dress lights up, tiny pins of light peeking through the dark blue fabric, like stars in a night sky.

"Wow. You look like the entire universe has been concentrated in one spot."

"I am not a supermassive black hole, Hunter!"

"No, but you're definitely making as much impact as the Big Bang tonight." He winks at me.

He winked at me!

I can't control the blushing or the wide smile that lights up my face.

CHAPTER 20

WAITING FOR MIDNIGHT

I hang out backstage by Hunter for a half-hour before I decide to head out to enjoy the energy of the crowd. I don't like crowds, but feeling them respond to aMUSEd is an experience I like to savor. Since the first time they took the stage together, they've owned every room they played, large or small, weeknight in a bar or New Year's Eve in a large club, or even a stadium with tens of thousands of people waiting to be entertained.

It's hard to describe to someone who hasn't seen them live, especially to someone who doesn't love music like I do. But there is an intangible quality to their performance that sparks passion and delight in everyone they perform for. I have never seen any musician take hold of an audience like they do. Except Mace. And if that's the only comparison that can be made, it's only a matter of time before they're superstars.

"I knew they'd be this good. And they're only getting better."

I know that voice speaking in my ear. But it's not possible...

I turn around to discover that it *is* possible. Because there's Aedan, standing in front of me, in his nice suit, with his hair fanned out around his collar, his eyes twinkling like the lights in my dress.

"Aedan! You're supposed to be in... Abu Dhabi?"

"That was yesterday."

"You're here!"

"I am. Just in time for New Year's Eve with my girl..." I want to object, but...

"Oh, Aedan..."

He pulls me into his arms and kisses me sweetly.

"You look amazing, Brighid! Not that you don't always. But I'm going to have to steal you away from here just to keep all the other guys from ogling you."

"I have a strict limit on ogling. One person only."

"I'm pretty sure you're already over your limit for the night. Hunter's distracted. And he's never distracted on stage."

I glance back up at my best friend. Aedan's right. He's glancing around the room, as if he's looking for someone or something.

"You want me to go? See if he'll finally wake up after seeing you in bombshell mode?"

"Aedan... I..."

"It's OK, Brighid. Regardless of what's going on with us, I can't begrudge you going to him if he's waking up to who you really are to him."

"And I won't begrudge you being with Cat when she decides that's what she wants."

"That's not now, nor anytime soon."

"I didn't dress up for Hunter, Aedan. I didn't dress up for you, either, since I had no idea you'd be here. I dressed up because I wanted to feel beautiful and confident and sexy."

"And you succeeded admirably. That confidence is what adds to your beauty. Not the makeup or the clothes. You're truly striking tonight, because you're your confident self."

"Thank you."

"So, should I steal you away? Or should I retreat to give Hunter a chance to make his move?"

"Neither. I wanted this night to be special. I wanted to think I might finally be able to dance with someone. That a kiss at midnight wasn't a ridiculous dream. That going into a new year feeling positive was a real possibility. And I didn't realize all of that until just now."

"Then let's make that happen."

I pull Aedan off to the side of the dance floor when the guys take their break. Since aMUSEd isn't exactly known for their slow-dancing ballads, the event organizers have packed slow songs into the breaks, with the DJ encouraging everyone to bring "that someone special" onto the dance floor, while anyone who's solo or not in the mood can visit the bar before the band gets back on stage. I'm loathe to admit it, but I've never had the chance to slow-dance with anyone, and I'm a little nervous.

But Aedan's already getting some looks from a couple people in the crowd who seem like they might recognize him, so we find a spot where people are already busy chatting or dancing, and he pulls me in close, my head on his chest, his tucked alongside my neck. I fall into rhythm with him, the two of us dancing together here as naturally as we do in bed now. He hums along with the stripped-down version of Duran Duran's "Save a Prayer," and I'm a little surprised he knows it. It was one of my mother's favorites, and while it's fun to tease him sometimes about our age difference, he's too young to remember it on his own.

"How do you know this song? You were a toddler when it came out!"

"I learned how to slow-dance to this song."

"When you were 2?"

"When I was 8."

"Wow. You were a ladies man early, weren't you?"

"My sitter was a Durannie. She and her friends thought it was cute to teach me how to dance. If nothing else, I figured out very quickly how much impact a charismatic frontman and good looks have on how successful a band is. They each had a favorite band member, and they bought every poster, magazine and pin they could get their hands on. I also learned the value of a tightly produced live performance and of a well-produced album."

"And you put that all into play when you made your own bid for superstardom."

"I did. And Hunter and his friends will make it pay off for them, too. Though they could use a few ballads in their repertoire if they really want to sell themselves as sex symbols."

"Don't let Declan hear you say that, or all they'll write from now on is ballads."

Aedan laughs and kisses me, running his hands along my spine. We dance closely through another four songs, and I'm so turned on from having his hands on me like that that I'm ready to scrap the rest of the night and go to his hotel with him, even with less than a half-hour to go until midnight.

"You ready to go?"

"In more ways than one..." I groan.

A knowing smile travels across this face.

"You're giving up on midnight? It won't be long now."

The guys come back on stage, instantly revving the crowd back up after the break.

"Let's at least wait until midnight. Hunter said they had something planned, something they'd never done before."

We move off to the side of the dance floor to watch the band, Aedan's arms around my waist as I lean back into him.

"Hunter's still distracted. Are you sure this isn't you and that dress throwing him off?"

"He seemed excited about whatever they had planned. I'm sure he's just nervous trying something new."

"I'd expect him to be pacing if it was nerves."

"You know about that?"

"He's a very... fervent... pacer. Though I have to say he'd really settled down by the time they finished their opening stint. They all had. I'd like to have them back for a full tour, or at least a full regional run. They're a nice complement for us."

"Hunter will be thrilled to hear that."

"You can't tell him."

"I know. I couldn't explain to him how I knew before he did."

"I'll talk to the label about pulling them in on the next tour, let the suits handle it."

"I'd thank you, but..."

"You want them to have earned it on their own, not because of our relationship."

I nod.

"Don't worry — they did. And then some. We won't get them to open again after this next tour. They'll be headlining by the time that's over."

"I saw all of this coming... and..."

"And what?"

"Him pulling away, leaving me behind..."

"I doubt that would ever happen."

"I've already seen hints of it. Tonight... tonight was the first night I really felt like I was part of it all. And it took a makeover for that to happen."

"It wasn't the hair and makeup, or the dress. Trust me. I think you're more important to him, to *them*, than you can see. Don't underestimate yourself. If anything, it makes it more likely that *he* will undervalue you, that *they* will. You're important to them, whether they say that or not. You're important to *me*."

I nuzzle back into him.

"Thank you."

"No thanks needed. It's just the truth."

There's a murmur, a rush of chatter around us. I look around, expecting to find people staring and pointing at Aedan. But they're focused on their phones, their watches. Declan brings their song to a close and calls everyone's attention to the time. It's almost midnight.

"Come," Aedan says, pulling me by the hand back onto the dance floor. "It's almost time."

While nearly everyone is watching the guys on stage as Declan does his little holiday patter, Aedan is looking away, leaning down into me.

"Is he still looking for you?"

I peek over his shoulder. Hunter is definitely surveying the room, clearly distracted.

"I can't tell what he's doing. He's looking around the room."

"For you."

"Maybe."

"You want to go backstage and see if you can get your midnight kiss from him?"

"Aedan..." It feels wrong for him to even say it. I know it's not realistic, and he should, too. "You came all this way... I'm standing right here with you. Let it go. He doesn't think of me like that."

"You're wrong. But I'll let it go. Especially if it means I get to kiss you in public on this side of the Atlantic."

There's so much in his expression... affection, wanting...

He leans down and kisses me, and I return the kiss, my arms going around his neck, my hands threading up through his hair.

"Five... four..."

I hear Declan counting down from the stage, the people around us joining in, but Aedan and I are locked together, connected.

"Three... two..."

Aedan's hands slide up along my cheeks, holding my face gently in place as he licks at my lips. I open my mouth to let him inside, and our tongues tangle with each other.

"One... Happy New Year!"

"Happy New Year, Brighid."

"Happy New Year, Aedan."

"Let's rock this new year!" Declan yells, and Hunter dives into a rocked-up version of "Auld Lang Syne" with a guitar solo. I look up over Aedan's shoulder, but he pulls me back into a kiss, into his arms, the two of us swaying together to aMUSEd's take on the traditional tune, until Rhys kicks the song into second gear, and then third...

Aedan chuckles.

"He really is a madman, isn't he?"

"On that throne, yeah. The rest... is just Rhys being Rhys."

"Wouldn't have him any other way. He's odd, but he's talented, and a good guy."

"He is. He's been asking about you."

"He has?"

"About you and me, I think. I'm not sure if he thinks he knows something or not. It's hard to tell with him. But I think I threw him off the trail."

"Smart girl... Sexy girl... Come celebrate the new year with me? Please?"

How could I resist?

"Let me tell someone I'm leaving, so Hunter doesn't worry. I'll meet you by the bar."

The only one backstage who I know is Lisa. I flag her down as she's getting herself a drink.

"I'm heading out."

"You find a friend out there?"

"Something like that."

"He wouldn't be an auburn-haired rock god, would he?"

I give her a pleading look but don't answer.

"It's fine. I'll tell Hunter you ran into a friend and called it an early night."

I nod, unwilling to actively participate in whatever cover story she's concocting to try to cover up something that I'm hiding for reasons entirely different from what she thinks are the case.

I look back at the stage as I re-enter the crowd, finding Hunter fully engaged with their next song. It must have just been nerves.

I blow him a kiss he can't see.

Happy New Year, Hunt.

I step under Aedan's outstretched arm as he pulls me into his side, kissing my temple and leading me off to the car.

"You sparkle like the midnight sky tonight, Brighid."

I laugh.

"It's my geek-tastic dress."

"It's really not..."

My cheeks warm under his appreciative regard. I turn off the lighting.

"Yup. Still sparkling."

"You need your eyes checked."

"We need to find you a better mirror. Hmm... now there's an idea..."

"What?"

"You'll see..."

"Now I'm worried."

His face is full of mischief, but he stays silent as he tucks me into the car and we head off to his hotel.

"**C**ome with me..."

Aedan offers me his hand, and I take it, following him across the spacious room to the bathroom.

"I do like shower sex..."

"I know. But that's not why you're coming in here with me. At least not this time."

"OK..."

"Do you trust me?"

"You know I do."

"Then come here."

He gestures in front of him, where he stands against the wall in front of the wide sink. I walk up to him, and he turns me around, facing the mirror, pulling my hips back against him.

"What do you see?"

I frown at him in the mirror.

"I don't need *my* eyes checked. I'm not sure we can say the same for you."

"We're about to find out. Tell me what you see."

"Me, dressed up as much like a '40s pinup as I can be made to be through the arts of cosmetics, hairdressing and ample amounts of fabric."

"You know what I see? A beautiful, intelligent, sexy young woman."

"I get it, Aedan. I can't help it if I'm a realist about my body."

"But you're not. You're the self-confidence equivalent of the glass half-empty."

"And you're the glass half-full guy."

"I've seen women of all sizes, shapes and ages, Brighid."

"And you've *had* all of them, too, I presume."

"Is that slut-shaming I'm hearing from you?"

"No! You're not Declan." He barks a laugh. "I'm just being a realist. You've made it clear that you're an equal-opportunity lover. Much to my benefit."

"I am. Which makes me an excellent judge of what I find attractive. So you want to know what *I* see? I see a beautiful, sexy young woman." He caresses my shoulders inside the portrait collar of the dress. "Incredible shoulders — strong, smooth, feminine without being too delicate." My eyes slide closed and I lean back into the sensation.

"A lovely long neck."

His hand traces up along the side of my neck. Watching his hands on me is magnetic.

"That glorious flaxen hair, which reminds me of a sunny day on the beach, full of waves and light, reflecting like tiny specks of glass." He twists a lock of my hair in his fingers.

"A strong face — expressive, interesting, unique. Striking."

And I recall having told myself the same thing the night Aedan and I met, wondering why Hunter doesn't see it, doesn't see me that way.

"And those lavender eyes... You don't see that often, if ever. And so full of intelligence, warmth, wisdom, caring."

His hands slide around my back, and the zipper of the dress slides down with his fingers. He undoes the hook-and-eye fastening at the top, sliding the wide collar down around my arms, then past my elbows as the unzipped dress falls to the floor. Once again, I'm standing nearly naked in front of him, only my panties left, with Aedan able to see me both from behind and reflected in the mirror.

"A perfect handful of breast," he continues, cupping one in each hand. "Tipped with those wonderfully responsive nipples." He proves his point by pinching them between his thumb and forefinger, and they tighten under his touch.

"A slender waist." His hands slide down my sides, and I shudder in response. "Complementing those feminine hips..." His hands transit cross my hips, below my belly, and I find myself glad the mirror stops at the top of the sink's backsplash. His hand brushes across the front of my panties, and I wriggle against him.

His hands go back to my hips, and I expect them to slide under the sides of my panties. Instead, he turns me sideways, and I realize there's a second mirror in this room. A full-length mirror. He planned this...

"Take them off for me."

Aedan's already shed his suit jacket, shoes and tie. He's standing behind me now in his dress shirt and slacks.

"Take them off," he urges.

I watch him behind me, his reflection in the mirror, as he unbuckles his belt and draws it through the loops of his slacks. He tosses the belt aside and starts unbuttoning his shirt.

"Take them off, Brighid," he murmurs in my ear. I swallow and slide my hands under the lacy sides of the dark blue panties. Aedan's face is rapt, his hands stilled on the buttons over his abs. I lift the sides and slowly slide my panties down, over my thighs, to my knees, letting them fall to my ankles. Aedan's breathing is fast as I step out of them and the low pumps that are as close to heels as I get. I pick up the dress, too, and place all three by the sink. I turn and help Aedan with his shirt, undoing his cuffs while his hands linger over those last few buttons. Then I unbutton his slacks, sliding down the zipper with a glancing caress to what lies beneath.

Aedan grabs my wrist, pulling my hand to his mouth and kissing my palm. He turns me around again, quickly shedding his shirt and slacks while his eyes remain fixed on our reflection in the full length mirror. His hands run down across my hips to the insides of my thighs, tracing back up the creases on each side of my mound. He pulls me back against him, his cock pressing against my ass and his hand cupping my pussy. His other hand slides south again, caressing the flesh of my thigh.

My eyes slide away.

"Look at my hands, Brighid. Look at them caressing you, your thighs, your pussy... Look at my fingers enjoying the sensation of your skin, your flesh..." He murmurs in my ear, and the sensual tone makes my blood race.

He sucks hard on my neck, leaving no question that he's marked me again, and I moan, both from the sensation and from that knowledge.

"I want you to come on my hand. And I want you to watch yourself come on my hand. No closing your eyes. You watch every moment of it, see how beautiful you are, see how much I'm enjoying watching you." He turns my head to the mirror. "Watch."

I don't have a choice in this. I don't let myself have a choice. I know I have to watch. I need to watch. And I need to try to finally get over the self-consciousness. My body may not be everyone's cup of tea, but it's the one I have, and I enjoy being in it. And it seems to be enough for Aedan, who could have pretty much any woman he wanted. And I owe it to myself to treat it with the same kind of reverence he is.

He draws his fingers across my opening and upward, using his thumb to circle that delightful little spot just above. Then he slides his fingers inside, cupping his hand around me, working me with fingers and thumb working in concert. His other arm slides around my waist, then up under my breasts, holding me tight against him. And that's good, because already my knees are threatening not to hold me up.

"Watch," he purrs against my ear.

I hadn't even noticed that my eyes had slid closed again. I'm so caught up in what I'm feeling that seeing isn't even a factor. Until he insists. And I watch as my skin flushes, my breathing speeds up, my hips rock in time with Aedan's fingers moving inside me. My eyes drift upward, watching him behind me, his hair caressing my shoulder, his eyes rapt. Watching us. Watching me. Watching me...

And I roll over, floating on waves of pleasure that pulse through me, slowing ever so slightly between each wave, until, finally...

Aedan urges me forward, toward the mirror. My legs manage to get me there with his hand on my hip and his other arm still around my chest, until I'm close enough to see my pupils, big, relaxed, looking as blissed out as the rest of my body feels.

Behind me, Aedan's are almost as big, and as my body presses into the cool glass, his warmth presses into my back, and I can feel him, hard, erect, eager. He drops a kiss to my shoulder, and I savor the feeling of his lips against my skin.

"Beautiful."

"I want to watch." I do. I want him to take me here, where I can watch him, watch us, as he takes his own pleasure in my body, in me.

"It's not a dressing room in a lingerie shop, but I've been fantasizing about this for a long while, watching us together like this..."

His hand strokes along my hip. His own hips rock against me. I close my eyes to savor the sensation. Aedan fits himself against my opening and slides slowly in. Gathering my hands in his, he presses them to the mirror on either side of us, our fingers entwined. He catches my eyes with his own, and then he starts to move, first slowly, then faster, until he's driving into me, the room filled with the sounds of his exertion, flesh on flesh, our breathing, the mirror fogging until it obscures my reflection but leaving me free to watch Aedan's face as he latches onto my neck with his lips and marks me once more. It sends me over again, pulsing around Aedan, which tips him into his final throes. He stills, panting in my ear.

"Gods... that was just..." He stops, still panting, leaving the sentiment unspoken.

"Yeah. Just..."

CHAPTER 21

SOMETHING'S ALWAYS WRONG

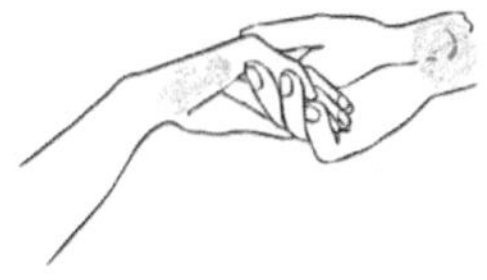

Aedan's phone rings, bringing us both out of a light doze. "Sorry — I meant to turn it off."

"It's fine."

"I should take this, just in case it's urgent..."

"No — go ahead. You've got the tour to deal with."

He picks up his phone and heads into the bathroom.

I go to the dresser next to the door and pick up my phone. I really owe Hunter a text, at minimum. Especially when I bailed on him without saying goodbye in person.

Ellie: *Sorry I had to leave early. You all were SO good tonight!*

I set the phone down again. Aedan's voice drifts through the half-open door.

"Are you OK? ... And you're cleared to fly? ... No, don't go home first. Not by yourself. Just get your passport and head to the airport. I've already got a flight to Rio booked for tomorrow. I'll meet you there. Tell the band to follow. I'll ask Marina Matthews to pull some strings and add a second opening act for the first set of dates, since the venues are bigger. ... It'll be fine. Don't worry. I'll be there soon enough."

There's a moment of quiet, and I realize I've been eavesdropping. I go back to the bed, curious but too embarrassed to even consider asking Aedan about the call. A minute or two later, he comes back out into the room.

"I'm set to fly out for Rio tomorrow afternoon, Iz. Let the label handle things on their end until then. I'll take care of the rest when I get there. ... No. Don't. I don't want things blown out of proportion. Just keep an eye out in case something comes up, OK? ... Thanks. I'll call you when I get in. Take it easy, man."

"Problems?" Something feels off.

"Yeah. Another opening band imploded days before the next leg of the tour was to start. Remind me next time — no more opening acts with exotic pets. I'm starting to think we're cursed."

I knock on the bedside table three times. "Don't jinx yourself. And remember — it all worked out OK when you called aMUSEd in at the last minute. You could end up glad this happened."

"You're right. And I like the glass-half-full attitude."

"I had a reminder to make sure my realism was tempered with optimism. And I've seen how this works with you all. It'll sort itself out, even if you have to do a little extra work to make it a success. Just like with aMUSEd."

"You know, if they'd had you managing them, they'd be even further ahead than they are now."

"Oh, I don't think so. I'm terrible with people. I can't even talk to strangers without things getting awkward."

"Tell that to Gráinne and those girls — who adore you, by the way."

"That's different. Gráinne and I have common interests, and the girls were fixated on *you*."

"That may be, but you have a strong belief in Hunter and aMUSEd, which is a key factor in a good manager. And you're practical, and organized."

"Which my parents insisted on for my grades' sake."

"And you have an ear, and an eye, for musical talent."

"Just because I knew Hunter had the *thing?*"

"Is that what you call it? '*The thing*'?" He chuckles at me.

"What? It's not exactly charisma. It's beyond that. It's an energy that draws people in and makes them want to watch, listen, participate, makes them feel passionately about what you're doing. You're basically a font of the stuff."

"And that's why you'd do very well in this business. If not in management or A&R, then in scouting talent. You know that X-factor when you see it."

"I don't have any desire to be in the music business. I just want my own shop, where I can sell my yarn and my weaving."

"You could dream bigger. Tour with aMUSEd. With me..." He purrs those last two words into my ear. And I melt. Until I start picturing myself traveling around the world with Aedan... with Mace, the rockstar... me, the secret girlfriend... the paparazzi...

the groupies... Something feels off... *He belongs with someone else...*

"I can't, Aedan. Please."

"OK. No pressure. I just want you to realize how valuable your insight is, how much you have to contribute — especially where music is involved. I mean, I'd trust you to pick an opening act for us, sight unseen. The first time I saw aMUSEd live, I knew they'd make it. Because of you."

"What? How because of me?"

"I saw how you responded to the crowd when they talked about the band — the people who hadn't seen them yet, the ones who had but didn't know whether they'd come into their own yet, the ones who thought Declan might just be as good — or better — than me... You had that proud, confident look on your face, a light in your eyes that told me those people hadn't seen or heard anything yet, but they would that night."

"Wait... How do you know any of this?"

"I was there that night. Standing right behind you. You knocked my hat off when you turned around to listen to the crowd talking about the band."

I can feel my jaw moving, but there's nothing intelligible coming out of my mouth. Aedan laughs.

"You can't tell them. Marina Matthews sometimes asks me to scout new talent. She sent me to check them out that night. She'd heard about Hunter, Declan and David when they were still in Delaware. She wanted my opinion on where they were headed."

"That was you? The guy who was standing behind me? That first night they played with Rhys?"

"It was."

"So that was how..."

"How they ended up opening for Telltale Signs. Yes. They were the best young band I'd seen in years. But it was the look on your face that sold me on them. So when our opening act imploded, they were the first name on my list."

"And I can't tell them."

"Please. Marina sends me out because she trusts my judgment, but it skews things if bands know I'm scouting for her in person. I have to stay incognito while I'm doing it."

"Well, you managed it that night. I had no idea, even after I bumped into you. Almost a second time. Sorry — belatedly."

"I was standing too close. You were almost as compelling as they were." *Something feels off.*

I look up into those sea-blue eyes of his and... my breath catches.

"You knew who I was before we met."

"Not as such. I suspected you had a connection to the band. I had no idea you'd show up at one of our gigs. But when I saw you that second time... It was like fate had dropped you right in my lap."

This should resonate with me. This should give me a feeling of rightness in the things between the two of us. But it doesn't. *Something feels off.* I feel just a little... manipulated. And now I know Aedan hasn't been honest with me about something else. *Something feels off.* It isn't just his feelings for me, which he's now owned. It isn't just his past with Cat. It goes all the way back to when we first met. He could have told me then. Or at any point since. And he chose not to.

"Brighid? Are you OK?"

"I... I... uh... No. Actually, no, I'm not. I'm... I'm sorry, Aedan — but I'm not... I'm not comfortable with this. I'm not really sure of my perception of a lot of things at this moment, and I think I need some time to absorb this, think about how things have come to be, where I want them to go. I'm really sorry. But I think I need to go."

"Wait. What? You're upset about this? That I didn't tell you I'd seen you once, at a gig, months before we met officially?"

"It's not as simple as that. And that's not all of it. I... this talk of me doing something 'bigger' with my life, something other than the dream I've been working toward for years, of coming on tour with you. I appreciate your belief in me. Aedan, and I appreciate you wanting more time with me. But we talked about keeping this casual, and none of this feels casual. It feels a little like you're trying to replace Cat the rockstar touring with your band with your vision of me as part of your entourage. And that's not something I can be."

"No, Brighid — it's not like that at all. I swear."

"I believe you believe that. I know you wouldn't swear to it otherwise. But that doesn't change the fact that I'm not comfortable with any of this right now. And you're leaving tomorrow anyway." *Something feels very off.* "I think it might be good for us to take a break, get some distance, re-evaluate what we really want, because either it's not really as casual as we'd talked about or it's fitting itself to a shape that has more to do with the relationships we can't have than the ones we do."

He gives a deep sigh.

"I think you're blowing this out of proportion, Brighid. But I understand that you're upset and want some space." He cringes.

"I'm not Cat, Aedan. And I promised you we'd stay friends and work through our issues. I'm not reneging on that promise. But I need a little while to decide where I really stand, with you and with what I want in my life. You spent half the night tonight suggesting maybe Hunter was ready to have something more with me — after you flew in, literally from Abu Dhabi, to spend New Year's Eve with 'your girl.' You use the words 'casual' and 'I love you' in basically the same sentence. So, I think maybe you need the time to consider things just as much as I do. Am I wrong?"

He's quiet, introspective. I let the silence continue, waiting for him to answer. He sighs again.

"No. Not entirely anyway. And I'm embarrassed to admit that I should have seen it myself. See — you are wise, insightful, glorious. No wonder it's so easy for me to fall for you." He smiles warmly at me, no indication of the resentment I expected to feel from him. And yet, still... something feels off.

"We were perfectly suited to be each other's rebound people, despite the fact that neither one of us actually had the relationship we're rebounding from." The realization hits me as the words fall from my mouth. "It was inevitable that things would get more complicated than we planned on."

"And it would inherently beg the question of what both of us want from this, because it lends itself to feeling more deeply than either of us wanted. We thought we knew what that was, what it would look like, and it seems it's a bigger thing to consider than what we've done."

"Exactly."

"And you want to go now?"

"Need, not want. I'm trying to make an adult decision here."

"There's that priestess... wise beyond her years."

"I really am sorry, Aedan."

"Don't be. You're right. I'll take you back to the dorm."

"No. I think I'll catch a cab. There'll be plenty out tonight."

"Will you let me know you got back safe?"

"Of course. Will you let me know you got to Rio safely?"

"Absolutely. Can we keep in touch?"

"We're still friends, Aedan. I meant that. Let's just get a little space for each of us to figure things out on our own. Text me if you need to. Call if need be. But maybe no daily chit-chat until we both agree that's what we want?"

"I'm going to miss hearing from you every day."

"Me, too. But it's temporary. And you're going to be busy with the tour and I'm going to have school."

"I'm still going to ask aMUSEd to tour with us."

"I would hope so."

"You'd kick my ass if I didn't, wouldn't you?"

"Probably."

"You'll keep all of this to yourself?"

"Of course. This is between us."

I stand up and go into the bathroom, closing the door behind me. I feel a little like I've been hit by a bus, and one glance in the mirror proves I look like that, too. I look more than a little stunned. And I can't shake this feeling that something just isn't adding up, almost like Aedan still hasn't been totally honest with me yet. I gather up my clothes and shoes and get dressed, cursing when I realize I need help zipping up my dress. I walk back out into the room, finding Aedan dressed in jeans and a T-shirt, his feet bare, his expression bleak.

"I'm sorry, but could you...?"

I turn my back to him.

"Of course," he says, reaching for the zipper. His other hand grasps my waist, and he pulls me wordlessly against him. I sigh and close my eyes, leaning into him like it's the most natural thing in the world, which it nearly is, or was. Only Hunter's arms feel more like home. After a moment, I pull away, and he zips up my dress, refastening the top hooks. I grab my phone and tuck it into my pocket with my key, and I head to the door.

"Let me know you got home safe."

"I will. And you..."

"I will."

He walks quickly up to me, a brief kiss to my lips and a squeeze of my hand, which I accept gratefully. For a moment, I question this decision, but in my heart I know it's the right thing. I grab the door handle and pull it open, sliding through the narrow space as Aedan's stormy blue eyes meet mine and the door shuts between us.

Five minutes later, I'm sitting in the back seat of a taxi, praying the driver will read me well enough to not talk any more than strictly necessary. He does. My mind remains blank, too stunned and confused to process what has happened. I give the driver a hefty tip and head back into the dorm, collapsing on my bed, still dressed and unable to figure out how to get the dress back off with no one here to help. Already, I'm missing Aedan. Even though I know this has to happen.

My phone pings, and I cringe. I need to tell him I got back in safely.

Hunter: *Happy New Year, Elle! Tell Maire I said hi.*

Oh, gods... Hunter. I don't know what Lisa told him, but he clearly thinks I ran into Maire and left with her. Every instinct tells me to beg him to come keep me company in my misery, or at least help me get out of this dress.

Brighid: *I'm back safe and sound. Have a safe trip and a good tour.*

Aedan: *I'll let you know when I'm on the ground in Rio. I hope your classes go well. Please keep in touch.*

I exit the text thread.

I remind myself I can still ask Hunter to come over. And I text him back.

Ellie: *Happy New Year to you, too!*

They say whatever you're doing at midnight on New Year's is what you'll be spending the next year doing. Somehow, I'm doubtful there's going to be much kissing and dancing in my year to come. On the other hand, crying into my pillow is seeming like a really good bet.

Two months later

There's a knock at my door. Not at the window, so I know it's not Hunter.

"Just tell me if you don't want to know, and I'll leave and go stick this rag in the trash."

Lisa.

This isn't going to be good.

"What don't I want to know?"

"Who Mace has been photographed with. Hot off the presses."

Aedan and I have texted each other a handful of times in the last two months. Mostly just asking each other how we're doing. Boring and as distant emotionally as we are physically. If he's seeing someone, I don't know, and it's really none of my business since I'm the one who asked for space.

But Lisa assumes things are a lot less complicated than they are, treating me like the jilted girlfriend of a college quarterback and not the sometimes secret lover of the Sexiest Guy guy.

"I'm really sorry — but I know I'd want to know if it was me."

She practically smashes the tabloid pages in my face, but I see enough in that split second to recognize the long golden-blond hair of the woman Mace has been photographed kissing. An inset photo shows the woman's face.

Chills run down my spine.

It's the face of the mermaid in my vision. Exactly as if they'd pulled the image from my mind. Her hair isn't down to her ankles, of course, but it's well past her waist, as it was in August.

"Mace and Cat caught canoodling in Manhattan," the headline reports. "'Sexiest Guy on the Planet' Aedan 'Mace' Mason, lead singer for Telltale Signs, has been spotted smooching with sometime paramour Catriona 'Cat' Connolly, lead guitarist and lead vocalist for hard-rock trio LandSeaSky. The pair are believed to have reunited during the bands' Latin America tour together, which included the filming of the video for Telltale Signs' new single, 'Diving in Deep,' in which Mason describes a passionate and secretive affair with a blond woman."

Aedan hasn't mentioned the new single. Which I would kind of think he'd have done if he'd written a song about me. I'm sure it's *not* about me. Right? Of course, I'd also have expected him to tell me he was back in the country. And if Cat had come around. Apparently, I was wrong on at least a couple counts. But I was apparently right that something was off with him.

"Thanks, Lisa. But Mace and Cat are old news. I wish them the best."

"Back with Hunter, huh? Well, I still prefer redheads, but Hunter's not hard on the eyes. Good for you!"

She leaves without another word.

I sigh.

I go back to my weaving.

A while later, my phone rings. I can see from my chair that it's Mace calling. I opt to continue working at my loom. A few minutes later, it rings again. I ignore it.

A few minutes after that, the text tone pings.

Aedan: *Dammit. Brighid — pick up the phone. It's not what it looks like! I promise!*

I contemplate what else Mace kissing Cat might mean, especially after he so glaringly omitted telling me that she was on tour with him again. Apparently willingly this time. And I'm having a really hard time coming up with anything that might mean that doesn't involve them having gotten back together. Maybe he's calling because it didn't last. Again. Maybe he's afraid she'll dump him again sometime soon, and he wants to make sure he's got his rebound girl ready.

Too harsh? Maybe. Probably.

But Gráinne's words keep ringing in my mind. *He belongs with someone else.* And I refuse to stand in the way of that, just as I'm sure he'd refuse to stand in the way if Hunter had kissed me. Heck — I *know* he'd have gotten out of the way, because he'd tried to do that on New Year's Eve, when Hunter hadn't even expressed an iota of interest in me. And I'm not going to let him blow a shot at happiness with Cat just so he can try to preserve whatever this is between us. All it took for them to get back together was me telling him I needed space. That's pretty clear proof right there.

I sigh. I pick up the phone. And I block Aedan's number.

It's painful. But it's necessary. Whether he realizes that or not.

CHAPTER 22

DISILLUSIONED

One year later

Hunt left yesterday on his tour with Telltale Signs. A full two months on the road. He's been hovering, almost as much as he did after Mom died. I keep telling him I'm fine, but he doesn't believe me. Heck — I don't fully believe myself.

It was a rough six months, cutting off contact with Aedan, then with my dad, and then The Incident with Hunter and the groupies. I ended up in a better place, physically, with my little apartment above Kara's shop, but emotionally... Well, I've been struggling.

There have been some bright spots that have kept me going.

Hunter came to me and asked for my — and Her — help with that song he got stuck on. The resulting track glued together the EP that aMUSEd had struggled with for months, becoming its title track and their first big single.

The winning bidder for "Soul of Ireland" sent it back to me, just as anonymously as they'd bought it, with a cryptic note that spoke to its powers of inspiration — and it has been inspiring. Hanging on the wall above my bed, alongside "Soul of the Hunter" and "Soul of Inspiration," it's been watching over all of the work I've been doing at both spinning wheel and loom. With plans for a gallery show in the spring, I've been spending a lot of hours at both.

I have to admit, I was just a little surprised by Hunt's news that they'd be opening for Telltale Signs on their spring tour — thirty shows in two months, Telltale Signs' sole opening act for the U.S. tour. It'll give Hunter a taste of the full touring experience. And it'll give me a taste of what it'll be like when they're gone on a tour of their own. That day is coming, and it's not too far off. Aedan predicted as much.

Despite that, I had still wondered whether my cutting off contact with Aedan would impact his decision to have aMUSEd open for them. Either it made no difference, or it reinforced his desire to have them as openers. I just hope Aedan wasn't expecting me to turn up at the shows. I didn't even want to go out for New Year's Eve. I'm definitely not going to a Telltale Signs gig, even with Hunter opening.

I just don't have it in me anymore. My feeling that I didn't belong in that world was only reinforced that night with the groupies. Megan's cackling still rings in my mind when I think about going to another gig. I find myself comparing my body to that of the groupie with the purple-streaked hair. I don't come out ahead in that comparison.

Aedan tried very hard to build my self-confidence, but in that one respect, I'm not sure I'll ever get there. I've taken too many blows to my self-esteem, especially with The Incident coming on the heels of seeing Aedan back with the very conventionally attractive Cat. I don't think he lied to me about finding me attractive. I just think that no matter how well we clicked, given the choice between my body and hers, what sane man chooses me?

And then Dad's comments about my naiveté and lascivious rockstars slide back to the forefront of my mind. Was I looking at things with rose-colored glasses when I took Aedan at his word that he genuinely wanted to be with me? That it wasn't about me giving him my virginity or being the easy rebound hookup, the guaranteed partner he could mold to his preferences and then dump when Cat came back? I don't think so. My instincts about people are usually pretty good. But then anyone who was truly good at fooling and using people would most certainly be good enough to fool nearly everyone. And perhaps an inexperienced girl with self-esteem issues more than anyone.

There — see? This kind of mental loop is where I get stuck these days. I'm much better off not even thinking about going out. I can stay home and work on pieces for the show, meditate, read, get my mind off of Hunter being gone for two months, with

Aedan. And then I picture what the post-show parties must look like. Yes, that's exactly why I need my mind off both of them.

Three months later

I can't decide whether to be thrilled for myself and Hunter, and our successes, or miserable that we're officially moving in different directions. Literally. He's moving to New York, and I'm headed back to Delaware to take over Lindsey's yarn shop, thanks to a stellar gallery show featuring my work, all of which sold for prices in nearly the same ballpark as the ones in the college showcase. I just wish I knew who'd bought "Soul of Ireland," so I could return it to them before the move is complete. It's brought me tremendous luck in my professional life. Would that it had brought as much luck in my personal life...

But that's neither here nor there.

Kieran — aMUSEd's new lead guitarist — is a puzzle. He's got secrets he wants kept hidden, and through an odd bit of happenstance, I discovered more than he wanted anyone to know. Except Aedan, as it turned out, because Aedan was one of just two other people who knew Kieran's secrets. And, likewise, we had both urged him to join the band, despite his reservations. I don't know whether it was Aedan's insider's insight or my fervent urging based on intuition alone, but one or both of us were persuasive enough to convince him. Or maybe he just changed his mind about being in a band.

Either way, he's part of aMUSEd now, and I've actually spent almost as much time lately talking to him, practicing my Irish, as I have with Hunter. I'm not sure I'd call us friends. He's really too closed-off for that, but we're definitely friend*ly*.

And Hunter... Like I said, I talk to Kieran nearly as much. Which isn't a lot. Hunt's busy. I'm busy-ish. Trying to keep busy to keep my mind of the reality that I've been dreading for years: Hunter's life and mine don't fit together anymore.

A year and a half later

I'm staring at my phone. It's not ringing. I don't expect it to ring. But the fact that it's not ringing still bothers me. Even though it was my idea.

My first trip to New York City was a bust. Beyond a bust. It was an epic disaster worthy of a B-grade TV movie. It cemented everything I'd ever feared about how I would end up cast off once Hunter's career really took off. I wasn't thin or pretty, or talented at glamorous things like music or modeling. I don't even deal well with people half the time. OK — more than half the time. But out of loyalty and nostalgia, and maybe pity, too, Hunter had coddled me, let me hang around him and his band when I didn't have any business being there. Until that glamorous life became his whole world, and then there was no room left for me. The man I saw that night wasn't a Hunter I recognized. And the miserable creature he'd kicked the legs out from under wasn't a Brighid that I recognized or wanted to be.

So, I took a page out of his book from years ago and asked for space. And time — time to get myself to a place where I could stand on my own two feet. No more relying on Hunter for my social life. No more falling back on his support when things go awry. No more letting my world settle into an orbit where Hunter is the sun. I have a business to run, a house to bring a little further into the 21st century, then a home to settle into, a beach to enjoy, a faith to practice, maybe a book or twelve to read. But no movies. I can't take the reminders of Hunter right now.

And that, of course, is why I'm staring at my phone. Because I can't allow myself to pick it up. If I do, it'll be dialing Hunter's number in a heartbeat. And I can't do that.

I never thought Hunter would be a habit I'd have to try to break. I knew the day was coming when he wouldn't be in my life much, if at all. I just never thought that I'd be the one who'd made that happen. But it was necessary. A line had to be drawn. A life — and our relationship — had to be reshaped, rebalanced and, maybe, someday, rebuilt. On a healthier, less codependent model. And if that's going to happen, I cannot call Hunter.

I leave the phone sitting on the coffee table, where it has the grace, in its inanimate way, to look a little guilty, though I'm not sure if it's feeling guilty because it's taunting me to call Hunter or because it's not already ringing with him on the other end of the line. But it can stay there, like a child in a time-out, because I'm not having anything to do with it right now, either way. So there. I stick my tongue out at it. Yes, literally.

I give a longing glance at my shoes by the back door. I'm going to want them, but I'm not going to need them where I'm going. Better I don't even take them. I bundle up in my oversized cardigan made of the most recent batch of Irish wool Gráinne sent, undyed, a classic creamy Aran color, spun by me and knitted by my own hand. (It's amazing how productive a knitter I can be when I'm trying to keep my hands from picking up my phone.) And I head out the door, down to the beach.

No one's down there. It's late afternoon two days before the winter solstice. It's cold, overcast and a little blustery, the wind sweeping the old year out the door and making way for a new one. I can't decide whether that's a symbolic plus or a terrifying thematic overlay to my current life dilemma.

I need answers. I've found them on the beach before. I've found certainty there, even when I didn't like the things it made me certain of. And I need that now. I need some sense of resolution when my soul is crying out for things it can't have and maybe shouldn't even want.

My bare feet ache as soon as they hit the sand, the cold biting into them, straight to the bone. It's a momentary distraction from the ache in my heart. And I sit my butt straight down on the sand, watching the winter sea churning lightly a dozen yards away. The wind kicks up, and I close my eyes against it, tuning my senses to the sounds of the water.

As much as I've always been a beach girl, Herself isn't a sea goddess. But still She comes to me sometimes when I sit here, usually when I'm most in need of Her. And today I sit here, waiting, hoping for anything — a sign, an omen, silent guidance, a warm touch to let me know there's a way forward from this moment where my path seems so utterly blocked. And... nothing.

My eyes open again, the sea looking much the same as it did when I closed them. The rush of water in my ears. An empty beach. Half-frozen toes. I reach for the hood of my sweater and pull it forward to shield my cheeks from the wind. And then I see it — a massive flock of gulls. Herring gulls. In summer, they'd be menacing tourists and stealing fries, whether plain, doused in vinegar or sprinkled with Old Bay. In winter... they land ten feet in front of me and start scouting for any unsuspecting creature, or remnants of one, left on the sand as the tide creeps back out.

Hardly the omen I was hoping for. A ubiquitous bird, scavenging for whatever sustenance they can find. Making do until a more bounteous time. One they can't ever know for certain is coming, being dependent on wind and tide. It's the nature of their life, untethered, unsure. I sympathize, especially these days. I've finally found a spot to call home, and the one anchor I've had for the last twenty years proves to be something — someone — I can't fully rely upon.

And it seems the gulls can't rely on the sea to provide right now either. They're gone in a flash. No — correction. All but one. She's still at it, searching, determined. And... there. She's found something, downs it whole. If a bird could smile... She can't, but she calls out, triumphant, and then takes flight. Amazing how the other birds in her flock had to fly off somewhere else before she found what she needed...

If Herself was human, She'd smack me on the back of the head. As it stands, there's a solid grasp on my shoulder that as good as says, "Wake up, kiddo — there's your answer."

I told Hunter I needed time on my own. I told myself I needed to find a way to stand on my own two feet, without him. I knew that. I know that. I may not want to listen to that advice, but I've not only already said it — I've now been reminded of the value of it, of letting go and standing alone.

I ignore the phone when I get back inside, warming my toes in front of the fireplace, plugging in the lights on the tree that sits in the bay window of the front porch. It's the first time I've let myself do it since I got back. Symbolic — the return of the light, the evergreen's promise of life continuing through a harsh winter. I settle in on the sofa, perusing the patterns in the new crochet book that came in yesterday. I take a deep breath and let it out in a sigh, the tension that had gripped my heart slowly loosening.

And the phone rings.

I lay down the book and peer over at it.

Hunter.

It rings again. And once more.

I can do this. I have to do this.

I pick it up and answer the call.

But darned if I can think of anything to say. Even "Hello" seems like too much of a challenge.

"Bridge?"

I inhale and exhale.

That voice I so love to hear... It would be so easy to just let it go. To just pretend that day never happened. But then were would I be? Where would *we* be? Exactly where we were a few weeks ago, or a few years ago. And that's not a place I can go back to. Not until things change.

"Hunter."

"Bridge! Thank god. I was starting to wonder if you were still speaking to me. I know you asked for some time, some space, but... Listen — I know I messed up. Really, really messed up. I'm owning that. And I'm sorry. I got caught up in everything that's been going on here, and I just wasn't thinking. I owed you way better than that, and... I'm sorry. I'm indescribably sorry. I want to make it up to you, but you said you wanted space, and I kind of thought maybe you'd have called by now, but you haven't called, and I was starting to worry you weren't ever going to. And I... I can't lose you, Bridge. Maybe I deserve to. Maybe this was the last straw for you. But I need to fix this. Somehow. I can't have all of this great stuff happening for me and then lose you. I'll blow off the promotional appearances. I can be down there tomorrow. We can have Yule together. ... Bridge? Brighid?"

I take a deep breath and let it out.

"I'm here, Hunter."

"I'll get on the next plane out to Ocean City."

"No."

"No?"

"No. I know you haven't heard that word from me very often, but... No."

"No, I shouldn't get on the next plane out?"

"Yes — no, you shouldn't get on the next plane out. No, you shouldn't come down here. No, you can't come for Yule. And no, you can't fix this. Not like this. Not now."

My voice is steady, but I can feel the tears coming on. I have to do this. I know I have to do this. I just have to.

"Bridge... Please. I'm so sorry. I need to fix this. Tell me what to do. Tell me what I can do to fix things between us."

"Grow up."

"What?"

"Grow up, Hunter. That's what you can do. It's what I've had to do. I have a house, a mortgage, a business and a responsibility to the people around me, including you. And myself. And my responsibility to you, and to me, means, right now, that I have to tell you to grow up. And to stay away. Don't come here. Don't call me. Don't text me. Don't email me. Focus on your career, and on what you want in your life, who you want to be. If that's the asshole rockstar I saw in New York, then go do that, but don't expect to be welcome here or anywhere in my life. And if that person you decide you want to be... if he's my best friend — one who can truly act like my friend — then maybe, someday, I'll be ready for you to come back. But that day's not today, and I can't honestly tell you when that day will be."

"Bridge... Please don't do this."

"I have to, Hunter. For both of our sakes. If you come back now, if I let myself just forgive you like this was just another stupid mistake, I'd be doing a disservice to both of us. This had to happen, Hunt. It was meant to happen. Because you have needed to wake up for so very long, and I have needed to realize that I can't have a healthy relationship with you — a healthy friendship with you — until I know down to my bones that I can live my life without you in it and still be content. Don't think for a moment this isn't killing me. Because it is. And that's exactly why I have to do it. For both of us. I want us to be more than just the rockstar and his shadow. I need us on equal footing in our relationship, or at least a lot more equal.

"I'm not going to pretend that we can get there overnight. And I'm not going to pretend that just wanting it to be so will make it that way. So, yeah — I have to do this. I have to stand on my own two feet. And you've got to grow up, wake up, and realize you owe me better. You owe both of us better. I wouldn't be your best friend if I didn't tell you that. I've let it go for too long, for both of us. I can't stay this doormat I've become. And you've got to learn to get out of your own way, stop punishing yourself for things that happened when you were just a kid and be the person I know you really are inside. That's the guy I'll welcome back in my home. And in my heart. Find him, Hunt. For both our sakes."

And I hang up the phone. And I block Hunter's number.

CHAPTER 23

WINTER SOLSTICE NIGHT

The next night

I admit it. When the doorbell rings late in the evening on Dec. 20, the eve of the winter solstice, I instantly assume it has to be Hunter. I can't say that part of me wasn't desperately hoping he'd go against my stated wishes and show up here for Yule regardless of what I'd said.

So, when the doorbell rings, I really think it might be him.

It is not.

Before I can even process what I'm seeing, I'm crushed in a hug that feels like it alone could put my broken pieces back together. I recognize that scent before I make sense of what my eyes are seeing. It's a memory trigger, that wisp of ocean breeze, a hint of cedar and sandalwood.

"Aedan?"

It's been nearly two years since I've seen him. Almost that long since I've had any communication with him.

"Happy Yule! How's my girl?" He pulls back from the hug and hits me with that famous smile of his, open and warm and just a little bit sexy.

"Uhh... Not?"

"Not good? Not a girl? Wow, that would be a big change, but you've got to be true to yourself."

I roll my eyes.

"Not *yours*, Aedan. You have Cat. And I'm not getting in the middle of that." Nor purposefully rhyming in Seussian style...

The smile disappears from his face, like sand sifting through fingers.

"I don't *have* Cat, Brighid. I never did. Which you'd have known if you hadn't broken your promise that we'd stay friends and work out any problems together, no matter what."

Ouch. That hurts. Almost as much as giving up Aedan. Almost as much as giving up Hunter.

He's right. I broke that promise I made to him, to both of us. I hadn't even thought of it that day I'd decided to block his number. And now I'd done it again with Hunter. Both times I'd reacted on instinct. Maybe wisely in Hunter's case, but with Mace, I'd ceded him to Cat based on a tabloid photo and a two-paragraph story. I'd wished them well. I truly had. But I hadn't given him the chance to explain, and I hadn't lived up to my part of the bargain in our friendship.

"I'm sorry. You're right. I owe you an apology for breaking that promise. So — I'm sorry."

"May I come in?"

We're still standing in the doorway, Aedan's hands on my arms, our breath fogging in the winter air, which is substantially colder than it was even yesterday.

"Sure. Come in..."

Why do I feel like I've just invited a vampire into my house? Not that Aedan is a vampire, or parasitic in any way, but it feels like this invitation is symbolic and something that can't be taken back. Once he's inside, will there always be a little bit of Aedan Mason in my home, if just the memory of him having been here?

"Do you want something to drink? To eat?" Anything but bread and salt, because his non-vampirism aside, I can't risk cementing his presence in my home with that traditional bonding of guest-right.

"No. I had dinner on the flight down. But thanks."

We sit down on the sofa, Aedan sitting on the far end near the fireplace, flexing his fingers in the heat. I sit on the opposite end, keeping a careful distance between us. I don't trust myself not to cave into anything where Aedan Mason is concerned, just as I don't trust myself not to cave in where Hunter's concerned. Hence having blocked his number. Wisely. It was wise, right?

"How did you know where I was?"

Aedan shucks off his leather jacket, laying it over the adjacent armchair.

"I've always known where you were. I've got enough staff to keep track of one wool-weaving priestess of Brighid. I was just trying to respect your decision where we were concerned."

"And you're here now because...? What changed?"

"I ran into Alex when I was in the music store near my apartment the other day. I was shopping for a new piano. He was looking at a new synthesizer ahead of their next tour. He told me what happened, Brighid. With you and Hunter."

It's too fresh. Tears start to well up in my eyes.

Aedan eliminates the distance between us in an instant, moving over to pull me into his chest.

"I'm sorry, Brighid. As much as you've told him you feared being left behind, he should have known better than to alienate you like that. For someone so intelligent, he isn't terribly bright sometimes."

My inhaled breath turns into a sniffle.

"Listen..." He strokes my hair comfortingly. "You may not want to hear this, but I think you need to." He pulls my eyes up to his. "I called Hunter before I left this morning. I'd honestly planned to tear his head off — verbally, at least. But... Brighid — he's wrecked. It just wouldn't have been productive. He already knows he screwed up on an epic scale. And I think he may have finally realized he's got to make some changes and start working through his issues, especially where you're concerned. Time will tell whether he can make that happen."

He kisses my forehead.

"I'm not doing myself any favors here, but I have to be honest with you. We agreed on that long ago. So, here's my honest opinion: Colossal screw-ups aside, I know Hunter's a good guy. If he wasn't, I wouldn't have brought him back on tour with us, and you wouldn't have stuck with him this long."

I nod. If I didn't believe that, I wouldn't have given him a chance to sort himself out, even if I finally had to take the tough-love route.

"But, Brighid — you have to realize he's been abused, in more ways than one, and he's continued that pattern in how he treats himself."

I'm stunned. I've never even thought of it like that, and I'd known better than anyone how Hunter's father treated him.

"It may look like fun from the outside, but his life is a slow-motion car wreck with you as the bystander. You've got to get yourself clear of the wreckage before you're a second victim. You can't allow that to happen. I *won't* allow that to happen. But still, he's a victim, twice over — of his father and now of himself. He's also the only one who can hit the pause button on that crash scene and pull himself out of the metaphorical wreck before the damage is permanent. You cutting him off is like shouting at him, hoping he'll see the crash coming and steer clear of it at the last moment. But he's got to be the one to save himself."

Aedan's put into words something I've known for a long time but had never thought of in that context. Hunter's father wasn't just a horrible parent — he was verbally and emotionally abusive to his mother, and to a lesser extent to Hunter himself. And the pressure he put on teenage Hunter to live up to his warped idea of what a man should be... that was a form of abuse, too, and maybe the longest-reaching, since it seems to have shaped parts of his life in ways that just don't match up with the Hunter I once knew. Ever since then, Hunter's relationships with women have been kind of a benign version of his father's, the key difference being Hunter has consistently *refused* to commit to *any* woman, out of fear he'd hurt someone. Especially me.

"He called me yesterday to apologize," I admit. "He wanted to come see me. And I told him he wasn't welcome, that I wasn't sure he ever would be. That I wanted him to stay away." I'm one step short of bawling, even if that's the last thing I want to do right now. "Did I do it again? Did I cut him out unfairly, like I did with you?"

"Brighid, I've talked to him enough about you over the years that I know he cares about you more than nearly anything in the world, maybe more than anything at all. But he's still heavily burdened by his past. It's been making decisions for him that aren't worthy of him. It's subtle and it's self-indulgent in some ways, but it's definitely self-sabotage. He thinks he's not good enough for you, so he's unwittingly made himself exactly that. Truly, I think if he'd just stop being so stupid about the two of you, it would go a long way toward making him understand he's not doomed to become his father. As it stands, that's a huge burden that's keeping him from being the man he should be. For himself and for you."

There's that priestly insight Aedan has. Right on target once again. And he's clearly been serving, if irregularly, as priest for

Hunter in much the same way I do for my counseling clients. I wish I'd seen this as clearly as Aedan has.

"I couldn't bring myself to just let him off the hook this time. Even though he apologized for what he said. Which wasn't entirely untrue, even if it wasn't kind, either."

"He needs you not to let him off the hook. He needs to realize that he's in danger of losing you — and himself — not to rockstar excesses, but to the legacy of his father's abuse. And you're right to force him to see that. It may be hurtful to him, but he's hurting you both right now, the way he's been acting. He's the last person you should ever have to expect to treat you unkindly, my Lady."

I give him a small smile.

"I've missed that — you calling me 'my Lady.'"

"You prefer that to 'my girl'?"

"I..." I look at him helplessly. "I'm just not, Aedan. I can't be. I couldn't be before, and now that I've seen you and Cat — that was a lot more than a hug, Aedan. And I don't think you were totally honest with me about that phone call you got the last time we were together."

He grimaces, sitting back and releasing me.

"You're right. I'm sorry. I keep telling you I can't tell you everything about the situation with Cat, and I should have just told you that was another case where I couldn't say exactly what was going on. It's two years too late, but I will tell you that it was Cat who called, and she was in some trouble and needed refuge. I pulled some strings to get her band an opening slot on the Latin America tour, just so I could ensure she was safe."

"And then the video? The song about the affair with the blonde woman?"

"The video was the director's concept. She saw Cat when we were discussing concepts backstage before a show and thought Cat was perfect for what she was proposing. Cat and I agreed to it, simply because it reduced the number of unknown people around her and let me keep an eye on her while we did the shoots. We were there together, and it was an easy concept to film. But there was no inherent relationship between the song and the video, or the two of us — Cat and me — beyond what the director had us do on camera. As for the song... the song isn't about Cat. It's about you."

To say I'm stunned is an understatement. I mean, I'd considered for a split second that it could have been about me, but I dismissed it entirely in the context of the photo and the story that went with it. I'd never even listened to it.

"You wrote a song about me? A song that you turned into a single? And then you made a video with Cat playing the part of me? I can't decide if I'm flattered, intimidated or embarrassed. That poor girl, pretending to be plain, pudgy Brighid."

"Stop it! Right now. Not another word like that, or I'll have to pull out all the stops to remind you how alluring you are, whether you want to believe it or not... even if I have to revisit our experiment with ropes and such to make that happen."

My cheeks flame, remembering how desperate I was for this man that night, right up until the moment I realized things had become more serious between us than was wise and that a discussion was needed even more desperately than I needed that orgasm. My breathing speeds up just thinking about it.

"There's my girl... Admit it — you still want me." There's that smile again — warm, confident, sexy, with that touch of humor.

"A girl would have to be dead not to want you. Making the reasoned decision to have you is another thing entirely."

"I always loved that strength in you. Soft and warm on the outside, but a spine of pure steel underneath when you need it. Formidable."

I sigh. I'm needing that spine these days as I second-guess the decision to cut Hunter out of my life, even for a while.

"More foolish than formidable, I'm afraid. If anything's been proven to me in the last few weeks, it's that I too often let my heart lead, rather than my head."

"Don't say that. I'd trust your heart every time. It's full of love and loyalty and..."

"Don't say friendship. I am not a claddagh, despite the fact that I wear one."

He chuckles. "But it's true. You're an amazing friend. I know that. Hunter knows that. He'll work for your forgiveness, and he'll come back. He won't be able to help himself."

"You consider me a good friend? Despite my cutting you both off? And breaking my promise to you... both of you. I didn't try to work things out with you, and I'm not 'always there' for Hunter now that I've told him I need to put space between us."

"You're doing what you need to for yourself. I know you well enough to know you have a hard time doing that, always prioritizing what other people need or want. It's overdue for you to put yourself first."

"This doesn't feel like putting myself first. It feels... miserable."

He pulls me into a hug again.

"If anyone knows how it feels to put distance between themself and the person they love, it's me. I'm sorry it came to that with Hunter, but I think you made the right choice, whether it was your heart or head that led you to do it. Except for not letting me explain before you decided, it was reasonable choice when you cut *me* off, too. Though I hope you'll have changed your mind — about that and some other things — by the time I leave here."

Something about how he says that...

"That sounds like you came here with a purpose."

He nods.

"I did. Several, in fact. First, I wanted to make sure you were OK after the falling out with Hunter. You're miserable, but you're OK. Check. Second, I figured you might need a friend, and I wanted to see if you'd consider renewing at least our friendship, especially after I explained about Cat."

"You didn't explain that kiss."

"It was a reshoot for a scene in the video for 'Diving in Deep.' The director didn't like the angle when she was editing it, so she had us reshoot it. Someone on the set took a shot with their phone and sold it to the tabloids with no context. Probably got paid more for it that way — not that the tabloids care whether what they report is true. They had it in print within two days and posted it to their website at the same time the first copies hit the stands — maximum impact, for all involved. I called you the moment our PR people spotted it."

And now I feel even worse for having cut him off. He helped out a friend, the woman he loves, when she was in trouble, and he did his job, filming a compelling video for a song... a song he wrote about me...

"The song — it's really about me? About us?"

"Did you ever listen to it? Read the lyrics? Clearly, you never watched the video, or you'd have realized that the photo was from the video shoot."

"No. I didn't. I was trying to keep my mind off you. In my head, you and Cat were happily together, off living an exciting life of touring and video shoots, kissing each other every chance you got."

"We weren't. In fact, not too long after that story was published, Cat pulled away again. I haven't spoken to her since then. Not so much as a Yule card. The tree's beautiful, by the way."

He gestures at the decorated tree, lit today for just the second time.

"Thank you. Though, honestly, if I hadn't pre-ordered a white pine before I went to New York, I think I might have skipped it this year. Can't get them very often around here. But I liked Kara and Maire's white pines so much each Yule that I decided to go to the extra trouble."

"It's very nice. And I'm glad you did go to the trouble. I'm on tour so much, it's rare to spend a cozy Yule at home. I miss it."

Wait...

"You're spending Yule here?"

"If you'll have me. We've got a holiday break this year. No work until we go back into the studio in mid-January..."

His tone is pointed.

"You want to stay with me during your break?"

"Thank you for inviting me." He chuckles.

"That wasn't an invitation. It was a question about your intent."

"Then, yes. If you'll have me. You technically haven't invited me to stay for Yule yet."

"What are we doing here, Aedan?"

"That's the other purpose for my visit. Not just to renew our friendship, but to remind you of who you really are. Not the butt of a joke, not the friend who's been pushed aside during a life change, not the woman someone shallow didn't think fit in at a party — but the priestess, the artist, the businesswoman, the alluring seductress who's been on my mind more often than even I'd care to admit these last two years."

"Is that your way of saying you've been fantasizing about me at night?"

"Among other things." His grin is pure wickedness, nearly impossible to resist. Nearly.

"I repeat: What are we doing here, Aedan? I'm not in a position to pursue a relationship with you. I'm trying to refocus my life on my business, my faith... not on a relationship, whether that's with you or with Hunter."

"I know. I knew that the moment Alex said you'd asked Hunter for space."

I'd forgotten how well Aedan knew me, how much we inherently understood each other. Two parallel souls walking a similar path, just occasionally stepping off that path to come together.

"And you're OK with that, with me not being open to a relationship with you? You said you were before, but I don't think you entirely meant it."

His look is thoughtful.

"I didn't. Not a hundred percent. But I did mean it when I said I'd accept whatever you wanted to give. No pressure. Except to stay friends. And that really is why I came. You're my friend. I care about you. I wanted to make sure you were OK. And I wanted my friend back. I miss you."

His hand brushes across my cheek.

"And if I can remind you that you're an irresistibly attractive woman in the process, all the better."

"So you're proposing pity sex..."

"If you feel like I'm deserving enough of your pity that you want to have sex with me, I won't object."

The smirk he gives me belies the innocent look he's trying to pull off with his eyes.

"You know what I meant."

"I do. And, no — far from it. If we sleep together while I'm here, it's because we both want to. And I know I want to. The question is whether you do..."

Astonishingly, I have to think about that.

Call it introspection spurred by the upside-down state of my life after New York, or call it caution from getting my heart banged up a little both then and in the years before, but I'm going to look before I leap, this time.

"I don't want to sleep with you just because I'm upset about Hunter and..."

"Feeling a little lonely?"

"Yeah. I haven't made a lot of friends here yet."

"You're shy. That's to be expected. They'll come." He smiles encouragingly. "Be patient. With them and with yourself. Even I don't make real friends as easily as you might think. I mean

— look at us. We're here because I knew I could trust you with some of my secrets, including some I don't even talk to Izzy about. I make acquaintances as easily as I breathe. But real, close friends? I've got maybe a handful."

"Is that why you wanted to stay with me? Is there no one else you wanted to spend the holidays with?"

Again I seem to have struck below the surface and surprised him. He's serious now, almost somber, and then... earnest, looking me deep in the eyes.

"You're my safe space, Brighid. I meant it all those years ago — I feel like I can be myself when I'm with you. There's no pressure to be Mace the rockstar. You'd be content if I just sat around the house writing songs for Top 40 acts and taking walks on the beach with you, wouldn't you?"

"If we were in a relationship, it wouldn't matter to me what you did with your days, so long as you were happy. But you and I both know music would have to be a big part of your life if you were to be happy. And you do light up when you're on stage like no one I've ever seen."

"Except Hunter."

"Yes, except Hunter."

"You're drawn to that — 'the thing,' as you called it. Not drawn in by its power the way everyone else is, but to the people who have it."

"There's a sense of pride, of satisfaction, in being there for people who have a special gift like that. I don't have it. Far from it. I'm so socially awkward it's a wonder I can hold a conversation about the weather without alienating the other person. But I see that gift — and the gift to create music — and it makes me feel warm inside, even though it's not mine. My ability to perceive that and my need to support it — that's a core part of my being. Maybe it's Herself, Her gift of poetry. I don't know. But I know I wouldn't be myself if I didn't appreciate that in the people who have it."

"You really would make a great artist scout. That could be something we could do together, maybe. Sometime..."

The look I give him is skeptical.

"I'm happy to give you an opinion any time you want it, Aedan. But there's a reason *you* were sent to see aMUSEd..."

There's a reason he was sent to see aMUSEd... There was a reason... The words echo in my head, reinforcing that this is important information. But I can't take any meaning away from it. Not yet. Maybe I'm not supposed to. But I know at the core of my being now, that him being there that night was purposeful, beyond what it might have seemed on the surface.

"What? You've got that look again. Like you know something you didn't a minute ago."

"I'm not sure. You might want to ask whoever told you to go to the club that night what their real reasons were, the deeper reasons. It feels like they were — are — important."

"Marina Matthews sent me herself. It wasn't the A&R department or anything. She asked me to do it as a personal favor, said she'd heard the guys had been building a following in Delaware and wanted to see if they'd come into their own now that they were in Virginia. I took it at face value. She trusts my judgment about new acts."

"Ask her sometime. It feels important."

"OK. I will."

There's a feeling of satisfaction, like I've said something that needed to be said, set something in motion that had been waiting for just those words to be spoken. It feels like I've been freed from a responsibility. And...

If I'm Aedan's safe space, he's equally much mine.

"Did you bring condoms?" I ask.

"No, I didn't." He looks a little sheepish. "I was trying to be hopeful. But I didn't want to presume. And... I haven't... if you're still on birth control... I haven't..." It's unlike Aedan to have trouble expressing himself. What is he...?

He can't possibly be telling me what it seems like he's telling me. There is no possible way.

"It's been nearly two years, Aedan."

"It has."

"Are you... Are you saying there's been no one? Not even once? Not some groupie on the tour bus?"

"No one."

"That's not possible."

"I admit it was not the most obvious of choices."

"You didn't have to do that, Aedan. You *shouldn't* have done that, Aedan. There was no reason for either of us to expect..."

"It wasn't that I thought you'd expect it of me. I wasn't even sure you'd ever want to see me again. But... Listen — we've talked about how we are together, about not wanting some shallow hookup. There was always more than that between us. And I found myself not wanting to settle for anything less. Even if all it was was friends with benefits. I need that emotional connection. Anything less would have been unsatisfying. And something told me I might hope... that maybe the fates would throw us in each other's path again."

Dammit. Ninja onions. In my house. I look up, halfway expecting to see them clinging to the ceiling, halfway knowing it's to avoid letting this welling emotion fall from my eyes. He grabs my hand and squeezes it.

"I can't promise you anything, Aedan. I can't let you get your hopes up. I'm a mess. And I've got a lot of work to do before I can even consider a relationship, with you or anyone."

"I know. Like I said — friends. We'll start back there, at friends, and see where it goes. Friends care for each other." He expression shifts from sentimental to sly. "Now, about that pity sex..."

I can't help it. I crack up.

"Now you're laughing at me? I mean, it's one thing to pity poor me maybe enough to have sex with me, after two years with only my hand to keep my company. But you have to laugh at me, too?"

He's trying to keep a straight face, and failing.

"You're still such a goofball."

"You love that I'm a goofball."

"It's a vital component of my friendship checklist."

"So... friends? With benefits?"

"That sounds really good, actually."

"It'll feel really good, too."

And it does. It really, really does.

Chapter 24

Tell Me Why

Three weeks later

It's been an amazing few weeks — from greeting the solstice sunrise together on the beach to waking up in Aedan's arms, from having lunch together on my breaks at work to shuffling him, giggling and shushing, into the storage loft at the shop whenever customers come in, from doing dinner-and-a-movie nights to enthusiastic returns to bed after dark that kept us up until the wee hours of the morning, half that time spent talking and half... not.

On days the shop is closed, I work at my spinning wheel while he tinkers on the old piano that came with the house. Thank the gods I had it tuned when I bought the place, even if I could only plink out "Twinkle, Twinkle Little Star," like Grandma taught me the summer before first grade. He's started penning new songs for their new album, and I smile every time he swears and creates pure dissonance when it's not flowing as smoothly as he would like. It's just amazing to be in the room when great music is being created. I've missed that feeling.

After a particularly dreadful not-chord erupts from the poor piano, I finally risk disturbing him while he's working.

"Problems?"

"This is actually smoother than normal."

"Do you usually compose on the piano? You don't use keyboards much on your songs."

"As often as not. It depends on my mood and where the song wants to go, where I am when inspiration strikes."

"If you'd prefer to compose on guitar, I'm sure Logan down at Mystic Music would lend you one of his babies. He's an amazing luthier. He'd be honored to have you play them, I'm sure."

"I'm avoiding going in there. I don't want to start the local rumor mill going and end up with paparazzi on your doorstep. We've had enough close calls as it is."

Part of his time here in Mystic Beach has been spent with me introducing him to all my favorite things about living here. There are no bandstand concerts or movies on the beach or bonfires this time of year, but we attended the local New Year's Eve "beach ball" drop, enjoying another midnight kiss two years after the first. (If nothing else, that night taught me that the midnight superstition is a myth. That kiss was definitely not predictive of our year to come, even if we've come full circle two years later.)

The amusement parks are all closed, but the arcades just over the state line in Ocean City are still open on weekends. We have a very competitive game of skee-ball, which he wins, handing me a giant stuffed unicorn that he got as his prize. I demonstrate my skill with the crane machines, adding four more modestly-sized plushes to our haul. We take in the light displays at Winterfest more than once between Yule and New Year's Day, riding the repurposed boardwalk tram through the park with his arm around my shoulders and pointing out our favorite displays to each other.

I've taken him to my favorite restaurants, doing a coastal risotto tour — mushroom, crab and corn, pumpkin... with scallops (our favorite), shrimp, salmon, ahi... — and finding the one frozen custard stand still open in winter, along with the popcorn shops taking advantage of holiday crowds. He learns not to put ketchup on his boardwalk fries — salt and vinegar, or Old Bay if we're getting fancy.

And that's where the close calls came in. We spotted a few people taking surreptitious photos of him (and maybe me — *maybe*) before we called our touristy plans done for the day. The restaurants were all kind enough to seat us out of the way, so that was less of a risk. And the people he thought might have caught me on their phone cameras — Aedan introduced himself and asked them not to share those photos, in exchange for selfies with him that they could post as soon as we left. What can I say? The man is charming. There's hardly anyone who isn't willing to bend over backwards — or in some cases, forwards — for him if he but asks.

But his break is coming to an end, and our little holiday bubble is about to burst.

"Brighid, sweetheart..." he says on a rainy Monday morning, a week before he has to head back to New York.

"Hmm?" I ask sleepily, still recovering from another late night when we went to bed but didn't go to sleep for hours.

"We need to talk..."

I'm not sure that feels any better to hear when I know we established that a relationship wasn't in the cards before all of this started. I kind of get why he didn't like hearing me say it.

I sit up.

"OK."

"No commentary on that terrifying phrase?"

"It was all internal."

He chuckles and kisses me on the nose, just as I've taken to doing with him when he's being particularly cute. Yeah... we haven't entirely avoided the trappings of a relationship. I seem to have a particular gift for friendships with nebulous boundaries.

"How are you feeling about us?"

It's an open-ended question, but the implication is clear. I've avoided thinking much about it. No — scratch that. I've *tried* to avoid thinking much about it. I have not been successful.

"I... Aedan, I want you to know I'm grateful that you came to see me, helped me get through a really challenging time by being so supportive. I'm beyond grateful to have your friendship. I really did miss you, us... But I'm still not sure that we have a future that's more than that."

"What I'm hearing is you saying you're not sure we *don't* have a future that's more than that." He grins.

"Aedan..." I groan. "It's been five weeks since I've talked to Hunter. I haven't even really processed that yet. These last few weeks have been a Hunter-less life with Aedan-shaped training wheels. That whole 'You can't be happy with someone else until you're happy alone' thing? It's always made sense to me. I need to feel like I'm whole alone, not waiting around to be completed by someone else."

His expression is thoughtful.

"You're right. You haven't had that. It's the one big advantage of my being ancient," he observes, chuckling. "I've had years when I knew Cat wasn't going to be around, where I focused on myself, the band, my faith. I wasn't waiting around for her. I was too busy living to do that."

"And that's what I need to do. It's one thing when we're being friends-with-benefits. It's another when things start to shift into real relationship territory. 'Playing house' like we have for these last few weeks — it's been delaying the inevitable, when it'll truly hit me that Hunter's not around. And it's too easy for both of us to forget that Cat's still out there."

"*I* haven't forgotten. She's *not* around. She doesn't want to *be* around," his voice is full of frustration. "And I'm not getting any younger, Brighid. I'm losing patience with this dance. I shouldn't have to wait around forever for her. And you shouldn't have to wait around forever for Hunter."

"But that's how we got here — passing time until they recognized those connections."

"And things haven't gotten better in all that time. In fact, they've gotten worse. I'm having to ride to the rescue whenever Cat runs into trouble — which is way more often than a normal human — and you're stuck not telling Hunter that you found that farm in Ireland while he dates every model who bats her eyelashes at him."

That slices me to the core, and it must show on my face.

"I'm sorry — I shouldn't have said that. It was insensitive."

"So there's more than just the one?"

He sighs heavily.

"From what I've seen, yes. He already seemed to be moving away from groupies — he actually told me he was swearing them off entirely — but a handful of 'girlfriends,' most of whom are models."

"There was a girl at the party. She said she'd come in from Milan."

"I'd say it's a safe assumption she's a model."

"Do you date models?"

"I don't date anyone. Except you. I thought we'd established that."

And hearing that hurts, too.

"Oh, gods, Aedan. I'm sorry. See — this is what I'm talking about. I'm only beginning to deal with the reality of what's changed in Hunter's life, and mine. I haven't accepted on any kind of real level that he's a rockstar with no room in his life for me."

"I have room for you, Brighid. And I'd like to see if, with a chance to really get over Hunter, you have that kind of room in your life for me."

"I can't tell you that right now, Aedan. I'm still shuffling the debris of Hunter and me out the metaphorical door. I need to do that before I can take stock of what I need, or want, in my life. Including something potentially more than just friends-with-benefits with you."

He closes his eyes, his face telling a story of frustration and disappointment. And that's because of me.

"It's OK," he finally says. "I understand. I really do. And I promised you I wouldn't pressure you. And here that's exactly what I'm doing. I apologize. I'd just like to know where we stand before I leave, and that's not very far off at this point."

"I know. And I wish I could promise you a definitive answer in the next week, but I don't think that's realistic. I've got too much internal work to do. It's going to take some time. All I can promise you is I'll give it some thought this week and we can talk about it again before you go. Is that enough?"

"Of course. I'll try to be more patient. Maybe it's being too used to getting my way in nearly everything. Maybe it's me getting old and watching the moments of my life slip away like grains of sand in an hourglass."

"You're not old." I push his hair out of his eyes and press a kiss to his lips.

"I'm old enough. You just wait — you'll hit 35 and realize how fast the time has flown by."

"Is that really bothering you? Your age and not having accomplished what you want in your personal life? After all you've done in so many other ways?"

He nods. "It really is. Maybe it's a premature mid-life crisis. Only I'm wanting to push all stereotypical trappings of that away — no need for fast cars or nights in Vegas or..."

"Or young mistresses?"

He looks at me, startled. I meant it as a joke. But it's hit home with him, I can tell.

"I don't think of you that way. You know that, right? You're my friend and my lover, and I hope that might lead to more. But I don't usually think about the age difference. You're mature beyond your years. It's one of the reasons I was drawn to you in the first place."

"I know — it was an attempt at a joke. And a poor one. I didn't think it through."

And now it makes me wonder... Is that how Hunter felt when he realized I'd overheard his little jab at me? Like it was just a joke that misfired, and at the worst possible time? Did I judge him too harshly because it was a subject I was already hypersensitive about? Is he angry with me now, because I was upset with him over something he thought was trivial? Will he even bother with the soul-searching I asked him to do, or will he give it up as a lost cause? Will he even want to come back when I feel like I've established myself enough to ask him to come back? Or will he have forgotten me entirely by then?

I shake myself free of that thought train. It's not something that needs to be addressed right now. Aedan's here and he comes first. I have time to figure out things with Hunter. I hope.

I take Aedan's hands in mine.

"You and I have been pretty lonely, even with other people in our lives. In your case, even with millions of adoring fans."

"It's ironic, isn't it? I connect with seemingly everyone, yet in reality, I hardly connect with anyone at all. Not deeply."

"And I'm too awkward to connect with anyone who hasn't found good reason to appreciate me in all my awkward glory." I shake my head.

"You *are* glorious..." he says with a smile, running his thumb along my hand and then bringing to his mouth to kiss it.

"And you're amazing. But then you know that already." His expression is neutral. "You *do* know that, don't you?"

If anything, his expression becomes more distant.

No, he doesn't know that. It's one of those flashes of insight, which often seem to come more easily around Aedan.

All that charisma, all that charm, all that talent, and looks that have him on the front cover of magazines, and he really doesn't know that. Maybe on the surface, but down deep... And now this all begins to make sense...

"What happened to you?"

"What do you mean?"

"You know what I mean."

He closes his eyes. His expression is rigid. "I can't decide if it's better or worse that you understand me so well. Even when I don't tell you, you still know half the time what's going on in my head."

"Back at you..."

"Promise me you won't bail on me again." His eyes plead with me, and my heart hurts for him. "Other than Izzy, Robbie and Chris, you're all I've really got."

"You have more than that. But I do promise. We're good. No matter what happens, we're friends."

"How is it I came here to make sure *you're* OK, and now you're making sure *I'm* OK?"

"That's what friends do."

"Thank you. I... I'll—"

"It's OK. Tell me when you're ready..."

"You see — this is why I can't lose you again. No one else — not even Izzy, not even Cat — understands me like that."

"I'm not going anywhere..."

I cringe. Because I told Hunter the same thing. More than once.

"It'll be OK. He's coming back. He's stupid, but he's not *that* stupid. He just needs to grow up a little, wake up at least a little. And you do need this break. Both of you do."

"I'm going to have to learn to be without him. And I can't treat you like a substitute."

"You're not. To start with, you're not having sex with Hunter..."

His face is pure mischief now, and I have to laugh.

"No, I'm not. I *have* enjoyed not sleeping alone the last few weeks. But I can't deny that those extra benefits have been very enjoyable."

"The feeling is mutual. I've slept alone too often, myself."

"You don't have to. You know that, right? I meant that. We were apart for a long time. You really didn't have to..."

"Do you want me to sleep with other women? Have sex with other women?"

Before he turned up on my doorstep, I hadn't really thought about that. I had assumed he was with Cat all this time. I hadn't thought in terms of Aedan sleeping with groupies or dating models or whatever else he might have been doing.

I don't like the idea, now that he's forced me to consider it.

"I... I don't think I do. What I want is for you to be happy. If you're happy with Cat, I'm happy for you. But..."

"You'd be jealous if it was someone else."

"If I'm totally honest, maybe a little. Yeah."

"Then that's all I need to know."

He pulls me into a hug, kissing my forehead. "You thinking breakfast?"

"I'm thinking bed. We didn't get a lot of sleep last night."

"No, we didn't." His look is just a little smug. And then it's more. "Sleep's overrated. Let's not-sleep some more..."

"I could be persuaded."

"What? I have to persuade you now?"

"You do have a particular skill for it."

"I do, don't I?" he says, running his fingers along my side. "Just do me a favor..."

"What?"

He smirks at me.

"Don't give in too fast."

CHAPTER 25

THE STAR AND THE SEA

The next morning

"I thought I might find you down here." If anyone would know to find me sitting on the beach on this cold, overcast Sunday morning in January, it's Aedan. "You OK?"

"I'm..." I start to tell him "I'm fine," but I'm really not.

"Pensive? You look pensive. Not quite troubled, but pensive."

"Yeah. I've got a lot on my mind."

"Us?"

"Yeah."

"I can leave you to your thinking, if you'd prefer."

"No. Come sit with me. It's peaceful here. It's peaceful here with you."

He sits down next to me on the sand at the crest of the beach, the leather scent of his jacket blending with the cedar-and-sandalwood smell of Aedan, and the fragrance of salt in the air and on this priest of a sea god.

"Peaceful with me when you're not thinking about *us*."

"Yeah. But it's just rolling around in my head, over and over, right now. I could use some of that priestly placidness you carry around with you."

"I'm not placid all the time. You've seen that yourself these last weeks."

"We're human. Inherently imperfect. But you have that soothing quality... not unlike the waves lapping at the shore, really, which is why I came down here in the first place."

He wraps his arm around my shoulders, and I lean my head into his chest, a wave of cool quiet coming over me, like cool, crisp, clean sheets spread across a bed. I want to revel in it. That's what I think of when I talk about that placid nature of his. There's a comforting stillness to him, which is the perfect complement both to his energetic stage performance and my often overly busy mind.

Hunter... Hunter's sunlight shining on a wood floor on a chilly spring morning, a warm blanket fresh out of the dryer. You want to wrap him around you and cuddle in. He'll keep you cozy on a cold night.

Unless you've told him to stay away. Yeah...

My emotions must be naked on my face, because Aedan's giving me a look of concern.

"You want me to stay?" he asks.

"You just got here."

"I've been here for three weeks."

"Oh — you mean *stay*-stay. I thought you meant on the beach."

"I *did* just get *here*. But, yeah, I meant in Mystic Beach."

"You've got studio time in a couple days. You can't miss that."

"I can push it back a few more days."

"Why? Why would you do that? You've said it dozens of times — you've got people relying on you."

"A few days won't matter. And I don't like leaving you when you're still in turmoil."

"I'll be fine, Aedan. Really. You can't hold my hand until I forget about Hunter. I'm not sure any of us will live long enough to see that."

"I'm not sure the *universe* will live that long."

I look in those deep blue eyes of his, the same color as the ocean just yards away.

"I suspect it will be just as long before you forget about Cat."

"We're still a sorry pair, aren't we?" He kisses the top of my head.

"That's the thing, Aedan. I don't want to be. I don't want to be that sadsack, moping creature, miserable without him. He's not moping around, hoping I'll call, needing people to keep him busy so he can avoid thinking about how much he's missing me."

"I think you're wrong about that."

"I doubt it. But the bottom line is the same. I need to try being on my own for a while. I need to get to that point where I'm content with my life, even if he's not in it."

"Even if *I'm* not in it."

"I promised you, Aedan, and I'm not going back on that promise a second time. Our friendship isn't going anywhere, even if the rest is put on hold for a while."

"Is that what you want? To put things between us on hold? To just be friends? No benefits, no seeing where things might go?"

"I don't know. I just honestly don't know. I don't know what I want. Except I don't want to lose you to disappointment if I say I can't handle more than that right now... or maybe ever."

"You won't. You have *my* promise. Whatever you want — I'll be OK with it. I may not be thrilled about it, but I'll be OK. As long as I can keep my friend."

I squeeze his hand and give him a small smile to reassure him.

"I can't begin to tell you how much I've appreciated your support... I just... I have to be able to live my life without Hunter. We've been together since we were 6. Even when he moved to Virginia, we kept in touch. He lied to me about how things were going for a while, because he didn't want me to worry, but we still kept in touch. This... this is unprecedented. It's like someone's kicked my feet out from under me. I don't want you thinking I'm asking you to go away. I'm just asking you to step back, let me get my balance, see if I can walk under my own steam, not run a marathon on my own. Not yet. Are you sure you can deal with that? I don't think I could handle being on the outs with both of you at the same time."

"I can do that. I'm going to be checking in, making sure you're still doing OK. If that's alright with you."

I nod.

"So, are we just friends from this point forward, until something changes?"

"Would you mind terribly much if we keep things like they've been until after you leave? I'll understand if you want..."

His kiss is sudden but tender, claiming my lips, both of us tasting of salt after sitting so close to the breaking waves for all this time. He smiles that Aedan smile, sexy and sweet, gentle and passionate all at the same time.

"I like things how they are. I could definitely handle another day with you, like this."

Aedan and I share a dinner of risotto with butternut squash and scallops, crème brûlée for dessert. A glass of wine for him, and tea for me. But before my tea has cooled, he's tracing his thumb across the back of my hand in a sensual rhythm. He stands, pulling me with him, and leads me up the stairs to the bedroom. He lies down on the bed and pulls me along with him, settling me next to him and then wrapping himself around me, our legs entwined as he kisses me slowly, sensually, our bodies brushing against each other through our clothes.

His hand pushes up under my shirt, his fingers under my camisole, calluses rough against my nipples. My back arches, pushing my breasts against him, and my legs wrap around him, pulling him into me. His hips rock against me, and I can feel him, hard, aroused, through the layers of fabric between us. We find a rhythm, still clothed, but panting heavily as our bodies work against each other.

I run my hands through his hair, my mouth brushing against his cheek, licking the curve of his ear, and he growls, low and sensual, stripping me out of my top and the camisole in one move. I repeat the maneuver with his T-shirt and unbutton his jeans, sliding my hand down inside as I undo each one, stroking him, bare as he is underneath.

Aedan gasps as I run my thumb across his tip, sitting up and looking hard at me for a moment before he jumps off the bed and strips off his jeans. As he climbs back up the bed, he brings my skirt with him, pooling it around my hips. My panties reverse the journey, sliding down my thighs over my knees and calves, and off my feet, discarded, unnecessary, in the way.

He changes course once again, his tongue sliding slowly along the inside of my ankle, calf, thigh. When he reaches my hips, he pushes my skirt down and off of me, coming back to mouth his way across to my center before continuing upward. He takes a detour to suck each nipple into his mouth and then pull it free again, the suction tugging straight at my core. I moan, running my hands across his back and shoulders, over that beautiful painted landscape.

"I need this, need you, like this... tonight," he says, laying his body atop mine, fitting us together in the most simple of ways. "Just us, face to face, eye to eye..." He's looking at me with such intensity that my breath catches. "No magic, no visions, no choices to be made, no one else to consider... Just Aedan and Brighid, connected, in the moment."

"That's what I want, too."

"Good."

He pushes himself inside me, then pauses, looking down at me, before capturing my mouth with his own. From there, it's a slow, sensuous ride, legs and arms pulling us against each other, hips rocking together, tongues tangling, fingertips searching for purchase and the sensation of skin on skin. He nips at my neck, my jaw, and I lick across his chin, nibble at his ear when he turns to gather himself as our tempo swings faster and faster.

He rubs his thumb across my clit as he drives inside me, and it's a rope snapped taught in an instant within me, connecting every nerve in my body, every sense, every thought and feeling, all coming into a single line, feeding into me and into him. I cling to him as it all begins to feel like I might fly apart, spinning and breaking into a million pieces, and then, as he plunges one last time inside my core, it's not a shattering, but a condensing — all of it coming together in a single moment of time, a single molecule of space, one moment of ecstasy shared by us both before we collapse in each other's arms, speechless and yet with so much left to say.

Neither of us wants to go to sleep. It's like time is spinning away, like cotton candy, and we want to gather all those moments together to enjoy them, sweet and ethereal, barely tangible but all the more vital for that.

Aedan stokes the fire in the fireplace while I make tea, and I deliver his cup to him where he sits at the piano, tickling the keys quietly. He gestures to me to sit beside him on the bench, and I wrap my long sweater around me, sitting with my thigh pressed up against his.

"I want to play something for you... I don't think you've heard it before, and I know I haven't played it for you before."

"Oh?"

"Yeah. And I think you need to hear it, hear me play it while I'm sitting here with you right beside me."

"OK." I smile gently at him, curious about the intensity in him as he puts his hands to the keys and begins to play, the tone of the song almost bittersweet — more sweet than bitter, but a close balance that pulls at my heart before he's sung a single syllable.

My sweetest heart, my present
A gift of the past, the future hesitant
Broken shell washed up on moonlit coast
Can never exorcise that lonely ghost

His expression mirrors the feel of the song as he sings it, intense and emotional, but curiously distant, as if just feeling those emotions is too much.

The salt of your skin
A kiss to your chin
Flaxen waves of your hair
Like oxygen to my air

His voice drops lower, deeper, fuller as he begins what is clearly a chorus.

Ocean tide
And secrets locked deep inside
But she's all I can see every time I sleep
Oh, I'm diving, diving in deep

I've never heard this song before, but I know as soon as he's sung the words exactly what song this is. It's "Diving in Deep," the song he wrote for me, about me... the one where Cat played the role of me in the video. The video that resulted in the photo that led me to think they'd gotten back together, leading me to cut him out of my life for nearly two years, expecting that he'd just move on with his own.

Living not in shadow but in shade
Dreams dreamed and decisions made
Will the light of the sun ever shine
On my love, she's always on my mind

His voice gathers grit as he moves into the next verse, and my breath catches with the impact of the emotion he puts behind the words.

Roses and lilacs, her petals never fell
I'm torn in two, feelin' like hell
Water to the well
No, never my secret to tell

There's so much here to parse, and I can't even begin, swept up with him as he twists together ode and lament into a single song that's just as much Aedan as it is me.

Ocean tide
And secrets locked deep inside
But she's all I can see every time I sleep
Oh, I'm diving, diving in deep
'Cause she's all I can see every time I sleep
Oh, I'm diving, diving, diving in deep

As the last notes drift away, I'm left speechless, lost in his song, in my thoughts, in the raw feelings in his eyes. His hands lift from the piano and trace across my cheeks, wiping away tears I hadn't even noticed I'd shed.

"Oh, Aedan..." I whimper, unable to put any of what I'm feeling into words.

He kisses me sweetly, holding my face to his.

There is a choice that must be made. If I accept what Aedan is offering me — his heart, and there's no way around acknowledging that for what it is — I have to give up any dream I've ever had of Hunter and me together. I have to give myself wholeheartedly to Aedan, or I'll break us both. But could I ever give up Hunter? After just a few weeks without him, it feels like someone's hollowed out my guts and left me to bleed on the floor. Will that feeling fade with time?

There's no vision here to guide me. I haven't had one since before Aedan arrived. And what meaning can be gleaned from that? No joyous joining in flight from our physical bodies, nor that terrifying feeling of falling, of drowning, of not being able to save Aedan, or myself, or keep that maybe-Hunter on the beach from leaving me behind.

I've been left to puzzle this out on my own. Or, rather, I've been given time to lose my worries and bury my pain in Aedan until we reached this branch in the path of my life, the paths of our lives — all three of us. No — all four of us. Whatever I decide, it will shape the future for me and Aedan, and Hunter and Cat. There's no vision to tell me that. Instead, I simply know. If only the answer to this puzzle was as clear.

"Let's go to bed, my Lady. I want to sleep in your arms one last night before I go."

He kisses the back of my hand, and pulls me up with him as he rises, leading me up the stairs to the bed we've shared for nearly a month. He pulls his T-shirt off over his head, sliding my sweater down off my arms, where it drops and falls in a puddle on the bedroom floor. His fingers brush over the thin straps of my chemise, and it, too, falls to the floor at my feet.

I step into his arms, looping my arms up under his and enjoying the feel of his strong shoulders under my hands, the ink stretching from bicep to shoulderblade, across and down the other side. His callused fingers brush up the small of my back, and I pull him close, knowing this could well be the last time I have him with me like this, this close, this intimate, mine to touch and be touched by.

The kiss we share this time isn't sweet or gentle. It's a wave of emotion made tangible, as complex and bittersweet as the song Aedan wrote for me, just as grippingly beautiful as those notes floating through the air at my piano, which will now forever bear the mark of Aedan's song, just as I will bear it on my heart.

Aedan's hands slide down from my back to my hips, sliding my panties to the floor, where they join the rest of our shed clothes, and I match the move, undoing his jeans and sliding them down to leave him — both of us — as naked physically as we both seem to be emotionally in this moment.

He pulls me to the bed with him, sliding under the covers and waiting for me to join him before laying the blankets around us and pulling my back up against his chest. It sparks a memory, of that first morning we awoke together, in Aedan's hotel room in Virginia Beach, beginning an unexpected odyssey that has taken us so far, physically and emotionally. I'm not sure where we go from here, but I do know that it's been a necessary journey, for both of us. Where life takes us now, it has all hinged on each decision we've made, separately and together, during these years, and I'm kind of looking forward to seeing where the fates, and our gods, have in mind to take us.

I settle into Aedan's arms, once again absorbing that peace he exudes so naturally, but now touched with confidence that we'll both — we'll all — end up where we're suppose to be. It's going to be a ride, and probably a wild one, knowing how the flow of my life goes, but it's a journey I'm ready to take.

"**A**re you sure you're going to be OK? I really can stay at least a few more days."
He puts his hand over mine across the kitchen table, which has seen so many meals for two these last weeks. Today, breakfast is done, and now we're lingering over our tea, both reluctant to have this end, especially with things not entirely settled between us.

"You staying would be delaying the inevitable, Aedan. I have to do this. I can't keep putting off dealing with losing Hunter."

"You haven't lost him. Don't keep telling yourself you have." He runs his thumb over mine in a soothing rhythm. "You need to think of this as a positive step for you, making a considered choice to take care of yourself, give yourself time to heal and get strong again. At least where he's concerned," he amends. "You've never had a problem being strong with me." He chuckles sheepishly.

I laugh despite myself.

"I have had lots of times where I've been weak where you're concerned, oh, Sexiest One."

"And yet here I am, leaving, unsure if you'll ever have me back."

"You're welcome anytime, Aedan. And you know that."

"And still you're kicking me out..."

His puppy-dog eyes aren't nearly as effective as Hunter's. It's got to be the extra self-assurance. Hard to buy him as needing to beg, and yet... as he said, here we are.

"I'm asking you to let me handle this on my own for a while. My friends are always welcome in my home. So, no, I'm not kicking you out. As you well know."

"Can't blame a guy for trying." He winks at me. I shake my head at him.

"Gods help me — I do love you. I need you to know that. I'm not sure how to define that, but I know you've meant more to me than nearly anyone in my life. And you've been a tremendously positive influence on me over the years. I've learned so much about myself..."

"Have you finally accepted that you're deserving of a Sexiest award of your own? Have I at least given you that much?"

"I don't know about an award, Aedan, but you've boosted my self-confidence considerably. So if that was your only goal that night we met, you can consider it achieved."

"It wasn't all I was hoping for, at least not by the time you left. But you've given me so much more than I ever would have dreamed. I love you, too, Brighid, whatever the fates have in store for us. Remind yourself of that when you need it."

"I will try. Thank you, Aedan."

He sighs, fiddling with his nearly empty mug.

"I guess I should go, then. Get settled back in before I'm due in the studio tomorrow."

"Let me know you got back safe."

He smiles warmly at me.

"You're the only one who ever asks me to do that. Everyone else just assumes I'll be fine."

"I *know* you'll be fine. I just need to reassure myself that I was right. Every time." I laugh at myself. It's almost absurd. But it's true. I'm a worrier, especially about my people. It's one reason being out of touch with Hunter is so hard.

"Well, I'm going to be checking in regularly. So no blocking me or ignoring my calls and texts this time, OK?"

"I promise. For good this time."

"Good. Now come here."

He stands and holds his arms out to me, and I fall into them, nearly as comfortable there as anywhere.

"Love you, sweetheart. You take care of yourself. It'll all be fine. I promise."

"I hope you're right. Thank you. For everything. I'm glad I got my friend back."

"Not as glad as I am."

He kisses the top of my head.

"We could argue that point all day."

"And then I'd have to stay over at least another night..."

"Aedan!"

"OK, OK. I'm going!" He chuckles. Then he pushes back, looking at me like he's trying to memorize me for the rest of time.

Finally, he kisses me sweetly on the lips, takes my hand and pulls me into the living room with him, where he grabs his bag. With a squeeze to my hand and a warm smile, he heads out the door, waving to me as he gets into his car and drives away.

I close the door, leaning my forehead into the cold glass. I wait for the emptiness of the house to hit me, and it does. But it's not as bad as I feared. Maybe those Aedan-shaped training wheels worked after all.

A week later

The one thing I haven't let myself do since Aedan left is watch the video for "Diving in Deep." I knew it existed, for nearly two years, and I knew all that time that Cat was in it with Aedan. So I hadn't watched it, hadn't listened to the song itself.

I'd assumed that it was about her. It wasn't.

But there was a reason the world believed when seeing the two of them on the screen, and then in that photo, that they were really in love. Because — at least in *his* case — that was true. But was it true for Cat, despite her efforts to push him away?

That is a thing I need to know before I can decide whether Aedan and I have a real shot at a future together. It's the missing piece of the puzzle, because while Hunter has never wanted me like that, Aedan has certainly implied that Cat and he were truly together at one point. And, just as I decided when I first saw that photo, I really can't get between the two of them. I can't be the one who keeps them apart. I would be heart-stricken if someone was standing between me and Hunter — if we both wanted to be together. And I can't do that to someone else. So, if Cat feels at all about Aedan like he does about her, I owe it to all of us to step aside before this thing with me and Aedan goes any further toward a real relationship.

And the only way I'll know whether she loves him is by watching them together. Not that glimpse backstage when they were arguing and then he comforted her. But in the liminal space between the frames of a music video.

I pull the video up on my laptop. My fingers are hesitant to push the play button when I see the still image for the video — that same shot of Aedan and Cat kissing that ended up on the pages and website of that tabloid gossip rag. If nothing else, it still has an emotional impact on me.

I overcome hesitation with impulse, tapping on the play button before I can think about it any further.

The same melody that Aedan played for me the night before he left drifts from the speakers. It has a harder, grittier, edge in its finished form but is just as bittersweet as it was when he played it for me. The video tells the story of two lovers — meaningful glances exchanged across a room full of people... sneaking out to a grove full of trees, where they stand in each other's arms in the deep shade... fingers brushing lingeringly across each other as a microphone changes hands... They're all things I can see happening on tour between two lovers who don't want people to know they've involved beyond the professional.

Then I see Aedan press Cat up against a backstage curtain, heat pouring off both of them in the supposed privacy of a niche where no one can see. It strikes too close to home, and I pause the video. Is this a coincidence? A natural-enough happenstance when two lovers seek privacy at a music venue? Or did Aedan tell someone, perhaps even suggest a scene like this, like that interlude he and I actually shared? It feels almost invasive, even though I know Aedan wrote this song about me. I mean — why wouldn't he include scenes in the video like the moments we shared? It's not as if anyone suspected...

I press the play button again, determined to see this through. Thus far, the scenes have all had a certain intimacy to them, and a steamy, forbidden quality that not only suits the song but reminds me of moments Aedan and I had in real life. But they're not truly intimate. I don't see anything in Cat's face that tells me she truly loves this man. Until that kiss.

The camera peers at an angle over Aedan's shoulder, catching the look on Cat's face he as pulls her around the corner of a building, into a quiet alleyway, and pushes her up against the brick wall. There's an instant of almost coquettish shyness about her — not what I was expecting to see in the bold lead singer/guitarist for an up-and-coming band. Me, yes. But Cat? No. And yet I can tell just looking at her that it's genuine. Just as genuine as the look in her eyes when he takes her face in his hands and then kisses her gently on the lips. Hesitation, adoration, tenderness, and then pure, raw passion as the kiss shifts in an instant from sweet to burning hot.

The camera angles to catch Aedan's expression. He's lost in the kiss. I can't tell if he even remembers in that moment that there's a camera there, that it's a scene in a video and people are watching. I've seen him get lost in me at moments, even in public, but it was never like this. This isn't sex and heat overlaying affection. It's passion, and lava, and an all-consuming love. It's a wonder the two of them don't melt straight into the brick and take the entire block down with them. The entire world.

The video plays on, working into that final chorus, but I'm not paying attention anymore.

There's not a molecule of doubt in my mind. Cat loves Aedan. She's *in love* with him. Whatever the complicated scenario is that has led to this secret of theirs, this push and pull that draws them together and then forces them away from each other — it's meaningless in the face of what I've seen in both of their faces. Aedan is a man in love. With two women. The one he wrote this song about, and the one in the video with him. But he doesn't belong with me. *He belongs with someone else.* He belongs with her.

There's such a sense of rightness in that thought that I don't feel even a twinge of pain at the impending loss, knowing — Knowing — I have to give him up. It's the way things are supposed to be. And I cannot stand in the way of that. It would do me no good to stand in the way of that. Because it is inevitable. I would always have had to give Aedan up, one way or another, for one reason or another, in a day or a year or a decade. She will come back to him again, and one of those times, it will be for good.

And that *is* good. Because Aedan may be feeling impatient with her right now, but he'll welcome her with open arms when the time is right. Better not to complicate things further with what he and I have started to feel for each other. That will pass. It's a grain of sand in the ocean that is what those two feel for each other.

I may not be destined to get my happy ending with Hunter. But Aedan will get his with Cat. Somewhere, down the road. But they'll get it. And that starts today, with me getting out of the way.

CHAPTER 26

I AM MINE

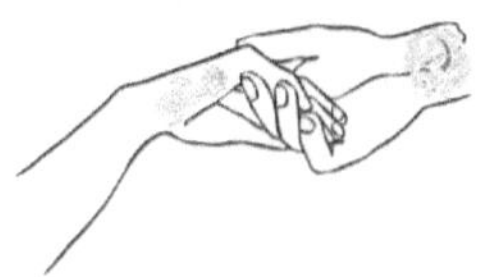

Two months later

The cast-iron bell over the shop door clangs, calling me out my inventory of the back room to attend to my customer. It's a quiet Monday in March. I might see five customers today, and I've already had four of them, but it gives me time to get some more books, candles and essential oils ordered, once I know exactly what stock needs topping up.

I wipe my hands on my skirt and get up off the floor, pulling aside the heavy velvet curtain that keeps this room secret, if a poorly-kept one.

There's a man standing at the counter, clad in jeans, a snug T-shirt and a leather jacket, his eyes hidden behind sunglasses, even though he's indoors now and not out in the bright spring sunshine.

I can't help myself. I smile widely. He's a sight for sore eyes, this man, gone away longer than I'd like, missed dearly. But my heart warms at seeing him here. A part of me was starting to wonder if he'd ever come back, after that last conversation we had.

"How's my girl?"

He slides the sunglasses off, laying them on the counter. The crinkles in the corners of his eyes mirror the mischief in them, the smirk garnering a shake of my head out of affectionate dismay.

"I'm not—"

"—Not my girl. Yes, I know. But still my Lady? After a fashion, at least?"

"I can accept that. Good to see you again, Aedan."

I step into his outstretched arms, a solid hug delivered that feels more platonic than any hug I've ever gotten from this man. And more platonic than most I've had from Hunter. But that's for another day.

"Good to see you, too. I've missed it. I got kind of used to seeing you every day. But I enjoy those texts of yours."

"That feeling is mutual."

I kiss the end of his nose, allow myself that small intimacy with one of my closest friends. Really, my closest now. At least at the moment.

"I recognize that look. You still haven't talked to him?"

I sigh.

"No. I've had almost two months on my own. It all still feels very... tentative. I'm not ready to even check in with him yet. I'm not sure when I will be."

"You'll know when the time is right."

"Thank you. For that and for not asking me to talk about it before now."

"You said you wanted me to step back and let you find your legs on your own. It seems to me you're doing that, making progress with it. And that's what you wanted, what you need."

"It feels like it."

"And no change of heart where we're concerned?" His smile says he's trying to charm me, just a little, but his eyes are more serious, if also just a little.

"That ship has sailed, Aedan. Didn't need oars or a mast. It went where it was intended to go, and that journey is done."

"Just like Manannán's boat. Lovely analogy, my Lady. I can't say I'm not disappointed, but I understood your decision then, and I do now."

"I'm glad. I didn't want to hurt you."

"Or Cat. You said." He chuckles. "I'm sure she'll appreciate your kindness, should she ever turn up in my presence again," he adds wryly.

"She will. You said it yourself the night we first met. It's just a matter of time. When the time is right, she'll be there. You, my dear, are just going to have to be patient a while longer."

"Hunter will come back, Brighid, and he'll be better for the time away. I'd be surprised if he didn't jump on the next flight the instant your number came up on his phone."

"I can't move forward expecting that. I can't move forward thinking about that. I'm not ready."

He pulls me back into his arms, leaning his cheek against my hair.

"I know. Give it time. Just don't give up hope. You have the control here. It's up to you to decide when you're ready, whether you think he's grown enough to be worthy of you. I just want you to know he'll come back."

"Intuition telling you that?"

He nods sharply. I take him at his word, thankful when I notice it relieves some of my anxiety over the whole decision to continue keeping my distance from my best friend.

"So, what brings you back to Mystic Beach? I thought you were in the studio for another month."

"We're done. The album is wrapped. Headed off for mastering."

"Wow. That was fast."

"I had a lot of inspiration for new songs this time. Things just kind of fell into place."

The look he gives me is meaningful.

"You wrote about me again, didn't you?"

He nods again.

"Forget flattered — I can't decide whether to be worried or terrified."

He barks a laugh.

"There's nothing identifiable. The closest I've come is that reference to your hair in the last one."

"I'm sure no one would think to connect the flowers from the song to the color of my eyes and the rose I had in my hair that New Year's Eve."

"Ah, you figured that out."

"I did."

"You're the only one. So I think you're safe. Assuming no one digs up that photo from Dublin."

"You're too cocky. Someday, you're going to find your 'No one will notice' plan hasn't worked as well as you thought it would. And then you're going to have to cover somebody else's ass, and not just your own."

"I think I did fine by your ass, Brighid."

He smirks again, and I roll my eyes at him.

"So... and this is definitely a segue to a different topic — I thought I might take a few days at the beach to relax, if you don't mind hosting me. Briefly, I promise," he says, chuckling. "I'll sleep on the sofa."

"That would be nice, actually. And you don't have to sleep on the sofa. I may not have gotten a bed set up in the guest room yet, but I've had some experience sharing a bed on a platonic basis. And this one is way bigger."

He gets a naughty little gleam in his eye.

"Oh, no — stop right there," I warn him. "Don't say a word. That joke I can see percolating in your head — not appropriate for a man who will be sleeping in my bed in a few hours, platonically."

"Spoilsport."

I shake my head.

"So, how soon do you think you can cut out of here? I'm in the mood for risotto."

"You're always in the mood for risotto."

"This is true. Good thing I burn off all those carbs on stage. Have to maintain my girlish figure." He turns sideways and puts his hands on his — rather slender — hips. I laugh and shake my head again. I did miss this.

"I can close up right now. This is the first Monday I've been open this spring. I'm not expecting anyone else to come in. I was just doing inventory in the back room."

"I love your little witchy nook. Does anyone ever wander in there, looking for yarn?"

"Actually, no. It's kind of odd, honestly. But they may just think it's storage back there if they haven't been inside."

"Someone's going to get a surprise one day, walking in on a tarot reading when they just wanted sock patterns."

I laugh.

"They'll be fine. I'll just offer them some pleasant-smelling ritual candles as a distraction and send them home with a bag of Springtime Serenade tea to try."

"And end up with another customer for life. Springtime Serenade?"

"It's meant to be serene, relaxing, placid, refreshing, like the waves washing over the beach on a sunny spring morning."

"And the musical name?"

"I might maybe have had a certain someone in mind when I was blending a tea designed to be placid and refreshing."

"*Now* who's milking our relationship for professional inspiration?"

I chuckle.

"No one's going to drink Springtime Serenade and think, 'Hmm... Tastes like Mace Mason.'"

"If they do, I've got bigger problems than your tea naming conventions."

We both laugh.

"Risotto, my Lady?"

"Yes, please."

"Scallops or ahi?"

"Scallops, I think."

"You love them."

"So do you!"

"That I do. And you, too."

He's not talking about the scallops now, but there's a purity to the words, no longer laden with heavy meaning or an unavoidably sexual intimacy.

"Back at you, my friend."

Seven months later

I don't dread a lot of days on the calendar, and I never dreaded this one, until now.

From the day I turned 6 until today, I've spent exactly one birthday without Hunter — the year he first moved to Virginia. And we made up for it the next year with a double-double birthday celebration, his in early October and mine just a few weeks later.

I've spent all day on tenterhooks, waiting, desperate for a call from Hunter, but dreading it just the same. It's been nearly a year since we've spoken. Has he worked to find my best friend inside the rockstar? Or did he give up and just revel in his new life?

After a quiet solo dinner of mushroom risotto and scallops, eaten while sitting on my sofa, watching "Return of the Jedi" in between answering the door for trick-or-treaters, and trying not to miss Hunter, I tuck into a book — an urban fantasy novel with an investigative reporter getting into some serious supernatural trouble. Not five minutes later, the phone rings. My heart catches in my chest. I check the screen, again dreading and hoping simultaneously.

"Happiest of birthdays, my Lady!"

"Thank you, Aedan. And thank you for the flowers. But aren't you getting ready to go on stage about now?"

"I have three minutes."

"You're not worried about making the audience wait?"

"Nah. They'll be fine. It's not like it's Madison Square Garden or anything... Oh, wait — it *is* Madison Square Garden!" He laughs uproariously.

"Aedan," I moan. "You can't do that! Go get on stage."

"You're getting bossy in your old age, my dear."

"Thanks for reminding me."

"Nice sarcasm there, Brighid. Another thing you've mastered in your old age."

"Aedan!"

"Love you! I'll talk to you tomorrow. Have a good night, and I hope it's a happy birthday."

"Love you, too, you crazy man, you. Go entertain the crowd! I'll talk to you tomorrow."

I hang up, still shaking my head. Aedan did invite me to come up to New York for my birthday, but I've found myself unwilling to go back there, still stinging from my last visit. And that's as good a reason as any as to why I still haven't let myself contact Hunter. And won't anytime soon.

A year later

There's an insistent knock at my door. I haven't even sat down after getting back from my birthday dinner at the new restaurant right next to my shop, where my new friend Callie is the chef. The other ladies — Amber the jewelsmith and Siobhan the tattoo artist, my other business neighbors — just dropped me off, still wheedling me to come out for drinks and dancing as I got out of the car.

"It's too late for trick-or-treat, kids! The candy was gone hours ago!" I announce, knowing that, at this hour, it's just the girls come back to try to change my mind about going out. "Seriously — I told you. I don't drink," I tell them loudly as I head to the door. "And I'm not up for dance—"

I swing the door back open, expecting to see the pair laughing at my determination to stay home. That's not what I see.

"Happy birthday, Bridge."

Hunter holds his arms out, a miraculous presence, like the gods have left me a birthday present on my front porch, minus the bow. I throw myself at him, bawling like a baby, soaking his T-shirt in seconds.

"I've missed you, Bridge. A lot. Let's never do that again," he says into my hair. He takes a deep breath and sighs. "I really am sorry. So, so sorry."

For nearly two years now, that's what I've needed to hear — but more than that... to know he really meant it, on a deeper level than just the words. I couldn't take him at his word when he'd called two weeks after that horrible night in New York and said he was sorry he'd let me become the butt of a joke. Because I knew then that it wouldn't change a thing if I didn't draw a line on our friendship, even if we had been best friends for basically our entire lives. In all those years, I'd never been able to stay mad at him, and it's been hard, building a life without him. But it was necessary. For both of us.

I needed him to do more than acknowledge that he'd screwed up and he'd hurt me. I needed to know that that mattered to him, that he'd really try to do better. And I needed him to pull my best friend of two decades out of the bullshit of the rockstar lifestyle and his tortured past so I wasn't stuck with the same asshole I'd met that horrible night. I wanted my best friend back. And this time, I couldn't be the one doing all the work to pull us back together.

"I missed you, too, Hunter." I sniffle. "But I can't keep doing this. I respect myself too much to accept being treated like that. By anyone."

"I never wanted to hurt you." He looks deep in my eyes, his own so full of regret that it tears at my heart. "I fucked up big-time. And I know it. When you stayed away, and I realized you might never come back..." He sighs, his breath catching on the way out. "I heard what you said that night I called. Really heard it. You kicked me in the ass that night. No — the balls. It felt like you'd clocked me in the nuts and left me gasping on the floor. And you didn't leave me much choice but to sit with it, absorb it and hold myself accountable for what I did, what I'd become. I've spent the last two years soul-searching. Trying to find a way to be better. For me and for you. Trying to think of a way to make it up to you, show you I've changed."

"And...?"

"I'm not sure I *can* make it up to you. That's how badly I messed up. I know that. I'm honestly not sure I can ever fix the damage I did to you, to us. And, knowing that, I finally decided maybe I should just come and try. Actually show you I've changed, even if I'm not exactly perfect. Show you that I've tried to become the grown-up version of your best friend, the best friend you deserve, not just the one you ended up with because my band got an album deal. I decided I'd just have to try to make it up to you, however I can, starting with a long-overdue apology from the core of my heart."

I pause to absorb his words, the emotions naked on his face. This familiar face, changed in our two years apart — older, his scruff grown out to a short beard, his hair longer, his emerald eyes haunted in a way that reminds me of the day I found out he'd been essentially homeless for a year, and also of... of a troubled man sitting on a beach in a dream I'd once had...

As the moments tick by, tension, fear, dread creep into his expression, alongside that regret. But he waits for me to respond. Maybe he really has grown in the past two years. And that image of the man on the beach... the one I've never been able to forget...

"Apology accepted." A wave of relief spreads across his face. "But the jury's still out on revised-rockstar Hunter. You're going to have to prove to me that it's my friend inside there, not that jerk who kept showing up in his place."

"I know. I don't blame you for being skeptical. I know I still have a long way to go to fix what I did. If I ever can."

I nod, accepting his honest self-appraisal.

"Come catch me up..."

He plays it down, maybe out of sensitivity to what happened that night in New York, but what he tells me of the last two years of his life is impressive. Sold-out shows at Madison Square Garden with aMUSEd, and in Paris, Sydney, Tokyo, Rio... A Best New Artist award for aMUSEd, and Song of the Year, the award for writing the best new song, for Hunter himself.

If he's seeing someone, he doesn't tell me, and I find it a relief.

I tell him about the shop, my ever-increasing clientele for healing and spiritual counseling, the friends I've made among my fellow business owners, far more of them Pagan or witches and such than odds would account for, since we're a pretty small minority. It's like something about Mystic Beach just draws people here.

And now it's brought Hunter home to me. Just for a few days this time, until he has to go back to the tour. But he's here, and this time, it feels like my best friend — my real best friend — is coming back. To Mystic Beach, and to me.

To be continued in "Dream Weaver"...

A NOTE FROM THE AUTHOR

T hank you so much for reading "Down to the Sea"! I hope you enjoyed this alternative-point-of-view novel in the Mystic Beach fantasy/rockstar romance series. There's so much more to come! I'm excited to have you join us in Mystic Beach, and I can't wait to tell you the rest of Hunter and Brighid's story, and introduce you to the other members of aMUSEd one-on-one, as well as some really awesome women and other friends you'll be meeting soon.

Please consider taking a few moments to leave a rating and/or a short review on and/or . Even a few words can help tremendously. Authors (especially independent authors) rely on reviews to sell books, and they're doubly important for a new author. Good reviews mean more readers, which means I can feed the voracious teenage boy who occasionally emerges from his bedroom to eat us out of house and home, and that I can provide sustenance for all the plot-bunnies in my head that are busy creating new novels in this series and at least one other. (Note: I am knee-deep in plot-bunnies. Send help. Preferably someone with editing experience.) Thank you once again for reading. I hope to see you in Mystic Beach again very soon!

Aislinn

Y ***our backstage pass:***
The conclusion (for now) of Hunter and Brighid's story, "Dream Weaver," will be released July 14, 2022, with David's story to follow later in the year. If you want to know all of what's happening with the members of aMUSEd and the... odd things that happen every day in Mystic Beach, be sure to sign up for the Aislinn Archer newsletter, the Mystic Beacon, which will magically appear in your email inbox on a regular (but not *too* frequent) basis.

You'll get backstage pass to the world of aMUSEd, with inside information on upcoming releases, teasers, behind-the-scenes details, giveaways, maybe even some original music and a surprise or two. Be ready for guest blogs from some of the members of aMUSEd and some exclusive stories on the band from our intrepid Mystic Beacon reporter, Aurora "Rory" Carmichael (provided she can find the time to do her day-job amidst the fantastical things that few even know happen in Mystic Beach).

And be sure to follow me on social media, at https://www.facebook.com/AislinnArcher; on Twitter @AislinnArcher; and on Instagram and Twitter @aislinnarcher. We'll have some goodies there, as well as on my website at AislinnArcher.com and MysticBeachRocks.com.

Thank you again for reading, and I'll look forward to chatting with you about the characters of Mystic Beach, all of whom are near and dear to my heart. (Yes, even Declan...)

What's Next

Dream Weaver

His rise to rock-and-roll stardom pulled them apart. Can a magical summer at the beach bring them back together, or even closer than they were before?

Hunter

After years of touring, it's time to go home. Not to NYC, but to my oceanside hometown. It's a working vacation — rest, relaxation and recording. But the label has roped me into a reality dating show. My relationship with my best friend, Brighid, has been the definition of complicated, thanks to her "visions." Putting her in the same room with my girlfriends is a recipe for disaster — one that just might need divine intervention for our relationship to survive.

Brighid

It's been years since Hunter has come home. While he's been off living his rockstar life, I've been building a life without my best friend by my side. Now that he's back, I just want some time together. But his reality dating show is making things more complicated than I can handle, especially when I'm the only curvy girl in a room full of models. This has disaster written all over it, and I'm not sure my visions and the goddess I serve will be enough to save us.

Two best friends.

Two soulmates.

His rock-and-roll dream has come true, but his best friend has faded into the background. With Hunter and Brighid both in Mystic Beach for the summer, it's a chance to reconnect, or for things to get even more complicated than they were. Will it mean the end of their lifelong friendship, or will it reawaken the connection that's existed between them for much longer?

The second novel in the **Mystic Beach Fantasy Rockstar Romance** series, "**Dream Weaver**" concludes the steamy best-friends-to-lovers romance that began in "Once Upon a Dream." It's time to return to **Mystic Beach**, where legendary status applies to more than the rockstars recording their new album there this summer, and where the friendship that helped spawn a soon-to-be-legendary band will need a helping hand of the divine variety if it's to survive a reality dating show. Hold onto your hats for a wild ride full of magic, music and romance, as Hunter and Brighid reconnect and discover whether they truly were meant to be more than "just friends."

What's yet to come

What's to come? Well, a lot more romance, plenty of laughs, a few tears, a bunch of secrets, a vacation at the beach, plentiful music and magic... so much more magic! So far, you've seen just the tip of the iceberg on the fantasy element of the series, so if you're hungry for more magic and myth, get ready for some real fun ahead! (And if you're wanting more "divine inspiration," you'll get that, too!)

Next up in this series is the official series kickoff, "Dream Weaver," the first of the series set in the present day and entirely in Mystic Beach. "Dream Weaver" continues where Brighid and Hunter's story left off in "," and now in "Down to the Sea," as we arrive in the present day and see how these two best friends have dealt with the impacts of a musical career on a trajectory to the stars, as well as their divergent takes on visions, fate, love, sex and friendship. Just to make things even more challenging, aMUSEd's label has decided to throw a reality dating series in Hunter's path, and since reality TV is an agent of chaos, it could unravel everything.

After Hunter and Brighid's story wraps up (for now) in "Dream Weaver," we'll get to know quiet, intellectual aMUSEd bassist

David Carter in a way no one ever has before, when he stumbles onto a secret that defies belief, let alone his understanding of science. Lives depend on how he handles what he discovers, and we'll see whether it's his legendary levelheaded response that wins out or the kind of passion that he usually reserves for his music.

His brother, and aMUSEd's resident diva, Declan, will take center stage after that, with a story that'll make you reconsider first impressions and assumptions made. That will be followed by an otherworldly Rhys Madigan drum break, and a mysterious Irishman's guitar solo that just might turn into a thrilling duet. Last (for now) will be our band-mom Alex's story, where we'll finally find out why our keyboard virtuoso is such a secondhand romantic and whether a shot at firsthand romance is finally in the cards for him.

Finally, I can't conclude this part of our story without noting that Mace *will* get his own book, which will reveal many of the things he couldn't tell Brighid, as well as why those secrets exist. I know many of you had already fallen for him before you finished "Once Upon a Dream," and you're probably even more enamored of him after "Down to the Sea." (I know I am.) His story is coming.

If you're ready to continue the journey with aMUSEd, your next stop is "Dream Weaver" (July 14, 2022). (And if you want to dip back into the past, sign up for my newsletter, the Mystic Beacon, and you'll be able to download the series prequel novella, "Good Golly Miss Molly," Molly and Logan's story, and the pre-prequel short story "Here Comes the Sun," which tells the story of that day Brighid and Hunter first met, at age 6.) Thanks so much for reading, and welcome aboard! I'm looking forward to having you along for this amazing ride!

The aMUSEd Series Roadmap

- Here Comes the Sun (Mystic Beach Fantasy Rockstar Romance series No. 0.25) — Brighid & Hunter, sweet pre-romance pre-prequel short story (newsletter subscriber exclusive, February 2022)

- Good Golly Miss Molly (Mystic Beach Fantasy Rockstar Romance series No. 0.50) — Molly & Logan, steamy series prequel novella (newsletter subscriber exclusive, March 2022)

- Once Upon a Dream (Mystic Beach Fantasy Rockstar Romance series No. 1) — Brighid & Hunter, series opening act and part one of the Brighid & Hunter duo (May 13, 2022)

- Down to the Sea (Mystic Beach Fantasy Rockstar Romance series No. 1.5) — Brighid point-of-view interstitial novel (June 17, 2022) (spoiler warning for "Once" and those preferring to remain in the dark about some secrets)

- Dream Weaver (Mystic Beach Fantasy Rockstar Romance series No. 2) — Brighid & Hunter, part two of the Brighid & Hunter duo (July 14, 2022)

- Smoke on the Water (Mystic Beach Fantasy Rockstar Romance series No. 3) — David (summer/fall 2022)

- Remind Me (Mystic Beach Fantasy Rockstar Romance series No. 4) — Declan

- Mad World (Mystic Beach Fantasy Rockstar Romance series No. 5) — Rhys

- Drawn to the Rhythm (Mystic Beach Fantasy Rockstar Romance series No. 6) — Kieran

- Carry Fire (Mystic Beach Fantasy Rockstar Romance series No. 7) — Alex

- Siren's Song (Mystic Beach Fantasy Rockstar Romance series No. 8) — (a secret, for now)

- To be announced... (Mystic Beach Fantasy Rockstar Romance series No. 9) — Mace

And much more to come...

Background Notes

A note on the many names of Herself:
There are literally entire videos devoted to the many variations of the names for the goddess (and saint) Brighid. Some are regional or more common to a period of time, others used as they seem appropriate to whoever is using them. Except to differentiate between the saint (Naomh Bríd) and the goddess, they're largely interchangeable. In Irish, Brighid and Bríd are pronounced pretty much the same — that H aspirates the G, leaving the I the only sound in the middle of the word that is pronounced — like "Breed." Brigid, on the other hand, is an Anglicized form and is pronounced like most English speakers pronounce the name. But, as you may have noticed, Hunter calls our Brighid "Bridge" for short. Brighid didn't start learning Irish until after she started exploring the legends around Herself, so she uses the Anglicized pronunciation, and that's what Hunter and everyone else use thereafter. Now that she knows some Irish, she uses the Irish pronunciation when speaking Irish and the Anglicized version when speaking English.

A note on Herself herself:

The veneration of Brighid, as both goddess and saint, is on the rise, both inside and outside of Ireland. As a recent New York Times Article ("As Ireland's Church Retreats, the Cult of a Female Saint Thrives," March 11, 2022) notes, even while the influence of the Catholic Church has waned in Ireland, veneration of Brighid — as both goddess and saint — has only increased. That's affirmed by the 2022 addition of an official government holiday honoring Brighid, observed on or around Feb. 1 each year, on the saint's feast day, which was itself aligned with the older spring holiday of Imbolc, or Brighnassadh, as I prefer to call it. The Brigidine sisters in Kildare seem to have greeted this phenomenon with open arms, welcoming Christians and non-Christians alike. It has seemed to me to be a hallmark of Brighid's devotees that they generally accept each other very freely. She has a pragmatic reputation in both her forms, so this is not unexpected. You do what needs to get done, with the tools at hand. If you're curious, there are numerous groups and websites online that offer further insight into Brighid in both her forms.

A note on this Irish vacation:

It's been vastly too long since I set foot on Irish soil. But I have to say that it felt like home the moment I got there. Like Brighid, I truly did fantasize about living off St. Stephen's Green. I spent far too long standing, full of hope, in front of Windmill Lane Studios, seeking to repeat my prior run-in with a particular group of Irish musicians. (Sadly, my timing was off.) I loved the music and the shops and the food and the people, and the city of Dublin itself. I haven't made it nearly as far afield as Brighid went, but I hope that my broad sketch of her travels, the people, and most particularly the shrine at Kildare, ring true. The farm in Brighid's vision may or may not exist in reality. I like to think that it's there somewhere, just waiting for two soulmates (and their dog) to return home.

A note to my fellow followers of Herself:

Please be assured that this book, and all references to Herself in any of my writings, are intended with the utmost respect. Much of what you will read is unverified personal gnosis (UPG), but a considerable amount is also based in actual research and reading the work of those much wiser and more knowledgeable than myself. I've been encouraged to pursue this project, this series, and am following the path that was laid out before me, so I hope it will lead to good things for myself and others. If you find anything within offensive or off-putting, please know that no offense was intended — only the best of intentions. May She bless the work and give those who read it whatever they may need.

FOR FANS OF MACE, AND BRIGHID...

I know we came into this book already having established a Mace fan-base, of which I am one (and the one whose head he lives in, so you can only imagine how distracting that is). He's had me wrapped around his little finger from Day 1, emerging from his role as a minor character for just a chapter or two to really trying to take over every scene and every book in which his name appears.

If you had hopes for him and Brighid to find their happily-ever-after together, I'm sorry if I got your hopes up. I tried to be pretty open about their fated partners from the moment I announced this book, which was always designed as a friends-with-benefits interstitial side story, even if it turned out there was more to it than I originally thought was there. But I know some people still clung to those hopes for Mace and Brighid to end up together. Migid-shippers, please, understand that there's a higher purpose, a longer and deeper connection between these two people and their respective partners that will be further revealed as we move through their stories. This was the story they gave me to tell right now.

But it's a vital story for these characters, in many respects, because it brings them both to places where they can find their true happily-ever-afters — wiser, stronger, a little more healed from some of their wounds and ready to have healthy relationships with their others (as soon as everybody manages to get out of their own way and makes it through some more drama, and at least a little comedy). This book is about patience and growth, friendship and love, recovering from hurt, the strength to stand on your own and the value of biding your time until fate delivers you to the place you belong.

It's also about self-confidence, body confidence and, yes, getting comfortable with sex. I can't promise you Brighid comes away from this with no remaining confidence issues, but I know she has a healthier view of herself than she did before. Mace was never going to heal all of her wounds, and it's unfair to both of them to expect him to. He said it to Hunter: some of these hurts aren't his to fix. But he opened the door for Brighid to work on accepting herself, healing herself. The next part of her story will give her a chance to cement that, in the face of some serious societal pressures, and for Hunter to show her (and the rest of us) that he's a good man capable of giving her what she needs and deserves.

I do want to point out that, no matter how many times Brighid is insulted or bullied about her size, no matter how many times she acknowledges that it may have shaped her life in ways she wouldn't necessarily have preferred, she never considers that a personal failing. She has a healthy relationship with food and eats dessert without any guilt, and none of the men in her life ever chide her about losing weight, getting more exercise or skipping that piece of pie. Outsiders may judge, but the people who love her never do. They just accept her for who she is and whatever makes her happy. And that's all she really cares about.

Acknowledgments

I'm finishing this book about a week after "Once Upon a Dream" was released, on a tight deadline with the release schedule for it and "Dream Weaver," (which, thankfully, is already done, except for final edits). It's been a wild ride to get here, and I'm pretty sure it's only going to get wilder.

So, I first have to thank two people who've been vital in keeping my new-author anxiety in check so that I could actually finish this book. Jill and Sandy, you two got me through the last couple weeks of fretting about reviews and sales and page reads, with some hope that what I've written will stand up and serve as a solid basis for this series and my writing going forward, that people are really enjoying it and will continue to. You also ensured that my last-minute course correction took things where they should have gone all along, so thank you. In addition to Jill (who went *so* far above and beyond) and Sandy (who ensured I listened to Jill), I also need to thank Heather and Lisa and all the other members of my writer's group who, despite being busy with their own lives and releases, always took a moment to give me a Like or a Care, or offer a word of support or advice.

Next, I have to thank Julia, who stopped in the middle of reading "Once" to tell me how much she was enjoying it (and Hunter) and instantly defused a mini author freak-out, even leaving me with a smile. Jaime also gave me a much-needed boost, despite coming onto my ARC team last-minute. Thanks also goes out to the Rockstar Romance Book Lovers group on Facebook, who have made me feel so welcome, both as a new author and as a fellow lover of the genre, even though my series is cross-genre.

Thanks to Liz, who was my first alpha reader/editor, despite all the other things going on in her life, and offered her insight as a veteran author. Thanks once again to my co-workers who have ignored my endless rambling about release dates and rankings and marketing, etc., etc., etc., and have in some cases even bought a book. (I promise, I warned them all this was steamy stuff. I just hope none of them gave that warning too little weight.) And the same goes for my other non-writer friends who've been so tolerant of my focus on the series as I get these first few books finished and released. Your patience is appreciated.

My dear friend and soul-sister Melissa gets extra-special recognition here, too, for offering me a glimpse, a flicker of insight, that sparked so much in my mind's eye.

And last, but never least, to my best friend, Al, who was the first one who really said, "You're a very good writer, and what you've written is good." And he said that *after* having read the work, despite it not being at all his usual type of thing. He then defused the near-daily author freak-outs and tolerated my discussing fictional people like they were people he should know and remember. (Well, there was that one suggestion of a suitable manner of death for one ridiculously handsome lead singer. But he was kidding. Mostly.) Al's a big part of the reason this series even exists, including giving me his insight as a working musician and tolerating me being the hanger-on at so many of his own gigs, as well as having brought me into work as a live sound engineer in my own right.

I'll also add here my thanks to Herself, who has kept pushing me along on this journey, even when I was plagued by doubt and second-guessing us both. She knows I've appreciated it, but it feels important to publicly acknowledge Her role in this work coming to life.

SUGGESTED PLAYLIST

This playlist is a product of my eclectic taste in music, and indicates the method and madness to my chapter titles. Sometimes they're ironic. Sometimes they're kismet. Feel free to listen along while you read, or just try some on for size and see if you end up with a new favorite.

Girlfriend — Matthew Sweet
Sea of Love — The Honeydrippers (Robert Plant)
Jealous Again — The Black Crowes
You'd Be Mine — Seven Nations
Sense the Adventure — The Fixx
I Had Me a Girl — The Civil Wars
Go Insane (Live, 1997) — Fleetwood Mac (Lindsey Buckingham)
Dream About Flying — Alexi Murdoch
Learning to Fly — Tom Petty & the Heartbreakers
Only the Lonely — The Motels
Lonely in Your Nightmare — Duran Duran

Welcome Brigid, Ode to Brigid/Ave Maris Stella, Poem to Brigit — Katy Taylor (These are the inspiration for the Irish-language music Mace got for Brighid and plays during their journey from Galway to Kildare.)

Paparazzi — Lady Gaga

Water to the Well — Sinéad Lohan

Memory Song — Robert Plant

Dreams — The Cranberries

An Cat Dubh — U2

Come to My Window — Melissa Etheridge

Magnet & Steel — Matthew Sweet with Fleetwood Mac (The original version of this song was written and recorded by Walter Egan, released in 1977. Fleetwood Mac's Lindsey Buckingham served as one of the producers on the song, while he and Stevie Nicks performed on the recording — Buckingham on guitar and background vocals, and Nicks with background vocals. The song was also reportedly inspired by Nicks. Matthew Sweet recorded a version for the "Sabrina the Teenage Witch" soundtrack, with Buckingham again on guitar. A live performance of that version of the song, with Fleetwood Mac backing Sweet and an amazing guitar solo by Buckingham, has also been recorded and that recording can be found online if you look. This one blew me away the first time I heard it and does every time I hear it again. If you want a Brighid/Mace theme song, this is it.)

Supermassive Black Hole — Muse (Note: I promise that aMUSEd's name wasn't inspired in any way by Muse, as great as Muse is. My aMUSEd is truly named after the Muses — the personified forces of creative inspiration.)

Save a Prayer — Duran Duran

Auld Lang Syne — Red Hot Chilli Pipers (read that name twice)

Waiting for Midnight — Seven Nations

Something's Always Wrong — Toad the Wet Sprocket

Disillusioned — Sinéad Lohan

Winter Solstice Night — The Dolmen

Why — Robert Plant

The Star and The Sea — The Waterboys

I Am Mine — Brooke Waggoner

Down to the Sea — Robert Plant

About the Author

Aislinn Archer

Aislinn Archer is an award-winning journalist, columnist and photographer, music and tech journalist, and editor, as well as a semi-retired live sound engineer.

She is in the process of writing two interconnected series spanning the urban fantasy and rockstar romance genres, set in her personal stomping grounds in Coastal Delaware. She is a member of Mensa and the Order of Bards, Ovates & Druids.

In her free time, Aislinn is an Irish language learner, persistent advanced-beginner guitar and bass guitar player, photographer, foodie, gadget guru, jewelrymaker and lampwork glass artist. She is a voracious reader of the urban fantasy, fantasy and rockstar romance genres, and dedicated music fan across many genres. Aislinn also loves visiting Disney World with her teenage son and her best friend, attending concerts and spending time on the beach.

For release updates, freebies, sneak peeks and inside details, sign up for her newsletter on her website at AislinnArcher.com, and follow Aislinn Archer on social media, at https://www.facebook.com/AislinnArcher; on Twitter @AislinnArcher; and on Instagram and TikTok @aislinnarcher. Visit her websites at AislinnArcher.com and MysticBeachRocks.com.

www.ingramcontent.com/pod-product-compliance
Lightning Source LLC
Chambersburg PA
CBHW061225310726
48971CB00007B/1945